Acclaim for Pepper Basham

SOME LIKE IT SCOT

"In *Some Like It Scot*, a travel writer explores her ancestral roots on a Scotland isle through the misadventures of an Edwardian experience. There, she finds a grumpy Scotsman, a charming bookshop, and the courage to write her own life story. Don't miss this lighthearted romp to Scotland, featuring a swoonworthy tale that's rich in legends and folklore!"

—Denise Hunter, bestselling author of *The Summer of You and Me*

"An utterly delightful read! Basham weaves the perfect blend of charm, humor, and heartfelt moments as a spirited woman and a hot Scot navigate life, love, and the power of faith. Their journey is inspiring and entertaining, offering readers a story filled with laughter and hope. A must-read for anyone who loves characters that leap off the page and into your heart!"

—Kasey Stockton, author of *I'm Not Charlotte Lucas*

LOYALLY, LUKE

"Readers, you are in for a pure delight! Luke Edgewood is, in a word, dreamy. At once tough and tender, guarded and vulnerable, he is a book boyfriend to rival all book boyfriends. And despite being a princess, readers will absolutely relate to Ellie's struggle to overcome her past, prove herself to her family, and make the noble choice—even if it means breaking her own heart in the process. Luke and Ellie's love story has the perfect amount of tension, chemistry, and tugging-at-your-heartstrings moments. Simply unputdownable! Even if this is your first trip to Skymar, you'll feel right at home in this funny, cozy absolute gem of a royal romance! To quote Luke Edgewood, 'I reckon the best kind of love is simple in one way . . . Choosing each other over and over and over again.' When it comes to this book (and the series), these will be stories readers choose to read over and over and over again."

—Emma St. Clair,
USA TODAY bestselling author

"With a hero who's better at texting and a princess who can wield a hammer, *Loyally, Luke* is 'peppered' with Ms. Basham's signature style of swoony romance and charming characters. She's also added a message we all need to hear and believe for ourselves as two unlikely people wonder if worlds can really merge and not merely collide. This will definitely be another fan favorite."

—Toni Shiloh,
Christy Award–winning author

"Fans of Pepper Basham's Skymar series will be thrilled and delighted with this much-anticipated third and final installment to the series. In pure Basham fashion, every page oozes with the magic of romance and characters you won't easily forget. *Loyally, Luke* is an escape many readers look for."

—Sarah Monzon, bestselling author of
All's Fair in Love and Christmas

"Pepper Basham has done it again! The author's sly wit and enduring tenderness make Luke and Ellie's story a (literal) love letter to the power of authenticity, hope, and redemption. *Loyally, Luke* is sure to hook new readers and delight those who already adore the one-of-a-kind Edgewood family. Prepare to fall head over heels for flannel and fishing!"

—Julie Christianson, author of the
Apple Valley Love Stories series

POSITIVELY, PENELOPE

"Basham is a rising star. *Positively, Penelope* is humorous and touching, and everything you want in the perfect summer read. Don't miss this one."

—Rachel Hauck, *New York Times* bestselling author of *The Wedding Dress*

"What do you get when you combine a lovable heroine with characters who have mastered the art of witty banter? A charming read. And that is what *Positively, Penelope* is."

—Sheila Roberts, *USA TODAY* bestselling author

"This book is a positive delight from the first line to the last. I adored Penelope in Izzy's book, and she screamed for her own book, so I couldn't wait to dive into the pages of this novel. Oh my goodness, it was a true, laugh-out-loud joy to read this book. The story was filled with twists and hiccups, but there was also such delight and fun. And fairy tales. And princesses. And Julie Andrews. And Gene Kelly. All the things I adore. In one place. And the kissing. Pepper does enjoy writing kissing books. I highly recommend this sweet, fun, romantic romp of a book. It was wonderful!"

—Cara Putman, award-winning author of more than 35 novels, including *Flight Risk*

"Like the character Penelope herself, this entire book radiates sunshine and magic. The banter between Penelope and her siblings kept me smiling. The theatrical references kept me humming and tapping my toes. And the overall joy that Pepper Basham exudes with her unique writing style and voice kept me engaged in a story I never wanted to leave. Simply put, this book is supercalifragilisticexpialidocious."

—Becca Kinzer, author of *Dear Henry, Love Edith*

"You won't want to put this book down! Pepper has a way of creating characters who are disarming and charismatic in all the best ways, while still reflecting our inner selves. Her stories are charming and witty, and I've never laughed so much while reading! You'll walk away with more joy than you came with and a heart full of assurance and encouragement about the power of our heavenly Father's heart for your love story."

—Victoria Lynn, author of *The Chronicles of Elira*, *Bound*, and *London in the Dark*

AUTHENTICALLY, IZZY

"A long-distance romance anchors this cute contemporary from Basham (*The Heart of the Mountains*) . . . Basham primarily tells her story through emails, texts, and dating app messages, a quirky approach that complements the adorable leads. Filled with humor and grace, this is perfect for fans of Denise Hunter."

—*Publishers Weekly*

"*Authentically, Izzy* is an absolutely adorable, charming, sweet romance that genuinely made me laugh out loud. A wonderful escape you're sure to fall in love with!"

—Courtney Walsh, *New York Times* bestselling author

"*Authentically, Izzy* is witty, endearing, and full of literary charm. Grab your favorite blanket and get ready to snuggle into this sweet book that will make you believe your dreams will find you."

—Jennifer Peel, *USA TODAY* bestselling author

"I can't remember the last time I've read such a truly wonderful romance. Basham's *Authentically, Izzy* was smart, funny, and adorably bookish. I smiled all the way through and finished it with my cheeks hurting. All the *Lord of the Rings* references were the cherry on top for me. Izzy and Brodie have officially overtaken Jane Eyre and Mr. Rochester as my favorite literary couple. You have to read this book!"

—Colleen Coble, *USA TODAY* bestselling author

"Pepper Basham is at her witty and charming best throughout the pages of this bookish delight! Fans of Katherine Reay will feel right at home between the covers of this epistolary treasure. Featuring a perfectly sprinkled smattering of Tolkien, *Authentically, Izzy* proves that the best reality sometimes begins with a little bit of fantasy. I hope you have as much fun with this one as I did!"

—Bethany Turner, bestselling author of *The Do-Over*

"In *Authentically, Izzy* author Pepper Basham has created a delightful cast of characters who quickly become your friends. Izzy beautifully captures the nerd in all of us who adores books and stories—sometimes more than real life. When a family member decides Izzy needs to live her own story, it sends Izzy on a fun romp that leads to a sweet, sigh-worthy romance. Grab this one today!"

—Jenny B. Jones, bestselling author of *There You'll Find Me* and *Sweet Right Here*

"This book was so much fun! I was drawn into the story from the beginning and loved the emails and text messages between Izzy and her cousins. What was even more fun was seeing how Izzy and Brodie's relationship grew from a few funny messages to a sweet relationship. I loved how Izzy grew throughout the story and learned to love herself and find her own strength and love. And her cousins were a hoot! Luke was my favorite cousin. His emails and text messages kept me in stitches. I highly recommend this fun and romantic book!"

—Amy Clipston, bestselling author of *The View from Coral Cove*

"You don't see enough epistolary novels these days, so the format of this being told almost entirely through emails appealed to me straightaway, and I wasn't disappointed! We follow librarian Izzy as she meets perfect-sounding bookshop owner Brodie online and wonders if he's too good to be true. Filled with the wonderfully warm cast of Izzy's family, and the swoon-worthy email exchanges with Brodie, I absolutely loved reading this book and felt like Izzy was a real friend rather than a book character! A book written by a book lover, about a book lover, for book lovers everywhere! I loved it! In fact, the only issue with this book is that my to-read list has grown exponentially from Izzy and Brodie's recommendations! It's a book lover's dream read!"

—Jaimie Admans, author of romantic comedies

Some Like It Scot

Other Books by Pepper Basham

CONTEMPORARY ROMANCE

Stand-Alone Novels

Authentically, Izzy

Positively, Penelope

Loyally, Luke

Mitchell's Crossroads Series

A Twist of Faith

Charming the Troublemaker

A Match for Emma

A Pleasant Gap Romance Series

Just the Way You Are

When You Look at Me

Novellas

Second Impressions

Jane by the Book

Christmas in Mistletoe Square

HISTORICAL ROMANCE

Stand-Alone Novels

Hope Between the Pages

The Red Ribbon

Blue Ridge Romances

Laurel's Dream

The Heart of the Mountains

Penned in Time Series

The Thorn Bearer

The Thorn Keeper

The Thorn Healer

Freddie and Grace Mysteries

The Mistletoe Countess

The Cairo Curse

The Juliet Code

Novellas

Facade

Between Stairs and Stardust

Some Like It Scot

a novel

PEPPER BASHAM

THOMAS NELSON
Since 1798

Some Like It Scot

Published in Nashville, Tennessee, by Thomas Nelson. Thomas Nelson is a registered trademark of HarperCollins Christian Publishing, Inc.

Thomas Nelson titles may be purchased in bulk for educational, business, fundraising, or sales promotional use. For information, please email SpecialMarkets@ThomasNelson.com.

Library of Congress Cataloging-in-Publication Data

Names: Basham, Pepper, author.
Title: Some like it Scot : a novel / Pepper Basham.
Description: Nashville, Tennessee : Thomas Nelson, 2025. | Summary: "She lives her life on the fly. His heart is double-knotted to home. Can two different souls create a life together?"—Provided by publisher.
Identifiers: LCCN 2024045478 (print) | LCCN 2024045479 (ebook) | ISBN 9780840716743 (paperback) | ISBN 9780840716750 (epub) | ISBN 9780840716767
Subjects: LCGFT: Christian fiction. | Romance fiction. | Novels.
Classification: LCC PS3602.A8459 S66 2025 (print) | LCC PS3602.A8459 (ebook) | DDC 813.6—dc23/eng/20240927
LC record available at https://lccn.loc.gov/2024045478
LC ebook record available at https://lccn.loc.gov/2024045479

Printed in the United States of America
25 26 27 28 29 LBC 5 4 3 2 1

To Beth Erin
Because of the Beards

Glossary of Scottish Terms

Bampot: an idiot, nutcase, or fool

Bap: Scottish bread rolls often filled with meat or jam and often used as a sandwich

Belter: great/excellent or eccentric

Bonnie: beautiful

Braces: suspenders

Bràigh: summit of a hillside (also brae)

Braw: splendid, or dressed well

Dafty: silly or foolish

Dauner: a walk

Dinnae fash yeself: don't worry yourself or don't worry about it

Dodgy: tricky or evasive

Doolally: crazy, out of one's mind

Dreich: dreary, gloomy

Fankle: tangle or ensnared

Feart/Afeart: afraid

Gallus: cheeky, mischievous

Gommy: simple-looking, idiot

Greetin': crying, weeping

Havering: babbling, pointless talk

Keek: peek

Ken: know

Numpty: lovable idiot

Peckish: hungry

Peely-wally: pale or sickly

Radge: a dangerous idiot

Roaster: someone who is obnoxious or a harsh critic; someone who is making a fool of themselves

Scran: food

Scunnered: annoyed, irritated

Shoogle: to shake or wobble

Snogging: to kiss, to caress romantically or amorously

Take the boke: get sick, vomit

Tidy: outstanding, lovely

Weans: children, little ones

Wellies: rain boots

PROLOGUE

I'd love to say I became famous because of my excellent writing skills.

Doesn't that sound like a superb reason for fame? Or, at the very least, a wonderful way to pay the bills.

"Hi, my name is Katie Campbell, and I actually write well enough to pay my bills." I know of dozens of excellent authors who'd love to make that claim.

But no, I am not one of the top travel writers for *World on a Page*'s international magazine because of my captivating prose (which is decent but not Austen) or my insightful descriptions (which I can do, sometimes) or my breathtaking narrative adventures (okay, breathtaking due to laughter). No, I am internationally known as a travel writer because of my *mis*adventures.

These have garnered me the memorable and somewhat embarrassing moniker Miss Adventure and have led to my popular articles, a few documentaries, plus an award-winning podcast titled *Where in the World Is Miss Adventure?*

What could have initiated such a claim to fame? A series of mishaps crossing three different countries and consecutively involving a one-horned bull (now he has one horn), an engagement ring and a sand trap (the ring wasn't for me), and a psychotic penguin (you had to be there).

I shouldn't really be surprised. My grandpa used to say that the only grace I had was the grace of God. If he could see me now, he would proclaim himself a prophet, because who *ever* gets paid for their clumsiness? Or making mistakes? Or being ridiculous?

Me, y'all. It's me. I'm the problem.

So here I am. Falling, quite literally most times, into life as a travel writer whose buffoonery makes money. Truth be told, trouble finds me in ways almost mythical. And though I enjoy a good laugh as well as the next person, living a story of successive blunders is starting to get a little old.

For me. Not the readers.

And to be honest, though the attention is nice, I'd really like to be known for more than my ineptitude, poor timing, and . . . bad luck. But traveling doesn't really equate with staying anywhere long enough to belong, so until I can get my children's books published, misadventures are my stories to tell.

And Miss Adventure . . . is me.

CHAPTER 1

Traveling is what I do, Dave." I pinched my phone between my shoulder and cheek, freeing my hands to grab my camera, and tapped my long-suffering taxi driver on the shoulder. "It's why you pay me, remember?"

Archie sent me a good-natured squint over his shoulder from the driver's seat. The friendly Scot had gotten accustomed to my picture-taking obsession about thirty minutes into our one-hour drive from the ferry drop-off on the Isle of Mull to my final location, Craighill House.

"And you're great at it." My boss's tone clearly hinted at a teeny bit of frustration at my reticence. "But you're also an excellent writer and encourager. You have a gift, and I've worked with you long enough to know you'd make a top-notch editor."

I gestured toward the window with my camera, where a sliver of aqua river split rows of mossy green hills in a curvy line, all cloaked in a halo of late-morning sunshine and mist. Surely we couldn't pass by the beauty without trying to capture another photo!

Archie pulled the taxi over to the side of the narrow road and met my gaze in the rearview mirror, a smile crinkling his face.

Well, at least he didn't mind stopping every five minutes.

"The view," I whispered. "Those hills, Archie!"

The driver offered an exasperated sigh tempered by the twinkle in his pale eyes. "It's the same bràigh as before, lass."

My grin took an upswing at the sound of the moniker. Why had I waited so long to take an assignment in Scotland? Me, of all people.

A third-generation Scottish American! I really should be ashamed of myself. Especially when the burr of that word *lass* brought back all sorts of the best memories of summers with my grandparents. The resident twinkle in Archie's eyes even looked a little like my grandpa's.

"But it looks different from this angle," I shot back, offering him a grin and an apologetic shrug before extracting myself from my seat belt. "Don't want my faithful followers to miss out on the exquisite beauty of the Highlands now, do we?"

I heard Archie's low chuckle brew beneath Dave's response on the phone: "Exactly."

Archie nodded and tapped his derby. "Dinnae fash yeself." His smile was edged with mischief. "I got all day as long as you got the money." He patted his digital meter on the dash and offered an impish wink.

I couldn't help but laugh. If the rest of the Scots oozed with such welcome, spending three weeks here was sure to be a blast. And why shouldn't Archie grin? My visceral need to take photos every five minutes earned him a pretty full purse!

"You're great at getting new followers, and I'm not contesting that," Dave continued as I slipped out of the cute, little blue Volkswagen into the breezy July air. You're one of the best travel writers I have—probably *the* best at bringing in new readers for the magazine, both online and in print."

"And why would you want to go messing with that success, Dave?" I switched the phone to speaker and tucked it into the top of my jeans so my hands were free to take photos, but truly, the pictures couldn't do this landscape justice. The stark contrast between the foreboding brownish mountains in the distance with the fog-covered, lush emerald hills in the foreground, all topped by molten gold as sunshine squeezed through some remnant clouds? Breathtaking. Otherworldly. My travel blog readers—not to mention the magazine audience—were going to be ecstatic.

I flinched as the teeniest bit of longing hit me square in the chest out of nowhere. With a deep breath, I rubbed my fingers into the spot. Grief often came out of nowhere.

Grandpa and Gran would have loved to see this.

I shook away the unexpected pull to linger in the feelings—maybe even in the view—and redirected my squirrelly brain.

I didn't linger places.

Never for very long.

Traveling is what I did. Traveling and story catching. Then I brought those adventures to life through words for others to experience. And I sometimes engaged in humorous misadventures along the way, which only increased ratings and readers.

These were only a few of the many reasons why Dave shouldn't distract me with an editorial position.

Editor?

The word hinged in my brain with cautious—and maybe a little unwanted—curiosity. Like trying food from a jungle tribe in the Amazon. Fifty percent of the time it was going to be tasty. One hundred percent of the time you didn't want to know what it was made of. But something about the idea of becoming an editor stirred a tiny bit of nervousness in my stomach.

"Because," came his voice from the phone, "when you see someone with talent in the right places, you want to put them where they'll make the greatest impact. If you were an editor, you'd improve half a dozen of our other writers within the first six months just because of your skills. That would increase our quality output exponentially."

I lowered my camera and sighed, loud enough for him to hear.

"This is your boss speaking, Katie." His tone deepened a little to prove his point. "With Carla retiring next month, I need someone with the skill set to take her place as associate editor for *World on a Page*. You're my top choice. I don't ever plan to ask you to stop traveling, but editing would give you the chance to grow as a writer and a professional. Give you some structure *and* options. Maybe even allow you to put down some roots."

Roots? I *had* roots. Sort of. Back home in Waynesville, North Carolina. In fact, I'd inherited an entire family farm (which I barely saw) from my grandparents—a place that held some of my favorite childhood memories. Those two amazing people had offered a much-needed sanctuary from my childhood home life with a passive-absent dad and a super society-conscious mother. And expectations no one, except she, ever met.

"Whoa there, Dave." I shook my head and took another photo. "I just turned twenty-eight. I don't think I've met my expiration date just yet."

"Seriously, Katie." His voice softened, pricking at my conscience a lot more than the "boss" voice. "I want you to consider this. I *really* think it would be good for you."

For some reason, when I thought "editor," I pictured Dave, who looked like a classic fiftysomething, small-town car salesman, who was one of the best guys in town and lived in a white picket-fenced house with his lovely wife, two and a half kids, and a perfect dog.

Settled.

Older.

Which really was ridiculous because I knew it wasn't true. So why did the idea stick like a splinter beneath my skin? Well, it was not so much annoying as . . . uncertain.

And this was coming from Dave, who'd basically mentored me from a crummy writer wannabe to now. He was a good-hearted, smart man who cared about me and my professional future. I couldn't disregard his instincts or faith in me. Gran always said that listening to the people who knew us best was a sign of wisdom.

But . . . editing?

"I'll think about it." I pulled the phone close to my mouth. "But you have to promise I'll still travel."

"I promise—if that's what you want."

If that's what I wanted? Of course it was. Why wouldn't it be?

"Over the next few weeks, I'm going to send some articles your way to edit."

"What happened to me *thinking* about it?"

He didn't even take the hint. "This assignment in Scotland sounds like you'll have some free time, so when you're not rummaging up stories or cosplaying like a Victorian, then you can stretch those editing muscles a little."

"Dave, it's the Edwardian time period, not Victorian. I've talked to enough historians to know it makes a difference. And it's not cosplaying. The brochure states—several times—that it's an Edwardian Experience." Whatever that meant. "No lightsabers or hobbit cloaks."

"You *still* dress in costume for a few weeks and pretend to be in a different era."

Three weeks, to be exact—a fact that still felt a little weird. Since beginning the whole travel-writing gig, I'd been careful to keep all my assignments to a week, sometimes less. It reduced the mess. No hard goodbyes, no super-deep conversations.

But Mrs. Lennox, the creator of this new specialty holiday house, evidently had not only an extremely rich, overindulgent husband but one who held some surprising connections in the media world. So various available and quality media influencers from across the travel-writing community had received an invitation to join her on the Isle of Mull for a first look on how to "live as an Edwardian."

With a media preview, especially if the reviews were good, Mrs. Lennox could start her new business on a successful trajectory. Word of mouth mattered. And influencers, bloggers, online personalities, and magazines had a way of making a big difference in spreading the news far and wide.

"Besides, you're a big fan of all things quirky, and I think this place might be right up your alley."

Quirky? To be fair, anyone who decided to re-create an entire era for tourists possessed a unique passion and determination that wasn't exactly normal, but the way he said *quirky* raised my internal alarm.

I looked down at the phone in my hand, trying to decipher Dave's comment. "How quirky?"

"I guess you'll just have to find out." Dave's voice took on a chipper ring. "You live for the adventure, so I couldn't think of a better person to represent *World on a Page*."

"Dave?" My voice cracked slightly, even as my boss exuded confidence.

"I look forward to seeing your articles on this assignment, Katie. And those edits!"

Dave's avoiding explanation did not bode well for my mis-adventuring future. "Do you know something about this place that I don't?"

"Gotta run, Katie! Talk to you soon."

"Dave!" I frowned down at the blank phone screen.

Not cool! Especially after I'd just been mentally praising his good-hearted attributes.

I raised my chin and stared back at the horizon.

I could handle quirky.

How bad could it really be? I'd been plenty of places, quirky and all, so a *Downton Abbey* cosplay didn't sound all that bad. The dresses, the hats, the handsome men in eye-catching suits.

I shrugged away the doubt and took a few more photos before climbing back in the car. Archie greeted me with "Just let me know if ya need another snap or two. I got all day."

I narrowed my eyes at him, fighting a smile. "I bet you do."

He laughed before steering the car down the hill.

I avoided asking him to stop yet another time within five minutes, although the views kept captivating me. Something inexpressible wove among the forests and mountains of this place. A strange sort of magic.

It had gripped me as soon as I'd stepped off the plane in Inverness and breathed the crisp, Scottish morning air for the first time. Kind of like that feeling I had right before a good cry when I wasn't at liberty to let the tears free yet. Not bad necessarily. Not good either. From the time I was knee-high to a grasshopper, my grandpa (a proud Scots-Irish Presbyterian who owned a kilt, collected historic Scottish weapons, and played a bagpipe poorly) raved about this country of his kindred, so maybe a little bit of preconditioned déjà vu inspired the strange feelings coursing through me as we drove through the diverse countryside. But I couldn't shake it.

I'd traveled to dozens of countries, stepped off even more airplanes, but had never felt as if I'd walked into a scene of my own life that had been waiting for me to live it.

Is it possible to feel a genetic link to a place you've never visited?

Whatever it was, some strange swoosh of welcome blasted through me as if every one of my grandfather's ancestors had risen from their battlefield deaths and shouted a hearty and ironic, "*Lang may yer lum reek!*" a phrase Grandpa translated as "May you live long and prosper!"—a Scottish version of *Star Trek*'s Spock's famous salutation.

Maybe "quirky" just went hand in hand with Scotland, which, for some reason, helped me feel even more prepared for the adventure ahead.

"You'll have to visit Tobermory once you get tucked in, Ms. Campbell."

I looked up from scanning over my photos and registered the village name in my mind from research. Aha! The capital of the small island.

"It's the place with all the colorful houses along the coastline, isn't it?"

"Aye," came Archie's warm reply. "But there are quite a few villages with the same. Glenkirk is no far from Craighill and is one of the few villages along Loch na Keal."

With the island being so small, I didn't imagine a massive number of villages, but as the hills grew in size and breadth, the wide-open emptiness of the vista resurrected the unsettling feeling I kept trying to ignore.

"There's Briggs Mussel Farm," Archie announced. "We're close now." He slowed the car's speed for my ogling pleasure—and likely a few extra coins in his purse.

Another mussel farm. Probably the fourth one I'd seen since disembarking the ferry at Craignure. Yep, this island maintained its fishing town persona. Maybe that's what gave it an untouched, old feeling.

The green hillsides framed the loch on two sides with taller, more barren mountains rising behind those in imposing hues of gray and olive. And yet, the desolation created its own sort of mesmerizing beauty.

I bit back another request to stop. Craighill House's website mentioned that Glenkirk was only a mile away, and Salen another five after that, but more populous villages like Calgary and Tobermory were over fifteen and Dervaig was upward of twenty, so I'd have to hire a car to visit places like the capital of the isle and perhaps Iona.

Besides, within a couple of weeks, Tobermory would be hosting the Mull Highland Games, and my readers/followers would love an inside look at something as classically Scottish as the games. But for now it was time to settle into my temporary home and—I braced my shoulders—the early twentieth century.

We followed Loch na Keal for another mile, and then we turned toward a forest, slipping into the shadows of trees. For some reason, the sudden darkness of the forest closing in on all sides caused my spine to tingle. Anticipation? Warning? Something else?

I stared into the passing woods. No—I released the hold on my breath—it felt more like the sense I'd experienced when I stood before the Giza pyramids for the first time or when I stepped inside Rome's massive Colosseum. The weight of centuries lingered in the atmosphere, lives lived and histories haunting the breeze.

The farther away from Craignure we drove, the deeper the sense of . . . something else pulled through me. Something old and familiar and just out of reach of identity. I shot Archie a glance, as if he could use his native powers to give me a clue, but he just kept his face forward as he whistled some happy tune.

The anniversary of my grandpa's death usually ramped up my emotions a few degrees, and with Gran dying a year before him—almost to the day—the twin losses turned me a bit more introspective than usual. And for almost five years now, I'd missed their presence. Something in the acknowledgment of the length of time they'd been gone, or the fact they'd have loved visiting Scotland with me, ushered in a deep longing. For the home I once knew with them, maybe? For their infectious love? Certainly.

A set of black iron gates appeared on the left with the letters *C.H.* embossed on them, though the gold had partially stripped off over time.

"Craighill, up ahead." Archie's gravelly voice pulled my attention away from the shadowed woods, and I barely held in a gasp. The trees spread aside like a curtain to reveal a magnificent structure rising up from the clearing. Gray and tan bricks created a towering edifice with jutting rooflines, towers with parapets, and even two turrets. No, it wasn't as massive as Russia's Winter Palace or Prague Castle with its fifteen hundred or so rooms, but the way the landscape behind Craighill House swooped into an almost cinematic expanse created a unique sort of captivation. As I looked behind me through the scattered tree line—a mixture of rolling hills and massive mountains of stone rushed to meet the rocky shore of the loch and tucked behind a hillside—I caught a glimpse of a steeple.

Perhaps that was Glenkirk.

At least living Edwardian came with an impressive view.

The clouds deepened, changing the landscape from magical to broody in a blink. Perhaps my emotions were just tracking with the weather.

"I'll collect your bags." Archie doffed his cap and then tapped his meter as a not-so-subtle clue for me to get his fee ready.

With a deep breath, I grabbed my purse and camera and stepped out onto the graveled drive.

The house rose four stories above me, the stormy sky bringing out more of the gray in the stonework. I gave an internal dare to a few of the resident ghosts, paid Archie for his excellent services, and walked toward the entrance with my bag rolling behind me, half expecting a procession of servants to greet me as they did on some costume drama.

After a few stops to take a picture or twelve, I knocked on the massive wooden door.

Nothing.

I scanned the front and then noticed a small, vintage-looking button to the right with the word *Press* at the center. A bell-like sound erupted from inside at my touch . . . followed by an indistinguishable call.

Maybe I was supposed to let myself in? The official start to the Edwardian world wasn't for a couple of days, so maybe they hadn't pulled out the butler and maids yet. I chuckled. I rarely dressed in costume for my travels, but as my viewers knew, I was always up for a new adventure.

With a look back at Archie—my only ally in Scotland—I pushed open the door, and someone immediately grabbed my arm and jerked me inside. My assailant turned out to be a small, dark-eyed woman, wearing something that resembled a maid's dress from an old-fashioned mystery movie. White lace collar, simple black gown, complete with apron.

"Close the door!" Her pale, wide eyes stared into mine, and she cried, "Merlin has escaped!"

Without another word, the young woman slammed the door behind me and dashed off down the hallway, tossing another entreaty for me to help find Merlin.

Merlin? As in the wizard? I stared at her disappearing silhouette as she turned the corner of a narrow hallway where a massive stuffed ostrich stood sentry. Ostrich?

Sure, the whole King Arthur legend was wrapped up in Scottish lore, but a maid searching for Merlin in a Scottish house with a stuffed ostrich? Had I fallen asleep in the taxi, and this was all a weird side effect of eating one too many of the Twirl bars I'd purchased from an airport vendor?

A vaulted white deco style ceiling rose two floors above me, carrying the woman's echoing plea through the room. On either side of the entry hall in which the maid had disappeared stood two suits of armor, both holding lances at their sides as if guarding the way forward.

Was I in Craighill or some sort of madhouse?

My face cooled. Perhaps they were the same.

Maybe I should take the advice of those armored suits and return to Archie's nice familiar taxi. But then I saw paintings. I released my hold on my suitcase and shuffled a few more feet forward on the glossy, checkered marble floor. Just up ahead the most spectacular floating stairway spiraled up and out of sight, but along the surrounding walls hung dozens of framed paintings of all sizes.

Visual art is my kryptonite. Okay, not my only kryptonite. I'm also a weakling to chocolate, masculine jawlines, fuzzy socks, and bruschetta . . . and a few dozen other things of lesser power. I'd never been able to create visual beauties like my sister, Sarah, but visual art had always captured me. All kinds—paintings, sculptures, handcrafts.

With a glance behind me for any other possible attacks from maids, I rounded the ostrich and slipped toward the stairway, taking in the intricate design of the wooden railing along with arched ceilings. Even the molding at the top of the arched entryways boasted unique designs of animals and flowers. The detail was remarkable.

And then one step led me closer to another painting and then another, mostly oils and landscapes.

I raised my camera for a shot of the amazing display of art and architecture.

"Merlin," came the cry again, except from an older voice. Very English and with a McGonagall-type authority. "I command you to appear at once."

My body froze at the incantation. And from an Englishwoman too.

I'd read my Agatha Christie and Sir Arthur Conan Doyle, so séances and weird magic fit into the Edwardian vibe, but I'm not sure I wanted to be a part of bringing Merlin back from the . . . wherever he'd gone.

I frowned. But wasn't King Arthur the legendary one who was supposed to rise from the dead?

I shouldn't have paused to contemplate. I should have headed directly for Archie and his overpriced taxi, but when I turned in the direction of the voice, my feet froze to the stair.

Coming toward me, wings outstretched and beady eyes capturing mine, flew a massive blue-and-yellow macaw holding a red hat in its talons.

But that wasn't the most alarming sight.

Running from the entryway in pursuit of the macaw emerged a small collection of three women. The lead woman wore a stylish Edwardian day suit and waved a broom in the air. The younger woman wore some sort of vintage gown with a red feather boa that flapped behind her like—forgive me—a broken wing. And the third woman was the maid who rushed ahead raising a sword.

What on earth was happening?

Or perhaps I wasn't on earth . . . and I'd opened the front door into another dimension.

My camera flashed as my finger reflexively squeezed.

The macaw closed in.

So did the women.

Keeping a firm hold on my camera, I pressed my body against the railing to give both the bird and the women as much access to pass as the stairway provided.

"Catch him!" The lead woman screamed. "That hat was given to my mother by the King of Spain."

Her English accent lengthened the vowels in an exaggerated way as she rushed forward, but my full attention focused on the macaw, who, without any hesitation, landed on my shoulder.

I held my breath, his weight surprising and the prick of his talons intimidating. With the slightest whimper, I pressed a little farther back into the stair railing, gripping the wood with all my might to keep from moving.

"Don't move." The elder lady slowed her pace, one palm outstretched and the other holding the broom.

"The broom will not work, my dear." A male voice sounded from somewhere above, much too calm for the situation. "It will only annoy him further."

The talons pinched more tightly into my shoulder as if to confirm the man's words, and two things happened at once. The bird took flight and a resounding crack reverberated through the room.

The railing gave way.

The nonexistent heels of my flats scraped the wood step in a vain attempt at slowing my demise, the English woman released a loud gasp, and my body lost its fight with gravity, sending me hurtling backward toward the ground.

My life flashed before my eyes, just as the sun split the clouds out the windows and haloed my face. My twelve-hour romance in Italy. An escape from a killer monkey in Africa. Grandpa's laugh. Gran's chocolate cake.

I resigned to my end, only disappointed that the last photo anyone would find on my camera would be of an oversize macaw carrying a hat with a barrage of Edwardian ladies in pursuit.

I hugged my camera to my chest with one arm—at least the photo of Dad wearing a duckbill for my nephew would survive—and tried to remember what I grasped in my other hand.

My body tensed for impact, but the back-breaking strike of the floor didn't come. Instead, I hit something firm and somewhat soft at the same time.

Another terrifying masterpiece by a taxidermist?

A grunt proved I'd hit something more human—and probably male—than stuffed and exotic. We both crashed to the floor, or rather, he crashed and I landed on top of him. I glanced up at the beautifully ornate ceiling and prayed to God I hadn't just squished a frail gardener or tenderhearted grandpa.

I wasn't the smallest of women.

With a catch in my back and a groan of my own, I sat up, my auburn hair blocking my vision for a full two seconds as my one hand gripped my camera and the other held—*wince*—a broken piece of the stair railing.

Some guttural rain of unidentifiable words rasped from the breathless man who'd broken my fall, and I scooted off his stomach just in time for him to come to a sitting position in front of me.

He was huge, and as a six-foot-one lady, that was saying something. My mom lovingly referred to me as sturdy, and my brand of sturdiness had succeeded in protecting half the female population in middle school from a notorious set of bullies determined to make small girls cry. But still, when this man sat up, I felt small and the sudden curiosity of watching him unfold into his full height distracted me from the current debacle I'd quite literally fallen into.

A wild array of mingled hues of brown curls splayed across his head in all directions. I tilted my head in closer examination. Maybe they couldn't be tamed.

My fingers twitched for a second.

His nose sat a little crooked, like it might have been broken once or twice. I cringed—hopefully I hadn't added a third. But what snagged my attention most were his eyes. A piercing light blue beneath those dark brows, and their intensity snatched the gratitude right from my brain. Who had eyes that unearthly shade of blue?

I tried to open my mouth to say something simple like "Thank you for saving my life," or a not so simple "How do you fit those shoulders through the doorway?" Or even something much less expected like "Your eyes are the same color as Chile's Lake Pehoe at sunset." But the only thing that came out was a squeak. It wasn't every day someone saved your life. I flinched at that thought. Okay, I'd had it happen three times, but how was I supposed to know that sharks were nearby and attracted to beef jerky if the scuba instructor didn't happen to mention it in his overview of the diving class? And the rock-climbing incident was due to poor directions on the guide's part.

The massive man's attention slipped from my face to my right hand, which clutched my camera, and then to my left, which held the incriminating stair rail. Those periwinkles of his flashed back to my face, and the shade of his cheeks moved from a suntanned hue to definite carmine within a span of two seconds. Something like a growl erupted from his chest, and he jolted upright, leaving me to stumble back and fall, unceremoniously, on my softest spot.

"You broke my stairs!"

The accusation blustered out beautifully in Scottish curls, especially the *br*, but with none of the warmth of Archie's welcome. I blinked, still trying to comprehend what on earth was going on, but comprehension wasn't emerging quite as quickly as usual. Or maybe it was and none of it made sense anyway.

My mouth dropped open again, resulting in another annoying squeak.

The man leaned forward, and I thought for a second he meant to help me stand, but he merely plucked the piece of railing from my hand. "I've worked on that railing for three days, and in five minutes you took out two meters of freshly hewn ash."

My jaw locked in a frown, and I released my own growl, though it wasn't nearly as impressive as his. *Fine.* He didn't seem the type to enjoy a sea sunset anyway.

Mesmerizing eyes or not, all six foot three hundred—or whatever he was—of him was Highland jerk.

"Are you kidding me?" I pushed myself to a quaking stand and barely stood as tall as his crooked nose. "The stairs?" I yelled back into his reddening face. "I am immediately accosted by some wizard macaw on the loose carrying a hat, followed by a collection of Agatha Christie actors, then nearly lose my life—not to mention my camera—by falling off a flight of stairs, and you're concerned about your railing?"

I considered taking the broken piece of railing back and poking his inflated chest with it.

Both of his too-bushy brows shot high for a split second and then crashed over his highly uninteresting eyes. "If you dinnae like the company, find a new place to stay and leave the rest of us and *my* stair railing in peace."

"I couldn't care less about you, this madhouse, or your precious stair railing." I reached for the broken railing to turn my thoughts into action, but the size of his hands wrapping around it distracted me for a full second. Were there giants in Scotland, along with faeries and dragons and birds named Merlin?

"Ms. Campbell?"

The pristine voice pealed through the cavernous room and pulled me from my near assault on Mr. Scottish Grump.

The lean woman wearing the Edwardian dress who'd been chasing Merlin stepped forward, smoothing a palm over her ruffled hair. Her lips seemed to wrestle with an expression, finally ending on a tight smile as she folded her hands in front of her.

"I'm Mrs. Elizabeth Lennox." She offered her hand. "And I do hope you won't base your opinion about Craighill House on this most unexpected initial impression."

My bottom lip dropped for a split second, and then I sucked it back up for a smile. "I'm used to stumbling into unexpected adventures, but never with a hat-stealing parrot."

Her manicured brow rose almost imperceptibly as she followed Mr. Highlander's march up the stairs. "Well, I can assure you, my husband's delinquent, Merlin, will remain well hidden for the extent of your and our other guests' time here."

I followed Mrs. Lennox's gaze to the top of the stairs where a middle-aged man, perched a floor above us, smiled, while rebel Merlin perched on his shoulder. The former offered a welcome—the latter . . . well, I avoided looking into those beady little eyes.

"At least this time it wasn't the weasel," the younger lady with the red boa offered. "Marzipan may not pinch anything, but he is notorious for trying to bite off people's heels."

Mrs. Lennox offered a nervous laugh. "This is my daughter, Ana, who will be referred to as Miss Lennox during the *experience*." Mrs. Lennox gave a flourish of her hands as she said the last word and a new glow lit her pale eyes.

The nervous feeling returned. I opened my mouth to say, "Maybe I'm the wrong gal for this sanatorium," but Mrs. Lennox continued, completely unfazed by my disarray, Mr. Giant's grumblings, and the way her curls had come loose from her bun and stood to electrified attention in contrast to the uniformity of her dress. "I just received the most delightful phone call from Dave Carson, and he raves about you. We are looking forward to the publicity your experience will provide."

My shoulders deflated. I'd promised Dave, assured him I could do this extended assignment. And in exchange, he'd promised me a raise, editorial position or not. "He's a great guy." Though saying it through gritted teeth sounded less believable.

"Oh yes, and he assures me you will help bring guests to Craighill and our Edwardian *Experience*"—again with the hand flourish—"to the magazine, social media, and even your personal blog. He shared that you often give more personal accounts on your blog, which lead to your articles in the magazine, reaching a broader audience."

My possible escape plan suddenly shrank to a sigh. I couldn't leave the madhouse. My and the magazine's reputations were at stake. I'd signed on for the long haul. I shrugged my shoulders and accepted my fate. I'd been trapped before, and this couldn't be as bad as the volcano.

My attention slid back up the stairs to meet a set of narrowed blue eyes, and my body instinctively prepared for battle.

I raised my chin and flashed Mrs. Lennox a smile. "I look forward to sharing Craighill and the Edwardian Experience"—without the hand flourish—"with the world. You can count on me."

CHAPTER 2

Graeme

"We've gotten ourselves into a belter of a disaster, Mum." I pushed my hand through my hair as I entered Mother's kitchen, the chaos from Craighill still ringing in my ears like an annoying song I couldn't shake. "I told you we shouldnae have let the house to them."

Mum didn't even look up from the sink as she washed up from supper. "They were the only ones who would pay the price we asked. You ken that."

"But they're numpties, the lot of them." I released a long sigh and leaned against the doorframe, replaying the afternoon, including a chase through the three-hundred-year-old MacKerrow family estate house in search of an escaped parrot. "They're mental, Mum. And they've turned our family estate into a madhouse."

"Graeme." Her gentle reprimand only fueled my arguments.

"The man playing the part of the gardener looks like he stepped out of a zombie apocalypse movie. Ana Lennox has her sights set on finding a husband and isnae being subtle about it." I cringed at the thought of her showing up wherever I worked in the house. "And there's a dodgy parrot with a propensity for pinching small objects. He even stole my hammer yesterday." I stared at my mother to emphasize the ridiculousness of the entire situation. "And that's only some of the actors taking over *our* ancestral home!"

Mum's chuckle did little to dim my ire. "Graeme, first off, we've no got the money to turn the place around on our own. It took everything we had just to purchase it back so it'd be in the MacKerrow family again." One of her dark brows edged northward. "And we'll never restore it as a venue or inn unless we earn the means to do so from people just like the Lennoxes."

I looked away from her knowing stare.

My parents and I—even my brother Calum—had already dissolved our collective savings to purchase the estate from German businessman Carl Newman after his great-grandfather bought the settlement from Duncan MacKerrow in 1919. Just after the Great War, many of the larger Scottish estates fought for survival. Increased taxes, business losses from the war, and tenants buying up their own farms led to grand estate owners forfeiting precious family properties.

The desire to repossess family land continued through each generation. Now we had it, but our ownership hinged on the edge of a knife if we couldn't earn money to pay for the mortgage and improvements.

And the weight of that knowledge hit my shoulders with added force because I was the primary manager of the estate. As eldest son, it fell to me, but I'd also been the driving force behind recapturing the property. And with Dad teaching history at university on the mainland, Mum running her local bookshop and helping take care of Lachlan, and Calum working and traveling as an editor by day and author by night, the task fell most naturally to me. And it made sense. I could run my wildlife sculptures and woodcrafts business from my home, continue my carpentry work among the islanders, and navigate the needs of Craighill's tenants as well as initiate restoration.

Plus, it gave me a chance to keep a keen eye on things at the house. Though, after today, I wished my eyes weren't so keen. There were things I couldn't unsee. Ana Lennox's eye makeup was one. Her father's parrot was another. And then there was the ostrich mount. What on earth would lead Mrs. Lennox to think the stately home of Craighill needed an ostrich?

I pressed my fingers into my eyes as if that might help remove the images and then stretched out my spine, my head nearly meeting the top of the doorframe. My back twinged with a sudden pain, reminding me of my failed attempt at catching the American woman falling from the stairs.

My sister had been a tall woman, but the American even bested Greer by a few inches. My throat closed off at the memory of the way her curves pressed against my chest as she'd landed on me before we both crashed to the floor.

All woman.

My head thrummed with a deeper pain at the thought. Now I was the one going full-on mental. Clearly, it had been much too long since I'd held a woman in my arms. And since the last one chose to leave and take my heart with her, I hadn't been in search of another. Still wasn't.

Especially some fiery-tempered American social media . . . whatever.

"Some barmy American broke the stair railing on the main stairs."

Now why did I feel the need to state that aloud?

Mum's other brow joined the first. "The same railing you're having to repair because it was already falling apart?"

I looked away and walked to a nearby window.

Too many things needed attention at the house, but I loved the work. Restoring craftsmanship my forefathers designed and constructed to showcase the love of their home fed my soul. There was a whole host of things I couldn't fix. Life had driven that point to the painful spot. But *this*, I could. Nevertheless, it was going to take money and a long time—I sighed—and I'd have to work around the Edwardian actors to do it.

What inspired a rich man and his wife to offer a historical experience for tourists with a penchant for wearing old-fashioned clothes and acting like rich people from the early 1900s, I had no idea, but from the extensive application the Lennoxes sent my family to justify their desire to let the house, the venture sounded oddly lucrative.

My shoulders slumped at the idea.

They were turning the beautiful MacKerrow estate house into a bathersome theme park.

The familiar view from the window of the village of Glenkirk calmed me with its more than a dozen buildings in a long line situated toward the rich blue hues of Loch na Keal. My gaze traveled over the lush green glen behind the village toward a hill beyond, where I daily trekked from my cottage hidden along the craigs above. I caught a glimpse of one of Craighill's turret tops peeking above the hillside. I'd stood upon that parapet on the first evening we'd purchased the house, gazed out over a view I'd known the whole of my life. But standing on the stones my forefathers helped carve to create the MacKerrow ancestral home caused pride to settle deep in my chest.

Home.

And even if it meant navigating a houseful of play actors trying to relive the past, I'd swallow up the frustration in order to keep it. I had to. We'd only had enough money to restore part of the house for the Lennoxes' costume drama, and that left half of the house with needs my family couldn't afford.

"So the guests are beginning to arrive?"

"Aye." I looked back at Mum. "Only one today. The charade doesn't start in earnest until later in the week, praise be."

"We want this to succeed, son." Mum approached, a smile on her face and a tiffin in hand. "In the long run, it will prove a good choice."

"Aye." I grumbled out the word again and turned toward her, taking a chocolaty biscuit from her fingers with a begrudging nod. I'd nearly keeled over at the amount Dad received from the Lennoxes to lease the house for six months. Up-front money. Enough to finish necessary repairs for Lennox to plan her venture, at least. Then they'd have to earn more through the rent to continue the restoration process. A long-term plan to turn the house into a wedding venue and inn, featuring local woodcrafts, artistry, and history.

But that was years in the making.

"I heard it's been an exciting day up at the big house."

Calum entered the kitchen in the same way he usually entered any room, as if waiting for applause. His dark hair, similar to mine, waved down to almost touch his shoulders. A grin always accompanied his defense of the length, followed by the comment "I'm an author," as if it explained everything.

He sauntered past the counter and snatched up a biscuit from the plate before sitting down in a chair by the small table between them. "Eileen from down at the pub said her sister told her of the great adventures of Merlin, an American, and a broken stair railing."

I stifled the grin edging for release at my brother's succinct and comical unraveling of the day's events. But Mum released a full laugh, which knocked my smile completely loose.

She had a great laugh.

One not as frequently in use over the past two years.

"Eileen said the American was some famous travel writer who has even won a few awards for her documentaries." Calum crossed his legs and took another bite of the biscuit. "I'd wager travel writing and novel writing have a great many differences, but it's always nice to share ideas with other writers."

Travel writer? And a famous one at that? No wonder she didn't so much as thank me for creating a buffer between her and the three-hundred-year-old oak floors.

I should have known she'd be trouble as soon as her dark red hair flew into my face. It smelled as fresh as yellow bedstraw by the sea—a combination of warm honey and cool coastal brine. Wild and unwieldy.

The vision of her hinged in place despite my best efforts. I'd never met a woman so tall. And those eyes of hers—as deep and dark as the loch. The fact she failed to back down to my, admittedly, poor manners only needled my annoyance at her return to my mind even further.

I nearly growled all over again.

"I suspect there'll be quite a few Americans since Mr. Lennox works in the hospitality business there and will use his connections." Mum returned to the sink. "For this first 'run-through,' as his wife called it, for the media outlets, she'll likely draw upon people who will speak highly of the experience."

"Well, I must stay out of the way to keep my air of mystery." Calum waved a biscuit toward me. "Part of my brand as an up-and-coming fantasy author is that no one knows the real face behind C.J. Cunningham, and my publicist thinks it's a boon for my growing popularity."

How could I let the opportunity pass me by?

"You mean the truth would frighten all the readers away, do ye?"

"No." Calum's smile didn't waver. "I'm afraid for all the poor hens' hearts I'll break at having to turn them down."

Mum's chuckle warmed the air, and I rolled my eyes, fighting my own grin. "Ah, you're haverin' now, are ye? What woman would want a pure dafty like you?"

That worked to remove Calum's satisfied smile and resulted in him sending the other half of his biscuit toward me. I caught it and tossed it in my mouth with a satisfied shrug.

"That's enough, lads." Mum shook her head and returned to her dishes. "We already know you'll keep your distance from the guests, Calum. And with Peter at uni, it will be up to me, Graeme, and your dad to smooth anything over."

"Does that mean you'll put on the historic breeches and neckerchiefs too, brother?" Calum snatched another biscuit from the plate on the table, tossing me a wink. "I'd pay a few quid to see that."

The heat left my face at the idea. I'd agreed to help with any problems that arose. Emergencies, if necessary. But that didn't include Mrs. Lennox's little dress-up party.

The only time I justified some similar tomfoolery was at the Highland games.

Or wearing my kilt for special occasions.

Otherwise, the idea of donning early twentieth-century suits and hats sounded more like a form of torture designed by women who watched too many costume dramas than a voluntary adventure.

"You'd lose money on that one, Cal." I walked over to Mum and pressed a kiss to her cheek. "I'll be back tomorrow to fix the back door. Have to make a new hinge for it tonight."

She smiled up at me in the way I felt all the way through. The way only a mother who had pride in her children could do, even if life hadn't always gone the way she'd hoped.

My heart ached a little as grief pierced afresh, and I rubbed at the spot on my chest as I left the room.

Some things could never be fixed.

But the madhouse on the hill wasn't one of them. At least if the Edwardians didn't destroy it in the process.

Katie

Some dresses are flattering to more voluptuous figures. After trying on four different Edwardian styles, I came to the conclusion that perhaps these weren't those sorts of dresses.

Okay, not "perhaps." Without a doubt. As my only high school boyfriend said, "*Some girls are more like a guitar, but you are definitely a cello.*"

Yeah, I dated one of *those* guys. Needless to say, we didn't date for long.

At any rate, the entire "cello" comment was coming back to haunt me as these dainty and elegant gowns found a hard time making it over the bottom of my cello. And since high school, I'd grown more into the top of my cello, so I had serious doubts about buttoning any shirtwaists too.

I rubbed at an aching spot on my temple and transformed my frustration into a chuckle. From the shapes of these gowns, rich Edwardian women were flutes.

And this cello was definitely not playing the right song for Edwardian England.

Emily, the young maid who'd attempted to dress me, alerted Mrs. Lennox of the . . . unfitting. The matron arrived to find my bed littered with discarded gown options and me wearing a pink day dress that hit too high on my calf and left an embarrassing pucker at my chest. With another lift of those manicured brows of hers, she ran a palm over her now perfectly smooth hair. "Well, you certainly cannot present yourself before guests with any bit of credulity in such a fashion. No high-bred lady would be caught like"—she waved a palm toward me, her frown deepening—"that."

It took me a full five seconds to comprehend her, but the intention rang as clear as her perfectly articulated diction. The little curl of her lip probably helped too.

"Which means you won't be able to participate in our activities until you have an appropriate wardrobe." She nodded, running her palm over her hair again. "It's a very good thing you arrived early enough for us to solve this little dilemma."

"You think you can?" I waved toward the bed and cringed a little at the mound of discarded gowns. "I could just watch from the sidelines."

"No, of course not." The words whipped out of her. "You cannot fully appreciate the experience without actually participating. We have classes on everything from meal etiquette to dancing, to the language of the fan." Her hand rose in imitation of a fan opening. "This is a fully immersive program that requires complete participation. How can you accurately critique our experience without comprehensive saturation?"

The fire in her eyes took a teensy tip toward crazy. "Sidelines are not an option."

Super. And fully immersive classes? Why did the idea stick somewhere in my mind between "run away" and "most embarrassing moment of my life"?

I kind of got the sense Mrs. Lennox was bordering on obsession when she gave me a ten-page booklet on the Edwardian Experience, which covered house rules and Edwardian etiquette.

Including how to handle romantic relationships appropriately.

I caught my snicker before it burst out. I didn't plan to meet my perfect match at some crazy baronial home dressed as a *Downton Abbey* character in the middle-of-nowhere Scotland. Oh no, no! I didn't need to compete with crazy in a relationship.

"Of course."

Her smile returned. "I believe one of my maids does some sewing, so perhaps she can alter these, especially since I hadn't fully considered needing clothing options for women with more"—her gaze rose from my toes to my erratic attempts at a coiffure—"stature."

And that was a nice way of saying what didn't need to be voiced.

It was true. My stature had been the bane of my existence since middle school, except when it came to me playing basketball, the one sport I wasn't afraid to try. (Note: I didn't say I was *good* at it, just not *afraid* of it . . . or rather, afraid of what my clumsiness might do to other people.) But as I grew taller . . . and taller than *all* the boys in my grade, plus the grade above me, the awareness of my size as a young teenager didn't bode well in the self-confidence arena. Being a tall woman is not for the faint of heart. In all my photos with friends, I'm the one standing beside the petite faerie maids like a lurking Frankenstein without the squarish head and sickly complexion.

Tall and "well-built," as my gran put it. Exactly the sort of thing a fifteen-year-old girl wanted to hear. Made me feel like a truck.

"Would you fetch Clarice at once so we can ask her about alterations?" Mrs. Lennox looked over at Emily and then back at me, her posture wilting a little. "Or full gowns?"

"Yes, your ladyship," the young woman curtsied and slipped from the room, keeping to her role of Edwardian maid.

With a deep breath, Mrs. Lennox folded her hands in front of her and approached me, giving off similar vibes to my mom before my first date. That vulture-like feeling that made you feel that if she looked a little too closely, she'd see the extra layer of eye shadow you tried to slather on without notice.

"Since we only have one additional guest arriving today and the others won't be here until tomorrow, we have some time before we initiate the full Edwardian Experience." She spoke the last two words with that familiar flourish of both her voice and hands. "Perhaps I could give you an extensive tour of Craighill, and then, since the day is proving a dry one, you might like to explore Glenkirk. It's a lovely village that we will involve in our experience by taking a few walks there, as any Edwardian household would have done during that time."

And the little tour would give me even more photos and stories for my articles, podcast, and blog. I'd learned to stretch every opportunity.

Mrs. Lennox proceeded by giving me a much slower tour of the massive baronial house than I'd had the day before and then expounded a half hour about the benefits that this historic experience offered. Evidently Mrs. Lennox had an almost terrifying fascination with all things Downton, which compelled her to convince her doting millionaire husband to lease the manor house and embark on this unique career adventure.

Though we hadn't seen much of her husband, she mentioned that he would be joining her and their daughter (whom I'd met during the parrot debacle) for the full experience. Due to said debacle, I hadn't properly met either one of them, but Mrs. Lennox took the opportunity to list her daughter's attributes and *lengthy* bout of singleness.

For a second, I began to wonder if Mrs. Lennox created this entire Edwardian Experience to catch her daughter a husband.

Props to Mrs. Lennox for going big for her daughter, but . . . well, there was matchmaking and then there was this—creating an entire fictional world for your child to find her early twentieth-century knight in knickers.

But in real life, meeting your match on a tiny island in an old manor house where everyone dressed up in costume? Probably not very realistic.

And then I replayed my sentence and grinned. Which part was realistic anyway?

As Mrs. Lennox left me to attend to some catastrophe in the kitchen, I glanced out one of the magnificent arched windows toward green hills and beauty. Sunlight beckoned me forward.

I always uncovered the *best* adventures when I went off on my own. And today I had time to explore, so why not go ahead and search for a story to share?

CHAPTER 3

Katie

I snatched up the book on Scottish legends I'd purchased at an adorable bookshop in Inverness and headed out my bedroom door, energized by the idea of possible discoveries . . . and from the excellent sleep I'd gotten the night before. The soft night sounds of crashing waves, a warbling bird noise, and an occasional owl created a soothing lullaby. And having the windows open to the cool island breeze sent me into a sort of comatose sleep state I hadn't experienced in years. Something about this quaint world fit me in a way I'd never imagined. A surprising match.

The same thing happened the first time I ate scallops. I was sure I was going to hate the slimy things but then had to practically redefine my future after wondering where they'd been all my life. This entire landscape Obi-Wanned me into self-reflection about why it fit, without providing any clear answers.

Weird. Captivating. And a little unsettling. Pretty much the perfect trio to describe my entire trip to Scotland so far.

I'd just pulled my backpack onto my shoulder when my phone buzzed to life in my jeans pocket. Dropping my pack down on the bed, I raised the phone and grinned at a photo of me and my closest brother.

I perched on the edge of the bed and raised the phone to my ear. "Whit like are ye, Brett?"

His chuckle emerged all warm and familiar. "Is that really a greeting from Scotland, or are you making it up?"

I settled into the conversation like a warm hug. In all my traveling, he remained constant. There. Just a little reminder that somewhere in the world, someone wondered about me and wanted to make sure I was okay.

"I heard it from a few of the locals, especially my taxi driver yesterday. You would have loved Archie. He'd make a great character in a book."

"Do you plan to put it into one of your *Katie on the Fly* stories, then?"

My chest squeezed at the mention of my secret project. Brett was the only person on the entire planet who knew about the middle reader books I'd started writing three years ago. One day while sitting on a beach in Australia watching a family make a sandcastle together, I'd jotted down a few lines of a story idea and couldn't stop. Fourteen-year-old Katie was much less accident prone and embarked on adventures to the places I'd traveled, only I'd sprinkled her stories with some fictional magic here and there. I'd just started writing book four: *King Tut's Impossible Tomb Adventure.*

Despite Brett's urging, I'd refused to send the stories to a publisher because, well, I wasn't a fiction writer. I was a *travel* writer. And I'd poured all this joy, hopefulness, and creative exploration into them. The idea of making an offering to the publishing gods of this intimate story, about the Katie I wished I were, felt way too vulnerable. Fictional Katie abounded with bravery, confidence, and certain happily-ever-afters, despite the dangers along the way. She didn't stumble around and constantly second-guess herself—rather, she knew who she was, what she wanted, and where she belonged.

I forced a chuckle through my tightening throat. "You know I'm trying to keep it authentic for the kids." I blinked out of my foggy emotions and gave the conversation a safe turn. "Speaking of kids, how are my favorite niece and nephew?"

"Your *only* niece and nephew," came Brett's unamused response.

"Which proves my point all the more." I shrugged, as if he could see me through the phone. "We both know it will take a miracle from God for Chase to find a woman to put up with his temperament. You may be the only hope for my aunt status."

"After being raised in a house with Mom, I think Chase is just afraid of the possibilities."

Weren't we all? Until Brett went off and met Jess, a wonderful woman from an equally wonderful and well-adjusted family, we three surviving siblings rarely spoke of our future families. Jess's entrance into our family seven years ago introduced a picture within our defunct family of a happily-ever-after possibility. At least for Brett. The relationship had not only brought out his smile a lot more but had pulled him out of his shell. She proved that the right person in one's life had power to influence that person for the good.

I shook the thoughts away. "How are Jess and the kids adjusting to the new apartment?"

His hesitation didn't bode well. "We need more space, but we just can't afford it right now. Jess is trying to make the best out of the situation, as usual, but I can tell she's feeling the pinch."

"Maybe moving away from Atlanta would help?"

"It's something we've talked about, but I'd need to find a solid job before we can even consider that option, and we can't count on an income from Jess for a while. It's cheaper for her to stay at home with the kids than pay for daycare."

"But that means you can't pursue your art like you'd hoped." His dream for years.

"I think I may need to hang up the hobby for a while. Mom always said it would never amount to anything anyway, and I want to be a part of my kids' lives when I'm home from the bank."

Unlike our dad. But Brett didn't say that. He didn't have to.

"You're a great dad. I just wish you could have a little freedom for your dreams too."

"Katie." His voice softened with acceptance that I didn't fully understand. "Sometimes one dream has to bow to another, and that's okay." He chuckled. "I love having my family to come home to, even if they're sometimes loud and stinky."

"Gross." I pushed levity into my response, but my heart squeezed a little. Home sounded sweet when he said it. "I'm going to tell Jess you called her stinky."

"Funny." Quiet passed between us as I looked out the window into Scotland green. "She's the best thing that's ever happened to me."

"Clearly one of a kind to put up with you and all your dad jokes." I felt that pinch in my chest again, but for a different reason. A weird sort of fight-or-flight battle against pressing into what Brett had. Something sweet enough to redirect dreams and plans. "But I hope you can pursue your art someday, Brett. You have a gift and you love it."

"I hope so too, Skeeter."

The nickname incited my grin.

"When will you be back at the farm? We'll come visit."

Oh, how Brett loved that farm. He'd never say it aloud, but we both knew he loved the old place more than I did. Why Grandpa and Gran left it to me, I'm not sure, except maybe as a way to link me back to my roots when I traveled more days out of the year than not.

"I have an assignment in Kentucky right after Scotland, and then I have a few weeks before the next trip. This time to Spain."

"Spain." He released the word with a puff of a laugh. "Someday you may want to land a little while, Skeeter."

The unspoken implication unearthed something Gran had told me once: "*It's fine to run away from home, but one day home will catch you.*"

"You find me a match as amazing as Jess and I might consider it." I rubbed my palm against my jeans and shook off the unsettling feelings I couldn't quite define. "Otherwise, I'll be off now on my little afternoon adventure to a quaint Scottish village in the middle of the most magical countryside you can imagine."

"Rub it in."

"Turnabout is fair play, brother dear."

With the sound of his familiar chuckle in my ears, I ended the call and started for the village of Glenkirk. My maid—which sounded really weird to voice even in my thoughts—had mentioned a path to the village cut through the garden on the back side of the house, so I started down the second floor (or first floor in the UK) hallway of guest rooms toward the back stairs. Reading about Scottish legends while rocky cliffs, ocean breezes, and ancient mountains surrounded me was sure to inspire my imagination for my magazine articles, not to mention my blog. I'd already written up a teaser to describe my introduction to Mull from the ferry.

And my books? This place breathed with some sort of otherworldly wonder.

I slowed my pace down the hallway to take a few photos of the amazing woodwork, which looked new but was so intricately woven into the existing crown molding that it fit perfectly. Those must be some of the renovations Mrs. Lennox had mentioned during the tour. And had she said only half of the rooms were in use? What did she have in mind once the whole house was restored? Surely not just a Downton stage. From the entryway to the views, this place nearly screamed for something more.

I'd just made it to the top of the back stairs when a strangely familiar voice broke into the silence from the direction of the main stairs. Considering an entire hallway separated me from the top of the main stairs and I could still hear his voice painfully clearly only proved the identification of the man all the more probable.

Mark Page, or at least that was his online moniker.

My entire body seized, and I pressed myself against the wall as if my jacket and jeans would somehow become one with the floral print wallpaper. I even pulled my ball cap a little lower on my head.

Why had he been invited to Craighill's media preview? He wrote sports travel articles. How on earth would he fit into an Edwardian Experience?

"Horseback riding?" His words barreled down the hallway toward me as if in answer. "Of course I know how to ride. Been doing it since I was sixteen."

I rolled my gaze heavenward and prayed for a secret passage to open behind me and transport me to . . . anywhere. Even that awful dungeon restaurant I'd visited in Belize.

Mark and I had only spent one evening together after a media event in London, and no amount of toothbrushing had removed his painfully thorough and unprovoked kiss from my tactile memory. Twenty texts (most of which I tried to ignore), a long and unflattering (to him) social media message, and five months later, he'd seemed to have moved on.

And now? I had to spend three weeks with him in this house?

My eyes narrowed on the beautifully ornate ceiling. Gran often talked about how God wrote the story of our lives. Hmm . . . Why did my personal genre look more like a book of jokes than a cozy mystery or sweeping adventure?

It certainly didn't resemble a romance. For one, living on the fly made it nigh impossible to meet a guy for more than two or three dates. My lips tipped. Except the delicious Egyptian in Cairo. Five of the best dates of my life, all along the Nile on a dahabeah.

But second, I'd never met a guy to stay put for. Finding one who was confident enough to encourage my travels but loved me in such a way to bring me home? Well, maybe he was as legendary and mythical as a sword in a stone.

Mark's voice drew nearer, so with careful, quiet steps, I descended the back stairs and turned the curve on the landing of the stairs, just as his blond head came into view. With a creak to the next step, I blew out the breath I'd been holding and dashed down the remainder of the stairs into a narrow hall, only to come nose to wood with a massive stair railing swinging toward my head. Before ducking, I did wonder how on earth a stair railing could fly, but with my introduction to Craighill, normal seemed relative.

The railing swung over the space my head recently vacated, and on the other side of it stood Mr. Scotsman from the day before. The railing balanced on one of his massive shoulders as if it were nothing more than a damsel.

I blinked.

Well, not that he seemed the sort to throw damsels over his shoulder. But with those arms, it probably wasn't a hardship.

Heat flooded my already hot face, and if my breathing came any faster, my head might take flight off my body like a hot-air balloon.

I stared up at the man from my crouched position on the floor, the brim of my cap blocking the top half of his expression, but his close-shaved beard framed an impressive frown. I braced myself as I rose to my feet.

Maybe I could get in the first word.

"If you're going to lug a tree through the house, don't you think you ought to wear a warning bell or something?"

Looking up to him still felt strange, but in a nice sort of way. I met his gaze, but the scowl I'd expected was surprisingly absent. Instead, his dark brows pinched together and he studied me as if he wasn't sure what to do next. Those eyes had taken on more of a stormy blue than the paler hue of earlier. And I lost whatever verbal defense I'd partially been concocting in my head.

The man didn't respond with words, but his gaze traveled from my face to the brim of my hat and then back to my eyes. The silence prickled over my skin, and I cleared my throat, gesturing with my book to his railing.

"Do you carry stair railings through manor houses often?" I placed my free hand on my hip to have something to do with it and looked away from his stare to the wood. The light filtered over it, highlighting the beautiful grain and reddish sheen. "Is that cherry? What an amazing finish!"

I reached my hand to smooth over the wood, noting the careful trim work on the lip of the railing. "And the detail. Beautiful. There's something about hand-carved wood that feels so intimate, isn't th—"

My words died on my tongue as I glanced back at his face and realized I'd been yammering on to a man whose sentence lengths so far made it up to five fingers. Maybe less. Plus, by stepping closer to touch the railing, I'd moved nearer to Stoic Scot than I'd intended. My pulse ricocheted in my throat. I breathed in to make a comment and caught a distinct sweet scent along with something tangy. Maybe wood finish or cologne? I nearly grinned. No, he didn't seem the cologne sort.

He blinked as if coming out of a daze. Again his gaze shifted from my eyes to my hat, then paused on the book in my hand. The crinkles on his dark brow deepened. "That book's rubbish."

Three words in that sentence. He was digressing. My yammering clearly impressed.

Yet the sentence and his tone of voice failed to match. There was a softness in his delivery, breathlessness, even, which slowed my comprehension.

"What?"

He cleared his throat and took a step back, nodding toward my book. "That book on Scottish legends. It's pure rubbish. If you want a good book on the subject, you can fetch Alec Frasier's *Lore and Legend* from Mirren's in the village."

Three full sentences. And in that Scottish accent.

Why did I feel like I'd just won an award while also being reprimanded? The way he curled his *r*'s sounded a whole lot different from Mrs. Lennox. Skin-hummingly different.

I tugged the book to my chest to protect it from his critique. True, I had only read the first few paragraphs, but "rubbish" seemed a strong insult for something that couldn't defend itself. "Are you one of the servants in this whole Edwardian Experience?"

Though Mr. Grumpy would have a difficult time making his six-seven, wide-shouldered, thundercloud-browed self unnoticeable.

"I'm not a servant." He grumbled out the words, his eyes narrowing.

My attention flitted down his attire of dusty white shirt and brown trousers, halting for just a second to appreciate those shoulders one more time. It was a rare thing indeed for me to meet a man who made *me* feel small.

"Are you quite done oglin' me?"

My attention snapped back to his eyes as sweltering heat coursed up my neck into my face and nearly evaporated through my eyeballs. "Um . . . you're *dressed* like a servant."

"I'm a tradesman." One of his dark brows needled northward. "BBC doesn't teach you everythin', Duchess." He ground out the last word like an oath and dipped his head, as if that made his behavior all better.

I stood up to my full height, which usually gave me more confidence than it currently did. "I'm . . . a writer." But with a baseball cap, jeans, and sneakers, the argument didn't quite sting. "Not a duchess."

Which fell flat, even to my ears.

He enacted the most impressive eye roll I'd ever witnessed, then released a growl—or that's what it sounded like—along with a grumbled string of words I couldn't understand. Giving me as wide a berth as a massive man and a stair railing could, he walked toward the ballroom.

I glared at the back of his head. "If you're going to insult me, at least do it in English."

And with a little twinge in my chest of something I couldn't quite identify and a glance back toward the disappearing giant, I marched directly out the back door toward Glenkirk and far away from grumpy Scots, arrogant sportswriters, and the promise of another embarrassing experience.

The fresh air slowed my pulse and pace as I stepped over the threshold from the house on the walking path through Craighill's back garden. Seven years as a travel writer taught me to heed that inner navigator and breathe in the day. Most of my best stories happened in the unplanned moments, and I tried to keep an eye out for the untold tales and less-trodden trails.

So I took a fistful of that experience to heart and pushed away my worries about Mark and the unsettling leftovers from Brett's call and stepped forward. A motto for life. *Move forward.*

Too many things in the past only slowed me down anyway.

So I embraced the moment. The early July breeze against my cheeks. The glints of sun through a veil of intermittent clouds. A slight mist sprinkling my face and the sweet scent of—what was it? Almonds and honey? A burst of white flowers clung to the rock garden wall lining the path toward a grassy field. In fact, though part of the wall disappeared beneath an overgrowth of vines and a few wild roses, my gaze trailed the length of the expanse, and the breadth of the garden took full shape.

What must it have once looked like? Because, from a little Google searching, it had been built in 1800 as the pride and joy of some great Scottish military guy named Duncan MacKerrow. I'd always bragged that the house I'd inherited from my grandparents was pretty old as a 1915 two-story brick farmhouse, but Europe redefined *old* for me. In fact, Craighill stood as a relatively young structure in the UK.

The garden path spilled out into a vast glen, the beauty of which caused me to pause my steps. My breath caught. A lush hillside slanted down to Loch na Keal, and hugging the edge of the water stood a line of brightly colored buildings, just like photos I'd seen of other Scottish places like Tobermory or Portree. Quaint, colorful, and waiting for a visit.

The path wove through a glorious field that looked like a carpet of gold. What a combination. Blue loch, green hillsides, azure sky, and a field of . . . I drew closer.

Buttercups.

Thousands of them blanketed the way toward Glenkirk, and the picture settled somewhere deep in my heart. With sloped mountains in the distance and a wide, blue sky paired with the golden field and colorful buildings, I thought for a moment that I'd stepped into a childhood story.

Grandpa had often commented on how the Blue Ridge Mountains reminded him of his childhood home in the Scottish Highlands. There was a similarity to the sloping backdrop of valleys, hills, and occasional rocky edges, but this landscape held an even more ruggedly beautiful aspect. And vastness with an ancientness I could feel almost bone deep.

I took some photos and short videos to use for later, then jotted down a few notes in my notebook before taking the path down the hill. A quiet surrounded the view unfolding before me, and I could even hear the wind move through the grass. I couldn't remember the last time I'd experienced such stillness. The world slowed down. I felt it in some strange way, like I felt the sluggishness of sleep start to take hold while sitting by the fire during an evening rain. And underneath the quiet, a strange sort of calm soothed me like nothing I'd ever known. Not exactly like sleep, but more like . . . well . . . like a loving caress over my soul.

Almost as if I knew this place. Like I'd breathed the air before.

But that was ridiculous. I'd seen hundreds of breathtaking views, some even more so than this one, but here in this place I felt an inexplicable tug toward memory and life and . . . what else?

I paused on the trail, wrangling a sudden rush of emotion under control. Grandpa's memory always hovered close, but ever since I'd stepped into his ancestral country, thoughts of him seemed nearer. I wrapped my arms around myself in a hug, bracing my heart for the squeeze of pain. The thinnest tether binding me to those Blue Ridge Mountains had snapped when my grandparents died. The sense of belonging to a place and people where I could just be myself had dissolved with each passing year that separated me from their hugs.

My sister's face rushed to my mind, unbidden, and my whole body tensed against the onslaught of failures. Of lostness. Of unspoken words and impossible expectations.

I shook away the thoughts and raised my camera for another photo or two, capturing the present. The moment. The beauty right in front of me.

As an adult, I rarely gave much credit to what Mom said, but in one thing she was absolutely right.

"You can't change the past, so just leave it be."

The village looked much closer than the half hour it took me to get to the first building on the main street. I traversed over damp ground and a bog that soaked my tennis shoes to such an extent that water squished out of the sides of them with each step I took along the pavement.

The effect of the rainbow buildings separated by a cobblestone street from the dark waters of Loch na Keal proved a striking example of nature and humans meeting in the middle to create a beautiful combination. The buildings of Glenkirk poised along the right side, and on the left a small man-made rock ledge lined with flowers buffered the street from a drop into the loch.

In America there probably would have been a guardrail to block folks from taking a fun tumble into the water, or if legend held, from being pulled under by a murderous mermaid or kelpie. But here it seemed the folks favored more natural beauty and less intrusion—either that or not enough people had fallen into the loch to cause a problem.

The shops looked even cuter close up, and a few small boats wobbled in the gentle waves of the loch. As my next step squished and my cold toes begged for relief, I scanned the nearest buildings for evidence of the shops' contents. Only nine or ten shops lined the road with a few more scattered along the hillside behind. They were different heights and widths, but all the same general boxy shape with white-framed windows surrounded by colors of teal, red, or yellow. I figured that since it rained so much in Scotland, the natives tried whatever they could to brighten up the atmosphere. Which made me like them even more. I was a sucker for dedicated optimists.

The Glenkirk Inn stood as one of the tallest buildings at the edge of the street, each of the windows on its three stories curtained with a patchwork of different patterns. A post office came next, followed by Lochside Café and then some sort of all-purpose shop called The Scot. Shona's Bakehouse and Sweeties was squeezed in between a charity shop called Second Go 'Round and The Haverin' Magpie, which didn't open until later in the day.

The shops seemed to have a little bit of everything, kind of like the colors of the buildings. A steeple rose from a church secluded behind a veil of trees in the distance up from the main street. Then my attention focused on a beautiful yellow building with the sign "Mirren's Books" on the front.

Mirren's large sign read: "Visitor's Centre, Books & Tackle."

My lips formed a smirk. Quite the combination.

The sudden jingling of a bell sounded behind me, spoiling the midmorning quiet.

"Comin' through!" came a youthful and somewhat frantic call along with the bell.

I turned just in time to see a raven-haired girl whizzing down the street toward me on a bicycle. Her hair flew in all directions as the bike approached at an alarming speed.

The earlier warmth of the sun dissipated from my body and I froze in place.

"Get out of the way! My brakes is gone!"

And that was the second time I saw my life flash before my eyes since coming to Scotland.

CHAPTER 4

Katie

Just as the cycling siren neared enough for me to see the whites of her eyes, my sloshy tennis shoes and I jumped to the side, landing in a magnificent mud puddle and clearing the way for the homicidal mini-cyclist to zoom past.

She shot a toothy grin over her shoulder, and I'm pretty sure my jaw slacked.

The little rascal!

If my eyes shot lasers, little Miss "My brakes is gone!" would have an exploded tire. I stared at the girl's retreating silhouette as I pulled myself from the tiny pond from which I'd landed and shook out my shoes.

"I see you survived Kirsty and her dreaded bicycle."

A woman about my mom's age stood just outside the door of Mirren's. She wore a patterned dress with a red cardigan over it, and her dark hair fell to her shoulders in waves.

"So that happens often?" I took a few steps toward her welcoming smile, the squishing-shoe sounds keeping time with my words.

"Aye." Her pale eyes twinkled. "Some of us thinks there's naught wrong with her brakes and she merely likes to terrify folks to an early grave. Like her dad, that one."

My grin responded to her humor without hesitation. Her accent probably helped too. "I think my heart might have stopped there for a second." I patted my chest and closed the distance. "But since my life follows a series of unexpected accidents, I think I'll survive." I looked back in the direction the little girl had left. "And I'll know to keep my eye out for her next time."

"Both eyes." The woman pointed toward her own. "If I was you, *especially* with that one."

Oh, I liked this lady. With a renewed smile, I offered my hand. "Katie Campbell."

"Campbell." Her dark brows rose as she examined my face and took my hand. "Have you tossed that name around the village much?"

My smile resurrected. "My taxi driver told me to be careful with it since I was in McClean country and might find myself on the wrong side of a claymore."

Her laugh burst out in such an infectious way, it made me want to hug her. "Aye, if you'd lived here a few centuries ago." She wiped her eyes and looked back up at me. "But I think you're safe in this century if you stay away from certain villages. Though, if you're keen to learn more about it, Duart Castle is the site of one of the many battles between the McCleans and Campells."

Had I seen something about Duart Castle on a map?

"It's naught a half hour drive from here and has a braw view."

"Then I'll definitely add it to my list of sites to see on Mull."

"I s'pose you have some Scottish heritage in ye?"

"Aye." I tried the word out. "My grandfather was a first-generation Scottish American and Scotland's biggest fan."

Her smile grew to crinkle her eyes. "Mirren MacKerrow, and this is my bookshop." She gestured inside before leading the way over the threshold.

For a book lover, bookshops held a similar ambience no matter where you were in the world. The shelves of spines, the scents of paper and baked goods—but in this case an added mild fragrance of fish blended into the overall atmosphere.

Again, unexpected.

"There's a bit of everything here, as you'll find with most of the shops in Glenkirk. Small, but we have a mind of how to use our space." She waved toward the room. "Take a look around, Katie, and I'll fetch us some tea."

Mirren slipped through a door in the back and left me to the wonderful quiet of the room.

The back of the shop boasted rows of books with a sweet little window seat along one part of the back wall and a cozy sitting area around a potbellied stove at the other back corner. To my left stood a counter with various baked goods on display and a couple of small tables directly in front of it. But to my right, a section of rain gear, fishing poles, and other fishy sorts of things waited.

My attention fell on a row of rain boots.

As if approving of my approach toward the boots, my shoes added a squeak along with the familiar squish.

"Ah, you'll be needin' some wellies, will ya noo?" Mirren appeared from the back room and gestured toward my feet. "I'm brewin' a fresh pot so we can warm you from your soggy socks up through the rest of you."

It was almost impossible not to keep smiling at the woman. Not only did her turn of phrase and accent make me think of my grandpa, but she glowed with a welcome and friendliness that put my whole body at ease.

"That is so kind of you."

"Pshh!" She waved away my words and returned her attention to my shoes. "Some fresh wool socks would set you right too, you ken?"

How could a simple phrase like "you ken" squeeze my heart in twenty places? Grandpa was surely grinning down from heaven as I stepped into the world he loved so much . . . and felt such an immediate kinship to.

"Pulling on a pair of those soft warm socks over my cold toes sounds like one of the best things I've heard all day." I pointed toward my shoes and wiggled my wet toes. "I'm afraid I didn't come prepared for Scotland in the footwear department."

"We'll take care of that." She nodded, then scanned me from toes to head as she reached for a pair of socks nearby. "And aren't you a tall one? You'd barely fit through the door of my cottage. My boys have to bend their necks, and you're nearly as tall as the shortest of the lot."

"You should have seen me in the Philippines. I nearly bowed every time I walked through a doorway."

A warm chuckle erupted from the woman as she handed me the socks, adding another charm to the list. She fit within these storied walls and the quaint shop. Her red cardigan over a simple dress. Her reading glasses topping her head. The resident twinkle in those pale blue eyes.

Everything fit together in a perfect sort of homey way.

"I suppose you're one of the media people who've come to Craighill for the next few weeks?"

"I am. I write for a travel magazine called *World on a Page*."

"So you travel for your job?" She lowered her glasses from her head to study me. "And write about what you see?"

"And any adventures or misadventures I experience along the way."

Her chuckle warmed the room again. "From that twinkle in your eye, I'd say you're keen on finding a few adventures."

"Or they're keen on finding me."

We rummaged through the few pairs of wellies and, to no one's surprise who has lived my life, the only ones close enough to fit my size 10½ feet were a bright yellow pair covered in hand-painted vegetables.

"Well now. I've hoped to sell those for a good three years."

I nodded down at my newly adorned feet. "I wonder what took so long."

"I cannae say. They've been my favorite pair." She offered a wink and then shuffled to the counter. "How do you find the folks at Craighill?"

I and my bright yellow wellies turned toward the books, measuring my response. "Surprised to find the Lennoxes are English instead of Scottish since the house is on Mull. But Mrs. Lennox has been pleasant enough." No need to mention the macaw. "And the house is fantastic."

"Aye, 'tis so." Mirren nodded her appreciation. "A lovely house. Historic. Over four hundred years old and in need of some repair. The upkeep for a house the likes of Craighill is no small feat."

I couldn't even imagine. The electric bill for the farmhouse back home was impressive enough. The idea of upkeep and heating for some stone manor house on an island in the northern hemisphere? No thanks.

A whistling sound erupted from the back room, and Mirren's head rose to attention. "Ah, the tea! I almost forgot." She raised a finger toward me. "Take a look around at the books, and I'll be back in a trice."

She scurried off, leaving me to pleasantly peruse the room some more, especially the bookshelves lining the back corner. All sorts. And many featuring Scotland in some way or other. Hmm. What book had the Hateful Highlander mentioned? *Lore and Legend*?

Well, he was Scottish, so at least I should consider his recommendation.

I skimmed over the spines of the books. A few popular titles faced forward, particularly a series involving time travel. Another highlighted series featured dragons and swords on the covers. A crimson cover embossed with gold caught my attention, and I slipped the book from the shelf. *Scottish Kisses and Other Romantic Secrets of Alba*?

My face grew warm just reading the title. What on earth would the contents do? And yet, after a glance over my shoulder, I flipped open the book. Despite my less-than-stellar romantic history and uncertain romantic future, a title like that slapped on a book practically compelled the most inane romantic to take a little peek—or *keek*, as the locals might say.

My gaze fell on a short paragraph near the top of the page.

> Though your typical Scotsman may appear standoffish to the stranger's eye, don't let his expression fool you. The Scots are a deeply passionate people with a love for family, story, drink, and an extended coorie or snogging opportunity.

I cleared my throat and sent another glance over my shoulder. I didn't know what coorie meant, but I sure knew what *snogging* implied. I'd read enough books to almost envision that one. My face reheated and I slammed the book closed but hesitated before returning it to the shelf.

I cleared my throat and slipped the book back open.

> The history and romance of Scotland is part of the lifeblood of its people. And though they may talk a great deal about their stories and histories, they'll not fail to show rather than tell when they find their *m'eudail* or *ghràidh*—darling or love, as the case may be.

A door snapped closed, sending me into motion, and I tucked the book beneath my arm to hide the title. Good grief. I didn't need *that* sort of distraction. Even though my thoughts had sufficiently dipped into the part of my brain that wondered how a wonderfully standoffish Scot might show his passion in a very non-standoffish kind of way.

And then a vision of the Sulky Scot's eyes and shoulders—in that order—popped to mind.

Ack!

"Here we go, Katie Campbell," came Mirren's voice as she emerged back into view, a tray in hand.

I snatched *Lore and Legend* from the shelf and shoved a smile in place, hoping my cheeks weren't as red as they felt. "You're so kind. Thank you. But let me go ahead and pay for these purchases so I won't forget."

Mirren placed the tray on a small center table near the bookshelves and followed me back to the counter, where I placed the wellies and the books out for her view.

She scanned my findings and looked up at me, a twinkle deepening in her eyes as she rang up the books. "Are you looking for a wee bit of lore and romance here in Scotland, Katie Campbell?"

The heat in my face took an upswing into feverish, but I shrugged and gestured toward the books. "Fictional suits me well."

"No beau back home, is there?"

Back home? I didn't even know where home was. And spending too much time trying to sort out the answer ended up hurting in places I tried to ignore.

"I appreciate that matchmaking twinkle in your eyes, Mirren, but I'm not really the type of girl a home-loving Scottish guy would want. I travel a lot. I'm a little nerdy and old-fashioned. Ridiculously clumsy." As my list grew, the twinge of loneliness in my chest grew too. "Prone to snuggle up by the fire rather than party in the pub."

My list didn't seem to deter that twinkle as much as I'd hoped. "Ah, so you've set your mind against finding true love here, have ye?"

"No, not . . . I mean . . . I'm sure there are some . . . braw Scottish men in want of a wife." And my cheeks may have started to sizzle a little. "But no guy wants a girlfriend who travels all the time, and very few are after a giant." I gestured toward myself.

Her brows rose.

"Not that I'm looking, of course." I scanned the room, searching for a diversion, and my gaze landed on some hand-carved fishing poles. "Oh, what are those? Aren't they lovely."

A smile crooked on the woman's face, letting me know she was not deceived by my attempt at distraction. "Aye, if you're looking for a nice souvenir, those would prove an excellent choice." She opened a wooden box by the door that housed a dozen or more long poles, complete with a simple string and hook. "My brother makes them, and all the proceeds go to support our local school."

I couldn't help the grin that pulled against my lips, grateful for the topic change. The simple poles reminded me of going fishing with my grandpa in the little pond at the back of his farm. We'd never caught too much with them—an occasional surprise or two—but rarely anything to take back home for supper. The whole art and experience of fishing provided the real goal: time—with him.

I glanced back at Mirren. "Proceeds go to the school, huh?"

"They do." She preened, clearly proud of her brother's work. "He's made 'em for over thirty years."

Though the poles were simple, the craftsmanship was not. Tiny curves and curls grooved into the wood. Swirls of Celtic variety. A simple silhouette of a dragon or a bird or a mermaid. My fingers glided over the indentations and smoothed over the arches of a few of the poles until I settled on my choice. The pole held carvings of flowers and the moon, and ended near the top with a beautiful woman, her hair and gown swirling down the wood to meet the flowers.

"Ah, you've chosen Aine." Mirren's grin crinkled.

"Aine?"

"Aye, the goddess of love." Her brows rose again. "Seems to be a theme. I wouldnae wonder if there's a secret desire in your heart, Katie-girl."

The *Scottish Kisses* book popped to mind and my cheeks went hot again. "Well, doesn't everybody want love?"

Whether we're able to find it or not is the real question.

She didn't answer but rang up my order while whistling some sort of magical tune that reminded me of a bluegrass ballad from my childhood. "This afternoon is meant to be a fine day, and the pools will be a good place to start."

"The pools?"

"Aye, for fishin'." She nodded toward the pole in my hands. "There are some nice pools down the trail with a few fish and a pretty view just waitin' to show off some of our island scenery for ye." Her suggestion, paired with the twinkle in her eyes, gave me the nudge I needed to take a little detour and indulge in a childhood memory placed quite perfectly in Grandpa's old stomping grounds. "I'd wager an adventure or two may wait there too."

Why did "adventure" take on a totally different connotation when paired with her mischievous twinkle?

"But first, we must have tea before it gets cold." She guided my newly wellied feet, my bag of books, and my fishing pole over to the little sitting area by the stove where she'd left her tray. "You won't want to become peckish while you're out near the pools."

I had just taken a seat and filled a little plate with a sandwich and scone when the bell over the door jingled someone's entrance. Four older ladies, a book and bag in each hand, entered the shop and, in deep conversation about some spy in a downed plane, found their way to the corner where I sat.

With a nod and/or smile in my direction and without any explanation, each lady took a plate and cup from the tray and joined me on the seats near the stove as if they'd been expecting me.

What was happening?

"So glad to have a new one with us today," said one lady as she welcomed me, took a seat, and opened her bag. "Not often enough we get new ones."

The next three ladies did the same.

From their bags, they drew yarn balls of various colors, knitting needles, and knitting projects in various stages of completion.

I looked over at Mirren as she took the vacant chair next to mine, her own knitting piece in hand. She leaned close. "This is our Wednesday morning Stories and Stitches book club."

Book club? I shrugged off the surprise and embraced the opportunity. "How lovely." Getting involved with the culture always led to some great blog posts and articles. And, like this, I usually stumbled upon them.

"And everyone will love to learn more about you and your history," Mirren continued. "All of us bring our own stories, don't we?"

My back stiffened a little. My own story? I wrote about other people's stories. Not my own. Some places weren't meant to be explored too deeply.

"I'm much more interested in hearing about *you* all."

"Oh! She's American!" exclaimed an older lady wearing a purple cloche hat that brought out the green of her eyes. "How lovely."

"Katie, this is Lori." Mirren gestured toward the hat lady. "And Bea." The woman beside Lori offered a gentle smile. Her beautiful dark hair spun up beneath a teal headband that highlighted her skin tone, which was only a shade lighter than her hair. "And there's Blair." The woman had a full white head of hair and wore round spectacles perched atop a narrow nose framed by two rosy cheeks. If anyone ever looked like Mrs. Claus, this was her.

"And I'm Maggie," announced the fourth woman, shaking her too-blond-to-be-real head of tight curls and examining me through narrowed eyes.

I pulled my gaze away from her to friendlier faces. "It's a pleasure to meet all of you. My name is Katie Campbell."

An audible response emerged in various ways from the little crowd but, apart from Maggie, ended in more sympathetic smiles than not, with Bea nodding and saying, "But those feuds were so long ago."

And I wasn't sure whether to nod my gratitude at not being in peril for my last name or laugh at the idea that my last name could put me in peril. In Scotland. Where stories and histories seemed to carry weight for decades and, maybe, centuries.

"What do you like to read?" This from Mrs. Claus . . . er . . . Blair?

"All sorts of things." Surely book choices couldn't be as historically controversial as my last name. "Fiction, travel, of course." I laughed. "History."

"And have you enjoyed your visit to Mull so far?" Bea asked, touching up my tea.

"There's this wild sort of beauty to it, isn't there? Otherworldly."

All the ladies, even Maggie, nodded in agreement.

I tipped my head to them. "And the people are pretty nice too."

"Well, I'll tell you now that we're not like some of the movies portray," Maggie offered. "It's not always raining here, and our men dinnae wear kilts all the time."

"But when they do, it's worth remembering," Lori added with a little glimmer in her eyes.

My lips twitched. *Go, Lori!*

"And I havenae heard one person say 'och aye the noo' in all my days." Maggie's gray eyes grew wider the more she spoke. "And there are a great deal of friendly Scots if one takes the time to learn us. We're not a crabbit group in the slightest. No matter what the movies say."

Though her deepening frown conveyed just the opposite.

"Maggie," Mirren interrupted, her lips tightening as if she fought a smile. "I dinnae think Katie is someone with a poor opinion of us, are you, Katie?"

"Not at all," I answered, smiling. "My grandpa was a first-generation American Scot, so I have all the respect in the world for my own kin." I tagged on an attempt at a Scottish accent on the last few words of my sentence and garnered some chuckles. But not from Maggie. "And I'm delighted more than I can say to spend some time here."

"And what's brought you to Mull?" This from . . . Blair, was it?

"I'm a travel writer, and I'm here for the Craighill House's Edwardian Experience."

All smiles fell, almost changing the temperature in the room.

"Not fans of Craighill?"

"It's no that." Blair adjusted her glasses only to look at me from over the rims. "Craighill is a part of our heritage here in Glenkirk. We love the *house*."

"And the gardens," Bea added.

"But it's Lennox we're not too keen on." Maggie mumbled out the phrase before taking a bite of scone. "The Sassenach!"

Lennox? Which must mean Mrs. Lennox? And I'd never heard *Sassenach* said in such an unflattering way. Mind you, I'd only heard the word mentioned by Jamie Fraser.

Didn't it mean English?

Mirren placed a palm on my knee. "It just takes some adjusting when any foreigner comes into your place with their own ideas, as you can imagine."

"And brings all her workers from England," Maggie added, before washing down her bite with a sip of tea. "Not one hire from the village. Why?" Her eyes narrowed. "Because she's too high and mighty, that's why."

Not such a great rapport to have for a new business, that's for sure. If Mrs. Lennox wanted to build her clientele, reputation mattered, especially with locals. My thoughts spun back to attempting to fit into dozens of tiny dresses, and an idea popped to mind. Maybe a little olive branch for both Mrs. Lennox and the ladies of Glenkirk would make this entire experience a little better for everyone. Besides, if I was going to make this assignment shine for Dave, then it couldn't hurt to put in a good word or two. "Would you happen to know of a good seamstress nearby who can work fast?"

All the ladies' attention shifted back to me, so I continued, "There's some trouble with a few pieces of clothing I have back at Craighill."

"Aye, Janie McTavish is one of the best here in the village." Mirren stared over at me, her expression making me feel all warm and cozy inside and, at the same time, a little . . . nervous. What was going on behind those eyes? "She and her husband run The Hairy Coo."

"Which is an excellent shop for wool wear," Lori offered.

"She hasn't a mind for wool wear, Lori." Maggie gave a shake to her head. "She's in need of a seamstress."

"I'll fetch Janie's card for ye." Mirren stood and stepped to the counter, leaving me alone with the knitters.

Which shouldn't sound as ominous as if felt.

"What does a travel writer do exactly?" This from Bea, her smile soothing over the earlier tension.

I took a sip of tea before answering. "Well, I travel around the world and collect stories to share, either through articles or podcasts or on my blog. I've even contributed to a few documentaries."

"You've been on the telly?" Blair's mouth dropped wide. "We've got a regular celebrity among us, don't we?"

"No, nothing like that." I laughed and shook my head. "And I'm really not interested in that kind of visibility."

In fact, the idea kind of crawled over my skin like Peruvian-sized cockroaches.

"Go to the pub of a Friday night and you're bound to collect more stories than you could ever use," Maggie offered with a smug look that let everyone know she thought she was clever.

"To be honest, I love getting everyday people's stories. Those are some of my favorites," I answered. "And sharing the history of an area, or the legends." I raised the *Lore and Legends* book. "There's never a dull moment with all these stories waiting to be told in a new way."

"Aye, Mull's stories are fathomless for sure." Mirren returned to her seat and placed a card on the table in front of me.

"I can't wait to learn about them." I waved toward the ladies. "I'm sure you all could write a book with the stories you know."

They nodded, a few snickering at the apparent delight of some of their memories.

"Our stories *do* tell a lot about us, don't they?" Mirren topped off my nearly full cup of tea. Her expression caught my attention, and I couldn't look away. Those pale eyes captured mine, delving deep, as if she saw all the way back to my broken childhood. "But if you're spending so much time on all these other stories, when do you share your own?"

My face went cold. People weren't supposed to see through me.

Especially not that quickly.

Which made me wonder about all those faerie stories about Scotland. And whatever magic powers Mirren, the bookshop lady, had. Because here I was, being held captive by Mirren's all-knowing eye like Frodo Baggins and Sauron. I flinched a little but tried to cover it with a rub to my arm. "I don't travel to share my stories." I laughed weakly. "People aren't interested in those."

"Then you've been around the wrong people, I'd say." Mirren didn't let go of me or the topic. "Every person's story is worth hearing, Katie-girl."

Katie-girl. The first time I thought I'd misheard, but here she went and said it again. The intimacy of the name paired with her knowing look twisted at my emotions. I cleared my throat. "Maybe my stories are just intermingled in the ones I tell." I swallowed through the lump in my throat and succeeded in pulling my gaze from hers, though I still felt her looking at me. Thankfully, each of the women rushed ahead, sharing some of their own life stories.

I drew in a deep breath, thankful for the distraction as I tried to wrangle in my emotions. Maybe I should skedaddle out of Scotland on the next ferry before I ended up spilling my heart to a faerie who would capture me in some sort of faerie world from which there was no escape. I looked down at the book in my hand and wondered if it would give me some answers.

As the ladies talked, I began to relax a little, commenting here and there, trying to sort out why my insides kept doing the shimmy every time I glanced over at Mirren.

Then Lori asked, "Where's home for you, lass?"

With only a slight hesitation and a tightening of my fingers on my teacup, I gave my automatic answer: "North Carolina."

"Do you have any siblings?" Blair blinked behind her glasses.

My throat closed up. "I have two brothers. Both older." Sarah's name waited on my tongue, but I forced the temptation away. "Brett, the brother who is closest to my age, would love fishing here. Chase would probably prefer the convenience of Edinburgh." Why was I chattering? I didn't chatter. "Where would you say are some of the best fishing spots?"

"Any of the lochs," Bea answered. "And my husband would be happy to show you."

I smiled and readied for another redirection of the conversation away from me when Blair asked, "Are your parents still with ye?"

With me? Ah, alive. "Aye," I added for levity. "They're in North Carolina. Actually, the mountains back home are similar to yours here in a lot of ways. I've heard there's a particularly large mountain on the island. What is it called again?"

"Ben More," Maggie said. "And if you walk to the top of the bràigh behind Craighill, you'll catch a fine view of it."

"I have a nephew who'd be keen on a lovely lass like you," Lori offered with a dreamy sigh.

"Oh." I steadied my feet against the floor, readied to stand. Escape. Possibly run. "Well, that's nice."

"Do you have a sweetheart back home?" The angle of Blair's glasses now made her eyes larger. Or maybe I was just paranoid. Like all of them were trying to peer into my broken and very private past.

"No sweethearts." I set my teacup down on the table and pulled my books up into my arms, tilting just a little bit to measure how far away the front door was. If I could jump over Bea and her tall hair, I could probably make it in less than five seconds.

"I cannae believe a lovely lass like you hasnae a lad of your own." Bea shook her head as if she'd read my mind about the escape plan. "There are some strappin' lads here who'd love a tall lass like yourself. You look like you could weather a few storms, and that's a fact."

My mouth struggled with something between a smile and a whimper. Why couldn't I shake these ladies? They were harder to elude than a bloodhound on the hunt. My breath caught. Maybe they smelled my growing fear.

"Do you miss bein' away from home?"

I looked over at Mirren, my trained response waiting on the end of my tongue, but the look in her eyes stopped me. Her gaze probed, sifted, and somehow pulled truth out of my mouth. "I . . . I miss what home could be, I guess."

My face paled. Had I just said that out loud?

And what was worse? I actually *meant* it. I hadn't even sorted out what home was yet. How could I miss what it *could* be?

If I stayed here much longer, I'd break down into a weepy mess in front of a bunch of strangers, and to my shock, all I really wanted to do was curl up inside Mirren's arms and cry like a baby on her shoulder while she cooed sweet Scottish comforts in my ear.

But that was insane.

That I actually felt the desire to bare my soul to the lovely bookshop owner.

Whom I'd just met less than an hour ago.

Suddenly the door of the bookshop opened and a familiar, broad-shouldered silhouette framed the threshold. My heart crawled right up into my throat and closed off any air I'd planned to breathe, as a terrifying realization dawned in my befuddled mind.

I didn't necessarily *need* it, but I desperately *wanted* a grumpy, barrel-chested, blue-eyed Scot to rescue me.

CHAPTER 5

Graeme

I've never been a fan of surprises.

Even when a lad.

But as soon as I walked into Mum's bookshop, I was gobsmacked by a ginger-headed surprise. The very American I'd hoped to avoid as much as possible sat cooried up next to Mum in the corner of the bookshop with the granny book club crowding in on all sides.

Like she somehow belonged right in the midst of them.

And what was worse? The poor hen looked as feart as a rabbit in a wolf's den. Those murky blue eyes of hers met mine as I entered the shop, all hints of the fiery lass from earlier that morning gone, replaced by a desperate vulnerability. Something in my chest twisted into a Double Davy knot.

She needed to be rescued.

My shoulders drooped as the realization unfurled into an ache behind my rib cage. And I would be the eejit to do it. I only fought against retreat for a second. The hardest thing about planning to rescue someone was when you couldn't. No matter how hard you tried.

My heart had been soundly throttled by the last woman I'd rescued. After two years together and a short engagement, her wandering heart not only found someone new but led her to a new life in Edinburgh. I'd thought we'd come to a compromise to make it work. But somewhere along the way, without letting me know, she'd stopped loving me and the idea of Mull in her future.

Then she left.

Like Greer. Except God alone could have rescued my sister. And He had. Just not here. The knot in my chest tightened to the painful place.

Playing hero proved a dangerous game between hope and failure. And I was full-up of failure.

My attention focused back on the ginger-headed American, and my jaw tensed with added resolve. Well, at least this rescue didn't involve hearts or cancer. I could manage this one—my attention swept the gaggle of ladies who'd known me my whole life—maybe.

"How did you trap one of the Craighill guests here already, ladies?"

All eyes turned toward me, but my focus remained on the American. She sighed and mouthed the words *thank you* before unfurling a smile I felt all the way to my spine. I should've turned back right then. The parrot and stair railing episodes gave clear warning, but instead, my feet stayed glued to the pine floors of the bookshop, confirming how mental I was.

"Well now, Graeme MacKerrow, what are you doing stopping by this morn? Come for your regular cup of coffee?" Mum stood, bringing the American with her. "Katie, have you met my son? He's up at the house something regular working on the repairs and stairs and such."

Katie's grin wobbled, as if she wrestled with it. "We've bumped into each other once or twice."

She raised her brows in silent amusement about her pun, and I forced my grin under control. Getting friendly with a social media personality from America wasn't on my to-do list for the day . . . or year.

Or ever.

She practically breathed "wandering heart." And crazy. Add social media to the equation and I was beginning to regret ever stepping foot in the village this morn.

"Aye." I tipped my head to her and then cleared my throat, dragging my attention back to Mum. "But nothin' proper since I'm there to do work and—"

"Well, she's a travel writer, a podcaster, and a blogger. She's even been on *television*."

Perfect. I ground my teeth and realized, yet again, how Mum didn't make the same connections in her brain as I did in mine. Being on television was one of the things that pulled Allison away from me and gave me another reason to refuse to turn on the telly for anything other than the local station of an evening, lest she pop up on the screen.

"But only documentaries, so keep those expectations duly measured, Mr. MacKerrow." Katie raised a palm as if to calm the rising praise. "I'm more of a behind-the-words type of gal."

"She collects stories, Graeme," Blair MacKay added, her eyes bright. "And wouldn't it be grand to share all the stories we know from—"

"I'm afraid the other guests have arrived at the house." I sent a weighted look to Katie, testing out her own nonverbal communication comprehension.

Those large eyes of hers widened with awareness, her bottom lip dropping a little, and the knot in my chest twined a wee bit tighter.

I looked back to Mum but then realized every set of eyes in the granny book club stared at me with various shades of amusement on their faces. Heat made a steady climb up my neck, so I rubbed at the spot and took a step back toward the door. "I thought you might want to know, Miss . . ."

"Campbell," Katie offered, reaching down to grab her jacket.

My lips tightened around my growing frown. Campbell? Och! Of course she was a Campbell!

"I'd better get back up to Craighill since Mrs. Lennox wants to meet with all the guests once everyone arrives." Her smile widened as she swept the room with an appreciative glance and tucked her hair behind her ear, only to have it slip right back in place against her cheek.

I rolled my eyes. Why would I even notice something like that? Eejit, indeed.

"Thanks so much for letting me spend time with you today." She held up the books in one hand. "And for the books." And raised a fishing rod. "And this." Then gestured toward her feet. "And the wellies." Her laugh bubbled out. "I'd say I've made a sufficient dent in your sales for today, Mrs. MacKerrow."

"Mirren," Mum corrected with a touch to the woman's shoulder. "And you're welcome anytime, Katie-girl."

Oh no! Mum already gave her a nickname, which meant the next statement would be—

"And you should come to my cottage for tea while you're on Mull," Mum continued, walking over to the counter. "I'll give you my address here, but Graeme can point out the path from the top of the hill as he walks you back to the house."

I raised my head to alert. Walk her back?

I looked over to find Mum's knowing gaze burrowing into mine with a warning that brooked no refusal. "Since you're sure to do more work there this afternoon?"

"I don't want you to go to any trouble." Katie looked from Mum to me as she picked up her pace to the door, tugging her rucksack on her back. At least the one thing I and the American had in common was the need for a quick escape from my mum. "I'm sure I'll be fine on my own."

"None of that, hen," Mum cooed as she placed a paper in Katie's hand. "And which days work in your schedule for tea?"

Katie's mouth opened in surprise, highlighting those pink lips of hers again, and I had the sudden urge to take out my eyeballs and toss them into Loch na Keal. Perhaps the local pixies were at work with their mischief, because I hadn't experienced this much difficulty ignoring a pretty woman in a while.

It must be the hair.

Because it *certainly* wasn't the accent.

Katie shifted her attention from Mum to me, as if I had an answer for my mother's behavior.

I never had an answer for Mum's behavior. She found new friends on an hourly basis.

"How . . . how very kind of you." The woman looked genuinely flummoxed by the admiration and attention. I suppose my opinion of the celebrity type was stained a little after Allison's promotion to lead fashion designer for some top brand in Edinburgh led to her departure.

And right after my sister had been diagnosed with cancer too.

As if my fiancé took the opportunity to run away from my family's grief, this simple life of Mull, and our future all at the same time.

"Would you mind if I got back to you on that answer after meeting with Mrs. Lennox today?"

"Of course." Mum stepped back. "Now off with you." Mum waved us away, but not before grinning at me with that crafty twinkle in her eyes.

Not again.

The look nearly gave me the boke. Could she and the entire book club become any more obvious or desperate in their matchmaking plans? I quelled the nausea and stared back at my mum as I held the door open for Katie to pass.

No! I inwardly shouted in hopes of transporting the clear message to her brain, but it bounced off her growing smile like the sprite-hearted woman she was.

Katie would be the fourth attempted match in as many months.

And Mum was no respecter of sons. Calum and Peter bore the brunt of her desire to see her weans married off and populating the whole of Mull.

And despite her grand boasting, none of the matches stuck.

Ever.

Especially the accountant from Inverness. What had Mum been thinking? The woman could talk the bark off a tree without a stop for breath.

I held Mum's gaze until the door clicked closed, attempting to communicate the futility of her habit. But I knew my attempt was even more futile than hers.

Drawing in a deep breath and bracing myself for the walk, I joined Katie along the street toward the house while keeping a very non-romantic distance between us.

"Thanks for rescuing me back there." Katie tucked the books she held against her chest and gestured back toward the bookshop with the fishing rod. "I mean, I know you were just sharing a message from Mrs. Lennox, but you arrived at the perfect time."

I gave my head a shake. "I dinnae think Lennox even knows you're in the village."

"Oh." Her narrow auburn brows took an upswing as that gaze turned back on me with newfound curiosity. "Well, thank you for rescuing me anyway."

"Rescue?" It sounded worse when she said it. "Dinnae think that, Katie Campbell. I'm not the heroic sort, but I do know that those ladies can prove a wee bit overwhelming. No one should have to manage them on their own for too long."

"So their . . . excessive welcome is a common occurrence then?" She released a long sigh and then chuckled. "I don't think I've ever been quite so—"

"Interrogated?"

She snorted and my lips twitched at the ungodly sound. "Um . . . I was going to say enthusiastically interviewed, but your word might fit a little better."

Sunlight brightened her hair to a fiery hue, a color not extinct from the western isles but still uncommon. And made even more noteworthy by its darker shade instead of the usual bright ginger color.

I rolled an annoyed gaze heavenward at my own thoughts. Shoving my hands into my pockets, I looked ahead and kept my attention away from the lass beside me turning from the road to go up the hill.

"Well, thank you again. I figured with the way we started off, I'd be the last person you'd want to help."

I stifled my wince, my shoulders drooping just a moment. Being mistaken as ill-mannered may be worse than being dubbed heroic.

But only slightly. "Those book club grannies are not to be underestimated."

"Book club grannies?" Her laugh burst out. "You realize I'll never be able to think of them as anything else now." She snickered and then sighed. "I don't know what happened back there. Usually I'm better at handling myself, but I think they caught me off guard with their exuberant friendliness and curiosity." Her eyes sparkled as she looked over at me. "Either that or there was some kind of truth serum in the tea."

I coughed to hide my laugh. Few things appealed to a Scotsman like a keen sense of humor. "Does it take a serum to get the truth out of you then, Katie Campbell?"

I'd only meant to match jest for jest, but the smile fell from her face. She looked away, recovering with a new grin that didn't reach her eyes. "I just assumed it was a regular occurence, considering the folklore and legends about this part of the world. A few faeries here, a mermaid there, occasional book club grannies brewing up trouble with magic tea."

She took a few steps to get ahead of me, not by much, but enough to notice. What caused such a reaction?

I ground my frown and resolution into place again. I didn't care. Rescuing . . . er . . . helping the lass didn't mean I had to know anything else about her. Nothing. "Then I'd give Mirren MacKerrow a wide berth if I were you."

Katie stopped altogether and turned, brows rising in unison. "Isn't she your mom?"

"Aye." Keeping my smile in check grew harder the longer I spoke.

"Which means I should know her better than the others. She's the most dangerous one of the lot."

The humored light returned to her eyes, and I flinched a little at the sight.

Humor looked good in those eyes.

The hill grew a wee bit steeper as we climbed, leaving the shelter of the surrounding trees and hills to allow the ocean breeze a more vigorous welcome. The air carried with it the feel of home and life. The blend of salt, buttercups, and phlox.

I paused. But something new today? What was it? A foreign warm scent. Vanilla? Honeysuckle? Something warm but distracting.

Her hair blew untamed beside me, wisping in my path and bringing a renewed hint of that scent.

Was that her?

I drew a deep breath of cool air and honeysuckle into my lungs.

"If I hadn't spent a good half hour with your mom *and* you weren't working so hard to fight a smile, I might believe you." Katie tossed me a look, lips crooked. "But I should probably forgo the tea at her house for fear of baring my soul or, at the least, buying more books than I can carry on my next flight."

She kept my pace up the bràigh, her breaths pulsing in time with mine, so she was used to similar activity. My gaze skimmed down her—her legs lean but strong. A tactile memory of her in my arms rushed to the forefront of my rebel mind. And the fact her stride nearly matched mine, highlighting those long legs, sent enough heat into my face to make my beard itch.

"This is a different path than the one I came down to the village on." Her words came a bit shallow, so I slowed my pace a little and pulled my brain away from long legs back to cool disinterest.

"Aye, it's a steeper climb along the back of the bràigh where I can point you toward Mum's house."

"Does she often invite strangers for tea?"

More than she ought, to my mind. "She tends to collect strangers like pets, and I suspect you're a particular curiosity with your"—I tried to sort out the right word—"career choice and stories."

Her pace slowed a little. "There aren't many exciting things to learn about me, but I have a whole lot of stories I can share about other people and places."

Did she often deflect from herself? I caught another glimpse of the lost look I'd seen before, rounded eyes like a wounded creature tugging at my dafty heart.

Och! I turned back to the climb. "What is it you're doing at Craighill besides writing articles and breaking my stairs?"

The gruffness in my voice failed to disarm her.

"Breaking your—" She narrowed her eyes at me in a mock glare. "Very funny." She shook her head, loosening her smile again. "What do you think I'm doing? I'm here"—she opened her arms wide as if to embrace the sky—"to immerse myself in an Edwardian Experience."

The way she attempted to mimic Mrs. Lennox on the last two words caused my grin to burst forth again. Ridiculous woman.

"I s'pose since you've been invited to the media preview of Lennox's . . ." I tried to find the right word. Circus? Spectacle?

"Experience?" Katie tipped her head, expression expectant before she dissolved into another easy laugh. "Believe me, I've been on a lot of trips around the world, but I've never been attacked by a parrot, nearly killed by a little girl on a bicycle, or tried to fit into dresses made for women half my size, all within two days. So Scotland has already proven to be an . . . experience," she repeated before pinching her eyes closed. "Humbling and a bit terrifying."

"Don't judge Scotland based on Craighill." I shook my head. "Or Kirsty. Or the book club grannies." Why was my life filled with such mad people? "You'd miss out on much better wonders."

We'd reached the crest of the hill when Katie came to an abrupt stop.

"What a view!" Her palm flew to her chest, and her head took a slow glide from one direction to the opposite. "And the lighting behind the clouds is just perfect." She began shaking off her rucksack and then frantically unzipped the bag. "I think this will do great as a first reel from Mull."

Reel?

She pulled a camera from her bag, removed the lens cover, and then proceeded to look around as if searching for something. My attention shot back to her fishing rod. Then realization dawned. Reel, as in social media?

She positioned the camera near her face and pointed in one direction, then another, continuing a little conversation with herself by saying things like, "Not quite that way," and "Almost perfect. Just a bit to the left, maybe?" and "Is that color green even real?"

I studied her a minute after the last question and then took another look at the view, trying to imagine someone seeing it for the first time. I never grew tired of it, especially on days when the sun brought out all the summer colors, so at least her awe proved Katie had a semblance of good taste.

Then, as if she found an answer to one of her questions, she took the camera away from her face and looked in various places near me, brow puckered in concentration. She shifted back and forth, staring at the ground.

Perhaps she fit into Craighill's *experience* better than I originally thought.

"Are you all right?"

"I'm trying to find a spot to set my camera so I can make a video."

My frown curled deeper. "Why?"

"Why?" She spun around, eyes wide. "Because you have this." She gestured back toward the horizon. "The combination of colors, atmosphere, and beauty. And I want to capture it as best I can. I just need to . . ." And then her attention grew in intensity, eyes narrowing on me. She tilted her head in her examination, her gaze starting at my forehead and trailing all the way down to my boots.

I shifted a step away from her.

I'd had Seamas, the crazy Highland cow, look at me the very same way, and it didn't end well.

For me.

She stepped closer, continuing to study me. "You're a great height for this, and I don't usually get to say that."

I'd be lying if I said I'd never been scared by a woman. Any red-blooded man who'd lived among the fairer sex for any time at all had had a little fear (even if he tried to hide it) of at least one lass in his life. They could change in a second. Or attempt to mind read poorly, and then men bear the brunt of their frustration over imaginary offenses. Or, even worse, they mind read well, which could cause even bigger troubles.

I avoided eye contact.

It hadn't helped with Seamas the cow, but perhaps it might with Katie the Crazy.

I crossed my arms and set my feet as if readying for battle. "A height for what?"

She stilled her approach. "For a video."

I tightened the cross of my arms. "I'm not going to be in one of your social media videos, Katie." And her name rolled off my tongue much too easily. A name well at home in these hills.

"I'm not videoing *you*, Mr. Grump." She pushed the camera into my chest, and one of my hands unfolded from its crossed position to catch the device. "*You're* videoing *me*."

Mr. Grump? I was not grumpy and would have told her so if she didn't just turn and walk back the way she'd come. "All right, I'm going to start walking toward the horizon, and I want you to push the button there, on top, and just follow me as I walk. I'll edit out any extras, but make sure you get the loch and the buttercups."

My body nearly bristled at her directives. First Mum and now some stranger telling me what to do. More reason to steer clear of women as a general rule.

She paused and looked back at me, her nose wrinkling with a frown like a little girl who'd done something wrong. "Sorry, I just bossed you around like you were a cameraman, didn't I?" Her shoulders scrunched in further plea, and all my grand resolve caved like the eejit I continued to be. "Would you please video me? It won't take but a minute."

I frowned like the grump I apparently was and raised the camera in answer.

Her smile flashed wide, and then she fluffed her hair so that it fell around her shoulders before proceeding to walk away from the camera. I pushed the button, and the numbers at the top of the screen started counting.

She continued walking away from the camera, legs taking long strides forward, and then she turned, raised a brow, and shrugged one of her shoulders, before waving toward the horizon in invitation.

Those eyes stared at me from the other side of the camera, dazzling and engaging, as if they looked directly into my soul. My throat squeezed against the awareness, the attraction.

A fleeting thing. Nothing to worry about. It had just been a while since a somewhat interesting stranger came through Glenkirk and into my world.

"Great!" she exclaimed, bringing her hands together as she moved back to me and plucked the camera from my hands. "Thank you so much."

She stared down at the screen, reviewing the video, and then cast me a look. "Great job. Usually when I have strangers video, I get more thumbs than usable content, but you focused right in on my face and the view."

I cleared my throat and shoved my hands back in my pockets. "Is that something you usually do for your work?"

She nodded, kneeling down to tuck the camera back in her bag. "I usually do three a week and have people guess"—she waved her hand in front of her as if displaying a title in the air—"what misadventure will I find today?"

"Don't you mean 'adventure'?"

"Nope. I make a living off my misadventures." She stood, pulling her rucksack over her shoulder before leaning down to collect her fishing rod. "So, basically, I get paid to mess up." A shadow passed over her features as she stood. "And it's something I'm really good at doing because I tend to mess up a lot."

Getting paid to bungle things? What a strange job!

And one I felt much too qualified for.

Without the videos and social media and travel parts.

Katie walked past me toward Craighill, its tower rising in the distance over the next hill, and I followed, mind spinning with more questions than I'd ever voice. From the longing in those eyes and the curb of sadness in her words, of all the people at Craighill, Katie Campbell's story may be the only one worth hearing.

CHAPTER 6

Katie

Walking into a live-action scene of a Clue game was odd.

Especially when one was dressed more like a lost camper than a 1920s Tudor mansion guest.

At least that's what it felt like as I turned the corner of the hallway into the lower salon of the manor house and met a collection of people poised as if waiting for the game to begin.

Not that I could pass for Miss Scarlet in the dining room with the candlestick.

Though Mrs. Lennox's daughter, Ana, certainly gave off Miss Scarlet vibes as she reclined on one of the chairs by the fireplace wearing an elegant red gown—especially the way she stared at the man by the bookshelf in a pinstriped suit. With his wire-rim glasses and slicked-back blond hair, he had to be Professor Plum.

I chuckled. Hmm . . . Who else?

The middle-aged man wearing a white button-down and beige trousers by one of the large windows gave off hints of Colonel Mustard—all the way to his shoe brush mustache—though he did have a bit of class about him.

Then there was the young woman with wild curly brown hair who looked like she was, well, examining a piece of pottery on the mantel with a magnifying glass in hand. Mrs. Peacock, perhaps. After extensively viewing as many seasons of *Downton Abbey* and *Upstairs Downstairs* that would fit on my lengthy flight from Australia, I could confidently say that her simple blue dress looked era appropriate.

My lips inched wide. Okay, I was pushing the Clue comparison a bit too far.

Three women, two men. Those numbers couldn't be right.

And then I remembered Mark . . . and my stomach cramped with annoyance. I'd known the man through our mutual contacts for a year, and apart from the disastrous moment on a streetlamp-lit evening under an umbrella in London, things had remained professionally distant.

But he'd rescued me, unintentionally, from a conversation with a horrendous travel agent by asking if I knew where the bathrooms were, and then we'd found a pub, had coffees, and . . . he kissed me. Well, tried to kiss me.

But sometimes the loneliness felt heavier than other times. And the atmosphere was somewhat romantic. And I was wearing a cute dress with flats, so we were almost the same height. And he'd complimented my hair.

I blame the ambience of lantern light on glossy pavement—it seems pretty powerful in classic movies.

Thank the good Lord for the double-decker bus distraction from prolonging the encounter or the kiss. Because the whole incident brought forth his true colors from beneath the umbrella and shocked me back to my senses. Loneliness was preferable to boorish and conceited company any day.

I tipped a little farther around the doorframe, my very un-Clue-like body half hidden, to get a better look for any other occupants in the room.

"Miss Campbell?"

I spun from my spot, nearly decapitating a bust of some possible war hero on the table nearby. Mrs. Lennox approached from the hallway, her peach lace dress giving off all the *Downton Abbey* vibes, though I'm not sure a white feathered stole matched the Crawleys, but who was I to say?

I currently wore vegetable-covered bright yellow wellies and carried a fishing pole.

Which may have been why Mrs. Lennox's smile tightened into some sort of terrifying imitation of my aunt Maude the first time I showed up at church wearing trousers. That *what could you possibly be thinking?* mixed with *wait until I speak to your mother* type of look.

"If I'd been able to find you, I would have properly prepared you for meeting the rest of the guests." Her gaze trailed down me.

"I still don't have anything to wear except a gown that's too tight in the chest and rises above my calf." I scrunched up my shoulders. "And I think I may break some sort of Edwardian rule by wearing that in public, because the men might actually *see* my calves."

Instead of the joke inspiring Mrs. Lennox's natural smile, her brows crashed together. "Oh, well, we certainly can't have that, can we? I do feel that the guests we have with us are the honorable sort, but I wouldn't put much stock in the staff to keep things aboveboard." She tapped her lips and gave me another once-over. "Well, until I can secure a seamstress, I've had Mrs. March order you something appropriate from"—she lowered her voice—"Amazon. They promise to deliver the items here within the next two days, which will bide us some time for any alterations of the other gowns."

"Oh, that reminds me." I tugged out the card Mirren had given me and offered it to her. "This is a local seamstress who comes highly recommended. And the clerk in the bookshop assured me she works fast too."

"Local?" Mrs. Lennox reached out to take the card as if it had leeches hanging from it. Truth be told, it did have a little blueberry smudge from the scone I ate at Mirren's, but nothing worthy of dramatics.

I glanced around the room and caught my eye roll before it started. Dramatics was the theme of this experience. "Surely you realize that one of the best ways to grow your business is through word of mouth?" I waved toward the room. "It's why social media works so well. But local reputation carries a lot of weight too, especially for this type of business. If you don't get the community behind you, then you're really missing out on free marketing, as well as some local support."

"But I don't *know* any of the locals, except the MacKerrows." She brought the card closer to her face to read it. "It's quite a small village though, isn't it?"

"It's big enough to spread the word about Craighill. Plus, the folks in Glenkirk will visit places like Tobermory and Inverness and other parts of Scotland." I shrugged a shoulder. "You want the folks in the village to have good things to say about you so the word will keep spreading, don't you?"

She studied the card and then looked back at my face, her brows dipping the teeniest bit before she gave her head a little shake and drew in a breath that straightened her posture. "We simply must do something about your attire, Miss Campbell, but now that you're here, it's time for introductions." She waved her hand toward me. "And you'll just have to make do as you are."

Strange how the statement came with a weird mix of barb and freedom. Being who I was had rarely been good enough in Mom's world of high class and higher expectations, especially after Sarah died. Distance helped.

My brain stumbled over the thought. I'd created distance from her for a long time. As soon as I was old enough to leave home. Death within a family hit hard enough, but even more so when the favorite child died. And measuring up to a perfect sister was hard enough when she lived. Measuring up to a memory was impossible.

"Come, Miss Campbell, let us meet the guests." Mrs. Lennox gestured me forward, and all eyes turned toward my navy-raincoat, yellow-wellies, mussed-hair self.

Miss Adventure in the sitting room with a fishing pole.

Exactly what the story had been missing all along. I chuckled inwardly. Except maybe a butler. I hadn't seen one of those, and a butler seemed necessary for any Clue-inspired daydream of mine.

Mrs. Lennox sashayed into the room, her smile sweeping the space and giving a bit of dramatic pause in her entry.

Ah! There was Mark, standing by a mounted elk on the wall and wearing some sort of vintage hunting pants, a white button-down, a vest, and a . . . noticeable glare.

At me. Which I didn't deserve. *I* was the one who was almost hit by the bus in London while he kept kissing me! If I hadn't pulled out of his iron-clasped hold when the bus blared its horn, my London misadventure may have been my last.

And no one wanted their last memory to be of a really bad kiss.

Even if it was in the rain.

"I am so pleased that you all could join Craighill for its very first Edwardian Experience." Mrs. Lennox's wrists twisted as if attached to the words. "Allow me to make introductions, and then we will discuss a few specifics." She gestured toward Colonel Mustard, her smile broadening. "This is Alexander Wake, who will be referred to as Lord Wake while with us. In his modern life, you may know him as the owner of Wake Trust."

My attention shot to the man. Wake Trust? Seriously? It was only one of the top marketing companies in Europe. How on earth did Lennox bag the owner of Wake Trust for her little costume drama?

"Lord Wake and my husband are dear friends, and he graciously offered his support for our little venture."

Well, that answered the question.

"The esteemed Miss Ana Lennox, my daughter, as many of you know, will assist me in offering some of her thoughts on Edwardian times. She is quite the connoisseur of historical movies."

"I'm fine if you'd prefer just to call me Ana. Especially as we become more acquainted." Ana stood and focused her attention one by one on each of the men in the room, giving her shoulders enough of a shrug to have the sheer golden shawl slip off one side to reveal her skin.

Hmm . . . subtle much? And then the thought hitched on the idea that Ana was the only child of the Lennoxes and, from what my servant Emily said, very wealthy.

Another reason to avoid going home. Mom always had some rich, uninteresting businessman with the glorious reputation of social status, dull personality, and high-maintenance mother for me to meet.

But I think Mrs. Lennox may have taken the wedding cake!

I shrugged a shoulder. Not sure what this said about me, but after the first few days here, the eccentricity of the choices of these people began to make more and more sense.

"Mr. Nigel Logan is well-known for his food blogs, articles, and weekly television show called *Tastes Around the World*." Mrs. Lennox nodded to him. "Our chef is particularly delighted to have you experience his culinary masterpieces, Mr. Logan."

Mr. Logan dipped his head, his pale gaze zipping from one person to the next, bouncing off Ana before landing on, or should I say, *rising to* me. To say he was unimpressed may have been an understatement. Which didn't hurt my feelings. Especially since dancing with the man might require a stepping stool . . . for him.

"I do realize all of you need to use your modern devices for your work, but *do try* not to allow them to negatively impact your overall immersion into this era. Photos and videos are encouraged, but please refrain from interrupting the natural process of our historical journey here at Craighill. And though you all have signed waivers to allow for your images to be shared, please ensure your fellow participants are presented in the best light." Her smile dipped into a delicate frown, as if she curated it for the speech. "We want everyone to experience the best of the Edwardian world with the fewest interruptions from the modern era or negative perspectives as possible."

"The full experience will truly be delightful," Ana Lennox added, her white teeth on full display for Mr. Logan.

"Next, we have Miss Estelle Dupont, known for her history articles and blogs."

The woman with the magnifying glass curtsied and preened, pushing her glasses up on her nose.

"I've also been a consultant for two historical movies." Her smile brimmed as she raised the appropriate number of fingers, her lush French accent curling over the words. "And I'm waiting to consult for another of even larger appeal than the previous." She searched the room with those large brown eyes of hers, her smile fading. "Of course all of you are doing marvelous things too. Even if it isn't . . . cinema. We all have important pieces to contribute—"

"Yes, certainly," Mrs. Lennox interrupted and spun to Mark, who straightened and flashed his perfect teeth. "Mr. Mark Page is with us as a sports and outdoor enthusiast who, I am sure, will find our equestrian and other Edwardian opportunities well worth note in his magazine and popular YouTube channel."

"I'm looking forward to proving my *visionary* skills." And focused the full weight of his comment on me.

What in the world? His comment didn't quite fit with—And then his allusion clicked into place. Right! We were both up for the Vision Award . . . again.

And clearly he wasn't too thrilled about it. Especially since I beat him out of the prize last year.

His competition levels rivaled most teenage boys or diva TikTokers. Just because we were finalists for the same international social media award didn't mean he had to try to burn my face with his scowl. Leave it to Mister Outdoorsman to take offense at us sharing the spotlight for the third time.

Another win would certainly help my chances of getting published too, wouldn't it? Prove to the publishers I had the credentials and skill to create great travel stories for children? And winning again might just prove the nudge I needed to take that chance.

I turned to meet Mrs. Lennox's defeated expression as she looked over my ensemble again, focusing for a full five seconds on my fishing rod.

"And this is Miss Katie Campbell." She tossed a limp wave in my direction. "She is known for her humorous videos and blog posts, insightful articles, and . . . entertaining documentaries under her moniker Miss Adventure."

At least she sounded more positive toward me than she looked.

"We are having a bit of trouble with her attire—" Mrs. Lennox seemed to think better of elaborating as she took a dramatic view from my wellies to my head. "But I feel certain it will all get sorted very soon."

My smile froze on my face. Yep, no need for anyone to wonder what she might be referring to.

"As stated in your packet, as part of the experience, each of the ladies will receive a custom-designed gown to wear to our Edwardian Ball on our last evening, and each gentleman their own Edwardian suit." She brought her hands together in pure delight. "And I will be guiding you through your process of immersion into the Edwardian world. As a former literature professor and an amateur historian, I feel certain I have set up this experience to give you a taste of the era, while also enjoying some modern perks. The natural beauty of Mull only enhances your discovery and allows you a natural break from many of the distractions common in more populous places."

She offered a self-satisfied chuckle.

"Though I do hope you increase the number of people you bring to the next experience, Mother." Ana scanned the room, her smile coy. "More *people* to meet."

"We shall see, dear." Mrs. Lennox's smile tightened as she stared at her daughter and gave her head a little shake. "I look forward to guiding you in your Edwardian Experience"—this time said with less flourish and no wrist swirl—"for the next three weeks. May you absorb the history and opulence of this marvelous time period."

She pressed her palms together as if in prayer, perhaps for me . . . or for herself on having to reform me into an Edwardian lady. I hope my expression offered my condolences.

"We will begin our first class at ten o'clock sharp," Mrs. Lennox continued. "How to dine like an Edwardian."

Even though I'd seen this class in the brochure, it still inspired my grin. I mean, how many ways were there to eat?

"Now, your assigned servants should meet you this evening after tea to ensure you have all necessary items to properly begin your Edwardian Experience in the morning." She paused, her expression dimming a little. "Two last items. My husband, Mr. Lennox, will be joining us for our meals and will assist as needed. His business expectations at this time do not allow him the freedom to enjoy all of our activities, but I am sure you will find him a charming addition whenever he is able to join us. And second, do not be alarmed if you should see a macaw flying about the premises or note a weasel in pursuit of said macaw." Her chuckle took a desperate turn. "It was not uncommon for the wealthy of Edwardian times to keep exotic pets, and we don't wish for you to be alarmed. It is our desire to keep the menagerie under amicable control." Her smile resurfaced and she gestured toward the room. "Now, please take some time to meet your fellow guests and enjoy your afternoon."

Since I felt a little unprepared for the current Clue game with my wellies and fishing pole on display, I started for the hallway, only to be ceremoniously thwarted by Mark.

"I can't believe we're finalists again this year." He folded his arms across his chest, the size of his biceps evident beneath the strain of his shirt sleeves. I was pretty sure those biceps were one of his few winning features, along with his impressive orthodontia. "You wouldn't even be in the finals if it hadn't been for the London incident you clearly planned."

"Planned?" Not even the biceps could save him from my glare. "Planned to end my life with a double-decker bus?"

"That 'almost' ran over you," he said, employing air quotes. Maybe his orthodontia wasn't so impressive either. "And then you conveniently landed in the arms of a passing policeman while the camera was running?"

"A tourist's phone camera, Mark. Not mine! That's the only reason it was recorded."

"Who just happened to follow you on social media?" One of his brows rose and my whole body tensed.

"Only after she realized who I was." I released an exhaustive sigh. "You are being ridiculous."

He returned to the folded-arm stance, hazel eyes narrowing. "Were you that afraid I'd upstage you?"

"Upstage me?" Though I had stepped away from him on the sidewalk after he claimed an unwanted kiss. "I could have died."

"Diva."

Now he'd thrown one of my least favorite insults. I lowered my fishing pole like a lance toward him. "You think I risked my life to get more visibility than you? Mark, I like my job, but not that much. You're the one who wants to perform life-threatening feats, not me. I only plan about 20 percent of the misadventures that happen to me. The rest of the time is just"—I exaggerated my shrug—"luck?"

"Luck." He scoffed and then leaned close. "I'm winning that award this year, Miss Adventure, and this trip is the award team's final look at social media ratings, content, and writing before they make their decision, so don't get in my way."

That award meant another boost in salary, which always came as a boon, but I didn't plan to wrestle, threaten, or swindle it from anybody. I'd win it fair and square, which was more than I could say for Meddling Mark.

"I don't even want to be in the same room with you, Mark." I pointed the fishing pole lance close enough to his chest to almost make contact. "And just because you feel threatened by me, my writing, and my humor doesn't mean that I'm trying to beat you. So get off your high horse."

"Your silly little cyberworld doesn't threaten me. I have plans, Miss Adventure." He knocked the fishing pole away and leaned in, nose flaring in the special way he had that resembled a frustrated horse. "Plans to push my ratings well above yours. So just stay out of my way."

With that somewhat anticlimactic warning, he turned and stomped from the room toward the kitchen. And with a look in Miss Dupont's direction and a half curtsy to Mrs. Lennox, I scooted right out of the room.

There would be plenty of time to meet the guests when I didn't look like a stand-in for the Goonies, but since I already had my fishing pole, rain jacket, and camera, I might as well take Mirren's advice and visit the pools, whatever those were.

Plus get a few more videos and photos.

Maybe, just maybe, I'd uncover a faerie or two.

I grabbed a quick bite to eat from the sandwiches Mrs. Lennox had left for the guests and ran to my room, avoiding Mark, who had thankfully found a conversational partner in Miss Lennox. Or rather, she may have found him.

Shrugging off my backpack and setting out my wet shoes to dry, I prepared for my trek to the pools. My gaze fell on my notebook in the internal pocket of the backpack, and I looked at my watch. It wasn't even one o'clock yet.

Definitely enough time to type up a few of my notes from the morning. My laptop looked a little out of place on the vintage desk, but I cozied up on the stiff-backed armchair (okay, not so cozy) and flipped open my computer. As the screen opened to reveal the last few documents I'd been working on, my attention caught on an open document at the bottom. *Katie and the Lost Scarab of King Tut's Tomb* shown as the title. I paused and then clicked open the page.

Talking to Brett about my dream of publishing these books always made me want to delve back into Katie's world. My grin tipped as I gazed over the first few paragraphs, tickled at my little creation's spunk and positivity. What little girl wouldn't love to embark on such literary adventures? Books saved my sanity long before they became my refuge. They introduced me to braver girls. Daring ones. Kind and generous ones. Girls with warm, welcoming homes full of love and laughter and belonging.

This fictitious fourteen-year-old Katie was all the things I loved best about young fictional heroines . . . and so much cooler than twenty-eight-year-old Katie. She dashed boldly into adventure, built relationships without fear. Fictional Katie knew where she belonged and traveled with the knowledge she'd return home after each adventure to a safe, welcoming world that embraced her as she was.

A twinge of discomfort wiggled its way up through my chest to tighten my throat. What must it feel like to belong to fictional Katie's world?

I closed the page and opened my notes, drowning out the thoughts with different ones describing my morning adventure in Glenkirk.

A half hour later, fishing pole in hand, I walked through the back garden again and took the trail behind the village toward the pools as Mirren had directed. The air smoothed over my skin with a cool touch, sending my hair flying about my face in a fury. I forged ahead toward some rocky hills beyond the village and not *too* far in the distance.

Well, they didn't *look* too far, but after walking a good half hour, I felt as if they weren't getting as close as they ought. Lucky for me, I stumbled upon an inlet of sorts and just a distance from the shore, over a strip of land, was a scattering of small pools of water surrounded by massive stones.

Very *Outlander*-ish stones.

Ah! This must be it. The Fey pools.

I paused to take in the view from the steep hillside and snapped a few pics, adding on a video to edit later. The scene beckoned me closer. I felt like Lucy Pevensie, being drawn deeper into the wardrobe to a world of magic and mystery. But this land wasn't in a book. It pulsed with life and age and an unidentifiable allure. Perhaps there was something to all those legends and myths. I poised my fishing pole against my shoulder and made my way to the pools.

Cliffs lined the horizon beyond the loch in the distance. Stones were scattered haphazardly among the pools, as if tossed there by a giant from one of the caves in the cliffs across the way. I carefully descended a small ledge, lowering myself to a patio of rock and sand with bits of tall grass peeping in between. The ocean whispered to my left, just over a hillside, so close I could smell the salty air. What a wonderful place an island was! One could find mountains, seas, lakes, and countryside all wrapped up within a thirty-mile stretch!

Certainly, if magic belonged anywhere, here seemed as perfect a place as any I'd visited.

A combination of rust-colored, brown, green, and gray slate mixed with sand and seaweed created my floor as I wove between the scattered standing stones to reach a set of three larger pools with a few smaller ones sprinkled in various spots among the stones. A larger one on the nearby hillside even spilled over to create a small waterfall.

Tossing my backpack on the ground and placing my fishing rod down on a grassy spot, I poised my phone against a nearby rock and pushed record. Why not give the viewers my fresh attempts at fishing? Sure, it had been a few years, but it wasn't a super complicated activity.

After a few maddening attempts at casting—and an episode of removing the hook from my hair—I finally succeeded in dropping the line quite perfectly in the spot I'd aimed for . . . mostly.

I squinted heavenward and sighed. Sometimes I wondered if God created me for comic relief. Oh well, it would be perfect fodder for the followers of Miss Adventure. Besides, fishing came with a much sweeter reward than a catch. My whole body relaxed into the warmth of sunshine, a cool breeze, and sweet memories.

After slipping off my wellies and socks to dip my feet over the edge of the rock into the pool, I basked in the glories of the day and the simple act of fishing. My grandfather had taken me fishing with him when I was younger, and though I caught more branches and weeds than fish most days, the whole point of fishing with Grandpa was enjoying the day and talking about something . . . or nothing at all. It wasn't until I was older that I realized it had never been about the fish. In fact, he'd been one of the few people in my life who just wanted to spend time with me . . . as me. Nothing else. I think I missed that freedom most of all.

Maybe being with him was the last time I felt anything close to home.

The sun blinked behind a few clouds, the sea-scented air fueled my lungs, and a quiet chorus of songbirds lulled me into reminiscing—an act I tried to avoid most of the time. Some memories didn't need extra space in my thoughts because they'd inevitably make it to my heart.

But Scotland drew out such feelings and memories with more force than other places. Perhaps it was because of Grandpa and his love for this country, or maybe it was the fact that I'd finally reached a point in my career where I could actually consider crazy options like being an editor or publishing children's books . . . or dream a little about finding whatever Brett found with Jessica.

Something worth redirecting even the biggest dreams?

I tried to shut down the thought, but a question rushed over me. Where would I *be* if I weren't traveling? *Who* would I be?

I wasn't sure how long I sat there partly trying to avoid my own introspection and partly mulling it over, but my little rod didn't gain one nibble. I squinted down into the pool. Like some of the other bodies of water I'd seen so far in Mull, this pool boasted clear water, but its depth kept me from seeing much except shadows beyond my purple toenails.

"You willnae be catchin' any fish in that pool."

The young voice pulled my attention to a little figure perched on a rock nearby, as if he'd just appeared out of sunlight.

Very sprite-like, which matched his overall appearance.

The boy stared at me with pale blue eyes, one brow perched high with suspicion. Dusty, strawberry-blond hair brought out the matching freckles spanning his nose from one cheek to the other. I grinned as his young voice curled his vowels and consonants in the most lilting of ways and made me think of a certain grumpy Scot.

Except the Grumpy Scot's deep voice caused those vowels and consonants to rumble in my own chest. Or, at least, that's how my pulse responded to the dips and curls of his accent. I ignored the tug to think about him—again—and focused on the little elf in front of me.

The boy's hair stood in all directions, and he had a smudge of dirt across his forehead. Just as a boy of eight or nine or ten should look. Like he enjoyed living life more than looking a part.

A veritable Peter Pan.

"I won't catch any fish here?"

"No" came his quick reply along with a shake of his head.

"And why is that?"

His brow scrunched as he examined my face. "There's no fish to be had."

I looked back at the pool and my unmoving line. "There aren't any fish in this pool?"

He released a sigh much bigger than his body should have been able to expel. "That's what I'm sayin'."

My grin started getting the better of me. "And why aren't there any fish in this pool?"

His face sobered even more. "Why, it's where the merfolk live!"

I felt my eyebrow rise and worked hard to subdue my smile. "Where the merfolk live?"

"Do you know nothin' at all?" His childish voice took on a great deal of adult frustration.

"I'm beginning to wonder."

He pushed up from his place on the rock and walked nearer, tipping his chin toward the water. "The merfolk eat the fish."

"Of course they do." Just like faux Edwardian lords collect thieving parrots. *Perfectly understandable.*

He shoved his hands in the pockets of his jeans and studied me so long, I pulled my feet out of the warm pool, drew on my socks, and tucked my toes back into my wellies.

"Ye cannae walk about the island when you dinnae know what you're doin', and that's a fact." He steadied his hands at his waist. "I'll show you the way."

The little boy gave out a much louder whistle than I thought possible from a person his size and then returned his attention to me as I stood to my full height. His freckled nose wrinkled with a frown when he set his focus on my wellies, but he didn't say anything because at just that time a border collie bounded from where the boy had come, taking a minute to sniff the air before prancing down the hillside toward us. As the dog grew closer, he tilted his head, staring at me with one blue eye and one brown.

Love at first sight may not be real for humans, but it sure was with dogs. I *loved* dogs. It was the first thing on my purchase list when I *did* finally settle down one day.

"That there is Witch" came the boy's faerie-like voice.

The dog's name was Witch? At this point, I was surprised at nothing. I mean, there evidently were mermaids.

"Witch?" I repeated, kneeling down to stroke the dog's fur.

"Not Witch, *Widge*," he corrected, but it didn't sound much different than before.

I racked my brain for another option.

The boy released an enormous sigh. "Like something's stuck between two things. Widge."

"Wedge!"

"That's what I said." The boy rolled his gaze heavenward as if sending a silent prayer.

The dog licked my nose, rewarding my eventual comprehension.

"We found him as a pup out on the moor wedged between two rocks."

I laughed and stood, giving the dog's head another pat. "And do you have a name as interesting as your dog's?"

The boy shook his head and studied me with those curious eyes again. "Lachlan."

"Nice to meet you, Lachlan. My name is Katie Campbell."

"Campbell?" His strawberry-blond brows shot high. "Well, no wonder ye dinnae know what you're doin'."

I stifled my chuckle and pulled my pack back over my shoulder. I'd already heard on more than one occasion that Mull was more McClean territory than Campbell but had hoped the conflict between the two clans died down a few hundred years ago.

Grandpa always said memory was long in Scotland.

Suddenly Lachlan dipped his chin as if he'd made some sort of decision. "If you want to be catchin' fish, you need to go on the other side of the hill."

The other side of the hill? I raised my gaze to the green and rocky separation between where I was sitting and what I supposed was the other side.

"Come on, now. I'll show ye the way." He jerked his head toward the hill. "I don't think you're fit to find it on your own."

His ready confidence and adorableness had me picking up my flimsy fishing pole and following the boy up the hillside to who-knew-where. But that was one of the perks of travel writing. Many times the best stories came in the most unexpected ways, and following that hunch had defined my career.

So off I went, trailing behind a boy named Lachlan and his dog named Wedge over a hillside on an island called Mull, wearing my vegetable wellies and carrying my fishing pole with carvings of the summer goddess of love. It sounded exactly like the makings of a Monty Python movie . . . and a perfectly quirky excerpt for my travel blog.

I didn't have to find weird. It always seemed to find me.

And an hour later, the only thing I'd truly caught was a sunburn and a dozen Scottish tales from my new buddy and his dog, before he headed on "aff to home" and I returned to Craighill with my heart surprisingly full and a story or three tingling my fingertips.

CHAPTER 7

Graeme

I took the wood-burning knife and carefully detailed the intricate feathers of the European roller I'd carved for my latest commission, allowing my fingers to trace the familiar path along the wood. The slope of the bird's head and neck awaited more detail, but the glass eye was already set in place, staring at me to ensure I gave appropriate attention to my task. The tiny, detailed scapulars required some of the most intense concentration as they were the smallest feathers on the bird, but the lengthy, crouched position required of me was worth the results.

After all, over the past five years this little hobby had taken on a life of its own. Not enough to take it on full-time—so taking on other carpentry jobs along the island proved necessary—but it had, at least, allowed me some cash to add into my family's collection to purchase back Craighill.

In fact, it had taken *everything* I'd saved, so I'd cut back on a few purchases the last several months just to make ends meet. And unless I could increase my sales or get more carpentry jobs, I'd have to keep costs low for a while yet. Making renovations to Craighill in my free time had cut into my sculpting, leaving less to offer potential buyers.

I adjusted my hold on the knife and glanced around my workshop as late-afternoon light bathed the room. Various wildlife sculptures hung or posed in different spots, either waiting to be purchased at the next local sale or awaiting shipment to their owners. An entire collection of creatures from Scottish folklore was positioned along a table by the back wall—my first attempts at anything other than the fowl I observed on Mull.

They'd sold well so far online. Selkies, mermaids, caoineag, Nessie, of course, and kelpies, faeries, the Ghillie Dhu, and even a dragon. Seemed folks wanted their faerie-tale creatures in sculpted form, as well as written.

I rolled my shoulders and sat back, returning my attention to the European roller and envisioning the finished product. Bright teal for the native bird's head and stomach, complemented with brown and perhaps black tail feathers? This wooden sculpture was much larger than the last life-size swallow I'd made for a professor in Edinburgh. I tilted my head, taking in the half-finished fowl, seeing beyond the basswood color to envision a fully painted product. Hmm . . . and perhaps I could add a tiny bit of darker blue to highlight a wing tip or curve of the shoulder.

Dark blue. Winter loch blue.

An image of Katie Campbell flashed to mind and my lips tilted in an upward curve. She was a pretty woman with her auburn hair and large eyes. Even the freckles scattered across her nose seemed to call out for my attention. Ridiculous, really. Freckles were commonplace enough. Even I had a healthy dose of them, generously handed down from Mum.

But whatever hid behind those eyes drew me. She was witty and, if I had to hazard a guess, fairly stubborn. My lips twitched again. And the way she quickly apologized for bossing me around, then laughed at herself, came with its own appeal. Yet something about our interaction pointed to carefully protected wounds. Wounds hidden behind her smile and humor.

I pushed my frown into place and gave my head a severe shake before standing and stretching my back. I'd barely made it to my feet when my workshop door burst open.

"This is the fourth one, Graeme." Mum stepped over the threshold waving a piece of paper. "You can't keep ignoring the opportunities God's clearly sending your way."

The red header on the page flashed clearly enough for recognition. I sighed and turned back to my worktable, putting away my tools to have something else to do with my attention than look at Mum. "Last I heard, the post was private, Mum."

"I didnae pilfer your post, son." She pointed the paper at me. "Lachlan collected the mail and"—she shifted her attention away from me, clearly guilty—"I merely helped him carry the post into the house and noticed another letter from the London Artisan Festival requesting your presence since . . ." With a flourish of her wrists, she flipped the paper in front of her and began reading, "'Your work has been reviewed by our esteemed artisans and found to be of excellent quality and craftsmanship. We request the honor of displaying your work in our upcoming festival, as well as encouraging you to submit a piece to the annual contest.'"

Her sudden quiet turned me around, and her look needled my conscience like a barb. Mothers had superpower stinging abilities.

"Weren't you sent a similar invitation from Germany two months ago?"

I walked around her and turned off my band saw, hopefully communicating that I didn't have any intention of talking about this invitation, the last, or the two before it.

"What are you afeart of, Graeme?"

Afeart? "I'm not." My shoulder tensed at the implication, and I pivoted toward her. "I just dinnae have a need to travel to those places. My online orders are growing enough for now."

Her silence hit harder than her nipping. We both knew money was tight. And I refused to take any from Dad or Mum, not when they already did so much to help me care for Lachlan. "But this, Graeme . . ."

The hope in her voice, the faith, urged me far out of my comfort zone. "This will not only get your work out to more people, but it's what your sister, your brothers, your dad, and I had hoped all along. That others would see your gifts."

Though my family talked about Greer often, the reference to her in this context hit me in the chest. Parents weren't supposed to lose their children, and one twin wasn't meant to lose the other.

But cancer was not a respecter of persons.

"I'm needed here and I want Lachlan to have consistency." The excuse kept growing weaker with each month after Greer's death, but the idea of expanding the dream we'd shared didn't feel right without her. Besides, she'd given me custody of Lachlan for a reason. She knew I'd keep him near the family, raise the boy as my own in this world he'd always known.

I didn't *need* to leave.

The realization ground even deeper. I didn't *want* to leave.

I looked over at Mum as she followed me to the door, but she didn't press the issue. She recognized the weakness in my argument too. Part of me knew it would be good to step back into a life beyond this island, as if Greer hadn't died, but the other part . . . well, I wasn't certain. What held me back? What part of Greer's death and Allison's leaving grounded me here?

"Exploring possibilities"—Mum's voice came soft behind me, almost a whisper—"doesnae mean you love her or her memory any less."

I pinched my eyes closed for a second, then crossed the small distance from my workshop to the blue front door of the cottage. Was I afraid? And if so, of what?

I opened the door for Mum to enter before following her inside, but she didn't continue the conversation. The question still waited in the air for me to answer, mixed in with the perfume of wild orchids wafting through the open windows and the scents of coffee and breakfast rashers.

I breathed it in. The blending meant home.

Greer's spirit still touched this place. Every time I stepped into the cottage, she met me in each corner.

She'd redesigned this house when Lachlan was born, intending to keep some independence while remaining close to family as she raised her son on her own. I'd moved in when she got her diagnosis, to help manage the heavy lifting of caring for the house and Lachlan and . . . her. Dad and Mum assisted with medications, transportation, and meals.

Calum and Peter pitched in too, as well as various members from Glenkirk and especially our church.

Family extended well beyond blood kin on Mull.

And those were the people to trust, the individuals to pour back into instead of spending my time gallivanting to London or Germany or wherever else.

"Where is Lachlan?"

Almost as if called, the lad walked through the kitchen doorway with an old fishing rod in his hand, Wedge trailing behind him as always.

"Have you been in the storage shed for the likes of that?" I gestured toward the pole, more to keep Mum off topic than about any real curiosity.

"Aye." My nephew, strawberry-blond hair in all directions, nodded. "I've caught myself a lass."

"With a fishing pole?" My brows raised, and the boy's eyes glistened with a hidden smile. "I dinnae think you want that type of lass, lad. She's the sort to eat ye or return to the sea once she's found her skin."

The boy's grin peaked with slow comprehension.

We'd grown to know each other even better since Greer's death. Relied on each other.

And there was no one in the world I loved more than that lad.

"I dinnae need to catch her. She's no mermaid or kelpie. They'd know better about the island than the likes of her." His grin finally brimmed. "I found her at the pools, and she plans to meet me again next week to practice fishing."

At the pools? Sounds like the making of a faerie story.

"Does she now?" This from Mum. "Do you suppose she's one of the fey then?"

"No, Granny!" He contorted his face into a grimace. "The pools are too close to the sea for the likes of them."

I sent Mum a wink, thankful for the detour of conversational topics. "Did you search for a seal skin then, lad? Just to be sure. Selkies are known to swim into these parts."

Lachlan rolled those pale blue eyes, his grin falling into an expression that let me know I'd not mastered my humor well enough for him.

"She talks fine, Uncle Graeme, and in English, so she cannae be a selkie." He sighed, his narrow shoulders falling a little as he seemed to reconsider. "Though she did seem to have trouble understanding when I talked, so . . . maybe she *was* a selkie."

I pinched my lips to keep my smile hidden.

"No, she's not." He gave his head a firm shake. "But I dinnae think she's been here before, so I took her to one of the best fishing spots and mean to take her to the rocks next."

Had a new family moved into Glenkirk and Lachlan met the girl at school? The island, and its natives, took some time to learn.

"If you take her to the rocks, lad, you'd best mind the cliffs down to the fishing post. Any new person won't know the path like you."

He nodded at my recommendation. "And I've a feelin' she needs a lot of help. When I found her, she was trying to catch a fish in the pools. It's a good thing I came along when I did, or else she might have been caught by a mermaid, and then where would she be?"

I loved that the lad still nursed alive those folktales Dad and Mum loved recounting. Of course Greer did too. As a schoolteacher, one of her delights came from helping children fall in love with books, and specifically the books that celebrated our culture and country.

"True that, lamb." Mum placed her palm on Lachlan's shoulder. "And I know you've grown up on the cliffs and glens, but you mind those feet and head of yours too."

"I have Wedge with me, Granny."

At his name, the dog perked up from his regular spot on the hearth rug.

"Aye, and though he's clever enough to protect ye, he's no good to keep you from falling, so"—she tapped her temple—"mind your way, aye?"

"Aye." He sighed out the word, as if his granny had no faith in him whatsoever.

I felt a little of his pain. The lad and I had grown a lot over the past year, but there was no doubt still a lot of growing to do.

"I've got to start some homework." Lachlan stepped close, knowing Mum would never let him leave without a hug. "I dinnae see why Mrs. Leeds gave some. There's only a week left of school."

"She wants to make sure you don't miss anythin'," I offered, but Lachlan only shrugged his shoulders before stepping into Mum's arms.

"My head's already full of the math she taught last week. I dinnae ken if I have room for more."

"I imagine a good night's sleep will make more room." Mum shot me a look over Lachlan's head as she held him in her arms. "And are you at Craighill tomorrow?"

Lachlan dashed up the narrow stairs to his room and a twinge of jealousy twisted up through my chest at the thought of escape. But Craighill was much easier to discuss than going abroad.

"Aye." I walked to the kitchen with her following, which meant she wasn't finished with her conversation. "The MacGregor boys are coming to polish the ballroom floor on Saturday, and I need to fix a few places in the floor before they arrive."

I took the kettle and placed it beneath the tap.

"Will Mrs. Lennox need you this week since everything starts tomorrow? Perhaps to finish off a pair?"

Her reminder of my involvement in the Edwardian scheme did nothing to help me feel better about the conversation. I put the kettle on and turned toward the cupboard for an opened package of oatcakes. "Last I heard, she has her three pairs set, so I willnae have to take part in any of Lennox's nonsense." I leveled Mum with a look to detour the matchmaking thoughts before they took off. I had only agreed to be an alternate this first time because I knew we needed the Lennoxes' ridiculous plan to be a success, but I regretted the agreement more with each passing day. Calum would have been a better choice all around. Even Peter.

The glimmer in Mum's eyes proved my attempts were in vain. "You've always been a good dancer though, Graeme. And I remember you performed well in some of the theatrics at school."

Now she was merely lying. I hated the stage. I pulled some cheese and jam from the refrigerator. "I doubt Lennox is teaching cèilidh dances, Mum."

"Some of our country dances aren't too different than English dances of old. Where do folks think the dances came from, after all?"

Mum readied the tea while I set out the food on the table, hoping the slim choices might keep the conversation slim too. I had more wood crafting to do, along with helping Lachlan with the math he hated.

After a few moments of silence, we settled at the small table and chairs with Mum pouring out tea for us.

"Katie Campbell seems to be a lovely lass."

"Och, Mum." I'd just taken a bite of oatcake and proceeded to push the contents through a hard swallow followed by a drink of tea to wash it down. "Can you stop with the matchmaking? I'm thirty-two years old and can manage my love life on my own."

She took a drink of her tea, brows rising as she looked at me over the rim of her cup. "Where? When you rarely leave our village, let alone this house?" She reached for an oatcake and wagged it at me. "Which means, all the more, you have to make do with who God brings your way."

I shoved the rest of my oatcake in my mouth with a growl.

"You don't have to marry her to get to know her, Graeme."

"She's passing through." I drew in a calming breath, only to choke on the remains of my oatcake.

Mum quietly refilled my teacup while I coughed out a lung. "None of us knows for certain the choices we'll make to change our futures. I lived in Inverness and had no plans to even work at the restaurant on the day your dad came in for a bap. I wanted to move to Yorkshire where my beau lived, you ken?"

The story she'd recounted a million times. Dad chatted her up for two hours, both sharing a love for family, faith, books, and animals. By the time they parted ways, she'd ended things with her current beau and Dad had her phone number. I washed down my cough with a drink of tea. "She's a travel writer, Mum. You know what that means?"

Mum's eyes narrowed at my implication. "She travels and writes about the stories she uncovers."

"Aye." I took another swig of tea. "She *travels*. It's her job."

"And evidently she's good at it, if Mrs. Lennox has brought her to Craighill."

"Which means, she hasnae plans to stop traveling and settle down." I raised my mug to her to emphasize my point. "Does she?"

"Are the two things mutually exclusive, son?" The way she voiced the endearment held very little "dear." She studied me with her X-ray vision and slowly lowered her mug to the table. "I see the way of it. You have the same mindset you had with Allison."

Allison. "What on earth—"

"I love you, Graeme. And I'm not sayin' Allison was right in all her choices, but you gave little room for compromise." She stood, firing shots but unwilling to see the damage her bullets made. "Just because your heart is tied to Mull doesn't mean everyone else's will be." She took a step back, holding his gaze. "The point is that her heart is tied to *you*."

"Allison chose someone else. Someone who fit her career." I pushed back from the table. "Right when our family"—my throat burned—"was going through so much. Greer had just gotten her prognosis, Mum."

Death sentence. Maybe a year.

And it had been. Almost to the day.

"Aye, but Greer's cancer wasn't Allison's fault."

I looked away.

"Allison was wrong in her choices too, and I'm glad you saw that before you tied yourself to her for good. Her love for you wasnae the same as your love for her." Mum's expression softened. "But loving her job and wanting you to go with her to the mainland wasn't a fault; it was a difference. One you *both* chose not to work out."

I started to argue, but she raised her palm, stilling my rebuttal. She, of all people, knew the pain Allison left behind, and the only reason I'd healed as well as I had was because of this place. These people. Not Allison.

"The real problem isnae out there, Graeme, wherever *there* is." She waved toward the window. "We live in a broken world where people leave and the ones we love die. In our modern times, death is skirted off the stage where we don't see it with such clear eyes as our forebears did in these bràigh and glens, but we saw. We lived it, and living through death changes us. It can make us afraid of the oddest things, like . . . the unknown. The risks. Maybe even our own dreams."

"I'm not afraid." I stood. "I'm angry."

"Don't you ken, son. Your anger looks more like fear with its feet dug into the ground. You're the only one who has the power to release the grasp you have on it." She tilted her head, studying me. "We've had to come to terms with this out-of-order death, with the grief of it all, but don't let what happened with Greer or Allison or anyone else steal what you have now. To nick your dreams. You're stronger than that, whether you believe it or not."

She turned and walked from the cottage. Leave it to a mum to dress down her bairn and leave them in the wake. I slid back down into my chair, fighting against her assessment. Allison *had* been wrong.

A flicker of doubt twinged in the back of my mind. But had I been wrong too? Had I been so afraid to trust our relationship that I'd "dug in" my heels to my way instead of giving her freedom? Had Allison been one of the casualties of me holding so tightly to keeping anything in my chaotic world that I'd blamed her—blamed anything—as a way to manage my grief?

The edge of London's *The Art Newspaper* wavered in the breeze coming through the window, sliding across the table a little from where Mum left it. Likely for an added barb in her argument.

Had I limited my dreams out of . . . fear? I flinched at the notion. I'd been justified in my anger toward Allison. Lachlan and this community warranted me staying close to home.

My palm tightened around my mug as the burning in my throat intensified. I raised my gaze to the window, where wisps of cloud floated across the blue sky, hinting of evening rain. What if, in some small way, Mum was right?

CHAPTER 8

Katie

Dining etiquette during the Edwardian era was highly dependent on rank." Mrs. Lennox stood at the head of a long table in the spacious dining room of Craighill, her golden gown shimmering in the fake candlelight.

Impressive with its vaulted wooden ceiling and wall of large windows, the room boasted of a time and place of grandeur that didn't quite match the simple ten-seater, but Emily had said the Lennoxes were continually having new furniture delivered in order to better match the era.

And the *experience.*

However, the structure itself already gave the sense of stepping back in time. Stone, woodwork, centuries-old paintings. Those things alone bumped the experience higher on the ratings scale, despite my somewhat loony introduction to the place.

Now, if only I could get my wardrobe to match the general ambience. I stared down at my simple floral dress, my only "formal" attire I'd packed since Mrs. Lennox assured guests that appropriate clothing was provided. The fact that my summer midi hit at my knee probably broke some sort of Edwardian rule and assured me of a future scandal, but what was a girl to do when she clearly didn't have the wardrobe to match the Downton vibes yet?

"We shall experience our first formal dinner tomorrow, with each guest dressed in *appropriate* evening attire." Her gaze landed on me as if my appearance earlier in the day, or maybe even now, was currently seared on her brain.

I sighed and looked away, only to run right into Mark's glare as he stood across the table from me. His smirk and very obvious perusal of my body only dug the sense of not measuring up even deeper.

Way to hit on my biggest insecurity, Mark the Menace.

"I assure you, not only will you enjoy the elegance of the dining, but our chef plans to prepare a feast that will leave you duly impressed." Her attention turned to Mr. Logan, who responded with a gracious nod.

"Dining for the rich of this time period was a three- to four-hour event."

Three to four hours? Well, back home in Appalachia, meals could last that long, but it was only because everyone sat around and talked forever. Were things the same in the Edwardian era? For some reason, I couldn't quite imagine someone in this setting resembling my uncle Dean, who would loosen his belt, lean back in his chair, and pick food out of his teeth with his pocketknife.

"And tonight I mean to set before you some of the rules of Edwardian dining so you will be prepared with your seating and basic etiquette for the rest of our time."

She waved toward the table, each place setting as immaculately ordered as if Mr. Carson himself stepped from the screen of *Downton Abbey* with his handy measuring thingy in tow.

"Wealthy Edwardian families, as we wish to emulate during your stay here, enjoyed a great variety of the best foods of the time, with an incredibly high volume of meat dishes, including fish, butcher's choice, and fowl in one sitting."

The carnivore within me offered an internal growl of appreciation . . . and then proceeded to echo a not-so-internal one. Loud enough to garner a crooked grin from Mr. Wake, who leaned in my direction. "Right on cue."

Despite the warmth in my cheeks, I grinned and shrugged a shoulder. "Accidentally being on cue is my forte."

His eyes crinkled with his smile, the exchange surprising me because it was the first normal encounter I'd had since arriving. Maybe Mrs. Lennox meant for eccentricity to be one of Craighill's charms.

Niche. I'd give her that.

"I hope the chef lives up to Mrs. Lennox's praise, because the cucumber sandwiches at lunch didn't quite do the trick." Mr. Wake patted his stomach.

"You didn't get a chance to try any of the salmon sandwiches?" I whispered back. "They were delicious."

"I'm afraid Mr. Page preceded me in line."

And without elaboration, Mr. Wake added another reason for me to send a frown to Mark's profile. Taking all the sandwiches before nice Mr. Wake had a chance to eat one? Boar!

"Pardon me." Ana Lennox raised a delicate hand in the air, and unlike the rest of the folks who'd either kept their afternoon clothing or changed into something less Clue-like, Ana now wore a glittering and possibly air-constricting blue gown. I had to admit the shade brought out the color of her eyes, which is where I tried to keep my attention since the rest of her skin strived for an escape from the confines of her dress in an unflattering way.

"I'm a vegetarian," Ana continued, blinking her fake eyelashes with extra gusto. "So I'll need the non-meat option."

Mrs. Lennox blinked back a few times, and then her smile grew tight enough to possibly bounce a penny. "When did you become a vegetarian, *dear*?"

"Two weeks ago when I visited Charlene at her home in Sussex. She's a vegetarian and swears that her hair has become glossier from the effort. I felt certain I should become one too since she made such a valiant case. As you know, I've never been a particular fan of beef or pork anyway."

The whole collection of people surrounding the table turned their attention back to Mrs. Lennox, whose eye may have twitched the teeniest bit. Her husband, however, offered a gracious chuckle. His good-natured glance around the room inspired the same feeling as when I watched any version of Mr. Bingley from *Pride and Prejudice*. Even his beige suit offered a more relaxed and welcome appeal.

"Ah well. I imagine this interest is as transitory as the last one, Ana darling. In fact, you may develop a sudden liking for steak before we even reach dessert tonight."

Ana's laugh bubbled out, apparently unaffected by the teasing, and she waved a dismissive hand at her father. "Now, Father, you're going to make everyone think I'm petty." Her blue gaze trailed the room, pausing on Mark, Mr. Wake, Mr. Logan, and even one of the valets, before returning to her mother. "I suppose a little chicken wouldn't hurt anything."

"There's the spirit, darling," Mr. Lennox offered with a raised glass. "Don't allow the legumes to have all the fun."

I caught my laugh with my hand and met Mr. Wake's grin.

"Tom's learned to keep a steady head and quick laugh when it comes to the ladies in his life." He tapped his temple. "Very clever motto, I'd say."

With a *Downton Abbey* reproduction and a husband-hunting daughter, both probably came in handy.

"There were not the same allowances of food choices in the Edwardian era, if we wish to be authentic," Mrs. Lennox continued. "However, I shall speak with Chef. Since there are upwards of seven courses, you should find a variety of options for any dietary needs." She drew in another breath and gestured toward the table. "As I was saying earlier, rank matters in all areas of the Edwardian life, and none other is so apparent than at the dinner table. As your hosts, Mr. Lennox and I will hold the places of honor at the center of the table, facing each other."

She nodded to her husband, who took his place, waiting to sit until she was settled.

Having watched way too many Regency era movies, I'd expected the hosts to sit on either end of the oval-shaped table instead of in the center, so this would be an interesting fact to tell all of my Austen-loving followers later.

"Now, the highest-ranking lady would sit on Mr. Lennox's right." Mrs. Lennox scanned the room, attention landing on Miss Lennox. "Which, my dear, I believe is you."

With another giggle, Ana sashayed to her place and slid down into the seat beside her father. "I do hope you sit near me, Lord Wake."

The man, easily Ana's father's age, may have smiled beneath his mustache. Maybe. But the quiet groan of annoyance I heard at his nearness suggested otherwise.

"The highest-ranking man will then sit to my left." Everyone's attention moved to "Lord" Wake.

He recovered from his discomfort (and perhaps he felt relieved at being all the way across the table from Ana) and offered a gracious smile to the room as he took his seat.

"The second highest lady"—Mrs. Lennox's gaze skipped right over me and offered Miss Dupont an encouraging smile—"will then sit to the host's left. While the second highest-ranking gentleman will be placed at the hostess's right." Evidently my fishing pole and wellies dropped my social status to the bottom rung.

At this, Mrs. Lennox appeared a bit uncertain as to next in line.

"I'll gladly take the spot, Mrs. Lennox." Mark stepped forward and bowed. With an arrogant tilt to his head, he walked past Mr. Logan and took the seat on the other side of Mrs. Lennox.

The man really needed his pride knocked down a few notches.

Mr. Logan and I filled in the other spots near the head of the table, with me sitting beside Lord Wake, and Mr. Logan beside Ana, which seemed to please her much more than him.

"Tomorrow evening it will be appropriate for each of the gentlemen to pull out a chair for the lady nearest him, as we do not have enough footmen to complete the task. However, in Edwardian times, if there were sufficient servants, they would have drawn out the ladies' chairs."

"I do believe we women are quite capable of pulling out our own chairs." This from Miss Dupont, whose expression wasn't as quiet as her usual disposition.

I wasn't certain, but I thought I saw Mrs. Lennox roll her eyes before turning a humorless smile on Miss Dupont. "Yet you all are here to experience the *Edwardian* era, so we will stay close to the rules of *that* time as much as possible."

"And pulling out a chair wasn't a sign of weakness as much as a sign of appreciation," Ana added and then tipped one of her bare shoulders. "And I think it's very dashing."

I suppose it could be dashing. However, I'd only had a chair pulled out for me by a man three times.

Once was on a date (and, I have to admit, it was a little dashing), once was on stage, and the other was by my oldest brother to see how hard I'd hit the ground. Despite the latter, I rather liked the idea of being treated like a lady, so that was a point for the Edwardian era.

"I am sorry to inform all of you that our butler, Mr. Reynolds, has been called away on a family emergency and will not be joining us for a week," Mrs. Lennox said. "It is a butler's usual occupation to organize those serving the meal, but we will have to make do with our two footmen for now." She waved to the two men standing against the wall on opposite sides of the room. "Do not worry; I shall have a replacement in the morning."

A replacement butler by morning? Sounded like a car. Were there just extra butlers for hire around here?

"Before we begin our meal, I should remind you that maintaining composure at all times is a sign of refinement, so if you feel yourself having high emotions, find a way to control them." Mrs. Lennox settled her attention on her daughter, and my wellies didn't seem so bad after all. "Or excuse yourself from the situation in order to collect yourself. Keeping your head is a true sign of nobility, whether you are royal or not."

Mrs. Lennox clapped her hands, and as if by magic, a set of doors to the left opened, allowing the two footmen, along with a lady, to reenter, each carrying a tray of food.

"Tomorrow we will have our hors d'oeuvres in the drawing room before we make our way to dinner, which is customary of the times. Tonight your meal will begin with the first course. Soup."

One of the servants placed a bowl in front of me filled with a green substance topped with croutons? Breadcrumbs?

"We begin with Chef's Vintage Pea Soup."

The servants moved around us in surprising synchrony, clearly well trained, even if the butler wasn't here. As soon as everyone had their soup, Mrs. Lennox raised her spoon and surveyed the room. "It was customary for guests to begin eating only after the hostess."

And with that, she took a taste of her soup.

The rest of us followed. I'd expected bland. But some sort of tangy flavor blended in with the typical pea taste, tumbling over my taste buds with a surprisingly pleasant richness.

"Excellent texture," Mr. Logan murmured as he stared down into his bowl with more admiration than any man had ever bestowed upon me. "The consistency is perfect."

"Chef le Blanc is most experienced," Mrs. Lennox preened. "And a good friend of Mr. Lennox."

"You should see him wrestle an alligator." Mr. Lennox nodded before raising his glass again. "There's nothing quite like eating what you catch yourself."

An alligator-wrestling French chef. It was a wonder that combination had never entered my mind in all my life.

"I couldn't agree more," Mark interjected with a satisfied grin. "I've had quite a few similar experiences, which I feature on my popular

YouTube channel, if you're interested. Especially the one about the kangaroo."

"You ate a kangaroo?" Miss Dupont nearly stood from her place, her face growing pale. "A . . . a kangaroo?"

"They're actually pests in Australia."

Kanga and Roo flashed to mind as they appeared in book form from *Winnie the Pooh*. I pushed through another swallow of pea soup.

"Pets?!" Ana gasped.

"No, *pests*." He bit down on the word. "The country is practically overrun with the creatures. It's legal and encouraged to attempt to cull the population. I hope to find some game here to show to my viewers. What would you suggest, Mr. Lennox?"

Mr. Lennox's pale brows rose and he leaned back in his chair. "I haven't the foggiest. Fish would come in plenty, I'd say, but you'd need to check with regulations before you go blasting about the island, Page. The locals may not be too keen."

"Of course." Mark nodded as if dismissing the man. "I always cover those bases."

"I've seen a few deer. Venison was once a widely consumed meal," Mr. Logan added. "Wild goat too."

Oh dear—and then I stifled my grin. Not a moment for puns, especially from the horrified expression on Ana's and Miss Dupont's faces.

"Not the deer." Ana dropped her spoon. "Oh, how could you?"

Looks like Ana's husband interests just decreased by one.

For now.

Without so much as a look in her direction, Mark turned to Mr. Wake. "Ever had elephant?"

Ana whimpered.

"I can't say my tastes have been as eclectic as yours, Mr. Page," Mr. Wake said, gesturing toward the bowl with his soup. "But I agree with Logan that this soup is one of the finest I've had."

Nice touch of redirection. A gentlemanly move.

"Perhaps it is more appropriate to discuss topics of more universal interest." Mrs. Lennox looked from Ana to Mark. "Perhaps the weather? Or the gardens?"

"The gardens here are certainly beautiful, Mrs. Lennox," I offered, just to help. "Did you design them?"

Her smile softened, and I caught Mark's glare from my periphery.

"I'm afraid I'm not so skilled, but the owners of Craighill are the true masterminds behind the design. With your permission, I shall give them your compliments."

I nodded.

"If you don't own Craighill, then who does?" This from Mr. Logan.

"A local family called the MacKerrows. The house is a part of their family history, but they have let it to us so that you all can have this experience." She waved toward the table, and the room grew quiet except for the tinkling of spoons and bowls.

The MacKerrows? As in Graeme and Mirren MacKerrow?

I reexamined the room. They *owned* a manor house?

For some reason, they didn't quite fit my idea of manor house owners. And Graeme didn't seem the sort to appreciate Mrs. Lennox's . . . creative venture.

Maybe it belonged to a rich grandpa or uncle MacKerrow. But then why would the owner rent their house to outsiders instead of using it themselves?

I took in the windows and woodwork. Envisioned the rooms I'd seen already.

The few historical romance books I'd read that hinted about owning a grand house always talked about cost. So, was it that the MacKerrow family needed money for upkeep? But there were dozens of ways to use this house instead of for an Edwardian re-creation. A museum, restaurant, inn, venue. Ooh, just imagine the wedding photos on those front stairs!

And Mull wasn't the easiest place to get to, so maybe that played a role in things.

Mulling—I smiled at my own pun—over the possibilities only left me with more questions. Questions I'd probably ask Mirren if I got the chance.

Fish came next—halibut in hollandaise sauce, to be exact—which Ana took, explaining how fish was acceptable for vegetarians. Perhaps the talk of eating all the other animals weakened her defenses against fish.

Again, the food tasted amazing, and I suppose it gave me some sense of false security, because when the unusual-looking main course arrived, I didn't even question the contents.

"This can't be," Mr. Logan exclaimed, his eyes wide with more emotion than I'd seen on the man's face since meeting him. "I can't believe you've provided this delicacy, Mrs. Lennox." His palm pressed to his chest.

I stared back at the meat on the plate, covered with some light gravy and long beans tastefully framing it. Was it beef?

"I mentioned to Chef that it was your favorite." Mrs. Lennox nodded. "Only the very best for my guests. And pig heart was quite the delicacy in Edwardian times, often served during Christmas festivities."

My smile stilled on my face. Had she said what I thought she said?

I looked over at Mr. Lennox on the other side of the table, and his smile only broadened. Miss Lennox tilted her head slowly to the right, her brow growing increasingly more wrinkled beneath her blond curls.

Pig heart?

Mrs. Lennox began eating, and Mr. Logan joined in with gusto, so I decided to ignore the people around me and focus on the "delicacy." After all, I'd tried a whole lot of different foods on my travels. Most of the time, though, I preferred the stranger-looking dishes to remain anonymous.

Charlotte's Web flashed through my thoughts, but I forced the notion far back into the recesses of my brain, along with my sixth-grade band concert first date, and the embarrassing moment when Mom called me by my sister's name in front of an entire auditorium.

My mouth went dry as I stared down at my plate, trying to redefine the word *heart* into something like chicken breast. I could do this. So what if it was a pig's heart? Logan, the food expert, called it a delicacy.

I drew in a deep breath and slid my knife into the meat, but the slippery thing moved around a little on the plate as if trying to get away.

"It may require a bit of elbow grease." Logan gestured with his knife. "Depending on Chef's cooking methods."

My added fervor only succeeded in sending the pieces diving off the plate.

"Oh!" Humor to the rescue. "Seems this one's still alive."

Mr. Logan merely raised an unamused brow. Lord Wake's lips quirked.

Mark leaned around Mrs. Lennox to add a sneer, his eyes narrowed as if my poor dining skills personally offended him.

"Clearly, we will need to offer added lessons on cutlery use before dining tomorrow, Miss Campbell." Mrs. Lennox's hands squeezed together.

"If we have something like steak or pork chops, I'm a little more skilled than when eating"—I swallowed—"pig heart."

"Just a slightly firmer grasp on the fork there, I think." Lord Wake leaned in, bringing the sweet scent of cigar smoke with him. "It's actually quite delicious."

One of my quieter snorts burst out. "Well, I don't want to seem like a hog."

Lord Wake grunted his approval of my wordplay, and certain every eye was carefully watching me mutilate my meal, I tried not to saw the dish in half.

Then the strangest thing happened. Out of the corner of my view, I saw something shoot across the table from the other side of Mrs. Lennox.

A small, baseball-sized something.

My fingers tightened around my fork, which made a squeaky sound on my plate. Was that a pig's heart?

With a clatter of dishes, the item landed with a crash in Ana's plate, vaulting her pile of roasted vegetables in various directions.

She screamed and pushed back from the table. "Get it away from me. I can't stand it." And then she shot up from the table, knocking over one glass as another started to teeter.

Mr. Logan stood to catch the falling glass, and I rose with him to, well, I wasn't sure what, but the next thing I knew, Ana's hands flew up in an attempt to back farther from the heart and she hit Mr. Logan square in the nose. In his shock, he stumbled back into me, knocking both of us off-kilter. My foot twisted against the leg of my chair as Mr. Logan and I fell backward.

Unfortunately, Mr. Logan reached out for something to stop his fall, which ended up being . . . the tablecloth. It's amazing how life slows down for these particular misadventures, as if they are scenes from a movie.

Ana was frozen in midscream, Mr. Lennox's bushy eyebrows rose to attention, Lord Wake reached out as if to catch me, and Mrs. Lennox's eyes widened to dinner-plate proportions. All while a lone green bean made its legendary flight across the table, haloed in fake candlelight.

Then the moment passed.

With all the grace I've never had, I and the chair crashed to the floor with Mr. Logan landing to my side, followed by four sets of dishes, a candelabra with battery-operated (thankfully) candles, and a gravy bowl . . . which actually had real gravy in it that split its impact between my dress and Mr. Logan's white button-down.

Thankfully, my most cushiony side landed first, followed by the rest of me, so apart from a little pain in my derriere and the icky sensation of gravy running across my knees, I was fine.

Mr. Logan didn't fare as well. He sat up with a green bean dangling over his forehead, gravy from his chin to his naval, and twin blood trails from his nostrils. A culinary *monsterpiece*?

Not the time for puns, but they had a tendency to pop into my head regardless.

Ana seemed equally as horrified, because she took one look at Mr. Logan, raised her hands in the air with another scream, and fled the room. Lord Wake rushed to my assistance while Miss Dupont made her way to Mr. Logan's, and Mr. Lennox reached to grab a glass of wine that had shifted places on the table from the tablecloth rotation.

"I . . . I cannot believe this . . . this . . ." Mrs. Lennox's voice raised with the color in her cheeks as Ana's sobs filtered down the hallway. "Pandemonium."

She stormed from the room after her daughter, slipping on a bit of food, probably pig heart, as she went.

So much for Edwardian composure.

Lord Wake steadied me to my feet and then moved to assist Mr. Logan, while Miss Dupont waved a napkin in front of Mr. Logan's face, trying not to get near his nose. Poor Mr. Logan's face, apart from the gravy bits, was as red as his bleeding nose.

"I . . . I assure you. I have never had something like this happen to me in all my life."

One of the pros of living through dozens of embarrassing experiences was that my emotions mostly bypassed anger or humiliation and went directly to humor. But thankfully, I turned my laugh into a cough just in time.

I took one of the napkins from the table and dipped it into my glass of cold ice water, offering it to Mr. Logan as he stood. "For the blood."

Mr. Logan took the offering and began to wipe his face, eyes widening. "The . . . the blood?"

He looked from me down to the cloth he pulled from his nose, the smear of red undeniable, and with another glance to me, his face went white all the way to his lips . . . and he fainted.

Thankfully, Lord Wake was already in position to catch Mr. Logan.

Which brought Mr. Lennox from his seat, wine glass still in hand. "What a night!" He grinned and cheered toward them. "I thought Mrs. Lennox's little hobby would prove a bore, but this is exciting." He placed his glass on the table and moved to help Lord Wake with Mr. Logan's limp body. "And the food was excellent, don't you think?"

I looked from Mr. Lennox's clueless grin to Lord Wake's confusion, and back. "Perhaps someone should take Mr. Logan to his room?"

"We'll take on the task, won't we, Wake?" came Mr. Lennox's cheery reply. "What man hasn't been bashed in the nose a time or two and lived to tell the tale, eh? Do you remember that time in Africa?"

Lord Wake offered a resigned grin to his friend, and as Mr. Lennox recounted some story about a mischievous monkey and a teapot, he silently assisted Mr. Logan out the door.

"Men really can't stomach the sight of blood, can they?" Miss Dupont pushed up her glasses and placed her napkin back on the table. "It's a good thing we were here to assist him." With a sniff, she glanced toward the kitchen door. "I wonder if they plan to serve us the rest of our meal in our rooms?" And with purposeful steps, she headed toward the kitchen.

I stood there, one hand poised on the back of my righted chair and the other rubbing my softest spot, pondering if this was how the first night of our Edwardian Experience went, what was the rest of it going to be like?

Then the hair on the back of my neck stood on edge as I turned to find Mark standing from his seat. He hadn't moved the whole time. Not even to help.

Maybe Mrs. Lennox should feature a chivalry class. I bet Lord Wake could teach it.

Mark walked toward me, smug grin growing as he neared, and as he passed he leaned in my direction. "I bet this little fiasco I started tonight will overshadow your 'Falling for a Scot' post in no time."

Are you kidding me? *He* was the one who purposefully sent the pig heart toward Ann Lennox? What a jerk move! How on earth had I *ever* wanted to kiss him?

And my article's title was not "Falling *for* a Scot," it was "Falling *on* a Scot." I had no intention of falling for anyone on this trip, especially a Scot.

Mr. MacKerrow's blue eyes flashed to mind, and I quickly pushed them way far back behind a dozen years of memories. "I don't *plan* my situations, Mark! And I don't hurt people."

Usually. I mean, if someone does get hurt, it's completely by accident.

Except once.

"And look what you did to all of the chef's hard work." I gestured toward the destroyed table. "You totally missed the mark on this one. Not even *near* the target. The Vision Award is about a whole lot more than how many viewers you have. It's about content and personality too."

His eyes narrowed, his nose even flared. "I'm not losing the Vision Award to you again, and if it's misadventures I need to win, then let the 'mishaps' begin." He made air quotes, and I curbed the urge to slap down his hands.

Had he always been this annoying with air quotes?

"I don't play games that involve disregarding other people's safety, Mark."

"Logan'll be all right." He shrugged a shoulder and winked, but just before leaving the room, he turned. "The game is on."

Evidently the disaster from the night before failed to thwart Mrs. Lennox's plans. First thing in the morning, I found a card slipped beneath my door that read:

Miss Campbell,

Please meet our party in the drawing room after breakfast. The Edwardian Experience must go on!

Mrs. McTavish was able to add enough lace to the bottom of your green gown to have it cover your calves, even though it will still be shorter than is period appropriate. I'm sending this gown with Emily. She knows what to do.

L

PS: Two of your gowns should be in today.

The green gown? The one that was much too tight around my upper cello? Sigh. Well, this should be . . . uncomfortable.

At least my scandalous calves would be covered.

I dashed off a few lines to Dave, letting him know I'd received the pages he wanted me to edit, before checking to see how the post Mark had mentioned was doing. As soon as I opened the screen, I groaned.

World on a Page had titled the article about my initiation into the experience at Craighill as "Falling for a Scot." My shoulders slumped. Oh, my readers were going to have a field day with this. They'd been trying to cyber-match me for years.

I read through my own words, grinning a little at my turns of phrases and the hint of exaggeration in the description of the parrot-stair-railing incident. Then my highly complimentary and exaggerated description of the Scot who "caught" me.

Hmm . . . well, maybe not too exaggerated. He was handsome in a rugged, salt-of-the-earth sort of way. And the size of his arms served to advertise his work ethic . . . and strength. I cleared my throat. And he really shouldn't have eyes so soul-searching. Every time we'd made solid eye contact while we walked from the village back to the manor house, my brain stumbled on my next words.

Which probably meant I sounded like a complete imbecile.

But there was something about his direct look—I felt that he could see all the way back to my broken childhood. Maybe it was a magical Scottish thing passed down by the faeries or something, because his mom had the same ability.

To see me.

Except Mirren's stare hadn't shaken my pulse.

I rolled my gaze heavenward and pushed back from my chair. What was wrong with me? You'd think I'd never looked deeply into a handsome man's eyes before.

I paused on the thought. Had I really?

Like the soul-searching kind of look?

Maybe that came with falling in love, which I may have partially done while watching *The Lord of the Rings* for the first time, but I'm pretty sure it's not the same thing.

A knock at my door pulled me from my strangely hypnotic thoughts about Graeme the Grump's eyes and arms.

Emily greeted me with a smile and a good morning. As an undergrad student pretending to be a lady's maid for this Edwardian Experience, Emily seemed a pretty normal young woman. A history major at the University of York, she'd taken on this job for the solid pay, the research, and the chance to summer in Scotland. All tabs on her wish list.

To be honest, so far summering in Scotland fit my wish list too. A strange realization, actually. For some reason, I'd always equated "summering somewhere" with Italian villas or beachfront condos. Maybe that's why I'd never really summered anywhere before—because none of those places fit my preferences. Despite my mom's unswerving belief that I was an extrovert like my sister, I wasn't.

I enjoyed people in controlled doses, but I recharged in the quiet of my room or the solitary world of nature. Traveling matched me surprisingly well. I navigated my social requirements and then cocooned away to write my thoughts and make my reels. Though, as my career had grown over the past two years, I'd been more in the public eye than I'd originally wanted.

No one really talked about how being a "rising star" can burn you out, especially when the favorite part of my job was the story part. I enjoyed listening to stories and then re-creating them in my own way in my articles or inventing them from my own imagination like my *Katie on the Fly* series.

"I s'pose you read Mrs. Lennox's note?" Emily asked, entering the room with a garment bag in her arms.

I nodded. "Even though it means I'll shock the masses with my attractive ankles."

Emily's laugh burst out as she pulled the summer confection of lace and satin from the bag and grinned, her brown eyes twinkling. "I wouldn't be surprised if nations haven't crumbled over the look of a pair of fine ankles."

Yep. Emily was definitely the best lady's maid for me.

Forty-five minutes later, I slowly (being the operative word here) made my way to the drawing room since the hobble skirt style restricted my movements to baby steps. At least the color looked fine on me and brought out my hair and eyes, as Emily said. Which provided some consolation for the fact that running, dancing, and maybe even breathing were going to be in short supply. Attractive ankles couldn't save me from mummification.

I felt like a silk and lace burrito.

"My Morning as an Edwardian Burrito." Perfect title for an article.

With my Chicago-pizza-sized hat tilted to a "fashionable" slant—the food references just wouldn't stop—my ridiculousness was complete.

So much for Clue classiness.

Bring on Monty Python.

Everyone, except me, looked immaculate in their Edwardian attire as we gathered in the drawing room for Lady Lennox's next instruction. Well, everyone's *clothes* looked immaculate. Mark's smugness failed to look anything but annoying. And poor Mr. Logan's nose was bandaged, and a purple hue shone at the bridge with additional swelling and discoloration over each eye.

His linen suit was nice though. Brought out the blue . . . at the bridge of his nose.

"We've had a change of plans this morning." Mrs. Lennox's gaze swept the room. "Since the weather is expected to be very nice, I thought we could learn about the importance of daily exercise during the Edwardian era as we walk to the nearby village of Glenkirk. The fresh summer air is excellent for your constitution, and the village will allow you to do some shopping, as the clerks are well aware of our visit."

Well, giving the folks of Glenkirk a front row seat to this little Edwardian parade of personalities should be fun! And despite the fact that I inwardly shivered a little at the idea of Mirren's gaze delving back into my psyche, her warmth and genuine interest fed something in my heart I didn't fully understand.

I scanned the group again to gauge everyone's reactions, and my gaze caught on Ana. Of course no outfit rivaled hers. Her hat alone was big enough to land a plane, and her soft-pink gown was fitted to perfection over her ample curves. Ana was much more than a cello. More like a double bass.

Miss Dupont showcased a day dress with a skirt much less fitted than mine, and I fought envy at the freedom of her stride as I hobbled along like the burrito I was, grateful for my parasol to balance my steps between the mummy-skirt and the platter-hat.

Our little entourage took the longer (and less steep) path to Glenkirk, creating a spectacle for a few passing sheep, a lone cow, and a poor farmer who dropped his pipe right out of his mouth. As Mark kept with Mrs. Lennox and Miss Dupont at the front of the group, I happily stayed in the back, taking in the absolutely gorgeous day.

The floral scents wafted on the warm breeze with such vibrancy I could almost taste them. Buttercups, daffodils, and some beautiful blue flowers of the same delicate makeup. A few irises perfumed the air, and the world took on gorgeous hues of gold and green and blue and white. Bright. Happy. I soaked them in. Embraced them all.

On a distant hill, a stark rush of purple slipped in between the golds.

My smile spread. Heather. Just as Grandpa described it. And he'd told a story about the flower too, but I couldn't summon it. How could a memory connect me to a place like this?

Mark had shifted farther back in the group as the walk continued, thankfully oblivious to my placement in line since he was clearly speaking to someone via Bluetooth.

Way to get into the spirit of the Edwardian era!

Mrs. Lennox remarked on some historical features of Glenkirk with its excellent location on the longest loch in Mull. Fishing. Commerce. A little piracy and some clan battles. Oh, this world held so many stories. They whispered in the breeze to me, nudging me to linger.

Linger.

For some reason, the word took on extra strength, seizing my breath, and it wasn't just because my mummifying gown squeezed any excess out of my lungs. Scotland called for exploration, yes. But one of my grandpa's favorite words rolled around in my head.

Tarry.

Scotland called me to tarry . . . and the idea pressed in on my heart with the same mixture of terror and excitement as falling in love. The external marvel, the internal memories, and the inexplicable longing.

An attack on all fronts, and I wasn't equipped for the battle. Because everything kept calling me toward introspection, as if all of those things promised to help ease an ache I'd never even been able to touch.

With my slow pace, I brought up the rear of the group, Mark just ahead of me, still talking on his phone. Mrs. Lennox brought us to a stop at the entrance of the village near the edge of Loch na Keal to provide a little history lesson about the types of boats used in fishing villages during the Edwardian era. Then folks began to disperse to their shops of choice.

I glanced out over the glimmering loch, attempting to ignore Mark's conversation nearby, when a familiar jingling bell met my ears.

My face went cold. I knew that sound.

The jingling bells came again, followed by the distinct call, "Get out of the way."

I turned to see Kirsty barreling toward us, a wicked gleam in her eyes.

Definitely a pixie!

And Mark had no idea!

"Mark!"

He didn't so much as turn.

I tried to take a step, but my skirt caught my attempt, so I hopped the four steps over to him. "Mark!"

I grabbed his arm.

He flinched and looked over at me, frown deepening as he plucked out his earpiece in time for me to point toward crazy Kirsty. "Watch out!"

I should have considered his startle reflex. Truly. I should have. He tended toward exaggeration and overreactions, if the past few days (and my previous experience with him) gave any indication, but with the whole hopping-to-save-his-life scenario, his startle response wasn't the first thing on my mind.

And so, as he stumbled back, arms raised in defense at the oncoming threat-on-wheels, he hit me in the chest.

Remember, I'm a sturdy girl, so normally I would have been able to steady myself.

Normally, I wouldn't have been wearing the satin equivalent of cling wrap.

But with Mark's excellent encouragement and Kirsty's homicidal tendencies, I wobbled back toward the edge of the rock ledge and . . . tipped right over.

The cold water caught me, stealing my breath. I attempted to raise my arms, but the tightness of the gown constricted my movements. Weeds rose from the bottom and tangled in the newly added lace at the bottom of the skirt, snagging my attempt at escape.

I tried to paddle my legs, with what little movement I could, and raised my arms again, feeling the shoulder of the gown rip.

Sorry, Mrs. Lennox!

Sunlight glimmered from above, down to me like a beacon. I kicked at the water weeds, my boots weighing me down a little more.

And for the fourth time in my life, I wondered if this misadventure may prove my last.

CHAPTER 9

Graeme

The sound of voices outside drew my attention to the front of Mum's bookshop. I'd stopped in to shore up one of her beloved bookshelves as it had gotten shoogly over the last few months.

Occasionally we'd have a coach stop over for a bit to shop or have lunch, but most of the time a coach gave off warning by the sound of the engine rattling against the quiet hum of the everyday.

I placed my hammer on the shelf and walked to the front window, leaning over the newest collection of handcrafted walking sticks to take a wee keek at the commotion. A collection of people poised on the edge of the loch, wearing an assortment of vintage clothes, were creating quite the spectacle.

I rolled my gaze heavenward.

Barmy. The lot of them.

And then my attention settled on Katie Campbell. Her gown appeared less elegant than the others and so tight it easily highlighted her curvy silhouette. But her profile held the real mesmerizing quality. Shaded beneath that muckle hat of hers, all smiles had faded. She wore an intriguing look—distant. Maybe lost or a little lonely.

I shouldn't care, truth be told.

And she shouldn't draw my attention like she did. No more than the rest of the group with their fancy dress and saucer-sized hats. But she did. In a bathersome way. My attention kept pulling back to the ginger in the ill-fitting frock and an expression filled with unvoiced emotions.

Suddenly her entire body stiffened, and she turned, eyes wide.

Then I heard it.

The sound of Kirsty's bicycle bell.

Och! How on earth did the little imp plan these things? Did she keep watch for victims from her granny's front porch?

The girl made sport of scaring strangers, and with the last week of summer term in place, she'd likely have even more freedom. Usually her antics weren't a problem because she rarely disturbed the natives anymore, but when tourists came, it was like she had a radar out to find them. Wild one, she was. But with naught but her aged granny for family, she was left to her own devices . . . and amusement most of the time.

"What's all the noise?"

Mum's question fell on deaf ears as Katie grabbed a man's arm near her, clearly trying to get his attention about mad Kirsty. In one quick movement, the man shocked to attention, moving away from Kirsty's trajectory, but in the process knocked Katie back. Katie stumbled, attempted to keep her balance with arms flailing about like propellers, and then—my breath seized in my chest—she tumbled over into the loch.

Did catastrophe follow the woman?

"Good heavens, Graeme!" Mum called.

I rushed to the door and flung it open, Mum on my heels. Dodging two ladies in fancy dress, I ran the distance to the loch, passing the daft man she'd saved as he stared into the water without one step to help.

"I . . . I didn't know. I . . . didn't mean . . ."

The loch wasn't especially deep at the water's edge—perhaps twelve feet—but deep enough.

Katie didn't emerge, but I could see her silhouette below the water, her arms frantically moving but not making progress to the surface. Jerking off my jacket and tugging off my shoes, I drew in a deep breath and plunged into the loch.

The cool water soaked through my T-shirt and jeans as I swam in

Katie's direction and waited for the bubbles from my dive to dissipate. A pale arm flapped toward me through the bubbles, and then her gaze met mine. So wide, so vulnerable, pleading for my response.

And my heart squeezed an answer.

She pointed below to her skirt, and I swam lower, noting the trouble.

The bottom of her dress had interwoven with an old, disposed oyster cage. I dove lower and found the tangle, ripping the knotted lace to free her. With the last tug of snagged cloth, I rose, wrapping my arm about her waist on the way to the surface.

Her arms were wrapped around my neck, her body flush against mine, as we broke above the water line. I may have freed the tangle of her dress, but the knot in my chest only tightened as she coughed against my shoulder, her cold cheek pressing into my neck.

Greer had looked at me with such fear once.

Only once.

Near the end.

And I'd been helpless to save her.

But Katie trembled against me, a mingle of breaths and coughs assuring me of her fitness, and . . . well, I fought rising emotions until they stung at my eyes. I was a bloomin' fool, I was.

With a sweep of my arm, I brought us close to the rock wall lining the water's edge and steadied us against it. She coughed once more before shivering into my side. My hold instinctively tightened around her, and with one long sigh, her head dropped against my shoulder, fully trusting me and my strength.

The pressure in my chest tightened to the hurting point. *Don't trust me to keep you safe*, I wanted to say, but the words refused to form. Instead, I went completely doolally and held her a little closer.

Because . . . truth be told. She *was* safe now.

"Do you need help?"

I shook free from my thoughts and looked up. A gentleman about Dad's age leaned over the edge of the rock wall, holding the handle of a nearby ladder into the loch.

"I think we're fine," I called back and then lowered my voice near her ear. "Are ye, lass?"

Her breath quivered warm against my skin, and then she raised her head. Those large eyes of hers so fathomless, I lost my train of thought all over again. Damp hair uncoiled in dark ginger waves around her face, highlighting those eyes, drawing me further into the madness. The same need—ache—branched out through my chest as I willed to protect this woman.

No—more than protect.

To discover who she was.

Her bottom lip trembled, and my rebel heart pulsed against my rib cage in response.

"Y . . . yes," she rasped.

And my attention dropped to those trembling lips. Pale pink now.

It'd been a while since I'd kissed a woman.

Heat broke through the chill of my body. Wheesht! Ach! No!

I shouldn't have made eye contact.

I didn't need to start daydreaming about any lass right now. My gaze trailed skyward.

Heaven must be conspiring against me.

With a brief nod to let her know I heard her, I used my hand to move toward the ladder, keeping any more of my attention away from her eyes or lips.

Or face.

Or form.

Or hair.

Crivens! The water pixies were at work with their mischief, and no mistake.

Because I wasn't going to fall for some social media world traveler who had a penchant for trouble.

Cold stone wall. That's the way of it. Focus on that, mate.

"Trouble seems to follow you, Katie Campbell." The words came out harsher than I meant.

"It usually *pursues* me, not just follows m . . . me." She trembled again, and my treacherous arm tightened around her, her soft curves pressing up against my side. And she had curves.

Suddenly my breath felt insufficient. "I'd advise you to get better at hiding from it then."

"If you've got any advice on how to do that, just let me know." Her cough erupted like a sad little laugh. "Because I'm awfully tired of being found so often."

I looked back at her, only to catch myself in her stare once again. A smile waited in her eyes, apologetic. "Thank you, Graeme."

My name, rasped from those lips, shouldn't heat my blood.

It was just a word. Everyone said it, some with more friendliness than others.

But the tenderness in her expression, paired with the way her accent curled around my name, settled me and unnerved me at the same time. Aye, there was more to Katie Campbell than a trouble finder, but I hadn't the need to discover it.

I looked away, the ladder near and relief at hand. "You wouldn't have taken a fall if it hadnae been for the gommy eejit who pushed you."

"Gommy?" A blast of air shot from her in a laugh. "Yeah, Mark's not the most heroic gent in Craighill, that's for sure. And he's in competition with me, so that makes him even more charming."

My lips twitched despite myself. Her sarcasm carried a spine with it.

"But thankfully, chivalry isn't dead because you showed up."

I opened my mouth to protest my chivalry, but she continued with an added shiver. "Let's just say, I might have been knocking on some pearly gates sooner than I planned."

The humor in her voice didn't match the sudden tension around her eyes. Aye, she'd been afeart. Truly. Enough to curb her humor a bit. And perhaps she would have gotten free. Her skirt wasn't deeply enfolded in the oyster cage. But perhaps not.

The knot in my chest unraveled a little. And I was glad my quick thinking had proved helpful. Simply put. That was all. Something *any* man should have been ready to do, in fact.

"Try not to make it a habit of expecting me to come to the rescue." I growled out the words, attempting to create some sort of barrier between her and my infuriating, unwanted, and unexpected curiosity. "I'm not as fond of trouble as you."

Her smile fell for the briefest moment and then resurfaced. "I'll try to steer clear of you as best I can, but thank you nonetheless."

And with my name on her lips and a renewed sadness in those eyes, she released her hold on me and stepped to the ladder, while I internally gave myself a tongue-lashing. She climbed to the top, assisted by the earlier gentleman who'd asked if we needed help, and then I followed. I wasn't an utter numpty or a "grump" as she'd said. Not usually. But the way she weakened my defenses had me sounding like one.

"Katie Campbell, what on earth happened to you?" Lennox stepped forward, looking over Katie's rumpled appearance with a horrified expression. "Your dress is ruined. And where is your glorious hat?"

Dress? Hat? I reached the top of the ladder and fairly exploded. "You're concerned about the bloomin' dress when the woman could have died?"

"Died?" Lennox gasped, along with her daughter at her side.

I jerked my jacket from the ground and looked back at Katie. The thin material of her dress did little to hide those curves I'd only recently appreciated too much for my own good. I nearly groaned out my frustration, half at myself and half at Mrs. Lennox's daftness.

"Mr. MacKerrow was quick to step in though." Katie glanced up at me before she turned back to Mrs. Lennox. "So I'd say that's another great boon for loving Scotland, don't you? Handsome and heroic natives? A definite marketing feature."

A few scattered laughs followed her comment, but one look in those watery eyes of hers proved the humor a ruse. And if I hadn't been trying to suss out what lay behind her fake smile, I may have spent too much time on the idea that she thought me handsome.

"I would have gone in after her if *he* hadn't beat me to it." The eejit who'd pushed her waved toward me, but I refused to give his flimsy excuse a response. Instead, I wrapped my jacket around Katie.

Her expression registered surprise, and no wonder, with my less than noble reaction earlier. Well, if I was going to be a grump, at least I could be a decent one.

"Let's get her to the bookshop and into the dry." Mum wrapped her arm around Katie, a humorous picture, seeing as Mum's petite stature barely made it to Katie's shoulder. "Graeme can light a fire in the stove to help knock off the chill."

I walked ahead of them to begin my task, with the sound of Mrs. Lennox's voice in my ears. "Everyone, please carry on with your shopping. Carry on. We have the situation under control."

Indeed! I increased my pace and stifled a growl.

"Katie-girl, let's find you something to wear that's not soaked to the skin." Mum seated Katie on a chair near the stove as I worked with the wood. "Graeme, I'm going to the back to brew a pot and then ring Second Go to see what clothes Lara can send over."

She bustled away, leaving me and Katie alone in the room. I kept turned away from her as I worked, but the sound of her shaking breaths so near sent tingles up my back and sent me into quicker motion.

"I'd heard tea solved everything in Britain, but I hadn't experienced its magic until I came here."

I kept my face forward, lighting the kindling beneath a few dry pieces of wood. "That, or ale for some people."

"Oh, right." She chuckled. "Two drinks that cause two very different internal warmth responses."

"Aye." Though, the memory of her in my arms came with its own unwelcome internal warmth response. I pinched my eyes closed and sighed, then blew into the small flicker. The flame took hold, moving from the kindling to the wood pieces. I stood and turned toward her, her face paler than I liked. "Come a wee bit closer and you'll start feeling the warmth."

She obeyed. "You don't need to stay here for my sake, Graeme. I'm sure you'd like to get some dry clothes on too."

I ignored her dismissal and folded my arms across my chest. "Who's the eejit?"

"The eejit?"

"The radge who pushed you in the loch."

Her brows rose and then her lips. "Mark?"

"Aye, Mark. Why is he in competition with you?"

She shook her head and looked away. "We're both up for the same award for using humor and creativity in our social media presence. I won last year, so he's extra determined to win this time."

"You write humor?"

"Miss Adventure?" She glanced back up at me and waved toward herself. "That's me. I mean, my latest exploit, of which you played an integral role"—she gestured toward the door—"is just part and parcel of my brand."

"I thought you wrote about travel."

"I do. I write about travel tips and locations and people, but my followers are used to me sharing about the things that go wrong. Most of the time they're more humorous or ridiculous than life-threatening, but humor has always been a part of my life."

"Life can be hard. Humor is a good weapon to have in defense."

Her gaze held mine a moment before we both looked away. The crackling of the growing fire broke into the silence.

"I'm sorry for . . ." She shrugged.

"No." I raked a hand through my hair and took a seat across from her. "It wasnae your fault. And"—I drew in a deep breath, forcing out the words—"I was glad to be . . . a help."

Her eyes narrowed for the briefest moment, lips wobbling as if trying to sort out what to say next. "What do you have against the whole hero thing?"

Heroes saved the day. Kept the girl. Rescued the moment. My track record so far wasn't stellar. I couldn't save my sister. Allison left. And I'd had to reach near-poverty to secure purchase of our family's estate house. None of those things sounded heroic in the least.

I shrugged. "I dinnae have anything *against* it."

One of her brows needled northward, and I tried to ignore the prodding look.

"You say the word *hero* and people like you think Mr. Bloomin' Darcy or Jamie Fraser or Superman." I gave my head a fierce shake. "No *real* man can meet expectations like that."

"People like me?" She crossed her arms, brow still raised. "What's that supposed to mean?"

Heat rose into my face and I stood. "Fanciful." I waved toward her dress. "American."

"American?" Her laugh burst out, and then she shrugged, taking the jab with ease. "Okay, maybe you do have a point there." Her quick humor lit her eyes. "Let me assure you, I've met enough real men to keep my expectations pretty grounded. But last I heard, the definition of a hero has stayed pretty consistent in the fictional and nonfictional realms for millennia, whether you want to claim it or not."

We stared at each other again, her gaze refusing to give way to mine and me much too stubborn to relent. Hero? What lad hadn't aimed for such, only to fail miserably when real-life people proved much harder to rescue than in comic books and movies?

She looked away first, her brow crinkling. "And who's to say that sometimes a hero is exactly what a person needs, not just to save a life, but to remind them that there are still regular, everyday, non-superpowered good guys out there in the world? Maybe you're the one with the wrong definition."

Her words hit me in the stomach. First Mum and now Katie Campbell telling me I'm wrong? I steadied my palms on my waist, trying to think of a solid retort . . . and failing.

She raised her gaze back to mine. "You should take it as a compliment from a grateful recipient, not a challenge. It's okay just to be who you are, Graeme."

I swallowed my response and somehow felt taller all at the same time. How did she do that? Her faith in me? Her gratitude? It was as if her words skipped right over my arguments to stab directly into how I wanted to be seen. Even if I'd failed in the past. Even if I'd still fail.

I didn't know what to do with that information.

"Mr. MacKerrow."

The call pierced into my foggy thoughts, and I pulled my attention from Katie to find Lennox standing in the doorway of the shop. Her tight smile came with its own warning.

"Could I speak with you for a moment?"

The fact I wanted to linger near Katie only pricked my agitation all the more. And my curiosity. I really was bloomin' mad.

Maybe someone needed to rescue me from my eejit self!

I drew in a deep breath and tipped my head to Katie, nearly getting caught in those eyes again, before walking to meet Lennox.

"Mr. MacKerrow." She pressed her hands together in front of her as if she needed to brace herself for whatever she planned to say.

At least we both knew how to prepare for each other.

"I have a favor I must beg of you, and I'm willing to pay you handsomely for your services."

How could her request send chills and hope at the same time? A favor for her? Heaven only knew what that could be. But "pay you handsomely" had an extra nice ring to it. "Favor?"

"It would greatly improve the overall experience for our guests, thus improving visibility for Craighill, you know?"

She was trying to sell this idea much too hard. I prepared for impact. "What do ye need, Mrs. Lennox?"

She drew in a breath and her lips grew into an unnatural smile. "What I *need*, Mr. MacKerrow, is a butler."

Katie

I had a threadbare hold on my emotions.

And even that was unraveling.

The very idea of not making it free from the wire cage in time was branded on my mind. I shivered. Although I felt pretty sure about my eternal security, skimming along the edge of death wasn't a move I wished to make on a regular basis.

Despite trouble's fascination with me.

And then came Graeme, taking on trouble . . . and winning.

I watched him as he approached Mrs. Lennox, his body towering over the petite woman. The water had taken his loose curls and tightened them into ringlets to make any woman envious . . . or delirious.

Seriously, what was it about a massive man with a head full of curls?

His shoulders pulled at the cloth of his wet T-shirt, his arm muscles defined beneath the thin material, and I pressed a palm to the base of my throat, a frisson of warmth shimmying up through my midsection.

The way he'd wrapped those arms around me and brought me to the surface. The feel of his palm pressed against the small of my back and the way his pale gaze had searched mine, checking for my well-being. And then he'd called me *lass*. Heaven and earth! There was power in the way he spoke that word.

Sure, I'd seen my fair share of Scottish movies involving time travel or Liam Neeson, or even a dancing Gene Kelly, but none of those had breathed the word *lass* against my ear in a deep brogue I felt reverberating in my chest. None of those came with a very real, iron-clad chest and mind-blanking periwinkle eyes.

None of those had ever made me feel . . . safe.

And *seen*.

A tremble traveled through me again, but not from the cold this time. From the dangling carrot of something dangerous and hopeful and impossible packaged inside the fifty-foot gorgeous grump in the room. A man who had to be reminded that it was okay to be a hero.

I took in his tense profile, attempting to *keek* through his wealth of black curls.

Who was this guy?

I wrapped my arms around myself and squeezed against the warmth spilling through me. And why did I have to meet him? I hugged myself harder.

Sometimes it's worse to experience something you can't have than never to have experienced it at all. Kind of like eating generic chocolate after tasting name brand. Ignorance truly is bliss.

Maybe.

But like an addict, my heart wanted one more hit of that high. One more feel of his arms to see if what I'd experienced wasn't just the post-life-saving rush, but something sweeter.

I pinched my eyes closed. Nope. I didn't want that. I didn't *need* to want that. And besides, he clearly wished to steer clear of me. I was a fluke in his life. A trouble-making fluke. I'd leave in a little less than three weeks. Gone. An unhappy memory.

But my gaze pulled back to him, dipping my daydreaming into threatening territory that started with two very dangerous words: *what if.*

What if the way he looked at me was more than simple concern? What if my traveling around the world wasn't such a big deal? What if lingering long enough meant finding a dream even better than I'd imagined? My heart squeezed against the pull.

He was rubbing his forehead like he had a headache, his voice too low to make out the conversation. Mrs. Lennox nodded and handed him a slip of paper. His eyes widened.

What were they talking about? Whatever it was, shock looked pretty nice on him.

Despite the internal struggle, I wanted another conversation with him, if for nothing else than to press the hero issue. I fought a grin. Okay, and maybe just to see if he'd call me lass again. Because that was neck-tingly nice.

"Ah, here we are." Mirren's voice broke into my attempts to eavesdrop. She carried a tray laden with all sorts of yummy temptations, placing the bountiful offering on the table in front of me. "Tea and some biscuits. And Lara's collecting a change of clothes so ye won't have to stay in those wet things all the way back to Craighill."

"Oh, Mirren, you don't have to—"

"Wheesht, luv," she interjected, her smile as kind as the first time I met her. She had one of those looks like my gran. The type I tried to avoid but desperately wanted to be near. Her entire personality offered something even more terrifying than falling in a loch.

She offered a glimpse into how a mother should be. Of the possibility of feeling a connection like I once knew with my gran.

And that little teaser pricked razor sharp. Because it left. Or broke. Or . . . I'd never be able to earn it.

"None of that. It's naught but some items from the charity shop. They'll be dry at the very least." Mirren surveyed me with an assessing eye. "What are you? Five eleven? Six feet?"

Good guess. "Six one."

"And ten or eleven stones?"

"Stones?" I narrowed my eyes with my grin. "Um . . . I'd say my birthstone is a sapphire, but I don't think that's what you're looking for."

"Ah yes." Mirren chuckled and poured a cup of tea into a lovely teacup with blue flowers on it. "How much do you weigh? Or do you calculate it in kilograms?"

Did she just ask me how much I weighed? "Um . . . I know kilograms are used throughout most of Europe, but stones?" My grin wobbled a little wider. "By the way, I like the idea of saying how many stones you are much better than pounds." I laughed. "Kudos to Britain! I mean, it could really boost a girl's confidence to say something like, 'Oh, I'm measured in diamonds or rubies.' Nice way to spin the usually negative view on weight."

"You have a great sense of humor, Katie-girl." Mirren's smile spread into a chuckle as she offered me the teacup. "It does a heart good for the troubles of the world to bring some laughter into it."

I paused on the sentiment. Surely Mirren couldn't know about my history or how humor had rescued me so many times in my grief. But her sentence hit too near the truth. "It's what I'm paid to do. Make lemonade out of lemons, so to speak."

"Aye, so I've seen."

"You have?"

"Aye." She placed a cookie on a small plate and offered it to me. "I've started following your blog online." A twinkle deepened the blue of her eyes. "The most recent article amused me more than I can say. Only the smartest lasses want to fall for a Scot."

Heat infused my face to such a degree, I was pretty sure all the water still on my cheeks evaporated. "Well, the title was a great eye-catcher created by *my editor.*"

Just to be clear.

"Indeed." She waved toward the cup in my hand. "Drink your tea before it cools too much to do ye any good." She poured another cup. "A stone equals fourteen pounds, so ten stones are a hundred and forty."

I'm pretty sure I felt the hot trail of tea move all the way to my stomach, shooting warmth through my extremities like an internal hug. Gracious sakes, these Scots dabbled in magic. "Ah, well, then I'm closer to 12 stones." I leaned in, lowering my voice. "I take after my sturdy gran."

"More of you to love, is what my gran always said." Mirren offered a wink. "Besides, there's something to be said for a strong woman, isn't there? Outside and in." Her gaze took on a prodding look. "Able to weather the storms of life, only to come out the other side with a smile."

Sometimes a fake smile.

I'd mastered that. After all, authenticity and cyberland rarely walked hand in hand. Still, my smile wasn't always an act. Folks like her seemed to sneak beyond the superficial, straight to the heart, much too quickly for my defenses. Kind of like my grandparents, reminding me of something real and true. And good. A heavenly kind of love spilling down to earth.

Though sometimes I had to wrestle my doubts about God's love into submission when I viewed them through the lens of my fourteen-year-old self trying to come to terms with a loss my parents refused to discuss and the weight of responsibility no child should have to carry.

Humans! Why God kept loving us baffled me sometimes.

"So far, I've been measured in precious stones and told my healthy stature just proves more to love. What's not to like about that perspective?" I raised my teacup in cheers. "Mirren, I think you are my favorite person I've met in Scotland so far."

The woman's chuckle warmed me before her arms did, but when she reached over and gave me a hug, a barrier within my heart cracked a little. She smelled of baked goods and rose hand cream. She hugged like she meant it.

And despite every cell in my body screaming retreat, I . . . lingered. Right there in her hug. And fought the heat gathering beneath my eyelids. Just a moment. Long enough to create a memory. Because it couldn't be anything more.

Between Mirren and her motherly affection and Graeme and his . . . attraction, the sooner I slipped back up to crazy Craighill and away from all these temptations, the better off I'd be.

If I just steered clear of Glenkirk for the next two weeks, I wasn't as likely to see Graeme or Mirren as often, and the temptation to fall into a friendship with either of them would prove less likely.

Because if Mirren turned out to be as sweet and welcoming and wonderful as she appeared, and my heart got the smallest taste of that, no amount of generic may ever satisfy again.

And I didn't belong here.

CHAPTER 10

Graeme

I couldn't say no.

It was too good an offer.

Maybe.

But as I stood inside the drawing room wearing butler's livery and waiting for my first "assignment" as a play actor in this insane world Lennox had concocted, the cost felt much greater than the payment. I resisted the urge to tug at my bow tie again. When was the last time I wore something so useless? And I'd never worn tails. Or braces to hold up my trousers.

If I could just keep this annoying agreement from Calum, perhaps I'd retain a little dignity. He'd never let me live it down. And Peter would have shared the news with the whole island. The youngest MacKerrow never failed to talk, often, to everyone.

But the price Lennox offered was impossible to ignore. It promised quicker improvements and a faster opportunity to turn this house into a MacKerrow venue, not an Edwardian Experience.

I released a sigh to the ceiling and wished for pockets in this monkey suit.

Keep the future of Craighill in mind, mate. That's what must be done.

Right. Craighill.

My ancestral home was worth every inch of me looking like a puffin.

At least the view encouraged my mindset too.

The large drawing room featured oversize dentil crown molding with similarly framed windows and entryways. Fresh white paint for the trim and a deep blue for the walls brought out the oak grains of the wood floor and mantelpiece. Thankfully, one of the rooms was fit to showcase.

Large windows allowed light and views from two walls, and with all the furniture removed, the space offered plenty of space for Lennox's next assignment.

Dance lessons.

I heaved a sigh and slipped a finger beneath the starched collar of the button-down. At least I wouldn't have to dance. I'd only been brought on to play the part of butler and ensure the footmen did their work. Two things, despite my dislike of the scheme, I could do.

Voices neared from the hallway, so I straightened my spine, braced my emotions, and calmed my expression to neutral. Somewhat. Though my lips kept tugging downward into a frown. Because this was the most dunderheaded thing I'd ever done in all my life.

Lennox entered on the arm of her husband first. I didn't have anything against her husband, except the fact he gave in to all of Lennox's wishes, and now I was standing in a uniform pretending to be a hundred-year-old butler. A man I'd not seen before walked in behind the couple, alone. Their daughter, Ana, entered on the arm of the mustached gentleman from earlier. The one who'd offered to help. What had Lennox called him? Wake?

A younger man, not the eejit, followed along with a petite brown-haired woman with glasses. I tried to press myself as far back into the wall as possible. Most of the people in the room had no idea who I was. I'd remained invisible to them as the best "Edwardian" servant, moving around the house making repairs without notice.

Besides the Lennoxes, one *other* person saw me a little too well for my liking.

And she had the deluded idea I was some sort of hero.

The odd thing was, maybe I didn't mind her thinking so about me.

Katie appeared in the entryway of the room, camera against her face, but her clothes looked very different from what she'd worn earlier in the day. Gone was the ill-fitting frock with its high neck and short sleeves. Now she stood in a gown of pale blue, cinched tight at the waist with a ribbon and so open at the neckline, it gave a keek of her shoulders. The skirt fell loose and full to the ground. The fit highlighted the hourglass curves of her body.

Bonnie.

Hadn't Lennox mentioned the packages I'd delivered from the door belonged to Katie? Could they have been dresses?

I'd been the one to help her look like that? Lord, help me!

I gave another tug to my collar. I'd had a hard enough time trying to get the vision of her after the loch out of my mind, and here she came like some sort of faerie from the glen with all her hair twisted up and showing off the slender line of her neck. A dainty silver band, like a crown, decorated her hair and gave her an even more fae-like appearance.

I looked away and slid to the left, somewhat behind a rather impressive plant Mrs. Lennox brought for the charade. It was ridiculous to imagine I'd actually be able to hide in the middle of this roomful of people since I was the tallest person in the place. Hiding never worked out for me.

Katie lowered the camera and scanned the room, my somewhat hidden spot offering me a view of her face before she crossed the threshold. She pressed a palm to her stomach, smile absent, and expression . . . lost.

I shouldn't want to know what was happening behind those eyes.

I shook my head at my idiocy. I was a right muckle gowk, I was.

And then, as soon as someone called her name, her face shifted into a smile that didn't reach those eyes of hers. I'd seen the authentic one on the walk to Craighill from Glenkirk—watched it bloom all across her face like the wild orchids of summer.

I pinched my eyes closed. *Dinnae be so glaikit, Graeme. Keep yourself to yourself. 'Tis the safer place to be.*

"I'm glad everyone is here," Lennox announced as the group gathered around her. "This afternoon we will enjoy our first Edwardian dancing lesson. I thought we could work up an appetite before dinner." The woman gave a muffled chuckle and preened like a peregrine falcon, her gray gown suiting the analogy.

Well, at least all I'd have to do is stand like a block of wood against the wall while everyone made a spectacle out of themselves on the floor in front of me. Except Katie. And watching her dance in that dress might not be so bad.

But I didnae have to admit it aloud.

"Allow me to introduce you to Mr. Lane Craig, who has come from Tobermory to teach us our first dance. I thought that since we are in Scotland, we should learn one of the classic Scottish dances for our first lesson. Mr. Craig?"

They were dancing a cèilidh? Perhaps I didn't want to watch them mutilate a dance from my heritage, even if Katie would be worth watching.

The round middle-aged man, Mr. Craig, boasted a brown mustache as manicured as his matching hair. The impeccable suit he wore somehow made him more compact. For a wee man, his smile took up a surprising portion of his face. In fact, with a mop of hair, his mustache, and that smile, he barely had any other recognizable facial features at all.

"Today I plan to teach you one of the simplest and oldest Scottish dances we have. The Gay Gordons. It's a cèilidh dance, which means it's a wee bit more relaxed, works wonderfully with pairs, and can encourage some simple flirting betwixt the couples." He wiggled his brows. "If such romanticizing is to your liking, of course."

I rolled my eyes. *Latherin' it on, aren't you, Craig?*

Lennox's daughter, Ana, released a teeth-grating giggle, which only encouraged Mr. Craig's smile to expand so wide, his eyes disappeared.

Ah! A performer, he was.

"Now The Gay Gordons works well for any number of couples, but its simple steps are a good way to start your education on cèilidh and country dances."

I glanced around the room. And a good set of pairs to start too. Small number. Four men. Four women. I'd give Craig a point for his planning on that score.

"So let's see the couples."

I crossed my arms and leaned back against the wall as Mr. and Mrs. Lennox stepped forward, followed by Wake and Ana, then the other couple I'd seen enter the room. And there stood Katie, still near the threshold as if she wanted to make a quick escape.

"Oh look!" She waved toward the couples, her smile too bright. "I get to watch and learn. I like this plan."

"No, no, Miss Campbell." Lennox stepped forward. "It's unfortunate Mr. Page sprained his ankle on the way back from the village, or the two of you could have stepped out together."

Mr. Page? My frown deepened. The eejit.

Katie's expression complied with my thoughts too. Smart lass.

"He shouldn't have attempted to scale the rocks when you clearly told him not to, my dear." This from Mr. Lennox. "He seemed determined to engage in some nonsense."

"I videoed the whole thing," Ana said, raising her hand with another giggle. "He wanted something funny to add to his reels, or so he said. Something daring. But I don't think he intended on it leaving him nursing a wound for the evening."

"Not to worry." Mr. Craig offered his hand. "A substitute is quite ready and willing to join you, Miss Campbell."

I stifled my chuckle. Katie would stand a whole head and shoulders above the man. Watching him spin her should be humorous indeed.

Katie reluctantly stepped forward and took Craig's outstretched hand, her lips pinched as if she were holding her own laugh in check. My grin stretched a little wider.

Until . . . Mr. Craig started moving in my direction with Katie at his side.

Recognition dawned on her face, and her eyes grew as wide as mine must have been.

"Mr. MacKerrow has not only agreed to take on the temporary part of butler but also as dance partner when needed."

I looked over at Craig as if he spoke a different language. Wait. I had! But I didn't actually expect to have to follow through, and certainly not with Katie Campbell.

"The two of you will fit best with height."

As if that made everything tidy!

Heat rose beneath my too-tight collar, underneath my beard, and into my cheeks, as my rebel eyes took another gander at Katie's full height. I didn't need to hold her again to know just how well her stature complemented mine.

And the acknowledgment raised the heat in my face to scorching.

My mum would die of delight at this moment. Calum would die of laughter.

I wanted to die. Plain and simple. And perhaps I would if the heat in my face kept rising into dangerous territory.

My attention shot to Lennox, who sent me a *you promised* look, and with a deep breath, I braced myself for the inevitable battle. No, not battle. Katie wasn't my enemy, but this attraction warring in my chest certainly was.

And then Craig nodded and turned back to the room, as if Katie and I knew exactly what to do next. Well, she probably had a better hold on her emotions than I did. In fact, her slack-jawed expression gave off every indication that I was the last person she wanted to dance with.

"Butler now, huh?" Her lips trembled into a smile.

"It seems so."

"A carpenter-butler." She nodded as her gaze trailed down and back up. "Well, I have to say that the look isn't hurting you at all."

I tilted my head as comprehension dawned. Had she just given me a compliment? And why did I like it so much?

"It's temporary," I added, attempting to keep my expression neutral. Very butler-like.

"Though, you must admit the occupation 'dancing butler' does have a nice ring to it."

A twinkle lit her eyes, and I, begrudgingly, lost my war with my smile. "Not if it's about me."

"Not heroic enough–sounding for you?"

A burst of a laugh proved I'd lost all control of my emotions. "If a dancing butler is your definition of heroic, you're not watching the right movies or reading the right books."

Her grin brightened her whole face, and something in my chest expanded along with it. "True. I've never read a book or watched a movie about a heroic dancing butler."

I cringed at the phrase, and her laugh bubbled out in a strange intoxicating sort of way that snared my attention. I wanted to hear it again.

And the desire just annoyed me all the more, because first, I wasn't a dancing butler. Second, I wasn't about to fancy some American travel writer. And third, I wasn't a fan of trouble.

"To the center of the room, everyone." Craig waved to the group like a conductor attempting to rein in some unruly instrumentalists. "Let's create a circle of pairs."

My feet made reluctant steps to the assigned spot as Katie's honeysuckle scent followed alongside me. Craig gave a brief overview of the movements in the Gay Gordons and then pushed a button on his phone for the familiar music to begin. I started the steps, the one dance I'd known since a lad. And without much redirection, Katie kept to my side, following along with my movements.

Hmm . . . She'd done something like this before, I'd wager.

"Yes, everyone. Follow Mr. MacKerrow and Miss Campbell's lead. Taller partner on the left. Aye. Your other left, Miss Lennox."

A snort-like puff sounded to my right, and Katie sent me a look from her periphery that caused me to go to war with my smile all over again. Blasted woman!

"Miss Dupont, do allow Mr. Logan to lead."

At this, Katie let out another little snort. "We've got quite the winning group here, Mr. MacKerrow. Aren't you glad you joined?"

It was impossible not to smile back at her. Why did her humor have to be so appealing?

Because she wore it as well as that dress.

"Now, men, bring *your* right hand over the head and shoulders of the lady and take hold of *her* right hand." Craig raised his chin, examining the results as I went on to the next step and reached for Katie's left hand with mine to link across the front of our bodies. The action drew us side by side, near enough that I could breathe in her scent of honeysuckle and sea, a tantalizing and wild combination I'd never imagined on a woman. For some reason, it matched her. The wild hair, the soft warm skin, the stormy blue of those eyes.

And just when I was about to take the boke at my disgusting thoughts, her long, strong fingers gripped mine in a sturdy hold, the scent of honeysuckle and sea distracting me once again.

"Now, if you can count to four, you can learn the Gay Gordons," Craig announced. "But we'll start you off easy. You take three steps forward and on the fourth step you turn 'round. Let's try it then."

Katie and I moved forward and, with me giving only a bit of guidance, made the turn rather effortlessly and proceeded on to the next four steps, which were backward.

"After you complete the four steps forward and four steps backward two times, the men will give their lasses a spin for four beats."

Katie took my cues as I guided her away from me and she spun, her smile growing with each rotation, and then Craig called out, "Now, take a ballroom hold with your partner and do a polka for the other four beats, or if you don't know a polka, it just means spinning together in a wee circle."

It was like she was made to dance with me. Either that or she'd danced the Gay Gordons before, but from the way she watched me and anticipated my moves, I didn't think so. When her gaze met mine after the polka, my smile slipped much too wide for my liking.

Which I blamed wholly on her.

Because her cheeks were rosy, her eyes gleaming, and her breaths pulsed out from the exertion, and all I wanted to do was pull her closer the next round.

"Aye." Craig beamed at us. "You ken the steps, Mr. MacKerrow." Craig looked at the other couples who were in various states of entanglement. "Mr. MacKerrow and Miss Campbell are going to show you how it's done in a full rotation."

So, with all eyes on us, we went through the steps again, this time with even more ease than before, as Craig offered suggestions for modifications within the dance to give it more variety.

After some more guidance with the other couples and Ana Lennox nearly debilitating Wake's foot, Craig restarted the song and encouraged everyone to keep going through the rotation for its entirety.

"Does being a new butler here have anything to do with the rumor that a local MacKerrow family owns this place?"

I blinked at her question. It wasn't a secret, but I supposed I hadn't expected guests to know. "I'd prefer to keep with my tradesman position, but desperate times . . ."

She searched my face. "So your family *does* own Craighill?"

I hesitated. I wasn't interested in becoming a story splashed across the internet. "Does it matter?"

"Well, I certainly hope it matters to you. I just can't understand why you'd rent it to the Lennoxes." She leaned closer, dropping her voice to a whisper. "Correct me if I'm wrong, but you don't seem the type of guy who is into theatrics, stuffed ostriches, and hobble skirts. Though"—her gaze dropped to my feet—"your dancing skills are pretty nice, so you could be a closet thespian."

I narrowed my eyes at her, attempting to quell my rebel lips from turning upward. "I repeat, desperate times, Miss Campbell."

The resident twinkle resurfaced in those eyes. "Did you just wake up one day and say, 'Oh, I think I'll buy a manor house'?"

I searched her face, her expression offering simple curiosity, so I hedged forward into trusting her a little more. "It's our family's estate that was sold away at the turn of the last century, over a hundred years ago. We only purchased it back little more than a year ago."

"So it *is* your family's." She shook her head and glanced around the room. "You must have been pretty desperate to take on this Edwardian Experience in your family home then."

"It takes a great deal of money to make necessary renovations."

Her eyes widened. "And the Lennoxes are helping you do that. Smart. Good plan." She nodded and then tilted her head to stare back up at me. "Then what?"

"We'll see." I raised my brow but refused to elaborate.

She took the hint with a little raised brow of her own. "Fine. But this place would make an amazing wedding venue. Or hotel." As if she'd read my plans in my head.

She was a tricky one. And I was a fool for making eye contact again.

"So, is being a butler, woodworker, country house owner, *and* hero the full extent of your occupation, or do you teach dancing on the side too?"

Losh! The woman and her teasing! "This is a common dance, so I've known it my whole life." I gestured with my chin toward her feet. "But you're dancin' it fairly easily."

She shrugged a shoulder before I turned her in a spin, a rebel strand of her hair slipping loose from the pins and trailing down her back. When I brought her into my arms for the paired spin, she answered through puffs of breath. "I try to learn dances in any of the countries I visit, and this one is similar to one I learned in England."

The idea of traveling to enough countries to say "any" sounded tiring. "How many places have you traveled?" What a daft question.

"More than I can count."

We moved back into side-by-side steps. "I s'pose you have favorites?"

"A few." Her grin peaked as we walked backward. "Iceland is breathtaking. Italy is spectacular, and all that yummy food probably helps. Spain, Costa Rica, France."

She must have noticed my frown, because she laughed as I took her into a spin. "Not a fan of France?"

"Old habit." I shrugged off the way her grin inspired mine.

"New Zealand was definitely near the top." She leaned in as I pulled her back into my arms, her voice dropping. "Don't tell anyone, but I feel as though in another life I could have been a hobbit."

A laugh burst out of me as I took in her full height. "I dinnae know if your profession inhibits you from such a choice, not to mention your height. Hobbits are regularly prone toward adventure."

"Shhh!" She shot me a mock-warning look. "Don't blow my cover. I make a living off of helping others see the world when they can't get there themselves, remember? But there is a temptation toward the simple and sweet, in a homey sort of way." She wiggled her brows.

"Maybe I'm more like Bilbo, where I want the best of both—*truly* fictional."

When she shone her job in that light, it changed the hue of my presumptions a bit. Helping others see the world? I couldn't stop my curiosity. "If you're prone to home, hearth, and pipe, why travel like you do?"

I sent her into another twirl, and she returned to my arms, her gaze not meeting mine. "It started as chasing stories and then turned into a real career."

"And you want to keep chasing stories?"

"I love stories." Not quite an answer, but she flashed me a smile. "But a pipe now and then? Now that's a real draw."

Her pun took two seconds to register and shouldn't have made me grin like a bampot. "You think you're witty, do ye?"

"Better a witty fool than a foolish wit." She wiggled her brows as I turned her into another spin, and this time when I drew her back into my arms, I brought her a little closer.

"You quote Shakespeare to me?"

"You called me on a quote?" Her eyes widened with new appreciation, tempting my bathersome smile again. "Surprising."

My grin fell along with my chest. "Surprising?"

"I mean, you seem too grumpy to like Shakespeare."

This time my brows rose but the tilt in her lips gave her teasing away. "You're having a bit of banter with me, are ye?"

"If we're going to be stuck together in a dance, it's certainly more enjoyable to talk than silently suffer, don't you think?" She shrugged a shoulder as I sent her into a turn. "Besides, if you've been roped into playing the butler, the least I can do is offer some teasing as compensation. This conversation has been one of the most normal and delightful ones I've had in this house so far."

"Has it now?" The declaration shouldn't have brought me so much pleasure, but it did. Only partly because I reciprocated the delight.

Which I shouldn't have. Because encouraging this attraction was a certain disaster.

Instead of answering, her gaze dropped as we came back together for a polka. "What type of flower is pinned on your lapel?"

I followed Katie's gaze to my chest, the purple blossom striking against my black jacket. "Heather."

"Heather." She sighed. "Oh, I've heard about it my whole life, but no description can quite capture that scent, can it? Honey and . . . earth?"

Something in the way she looked up at me, in her appreciation for something so wholly Scottish, squeezed in my lungs. It's the only excuse I had for my next response. "Since you like stories, have you heard the legend of heather?"

"I try not to read too much into the places I visit beforehand so that I'm as surprised and awed as my readers, so no."

"So you know nothing about Scotland."

She rolled her eyes. "I know basic things, plus my grandfather was a first-generation Scottish American, and he bragged about his parents' home country until the day he died, so I've always felt a little connection to it." Her expression turned thoughtful. "I just didn't expect to feel . . . I don't know." She shook her head and squeezed my hand, grin resurrecting. "But I'd love to hear the legend."

I pulled my attention away from the way she tilted her head back a little as I spun her around, the sheer freedom in her movements almost mesmerizing. I faulted her Scottish heritage, for certain. She probably came from the faerie line.

"Very well." I cleared my throat and then drew in a breath for dramatic effect. "Legend has it—"

"Legend has it?" Both her brows rose as she laughed. "You're really playing into the Scottish heritage, aren't you?"

"Oh, aye!" I welcomed her back into my arms. Her breath caught as I closed in, a fascinating rush of rose blushing over her cheeks and matching those lips. Och aye, those lips. I'd paid them little mind until now but couldn't seem to look away fast enough. "Leave it to the Scots to put a better shine on a story than one you've heard before, lass."

The words rasped out of me, so low I thought she mightn't have heard, but she had. Her gaze softened at the phrase.

My mouth went dry.

It didn't make sense. It shouldn't be happening, but I wanted to kiss the troublesome woman.

And what was worse, from the way she settled so closely in my arms and glanced down at my mouth, she wanted me to kiss her too.

We were both mental!

A screech broke the spell between her lips and my brain and brought my feet to a stop as a massive parrot flew into the room. Och! *The* parrot!

Someone gasped. Another person cried out, but the blasted creature seemed to know exactly what it was doing. With precision, it flew directly to Katie and plucked the silver headband from her hair, leaving those fiery curls in a tangle over her head.

Katie's jaw dropped, and she looked from me to follow the trail of the bird. It took a flight about the room in time with the music, as if showing off its prize, and then, with another screech to mock us all, it flew back out the way it had come.

Ana screamed, a few seconds too late. The younger man with the brown-haired woman dropped down into the only chair in the room, as if the incident exhausted him.

"Robert!" Lennox swatted at her husband's hand and gestured toward the doorway. "Fetch that hairband. Merlin has stolen it."

Dazed Robert Lennox, with an equally befuddled Craig at his side, blinked a few times in response.

"I should shoot the bird myself," Lennox muttered under her breath in a very un-Lennox sort of way and marched past them. "Do something with your bird, Robert."

The room fell silent, and then a strange sound erupted from the woman at my side.

A cry? I braced myself as I turned. Katie's hair stuck out in various directions from the parrot's removal of the hairband, and her eyes were still wide, but then she broke out into . . . laughter.

"She's gone mad," Ana whispered, shaking her head in consolation. "Of course, if Merlin had stolen my tiara, I wouldn't have taken it well either."

Katie's laughter grew and she wiped at her eyes. "The parrot in the drawing room with a hairband."

"What?"

"Come on." She gave a tug to my arm. "You're the butler. Surely you can help rescue my hairband."

With that, she dashed off out of the room.

And being the numpty I was, I followed.

CHAPTER 11

Katie

I woke up early on Saturday morning because I forgot to pull the curtains closed the night before. And with a sunrise at some ungodly time, like five o'clock, the happy golden beams created a brilliant wake-up call.

I shrugged off the initial frustration and shot a smile heavenward. There were worse ways to wake up in the morning. Howler monkeys have their name for a reason.

And today was a free day for me, so why not take advantage of exploring, catching up on writing, and just enjoying the world of Mull. So I stayed in my comfy "modern" pj's and edited another article Dave sent me, wrote up my notes from yesterday, sent the latest article ("Thievery Most Fowl") to my editor, and wrote a few thousand words in my middle reader story, all before even changing out of my pajamas.

I wasn't 100 percent sure where I wanted to visit on Mull, but I planned to do some research after breakfast and pick my spot. Pulling on some jeans and a T-shirt, I plopped down on my bed just as a knock came to my door.

At my welcome, Emily entered with a tray of Scottish goodness. Seriously, I don't know if the Scots are in competition with every other country to make their breakfasts bigger and better, but from my first night staying in Inverness to today, the Scottish breakfast proved massive . . . and eclectic.

Of course there were typical breakfast items like sausage, bacon (called rashers), and eggs. Even a bowl of fruit. But then there were the additions of potato scones, called tattie scones (which makes me smile to think about), baked beans on toast (which doesn't make me smile to think about), fried tomato with cheese, oatcakes, and the traditional blood sausage and haggis.

I tried both of the latter.

I only liked one, and I chose not to learn the contents of either.

"And I collected these notes for you that were under the door when I entered, Miss Campbell." Emily handed me two folded pieces of paper—one card stock and the other looked as if it had been torn from a notebook.

Once Emily left and I sat down in front of my plate, I opened up the first, thicker paper. In almost calligraphic beauty, a schedule for the upcoming week marked the page.

Monday—a cooking class and lawn tennis
Tuesday—guest's choice: day visit to Dervaig or a free day
Wednesday—the Language of Fans, dancing lesson 2, dining outdoors early
Thursday—a special surprise event, to be revealed the day of
Friday—a morning at the beach, archery

Mrs. Lennox certainly offered an experience. Language of fans? I grinned. Archery? Well, at least on that one I wouldn't embarrass myself too much. Lawn tennis, however? I wish you got points for playing passionately, if not accurately.

I propped the card against the nearby lamp as a reminder of my upcoming week and readied to open the second paper, when my phone buzzed to life.

Mom: I hope you're enjoying Scotland.

My entire body stiffened. She never started texting like that without an ulterior motive. And what was she doing up at five in the morning in the States? I racked my brain to recall her schedule. Morning tennis at the club?

I slowly picked up my phone, and the screen blinked again.

Mom: I saw your latest video, Katherine. Don't you think you ought to do a little something more with yourself before you make those? Candace at the club barely recognized you in that ball cap. And were you even wearing makeup?

I lowered the phone back to the desk. How did she always seem to wound me no matter how far away I was?

Mom: You know, you've always liked the color pink. Maybe you could wear that little dress I got you for Christmas and make a new video.

Pink? Pink was my least favorite color. And depending on the shade, it looked horrible on me.

But it had been Sarah's favorite.

And I'd never measure up to her, no matter how hard I tried or how far I went.

And I had to respond to Mom, because if I didn't, she'd extend her texts through the rest of the day until I replied.

Me: Grandpa was right. Scotland is beautiful.

I waited, muscles tight in preparation for some other sting I couldn't stop. I'd tried. So had Brett.

And she wouldn't stop, fueled by the need to have the world view her family as perfect or the desire to keep Sarah's memory alive in unhealthy ways. Or maybe a combination of both?

When she didn't respond for a few minutes, my body began to uncoil from flight mode. Grandpa came to the rescue again, even from the grave, creating a safe buffer between me and my mom's criticism. He'd been the only one who held some sort of ability to redirect her stings or quiet her criticisms.

Heat rose into my eyes as I leaned back in the chair, running my palms over my face to get control of my emotions. Brett understood.

My gaze dropped to the time on my phone.

But it was much too early to call him.

I buried my face in my hands. "Please, help me."

I'd been on my own for years, but for the first time in a long time, the gravity of being . . . alone hit me. God felt so very far away.

The second piece of paper—the one that looked like it had been torn from a notebook—caught my attention on the desk, so I opened it to find only one scrawled sentence.

If you want stories, visit Iona.

My breath froze, and I reread the note.

No signature, but from the warmth spilling through me, my body knew.

And the stinging in my eyes became nearly unbearable.

Graeme showed up at the right time even when he didn't know it.

I sniffled and rubbed at my nose, allowing his unintended sweetness to settle into my hurting heart. Only for a second.

I knew the idea of dipping into this attraction was ridiculous. But I grinned down at the paper anyway, our last few meetings flipping through my mind like a movie reel. The loch rescue was one thing, but dancing with him yesterday and the unexpected note today only secured the very real idea that Graeme MacKerrow was dangerous.

Highly dangerous.

I could have blamed the eyes, which were fascinating. Or the shoulders. I sighed in appreciation. Or the accent and the way his voice curled around the word *lass.* Honestly, those were dangerous enough to a single American woman who'd never really been in love. But then you add dancing and banter and this weird sort of tug-of-war between sweetness and grumpiness?

The entire package gripped my unwritten list of Mr. Right qualities and dangled them in front of me like a carrot for a starving rabbit. My lonely heart clawed at the possibility. My mind kept screaming, *Whoa there, Katie-girl!* (But in Mirren MacKerrow's voice in my mind. Not sure why it was hers, but it was.)

I ran a finger over the words on the paper, imagining him taking the time to write it. What an anomaly he was. With his gruffness, I wouldn't have expected it, so what else was he hiding behind that devastating smile?

Whew. I fanned the paper in front of my face as my grin kept growing. I don't think I'd ever been so attracted to a real person so quickly before, and the idea sent another tremble to my terrified heart. Because of one very obvious thing: Scotland wasn't my home. And Graeme certainly didn't have plans to leave. He owned a manor house, for heaven's sake!

I was afraid all the way down to my walking shoes. Afraid I'd mess it up like I did so many other things, except I couldn't write my way into making it a funny happily-ever-after. I'd just get my heart broken all over again in a new way. Then what would be left of me?

My thumb trailed over the words on the paper. They didn't mean love. They were just a really nice sentiment from a hot Scot who gave off hot/cold vibes and leathery cologne. But still, they hinted at a connection I didn't fully understand.

I swallowed through the emotions rallying in my throat before they could turn into tears, a skill I'd almost perfected from years of practice. Tears didn't help. They didn't change things. They didn't make me feel any better or smarter. They just dripped down my nose and turned my eyes red so my face resembled a leaking tomato. And how many people really want to love on something like that!

Love?

Silly idea for someone who was on her way to the next adventure.

But then I reread the simple sentence, and a vision of Graeme drawing me close to him during the dance made me smile all over again. And caused an explosion of glorious tingles to travel up my arms. Then we'd chased the dreaded parrot through Craighill with an entourage of a few other guests running behind us.

I'd offered a helpful pun as we skated around a doorway into a ballroom. "Isn't this *egg*-citing?"

Graeme nearly stopped running to look over at me and then rolled his eyes, continuing the chase. But he did call back to me. "If my ancestors were here right now, we'd be eating parrot for supper."

As we raced up a flight of stairs, he asked, "Why would a parrot need a hairband?"

To which I replied, "Well, it doesn't look like much of a *bird*en at the speed he's flying."

It took Graeme a second, but then he did stop and turn all the way around on the landing of the stairs. "You're a bampot, you are."

Which then made me smile even more because of how hard he fought to hide his smile. He really didn't like to smile. What was that about?

"I've been called worse." I shrugged a shoulder and shot him a wink. "At least you didn't call me *quackers*."

His eyelids pinched closed along with the battle he kept having with his lips. And then the thought of a battle between his lips and mine sounded way too distracting and exhilarating and positively perilous, so I rushed past him on the stairs after the feathered felon.

When we finally found the bird's hoard of pinched items, sans Merlin, we distributed the findings to a very flustered Mrs. Lennox and everyone was sent off to ready for supper.

I probably should have tried to ignore Graeme the rest of the evening for no other reason than to preserve my blood pressure. But he cut such a fine figure in that butler's uniform, poised at the corner of the room to serve, I found my gaze constantly moving in his direction.

Me, my lips, and my blood pressure were in so much trouble.

And as I stared down at the note, realizing the grumpy Scot had taken my interests into account? Well, I kind of swooned. Almost as thoroughly as when he rumbled the word *lass* by my ear.

Ach!

Don't get me wrong, I've had plenty of swoony encounters—encounters I happened to accidentally and thoroughly botch like a pro. There was the time in Italy when a deliciously attractive native rode up beside me on his moped, lowered his sunglasses, and winked. I must say I did look rather cute in the red floral dress I was wearing. Though it was the last time I wore that dress, because instead of responding with the suave and alluring reaction I had in my head, I tripped over an overly excited cockapoo and landed in the middle of a café table, sending a few bellinis flying in one direction and a few stradiottos in the other, leaving me, the people at the table, and the cockapoo smelling like a winery and sufficiently splashed with enough caffeine to run a cappuccino machine. The liquid explosion even made it to the handsome moped driver's sunglasses. Needless to say, he drove off without a glance back at me or my wonderfully stained floral dress.

And then there was the instance where I almost strangled a very handsome Parisian vendor with my purse strap. I blame the pigeons. The only consolations to the fiasco were the excellent cream puffs and the fact that the vendor didn't press charges.

There was also the time in Mexico with the scuba equipment and the sea urchins. The doctor said the swoony instructor should heal without a scar.

I've clearly left a long trail of reasons (and hospital bills) to support my fear of romance. Not just for my own heart, but for my possible leading man's lifespan.

I rested my chin on my palm as I took a bite of my tattie scone. But Graeme looked like he could take the risk. If his massive shoulders and steely eyes didn't prove it, the six-foot-twenty rest of him should. Right?

What if he was my chance?

The possibility crept right back into my pulse, and like the coward I was, I packed my bag, scarfed down a few more bites of my monster breakfast, wrapped the oatcakes in my napkin for later, and walked out the door.

It's what I did.

Ran away.

From the note. From the attraction. From the possibility of seeing him today.

But I couldn't quite shake the nudge that one day I'd run too far away and miss out on something extraordinary.

"You need to bring Jess and the kids here, Brett. Your artist's heart would soak in the views and colors and essence of Scotland like food to a starving man."

"Touché." My brother's dry response pierced my conscience. His family was already financially struggling, and I had to go and stick my foot in my mouth all the way to my hip bone.

"That's not what I meant."

"I know." He sighed—a painful sound. "We'll sort it out, but Jess and I have been talking about options. Maybe moving away from the city. Cost of living is really hitting us hard."

And maybe space to resurrect your art? A talent recognized by Gran and Grandpa, if not the rest of the family . . . except me, of course. Because "painting" and "photography" didn't make a real job. Brett had second-guessed his gift since we were kids, and his insecurities became worse after Sarah died. Everything became worse after she died.

"So, this holy island. What's it called again?"

Deflection. Our primary language. "Iona, and there's just something about it. A feeling. I don't know if it's because we heard about Scotland our whole lives from Grandpa, or maybe I'm hormonal or whatever, but there's something about this place. As weird as it sounds, it does have a strange sort of holy sense to it. Like God is very close."

"Which I hear He is, no matter which island you're on, sis."

I sighed loud enough for him to hear through the phone. "You're *so* funny." The water rushed up to my shoes in an uncommonly beautiful shade of blue. "Well, it's nice" came my lame response. Even as a writer, my words sometimes failed.

"So, how goes the Edwardian Experience?" Kudos to his horrible impersonation of *my* impersonation of Mrs. Lennox.

Dancing with Graeme popped to mind, unbidden. "Unexpected, that's for sure." I stood on the shore of Iona, glancing the short distance across the water to Mull. A four-minute ferry ride from one island to the next. "Where have platter-sized hats been all my life?"

"We always had them. Mom wore them to the beach, remember?"

I snorted at that image, scaring a seagull who'd just landed a few feet in front of me. A mist fell. Not really rain, but certainly not dry. And the entire place conjured up thoughts of King Arthur and Merlin—not the parrot—and valiant knights.

Graeme pulling me out of the loch emerged in my head, so I turned back toward Iona Abbey to get my mind back on higher things. There was no shaking the otherworldly, almost sacred feel of this place, even more so than Mull. Mull—and Scotland as a whole—carried some sort of internal draw to linger. Iona somehow encouraged me to . . . pray.

"So in answer to your unvoiced question . . ." My brother's voice called me back to the phone. "What if Scotland is the place you've been searching for?"

"Searching for?" I knew what he meant but didn't want to say it.

"Home, Katie. We're all trying to find it." His familiar voice relaxed my shoulders, and I breathed in the clean, salty air. "Sometimes it's a place. Sometimes it's a person. Sometimes it's both."

He sounded just like Gran.

Silence followed his words as I stared back up at the Abbey, which was half shrouded in fog. I was a little afraid to ask God if Scotland was home. Afraid He'd answer yes, and then I'd have to figure out what home looked like exactly, how it would work, and how not to screw it up.

"Stop it. I can practically hear you beating yourself up about how you'd ruin your life."

I huffed. "My thoughts were not *that* loud."

"It's been a recurring theme for a long time, sis." His sweet endearment, so intimate between us, brought tears to my eyes. It never got old. That one connection to my family that felt natural and real and good. "You call me out on my insecurities too."

"Touché right back atcha." I wiped my eyes and started following the path up the island toward the abbey. For a July day, the island looked pretty empty, except for its colorful array of shops at the ferry drop-off point.

Whether it was my own thoughts about prayer, my brother's voice, or the place—or all three—a calmness settled over me. It was so easy to feel alone when I hopped from one place to the next. So easy to forget the important things that grounded me. So easy to convince myself I wanted this solitary dance of adventure.

But if you deflected your heartfelt thoughts long enough, maybe you'd convince yourself you were fine . . . when you weren't.

"By the way, did you know you're trending?"

I came to a complete stop on the path beside some beautiful stone ruins. "What?"

"The article 'Falling for a Scot' started this entire social media phenomenon of people predicting the future love life of Miss Adventure. 'Kelpies or Oyster Cage: Saving the Sassenach' just came out this morning, and it's already gotten millions of hits."

Evidently those night classes on marketing were coming in handy for Brett . . . and me. So glad he managed those things for me, and definitely a skill to add to his many, in order to find the right job that would allow him to pursue his art. Wait? Did he just say 'Sassenach'? "Ugh. Dave changed the title again! My original title was just 'Kelpies or Oyster Cage.' And I'm not a Sassenach! Sassenachs are English!"

"Well, it's only increasing your numbers. If you were hoping to make some changes to your travel schedule, your performance the last two years has given you leverage. Maybe Dave's offer isn't such a bad thing to think about. Travel and home? Haven't you always said that if someone could magically give you the best of both worlds, you'd settle down a little?"

Now why did he have to go calling me out like that? Brothers!

But he was right. I didn't think a possibility of both existed. And I still didn't, but what if . . . what if I found it? My diet had consisted of a healthy dose of wanderlust for so long, my brain didn't even compute "settle down."

I resumed my walk up the path, a little faster. Change could be good.

Change could be terrible.

"I'm going to send a few more photos to you, but you really need to come here in person, Brett. This place would inspire you."

"Katie." His tone lost all humor, bringing me to a stop again. "No matter where you run or how fast or far, you'll never outrun your own heart. Maybe it's time to stop trying."

Graeme

There was only one benefit to becoming a pretend butler.

A benefit I hadn't counted on and would probably lead to heart-break later.

But everywhere the guests were, so was I. Which meant I had the opportunity to observe Katie Campbell in a not-so-natural habitat. However, despite the charade and faux-Edwardian atmosphere, the real Katie kept showing up because, to be perfectly honest, I don't think she knew how to pretend.

Though she tried.

But her inability kept me looking in her direction too much for my own good. Adding the fact that she'd jerked off her shoes to help me chase after the pinching parrot while wearing her Edwardian gown and then proceeded to make devastating puns along the way, well . . . I don't think my brain fully knew what to do next.

Perhaps I just wanted to sort her out. She didn't fit my expectations or any mold I knew. Simple curiosity, it was. But the way my body came alive when our eyes met didn't match "simple curiosity" at all.

There were wounds behind those eyes. Perhaps even fear. All mingled together behind an innocence, intelligence, and—I pinched my lips against a smile—glaikit humor to create the most curious creature.

My gaze took in the simple white gown she wore, something Lennox called a sporting dress, but with her hair piled in curls atop her head, she resembled an elfish beauty. And then she shot me a grin as she came to stand beside me while the other two couples played the first lawn tennis round.

"I hear we're partnering up for lawn tennis."

All right. An elfish beauty and a pixie spirit. And she was slowly ensnaring me.

"That's what I hear too."

Mark, the eejit, sat nearby, cane at his side. Though he'd joined in the morning cooking lesson, his twisted ankle meant I had to step in as Katie's partner again.

This time with lawn tennis.

And surprisingly, I didn't mind my volunteer job as much as I ought, especially since Lennox gave me some slightly more comfortable clothes to wear than the uniform. A white linen suit. But how anyone could play a solid round of tennis in this without staining it from ankles to chin, I had no idea.

"You look"—Katie scanned over me and I sat up straighter—"classy."

"Classy?"

"That was a compliment, by the way. It's okay to smile at those."

I narrowed my eyes instead. "Lennox said the winner gets their choice of the desserts you made in the cooking class."

"I know." Her nose wrinkled with her smile. "Great incentive."

"So, are you any good at lawn tennis?"

"No," she answered without hesitation and then sighed. "I and most sports have a love-hate relationship, but especially sports involving running and hitting something at the same time."

Which ruled out 75 percent of them. And yet, I grinned.

And she noticed.

"Ah, I see my ineptitude charms you more than compliments." She dusted off her hands as if finished with a task. "If you find that charming, Mr. MacKerrow, by the end of this game, you should be downright in love with me."

My heart plummeted. *Love.* Even if she teased me, I shouldn't feel a twinge of panic at the idea that she held some sort of ability to wrestle me into actually . . . caring for her. But I was starting to doubt my head . . . and my self-control. So I decided to redirect the conversation. "Mum said she let you borrow her car to drive to Iona on Saturday."

"Iona was amazing." She turned her body to face me, smile in full bloom. "There's something spiritual about it."

"Aye, there is." I nodded, watching her emotions flash so openly over her expression. Her authenticity offered a surprising and refreshing change from what I'd known with Allison. Perhaps I'd allowed my hurt to discolor my idea of relationships. That realization nipped at my assumptions.

Perhaps it had discolored even more?

"But I'm pretty sure driving there and back improved my prayer life."

I coughed to hide my chuckle. "Did it?"

"Don't get me wrong. The overall hallowed feel of the island turned my mind and heart toward heaven, but driving along these narrow roads with little stone bridges the size of toothpicks?" She shook her head, eyes wide. "Definite prayer-inducing times, especially when I didn't want to add a dent to your mom's car."

Who would notice? She already had aplenty.

And Katie's open talk of prayer? Certainly not a common occurrence among most new folks I met. Interesting.

Too interesting. Especially since I was attempting to keep my interest as tamed as my smile.

And failing. At both.

When our turn came for lawn tennis, Katie's action proved her declaration true. Despite keeping step on the short walk from the village to Craighill, when it came to sports, she showed no athleticism at all. Half the time, her hits didn't even fly toward the net. The other times, she missed the ball altogether.

But I had to give her cheers for effort.

She swung at anything that came remotely near her, fumbling, falling, sliding, and ultimately laughing about it all.

"You *are* rubbish at this game, aren't you?" I reached down to help her up from her latest nosedive.

She wrapped her fingers around mine, and I pulled her to a stand. Her hair, which was once on top of her head, now fell in wild directions around her pinkened face. "You really know how to *serve up* the compliments, Mr. MacKerrow."

Her brows rose in expectation of me getting her pun, and my chest nearly burst with a restrained laugh. For over a year, life's wounds had been hard, smiles more difficult, and laughter almost nonexistent. My family's faith and love for one another had softened some of the edges of the grief and offered small steps back into a world where my heart didn't feel as shattered. But within one week, the stiff muscles around my heart, the ones in need of this joy, began to work loose again, one pun, one conversation, one smile at a time. "Next time I'll try a *backhanded* one."

Her bottom lip dropped open with her smile, and she released a laugh. "You're not challenging me to a pun war, are you? Because I can tell you right now, you've just met your *match*."

My grin crooked the slightest bit. Met my match? "I'm willing to *court* trouble in that case then."

"Trouble?" She got back into position for the next serve and batted those eyes with a mock look of pure innocence. "Are you calling *me* trouble?"

"Aye," I said under my breath. "A great deal of trouble."

Despite her being an American travel writer and me a well-grounded Scot, was it possible her pun held a little truth? Mad, barmy, completely insane truth?

Had I met my match?

CHAPTER 12

Katie

Craighill House and the whole Edwardian Experience thing was really starting to grow on me in a cozy, sweatpants-snuggle-by-the-fire sort of way. Especially if the snuggling included the fantasy of a certain Scotsman I couldn't stop thinking about. I mean, I had tiptoed into a little bit of flirting with him, which seemed to be going really well until . . . I hit him in the eye with a tennis ball.

Usual Miss Adventure stuff.

I was a disaster. In all ways, especially in romance.

Ana Lennox had screamed something like "Have you made him blind?" Mrs. Lennox ran forward, but not close enough to actually do anything. And Mr. Lennox had raised his glass in another cheer before giving a nod of acknowledgment.

What had Graeme done?

He'd grunted. Almost grinned. And then talked about a similar incident with a piece of wood and his ex-fiancée.

Ex-fiancée.

I was glad for the "ex" part but of course wondered why such "ex-ness" happened.

After writing up some notes, which included deleting about five hundred words that consisted of detailed descriptions of Graeme's eyes, lips, and physique, I decided some solid distance from the man was what my mind needed most. Because any attraction to him was simply based on a little harmless and somewhat inept flirting, a dance, and the saving of my life. Plus some good conversations. And the chasing of a parrot while punning.

People didn't build futures on a collection of moments like that.

Did they?

Before my head started to hurt from my attempts at solving future problems I may not even experience, I packed my bag, grabbed my fishing pole, and left my bedroom, only to run face-to-chin into Mark. My chin. His face. #tallgirlproblems

He stumbled back, swiping at his face as if my chin were the problem with his proximity.

"I didn't think you'd stoop so low, Katie."

I pinched the bridge of my nose and looked down at him. "What are you talking about?"

"First, you take all the attention by falling into a loch, and then you try to hit me with a tennis ball last night as if I'm not already injured enough." He waved toward his foot.

I stared a full five seconds, trying to comprehend his lunacy.

"Mark, if you'd been paying attention to the full match, you'd have realized I almost hit *everyone* at least once. I'm just that skilled. You weren't special."

He sucked in an audible breath at the statement. "I think you're trying to get me out of the way so I don't steal your spotlight because you know I'm a threat." He narrowed his dark eyes. "Did you train that bird to take your hairband too, just to have another story trend?"

I took another step away from him and all his ridiculousness, though the idea of my post having a solid viewing never hurt my feelings.

Now the matchmaking going on in the comments section was a little over the top. A guilty pleasure to my daydreams—but over the top.

"Sure I did, and for my next trick I'll teach him how to pick up ridiculous men who ask stupid questions and then shake some sense into them."

A movement behind Mark almost distracted me from my utter annoyance of his entire person. Was that gray rug on the floor . . . moving?

"It's not fair you're up two years in a row." His voice pulled me back to him, his frown deepening to such an extent his chin size doubled. "It's my turn to win the Vision Award, and you know it."

The rug moved again. And had grown a tail.

And slipped to the door of Mark's bedroom. Was that Mr. Lennox's weasel? What was his name? Caesar?

"Are you even listening to me?"

I looked back down at his face.

"Mark." I rolled my eyes so hard it hurt. "I am not trying to beat you, okay? I hope you win so you'll get whatever this"—I waved my hand toward him—"is out of your system."

"But you're trending. Trending!" he sputtered, running a hand through his hair and continuing to eye me with great suspicion. "How on earth did you take a fall in a loch and turn it into a social media sensation?"

Did this guy know nothing about social media?

"*I* didn't, Mark." I bypassed him and started down the hall, him on my heels. The last bit of fur disappeared around the threshold into Mark's room. I bit back my grin. One weasel for another?

Sorry, Caesar!

"Haven't you figured out how all of this works? The *viewers* choose what makes it a sensation, not us. Only *half* of any interest is based on good writing, story, and visibility."

"What's the other half?"

I stopped at the top of the stairs. "The right time, place, and topic, and no one really knows what and when that combo will hit to make a trend, Mark. It's up to the cyber faeries."

With that, I rushed down the stairs before he got another idea of how to blame me for something, bypassing one of the footmen poised on the stairs with a young housemaid in his arms.

"Take it downstairs, y'all," I murmured as I passed and slipped from the house on my way to meet my "fishing date" by way of Glenkirk. After all, I needed to pick up some bait, as well as a few snacks for lunch for the two of us. I figured Scottish fisherfolk spent the same lazy time fishing as I'd known growing up. Fishing easily lasted several hours, if not more.

I glanced back toward the house as I exited through the back garden, releasing my full grin into the foggy morning. Maybe Caesar would give Mark the big misadventure he'd been waiting for.

As if in answer, a loud male cry saying something about a "rat in my room" echoed down the stairwell toward me and ushered me right out the door.

Low-lying cotton ball clouds floated on a gentle breeze and offered a soft rainy mist to help wake me up even more. I loved the brisk feel of the morning air, all scented with sea and flowers.

Careful to check for the sinister cyclist, I made my way down the street and to Mirren's shop window. A single light glowed inside. I checked my phone. Hmm . . . only 10:30 a.m. Maybe she didn't open until eleven on Tuesdays?

I stepped back, sending another glance around the space.

A movement drew my attention to the counter. Mirren stood with her head down, going through some papers. A little tap on the window pulled her attention in my direction, and her entire face spread into a smile. Something twanged in my chest at the immediacy of her welcome, like she'd known me for a lot longer than she really had.

And she was happy to see me.

She walked over to the door, and the sound of a lock turning came from the other side. Then she flung open the door.

"Ah, good morning to you, Katie-girl."

The endearment etched itself into my chest. "I didn't realize you wouldn't be open yet."

"Och away! None of that!" She waved me inside to the inviting smells of baked goods, fresh tea, and books. Really? Was there any combination of smells quite so perfect? "Have you time for a cup?"

My answer popped out before my brain could stop it. "I have a little while, if you're sure I'm not intruding."

I wasn't quite sure what kept drawing me toward this woman. Probably the twinkle in her eyes that reminded me of Grandpa. And the sweetness in her expressions so similar to Gran's.

Whatever it was, being around her seemed to douse the loneliness and ushered me into a connection I didn't even realize I fully missed until I felt it. I followed her through the shop to a back room where a cozy office nestled. A desk poised beneath the window, a bookshelf stood against one wall, and a small table and chair sat opposite. A filing cabinet in one corner was decorated with a massive fern, and a tall lamp cast a soft glow over a multicolored rug on the floor.

What a sweet little haven.

"Rest your feet and I'll bring the tea." She gestured toward the table, and I obeyed, taking a quick inventory of the books on her shelf. Some had titles in Gaelic or were unfamiliar to me, but others were old favorites. Austen, Brontë, Doyle, Christie. I noticed a few newer spines—John Grisham, Joel Rosenberg, Erik Larson, and even a Jaime Jo Wright book! Mirren liked a bit of suspense, eh?

"I s'pose you're not joining the rest of the group for a day visit to Dervaig today?" She reentered the room, laden tray in hand, and sent a focused look to my fishing pole.

I stood and took the tray from her, placing it on the table. "I needed a little quiet and a whole lot of nature today. It's calming."

"Aye." Mirren sat in the chair opposite me and studied me for a moment. "'Tis a place to calm the troubled heart for sure."

"Well, I don't know about troubled, but my mind's been too busy. My heart too. So the fresh air and just the overall . . . I don't know . . . atmosphere brings a special something with it."

"Ah, now there's something my gran used to say about a busy mind." She pushed a plate of scones toward me. "A busy mind can come from a restless spirit."

I looked over at her, a burst of air puffing from my lips. "My grandpa used to say that."

"And he was Scottish?"

"Aye," I responded, causing her to smile. "I know it sounds strange, but he seems a little closer to me since I've been here. I think about him and my gran often, but since being here, things he used to say and memories of him seem to be everywhere."

"And that's good?"

"It's great." My eyes burned a little, despite my smile. "I'd never felt safer or"—the word came to mind like an epiphany—"more *settled* than when I was with my grandparents. They were the best people. They were welcoming and seemed to have joy and"—I looked over at her, trying to find the right words—"quietness in their hearts. Kind of like you, I think."

"'Tis a sweet notion and even sweeter reality." Her gaze searched mine again. My eyes stung a little more. "When you know you're loved, it changes everything."

That was it. So simple I should have figured it out by now. But the difference between being with my parents and staying with my grandparents boiled down to knowing without question that I was loved.

And that knowledge not only gave my heart a sense of belonging but gave me freedom to be me. "Yes." I swallowed through the growing lump in my throat. "It does."

"There's comfort in speaking about the ones we've lost." Mirren pushed a plate of "biscuits" toward me, encouraging me to share more than just the superficial I usually gave to the people in passing. She wanted more. "What sort of man was your grandpa?"

Some tightly coiled knot in my heart began to unravel at her question.

"Big." I laughed. "He had a personality that took up an entire room in the best way. People loved gathering around and listening to him tell stories. Gran was the same way, except a quieter version. And Grandpa always had a smile. Even after Gran died. When he'd speak of her, many times through tears, the sweetest expression always covered his face. It didn't take long for him to follow her exit."

The quiet softened the declaration.

"Love doesnae stop when bodies do." Her voice smoothed over the words. "It's one of the comforts in losing a loved one, ye ken? The love lingers long."

Unless it has squeezed you into silence or nearly suffocated you with unspoken words.

I pressed into the memory of how my grandpa mourned my gran. A sweet grief. A tight grasp with his heart but a loose hold with his hands.

But Mirren's words? Love lingers long.

I recalled the walk from Craighill to Glenkirk, everything from the breeze to the mist to the sea calling me to slow down and embrace the now. To take it in. To savor.

I took a bite of the delicious scone to have something to do. I understood her sentiment because, despite my parents' resolve to ignore loved ones' deaths in some weird way that meant we never talked about them, the love for my grandparents *did* linger. Brett and I would talk about them sometimes, which provided a sense of relief, even if Mom and Dad refused.

But talking about death always left me sore inside, even if I wanted to talk about them.

Their love did linger long inside me. "It's a good thing you were close to them."

I smiled and swallowed my bite. "Definitely. They're the ones who encouraged my writing when everyone except my brother, Brett, thought it was crazy." I sniffled and took a sip of tea. "And once they passed away, I took their encouragement and began to travel."

"And you fancy traveling?"

"I do."

She caught the slight hesitation because her chin tipped the least bit, so I rushed ahead. "I really do. Writing about where I go and what I experience comes naturally to me. And seeing different cultures and beauties fills my life with so much amazement."

"But?"

She did remind me of my gran, except a younger version.

"Well, sometimes, especially since coming here, I wonder what it would be like to . . . not travel so much."

How had she gotten me to admit something I didn't even know about myself a week ago? I narrowed my eyes a little. *Faerie magic.*

"And you're afeart of it?"

Afeart? My grin tipped a little. "I don't know." And my words tumbled out even more. "Maybe I'm afraid of it not being what I hope it could be." And with whatever Scottish magic she used, the confession slipped from me in a whisper. "Or if it's that I'm not . . ."

Her hand reached out to cover mine, pausing my search for words. She studied me in a way I felt all the way to my soul. My body readied for her words, braced for them.

"It seems to me we need to pray you find home, Katie-girl, because every wandering heart needs a place to rest."

A place to rest.

It sounded so simple, and yet it shook me.

Weren't people supposed to know where home was? Wasn't that *normal*?

And the idea of home being a restful place ushered up all the summers I'd escaped to Grandpa and Gran's for refuge. I'd belonged there as a teenager and young adult. My heart had rested on their farm, away from the impossible expectations and criticism I was met with at home.

But when they died, maybe I thought the beauty of such a place died with them. Brett's words resurfaced: "*Sometimes home is a place. Sometimes it's a person. Sometimes it's both.*"

Maybe the people were what made the place home. Like how Mirren transformed a simple bookshop into something more.

For some reason, Graeme came to mind and the way he held me as he helped me from the loch. Secure. Strong.

I'd read about that feeling in romance books and had tossed the notion away as mere fiction, but I'd felt it before my encounter with Graeme. With my grandparents. There was something inextricably grounding about my memories with them—of their love.

It wasn't as if I didn't believe my parents loved me in their own broken way.

They did all the typical "right" things, like call on birthdays, check in every once in a while, ask if I needed any money, and so on. But the relationship stayed shallow. We didn't discuss our grief or the people we'd lost. We didn't share our emotions unless they were positive ones; otherwise Mom's nerves would act up. And living with a mom whose behavior meant the rest of us had to walk around on tiptoe, and a dad who distanced himself emotionally—I suppose as a way to cope—cast a big, wide, and deep sadness over so many memories.

As an adult, I could now see it and attempt to make sense of it.

Mom deserved some compassion. Dad too. But anger still bubbled beneath my compassion. Alongside a deep sense of longing. Longing for whatever those warm, fuzzy movies portrayed about belonging.

Love lingered long, but so did wounds. But maybe I'd spent more time focusing on the wounds and running away from the pain than I had recalling all the love and allowing the good to heal me.

I gazed up into the sky on my way to the fishing spot. From what I believed and all I'd seen in my grandparents, love could change everything. But whether from the care of a mother figure, the camaraderie of a little boy, the kindness of a handsome Scot, or reminders of the truth in my faith, could I slow down long enough to let love make a change in me?

The morning's mild temperatures had taken a strange turn into cooler air and darker skies. I pulled my jacket closer around me and continued my walk across the grassy field, a foreboding set of mountains rising up in the distance like guards keeping watch over the island. One peak rose above the rest. The tallest on Mull.

What had the map labeled that mountain?

Ben More.

During dinner the night before, I'd overheard Mark talking with Wake about "bagging a munro." At first I thought they planned to go hunting, but then Miss Dupont, in her encyclopedic way, explained that a munro is a mountain in Scotland, and the phrase "bag a munro" meant hiking to the summit of one of the mountains.

I stared at the towering vista.

Maybe I could hike it next time I visited.

The thought paused me in my walk. Next time. Hmm . . . I didn't usually contemplate things like "next time" this soon into an assignment.

With a shake of my head, I followed the path over the next hill and saw Lachlan down below, already fishing. Wedge's nose raised to sniff the air, and he turned first, noting me and taking off in a run in my direction.

I rewarded his welcome with a solid scratch behind the ears. "Are you keeping a good eye on that little boy, Wedge?"

With renewed vigor at the mention of his name, he gave me a solid lick on the nose. "That's good to hear. Mull doesn't seem to be a crime capital or anything, but I'm glad you're around to keep things under control." I loved dogs. Hard to own one as a travel writer, but I embraced the moments I saw them along the way.

"It's about time you showed up, Katie." Lachlan shaded his eyes with his hand and called out to me. "Were you trying to wait till I caught all the fish?"

I grinned through a sigh and made my way down the hillside, Wedge running ahead.

"I had to make a stop along the way. How is the fishing so far?"

"Not bad." He shrugged a shoulder like a kid much older than ten. "But 'tis a dreich day and we're bound to get some rain."

The sky kept changing, almost by the minute. From partly sunny, as I started out that morning, to windy and overcast, to now . . . where the clouds held a shade of darkness to them, just waiting to release right on top of our heads.

"My grandpa told me that some of the best fishing happens in the rain."

"Maybe for the size of the catch." He wrinkled his nose with his frown as I walked up beside him. "But no for pleasure."

I chuckled, still enamored with his turn of phrase and the overall Scottish accent. It was delightful. Engaging. And if I thought about Graeme, utterly swoon-inducing. "No, fishing in the rain isn't much fun, is it?"

I set up my pole and baited my hook, receiving an approving nod from my fishing buddy. The mist carried from across the loch, where a few hills rose on the opposite shoreline, and that's when I saw them. The bane of my mortal existence.

Sheep.

A flock grazed just across the loch, thankfully distant. At least two dozen of them.

Sheep hated me.

And now it was reciprocal, but only because they started it.

My dozen experiences where "cute sheep" attempted to kill me proved the fact. The first situation that led to my moniker of Miss Adventure involved a rebel sheep, a tricky vine, and a ledge. There I was on my first solo assignment, minding my own business taking photos of the amazing views of the Andes, and a Criollo sheep decided I was his mortal enemy.

From all my knowledge of sheep at the time, which basically came from the Bible and children's nursery rhymes, these creatures exuded gentleness, tranquility, and maybe some recklessness or stupidity. But murderous intent?

I get the fact that red hair is unique and my American accent may not have been familiar to his Peruvian ears. But neither of those things constituted him chasing me across the hillside until I slipped over a ledge, at which time I grabbed hold of a vine that unraveled me far enough down that I only dropped about six feet onto a hillside and rolled the rest of the way down the mountain.

So there I was at dusk with a fantastic photo of a sunset over the Andes, a ridiculous story, and a broken toe.

Of course I required a helicopter rescue due to the terrain.

My advice: Don't let the woolly fluff fool you.

Their black eyes convey a soullessness not even Bram Stoker describes. I knew beneath that pillow-fluffiness dwelt sinister designs for my demise.

"You look a wee bit peely-wally, Katie." Lachlan slowed his pace and glanced from me to the terrifying creatures. "You don't like sheep?"

Even the word sent shivers down my spine. And if I had a heat vision–empowered glare, then Lachlan and I would feast on lamb chops for supper instead of fish. I'd developed a tiny bit of a vindictive fondness for mutton.

"I had a bad run-in with a sheep once." Or thrice.

"Aye, they're troublesome sometimes, make no mistake."

Now there was an appropriate use of the word *troublesome*. At least it was daylight. They looked less horrific in daylight. "They seem less alarming here than in Mongolia."

"Mongolia?" His tongue smoothed over the word. "Is that near Yorkshire?"

I looked over at the adorable boy, and half of my previous fear dispersed into a grin. "Not really. Are the sheep in Yorkshire scary?"

"I don't know." He gave a half shoulder shrug. "But the Scottish sheep are too dumb to be scary. Just troublesome. Dinnae fash yourself. Wedge and I will keep ye safe." He gave the dog a nod. "Won't we, Wedge?"

The dog yelped his agreement.

"Now." He tapped his temple and narrowed his eyes. "The one to keep a keen eye out for is Seamas."

"Seamas?" I repeated. "Is that a really fierce sheep, or is it something even worse? Like a banshee? I've heard they live in these parts too."

He pursed his lips as if in thought. "Banshee?"

"A female spirit with a horrible cry."

"You mean the caoineag. Aye." He nodded. "But she doesnae appear in the day. Not her."

He said it so matter-of-factly I almost laughed. But his very serious expression stopped me.

"Seamas is a hairy coo and a crabbit one at that."

Hairy coo. Ah, I knew what that meant. I'd been sharing photos on social media of the adorable Highland cows for a few weeks before my trip to Scotland. And I'd promised my nephew, Jake, I'd get some photos of them. And puffins.

"Are there more around besides Seamas? Nicer ones?"

"Aye, they stay up along that bràigh most of the time." He gestured to a nearby hill. "And there's a braw view of the Gribun cliffs from up there. If you pinch your eyes, you might even see Tragedy Rock."

The names in this place! They begged for more information. "Tragedy Rock?"

Lachlan's eyes lit. He already had storytelling in his blood and knew a willing listener when he saw one. "Isnae a happy tale, Katie Campbell."

I love how he used my full name so often. In fact, Graeme did the same thing.

"Well, I like all kinds of stories."

He drew in a breath, ginger brows raised as if warning me. "'Tis said a young shepherd named John came to Mull to marry his sweetheart, Rona. But a great storm brewed on the day of their marriage." He spoke with the eloquence likely passed down from his family and recounted the tale probably word for word as it had been told to him. So much like my Appalachian heritage. Stories. They'd been in my blood from a very young age too.

"The storm didnae stop the two from celebrating their union, and after the festivities they retired in John's nearby cottage built under the cliffs." He gestured back behind us toward the hill he'd just mentioned.

My body stiffened. I saw the next part coming.

"But the storm continued to rage through the night and loosed a rock, which came tumbling down the hill to land atop the wee cottage, smashing it to bits."

The last dramatic description was likely added for my benefit.

I released an appreciative sigh. "That is a sad tale."

"Aye, and their bodies were never found." His thin lips crooked the slightest bit. "Some say poor Rona is the caoineag heard across the glen in the night crying for her dear John."

I leaned forward and narrowed my eyes at him. I had to give the kid kudos for effect. "Are you trying to scare me a little bit?"

"You're naught the type to be easily afeart, are ye?"

Only of sheep.

And maybe a few other things that lived much deeper in my psyche than sheep.

"Not *easily.*" I waved toward the flock across the loch. "Except when it comes to sheep, but I must say you're an excellent storyteller."

His smile spread wide. "My uncle knows all the tales. Granny too." He sighed back against the rock. "But my uncle always says to leave a tale with a bit o' hope, if ye can. So . . .'tis said that although the remains of the cottage lay crumbled 'neath Tragedy Rock, flowers still bloom in John and Rona's garden as a sign that true love ne'er dies."

Love lingers long.

I studied the little boy. Leave a tale with a bit of hope? I grinned. A good life notion too.

We fished and talked a little longer. I took a few videos and photos of the scenery and the one tiny fish I caught. Lachlan encouraged me with all the gusto a disillusioned eight-year-old could muster. Clearly, I was not an impressive fisherwoman.

However, when I brought out the Irn-Bru and baps, along with some cookies, his admiration for me resurfaced.

"I was told a proper fishing excursion required a snack of baps." I raised the bread roll for his view. "I think there's bacon and eggs in these."

"Aye." He laid his fishing pole down and moved to my side, his grin crinkling up his freckled nose. "And some biscuits too."

"Right." I placed the bap and "biscuits" on a napkin in front of him and handed him one of the Irn-Brus.

"But they dinnae call them biscuits where you're from, do they?"

I shook my head. "We call them cookies, but they taste great all the same."

He nodded and took a bite of the bap. "And do you have Irn-Bru where you live?"

I looked down at the orange drink, a little skeptical. It came with its own online reputation. "Some stores probably sell it, but I've never had any before. It's not a common drink for Americans."

So he waited, brows raised in anticipation. Whew, the pressure mounted as he watched me taste the liquid.

And whatever expression I made as the bubblegum-flavored soda washed over my tongue brought the most surprised look to Lachlan's face.

"You dinnae like it?"

Nope. "I think it might take some getting used to."

His brows pinched and he took a large drink of his Irn-Bru, then sent me a look, saying, *That's how it's done.* I covered my laugh with a bite of my bap. If life involved friendships with witty and sweet eight-year-olds, then maybe I wouldn't be so . . . afeart.

Suddenly Lachlan's fishing pole started to jerk on the nearby rock where he'd placed it.

"I got one," he called, cramming the rest of the bap into his mouth and rushing to the pole. Wedge joined in on the abrupt excitement as Lachlan mounted the rock, but Lachlan must have jumped in a different direction than Wedge planned. The boy and the dog got tangled.

Lachlan fell hard on the other side of the rock, and Wedge yelped before dashing back a few steps. I set my drink down and rushed to the other side of the rock where the little boy was slowly sitting up, grabbing at his leg.

A whimper sounded from both the dog and the boy. Wedge drew close, sniffing at Lachlan's hair, his ears low. Poor fella. But Lachlan? A deep cut, already pooling with blood, marked from his knee down toward his ankle. At least four inches long. And deep.

"Hold on. I have some bandages."

I ran to my bag and brought it back along with me, the little boy's lips pressed tight as he tried to hold in his tears.

Oh! I wanted to hug him.

"Does anything else hurt besides your knee?"

He shook his head and tried to move his leg, then stopped with a wince. "My ankle."

I drew in a breath and stared up at the sky just as the first drops of rain fell on my face. We had—at least—a half hour walk back to Glenkirk, and that was without a little limping boy.

"I'm going to bandage up your leg, Lachlan." I started pulling supplies out of my bag. With my track record of clumsiness, I always came prepared. I opened my water bottle. "I'm going to pour some water over the wound. Okay?" He nodded and I took out my water bottle and cleaned off the blood as best I could. Ooh! That was a doozy of a fall. "We should have you cleaned up in no time."

And then he sniffled.

My hands paused as I started to wipe the wound with a cloth. "I'm sorry it hurts."

He shook his head and looked away.

"I'll try to be as gentle as I can, Lachlan, but I know you're a strong boy, and it's okay if you need to cry."

He looked up at me then, those large blue eyes of his glossy from a sheen of tears, and my heart squeezed at the sight. "My mummy used to say that."

Used to? I clenched my teeth to steady my emotions. "Well, she was right. Must be where you got your smarts from."

His lips tilted a little. "She didnae like Irn-Bru either." He sniffled again, a lone tear sliding down his cheek as he nodded. "But she loved Coca-Cola."

I began to wrap his wound. "She had good taste then."

"Aye." The word rasped out, and he wiped an arm over his eyes. "Grandpa said if heaven has all the things we love, then Mummy will have a big supply of Coca-Cola and sticky toffee pudding."

I could get along with this lady. "I haven't tried sticky toffee pudding yet, but I've been told I need to."

"Aye." He sniffed again, and this time his bottom lip wobbled. "You'd like it."

I tucked the bandage into place and leaned close, catching his attention. He probably knew this already, but it never hurt for a kid to hear it again. "It's okay to cry when we miss someone, Lachlan. When we have such a big love inside of us, we grieve big too. And it sounds like you have a really big love inside you for your mom."

He pinched his lips as if working through his emotions, and then sniffled. "I cannae hear her voice anymore." The words disappeared into a quivered sound. "Not even when I close my eyes very tight."

I didn't know if it was the right thing to do or not, but I pulled him and his trembling shoulders into my arms . . . and he cried. A quiet, aching little sound. A noise my heart understood all too well.

And Wedge did his best to press his nose in between us, finally succeeding in planting a solid lick on Lachlan's wet face. The boy wrestled the pup into a hug, his smile slowly returning, and then he made to stand.

With a whimper, he crumbled back to the ground.

And the raindrops decided to fall a little steadier. At least he hadn't bled through the bandage yet. That was a good sign about the depth of his wound.

"Do you live nearby?"

His eyes welled up again, but he answered, "Aye. Up the way."

I grabbed my bag and scooted closer to him, sorting out how to lift him. "Is that a *stone's* throw away? Or longer?"

Please say closer.

His brow crinkled. "I dinnae think my uncle could even throw a stone that far." And then his expression cleared as his eyes lit. "Ah, I see what you mean." He paused and then his eyebrows shot high. "But I *fell* for it."

I laughed. "Nice one." And it got his mind off his leg and his grief for the moment. "And I might add"—I shot him a wink—"you really *rocked* that fall, so I'm going to help you get home, okay?"

"Okay." His smile returned almost as bright as normal. "I've got a joke for ye."

"Do you?" I scooped my arm around his back and helped him to a stand, snatching up my backpack as I went.

"What did one eye say to the other?"

Perfect boy joke, right here. "What?"

"Just between you and me, something smells."

I laughed and looked toward the hill from where I'd just come. "Okay, Lachlan, which way is home?"

He adjusted against me and then looked up. "You just follow the rock fence up the next hill, and I live in the old wee cottage at the top."

At the top of the next hill—I braced my shoulders—perfect.

We started forward. "My great-granny used to live there with her pet sheep."

Her pet sheep? In her house?

I knew what my nightmares would be tonight.

"Any sheep still there?"

His lips twitched as I slowed my strides to keep in step with him. "Not *inside* the house." His delivery came slowly, like he was testing my response.

"You're teasing me, are you?" I narrowed my eyes down at him. "That's a really *baaad* sport."

His giggle burst out and hit me square in the heart, especially after watching him grieve.

"Speaking of sheep." No time like the present to resurrect my fourth-grade self and offer my own jokes as distractions as we continued up the hill. "What instrument do two sheep play?"

He looked up at me, expectant.

"The *tubaaa*."

His snicker followed. "What should you wear to a tea party?"

I shrugged my shoulders and his smile bloomed.

"A T-shirt."

"Ooh." I nodded. "That was a good one to have up your *sleeve*."

And after a pause, he giggled again. I tucked that sound close.

On we went, higher up the hill, each trying to think up another ridiculous pun or joke. At one point I looked behind me, and even with the rain coming down and the fog whisking past on the breeze, it failed to dim the majesty of the place. Was the island moody? For sure. Was it equally fascinating and mysterious and . . . calming?

Strangely, yes.

No wonder Mirren read Jaime Jo Wright books.

As we crested the hill, a cottage came immediately into view. Larger than most of the others I'd seen off the main road, this white stone cottage was a two-story rectangle. Three large windows dotted the second floor, with two on the bottom, separated by a blue door. A chimney poked from each end of the roof, and a little lean-to room was attached to the left side.

The rock fence trailed all the way to meet a fence at the back of the house, and one large tree branched out in the front yard. With a few flowering bushes and window boxes, it would look even more storybook.

Even in the rain.

I wonder what a starlit night looked like from this point. Marvelous, to be sure.

What a place to call home!

The rain began coming down even harder, and my body wilted a little beneath the weight of the little boy and our climb. But at least relief was near.

We hobbled up to the door and I knocked, but Lachlan didn't wait for an answer. He just shoved the door open and pulled me in with him, as he was still attached to me for support.

"Uncle Graeme!" the boy called upon entry. "Uncle Graeme!"

The "Uncle Graeme" part didn't register as quickly as it ought to have because I was immediately drawn to the fascinating collection of sculpted birds hanging in various places throughout the living room.

A seagull.

Kestrel.

A barn owl with wings spread.

Even a puffin stood on the windowsill.

All lifelike.

Where was I?

"Lachlan?" The voice came just before the rest of him turned the corner of the room, towel over the shoulder of his T-shirt and a pair of jeans that was doing him all kinds of favors.

His eyes met mine, then shifted to Lachlan and his leg.

"What?" He rushed forward. "What on earth did you do this time, Katie Campbell?"

Maybe hearing my full name wasn't so great after all.

"Me?" The warm fuzzies tingling in my middle fizzled to sparks at his accusation. "I helped your . . . nephew get home after a fall."

Graeme was the uncle Lachlan kept talking about with such adoration? My thoughts spiraled. So, was Lachlan's mom Graeme's sister? Or sister-in-law?

Graeme reached down and swept the boy up in his arms, carrying him to the couch opposite a cozy fireplace. "Did you help with the fall too, perchance?"

Okay, that was just going too far. I turned right back toward the door.

"You're not going to leave in this storm," his voice boomed from behind me. "It's only going to get worse."

"I'm just trying to protect the innocent." I shot him a tight smile. "If I stay in your house, it might get struck by lightning. Or blown over. Or"—I waved a hand in the air—"have a rock drop on it simply because I'm in it."

"Katie," he said, his tone softening over my name, but I was determined now.

I already failed at enough. I didn't need to feel guilty over something I didn't even do.

I pulled open the door and marched right out into a blustery burst of rain. The wind caught my breath and doused me with more water than a shower. The view looked a lot less inviting than it had a few minutes before. In fact, it had pretty much disappeared into a cloud.

"Get back inside, woman."

Woman? I marched away from the house in a direction I hoped was the right one.

"Och." Graeme's fingers wrapped around my wrist and pulled me back. "You're the most stubborn woman." He tugged me over the threshold, slammed the door, and then proceeded to tower over me in his grouchy, jacked giant sort of way. "You're not going back out in that storm when you havenae the sense to know where you're going or how to get there."

I raised my chin with more confidence than I felt. "I can find my way. Besides, aren't you afraid I'll bring some hurricane with me to take out your entire farm?" I turned back toward the door, the burn of tears surprising me.

What on earth was wrong with me? I was as moody as the weather!

His fingers tightened back on my wrist, and he turned me around to face him. "You're stayin' until the storm passes, and then I'll drive you back to Craighill." He studied my face, and I looked away. "It's not safe, and you're not in clothes fit to go ramblin' along the craigs waiting for death to find you." He growled . . . or was it a chuckle? "Because it wants to find you, Katie Campbell. I can practically feel it blowin' on your neck."

I opened my mouth to protest as my palm caressed the back of my neck—just in case. But with my track record so far, I'm not sure I had a solid argument against his accusation. At least I knew I hadn't done anything to hurt Lachlan.

I'd never.

"You just catch me at the wrong times," I offered in my weak defense.

"Heaven help me if I ever catch you at the right ones," he grumbled and released my wrist. "I might not recognize ye."

"I see the rain brings out your charming side." It was a weak shot, but there it was.

His pale eyes steadied on me, and the faintest hint of a smile tipped those lips crooked. And those warm fuzzies came right back to life.

"Come near the fire to keep warm." The way he voiced those words held more fire than I needed. Warmth spilled from my damp head all the way down to my muddy wellies. But I didn't want to like him right now. He didn't deserve it. I offered him one of my finest glares.

He raised a brow, and I looked away just in case he could read the very warm thoughts in my head. With a chuckle, he returned to Lachlan's side.

After a moment's hesitation and a strong chill skittering up my spine, I stepped around the couch and lowered myself to a small wooden chair by the fire, near Wedge.

Graeme's gentle tones pulled the whole story out of Lachlan.

The grumpy man bent over little Lachlan, his gentle movements unwinding the bandages I'd wrapped around the boy's leg, and the twinge of longing I'd felt earlier branched throughout my chest. So strong yet gentle. Caring.

His shoulders stretched beneath his T-shirt. Powerful.

Then he sent me a small grin over his shoulder.

And I knew that if I did fall for a Scot, he'd be the perfect one to catch me.

CHAPTER 13

Graeme

Someone needed to protect this woman.

Even if it meant protecting her from herself.

I sighed as I rebandaged Lachlan's leg and then carried him up to his room to rest with a video game. The wound wasn't bad enough to take him to an emergency room, but the sprained ankle would keep him grounded for a wee bit. Probably not long enough. The lad barely stayed down for long.

"Katie may not be good at fishing or like Irn-Bru, but she's good at tending," Lachlan said as I helped him out of his wet shirt and pants to replace them with dry. "Like Mum."

The declaration hit my heart with an added pang. I was already beating myself up about how hard I was on her when she'd shown up at the cottage with my wounded nephew, knowing full well the situation wasn't her fault. But adding thoughts of Greer to it?

A double stab. Guilt and grief.

Lachlan regularly arrived with scrapes and bruises. And I always fought against overreacting because, well, he was my responsibility, and I wasn't keen to see someone else I love hurt . . . or worse.

Certainly Katie had a tendency toward trouble, but it was clear she never meant to hurt anyone. And there was a sincerity to her that kept sneaking beneath my defenses and hitting my curiosity or funny bone or . . . heart.

"Aye, she has a bit of your mum in her." I handed him his video game controller.

"Though Mum knew the island better."

My jaw twinged from the effort to maintain my composure. "Well now, your mum grew up here, so she ought to know it."

Lachlan nodded, his lips tipping a little. "She's funny too."

"Aye." I rested my hands on my hips, and then the realization dawned. Her hair color. Her height. Both could easily remind the lad of his mum. "Is Katie Campbell your sweetheart, lad?"

The boy's eyes lit. "I'm still decidin'. She didn't make fun when I cried like a baby after I fell, and she gives good hugs. But she's an American."

He said the word like it was a deal-breaker, and the guilt in my chest deepened some more. Perhaps the wariness of outsiders had been something he'd learned from me, a struggle of my own I didn't even realize I'd communicated, especially after Allison left. Home and the familiar had become safe, everyone and everything else, suspect.

Children acted as mirrors for the good and the bad, and right now the reflection stung. I lowered myself to the end of his bed. "There's nothing wrong with her bein' American, is there now, lad? She cannae help it."

"It's not bad?"

I only hesitated a second, thinking of a humorous jab at Americans before stilling the inner comic. "All the things you liked about Katie are the important things, not where she's from." I breathed in the words, relaying them to myself. "Doesnae matter where she's from or where she's going if her heart is a good fit, does it, lad?"

"Aye, Uncle Graeme." His smile brimmed. "Mum always liked talkin' about visitin' other places far away. I'd wager she's looking down on them now like a picture book."

"That's a good thought." My throat closed off any other response.

"And I think she'd fancy Katie too."

I didn't trust myself to add more words, so I nodded and stood, tousling Lachlan's hair before placing a quick kiss to his head and leaving the room.

It took a full minute to collect myself as I stood outside his door, only partly because of the constant grief of loss, but even more due to the way I saw my own bitterness, and perhaps my own fear, in Lachlan's words. I'd lived in protection mode since Greer became sick, hemming in the family so everyone was close enough for me to see and protect. Trying to capture every last moment, hold to every family tradition, sieve through every drop of life left in her to share with Lachlan for years to come . . . and in my own way, keep her near. In the process I'd closed off possibilities and dreams and even a little faith I used to have in what lay beyond the borders of my world.

And aye, Greer would have liked Katie, as Mum did. Seen to her heart.

I released a deep sigh and took the stairs back to the living room. Perhaps Katie was good at making trouble on the outside, but I'd had trouble brewing within that spilled over to my actions and decisions.

And I needed to make things right.

Katie stood by the door, still wearing her wet jacket, and raised her gaze to me as I reached the bottom of the steps. "How is he?"

The concern on her face only pummeled my shame anew. "He'll be right as rain once he rests awhile."

"Good." She nodded her head of damp, wavy hair and stepped toward the door. "I don't want to cause more trouble, and the rain is lightening up a little." She thumbed toward the door. I glanced out the window, the downpour blurring the view entirely.

"So if you'll just point me in the direction of Craighill, I can—"

"I want to apologize."

She paused in her steps toward the door and looked back over at me, brows rising.

"I . . . I'm truly sorry for being an utter roaster when you arrived."

She glanced at me and then quickly looked back to the door, as if weighing her options. And no wonder.

I stepped closer. "It wasnae you; it was me. I know I cannae keep Lachlan safe all the time, but my sister entrusted him to my care before she died, so I . . . well, I can sometimes overreact."

Her dark round gaze flickered to mine, the residual timidity a devastating punishment for me. I'd never want to take the fire from her. To wound her. "I wouldn't hurt him, Graeme. I'd never want to hurt him."

"I know." I held her gaze, hoping she believed me, saw the desire to make things right. "Forgive me."

She stared at me, eyes near full from a sudden swarm of tears. I'd seen Allison cry before, usually when we argued, but something haunting and spellbinding entranced me in Katie's expression. Honest. Searching.

What did she see?

I hoped much more than the eejit I knew I was.

Her gaze probed mine for long seconds as rain pelted the windows. Then suspicion and hurt melted into something unexpected. A . . . tenderness?

No fighting back. No prolonging how she'd been wronged.

The gentle acceptance did something to my brain. Dazed me, maybe? Sent me off-kilter?

And ignited an indefinable connection to her. A deeper need to know her.

"I'm sorry about your sister," she whispered. "She must have thought you were pretty wonderful to choose you for Lachlan."

Her words pierced, almost stinging in a bittersweet way. "Or the least offensive of her options."

"I doubt that's true." She smiled and looked away. "I mean, I've only met Lachlan and your mom, but I'd say your sister must have thought pretty highly to choose you as a guardian over Mirren."

"I volunteered." My throat tightened around the words. "He was such a link to her, and I love them both."

Her lips pinched as she audibly swallowed, and I knew she understood grief, whether she voiced it or not.

Quiet invaded the moment, and I gestured toward the room to redirect how exposed my heart felt. "This was her house. I moved in to help care for her during her illness. There was no reason to leave once she passed. Besides, it's been a good place to heal." I cleared my throat as familiar emotions rose to snatch at my voice. "And who wouldn't want that view?"

I gestured toward the window, but the blinding rain dimmed my attempts at levity.

She smiled a little. Well, maybe the levity wasn't lost after all.

"Did she make all of these sculptures too?" Her gaze roamed the room, noting each carving's placement.

"She certainly encouraged wildlife sculpting." I pushed my hands into my jean pockets, bracing for her response to my answer. "But the sculptures are mine."

Her attention flashed to me, and then she took another look around the room. "Yours." She breathed in, almost in wonder, and then looked back at me. "*You* made these beautiful creations?"

One of my brows tipped. "It's a wonder, isn't it, since I've been so brutish to ye."

"Maybe I wasn't expecting such beauty beneath all that beastyness." Her grin tipped wider.

"Och, lass." I exaggerated a groan. "Dinnae say it like that."

Her eyes lit with her laugh, and the world tilted back into its rightful place. She walked over to the puffin on the windowsill. "What amazing craftsmanship, Graeme." Her fingers skimmed over the puffin before she turned back to me. "These are remarkable."

"Thanks." I'd been praised before for my work, but her sincere admiration melted through me like a perfect cuppa. "It started as a hobby I did with my grandfather, and then, over the last few years, it's become . . . more."

"Of course it has. How could it not?" She lowered to her knee to examine the puffin more closely. "Well, this knowledge adds a whole new twist on the idea of you as the resident handyman."

"And butler, don't forget."

She tossed a grin over her shoulder as she stood, the look branding my mind. "How could I ever forget! Every manor house needs a butler."

The way her eyes swept over me warmed me through. And I tipped my head in curiosity, only to have her face flush as she looked away.

She stepped forward to the side table by the couch. I followed her gaze to the paper on the table—the invitation to exhibit my work in London.

"And you exhibit your work?"

Why did this keep coming up? First Mum, now Katie?

I stepped over to her and shook my head. "I'm not much of a traveler. Not with Lachlan, Craighill, and the work." I took the paper and placed it over on my nearby desk. "Sales are good enough online for now."

"I bet they are." She stepped back to the puffin. "But think of how many more people you'd inspire if they saw these in person. I'm sure the visibility up close would only get your name out there even more and you could give up the butlering side job."

Her easy teasing after I'd been harsh humbled me, and niggled her suggestion a little deeper than I'd allowed before. Inspire people?

"How do you reckon I'd inspire people?"

"Doesn't beauty always inspire us? I mean, it does me. Inspires my imagination. It's one of the amazing parts of traveling." Her finger glided over the puffin's wing, slow and—though she had no intention of it—seductive. The movement and her admiration shoogled my pulse. "I've never seen a real puffin before, and they're such interesting-looking creatures."

"They're a curious lot," I offered, happy to move the conversation away from its current trajectory. "I'll have to take you to see them, because even in sculptures there's no way to do them justice."

"Well, you must have gotten pretty close to create such detail. They look so real. I can't imagine seeing your work and not feeling awe." She leaned close to the puffin. "So intricate. I've been all around the world, and your work is just as good as some I've seen, and better than most."

Her wonder kept settling deeper, softening the edge of my reserve. Making me want to . . . share. Could this be the way people responded when I shipped my sculptures to them and they unwrapped them for the first time?

"It's a joy." I hadn't meant to say it. I'd thought it hundreds of times but never voiced it to anyone, except Greer. The realization shocked me back a step. Why now? Why Katie?

Her smile rewarded my blunder. "Well, I think your joy certainly comes through in what you do. It's amazing how you can take a piece of wood and create such beauty. What a gift!" She stood and stepped to the kestrel resting on the lone bookshelf in the room. "It's special when you can find something that really feeds your joy, isn't it? I find it in bringing people's stories to life. Trying to find and highlight the beauty in them. I love knowing something I wrote or retold lightened someone else's day." Her expression sobered as she stared at the bird. "Too many real-life stories end so hopelessly, don't they? And it's a wonderful thing to unearth that one treasure in someone's tale to bring it to the surface."

Much like re-creating that one unique curve to a bird's beak or a fox's nose. Watching the wood come to life. And this was a glimpse into her heart? What a contradiction, for the woman who wanted to lighten others' burdens courted her own trouble on a daily, if not momentary, basis.

I studied her. But perhaps one fueled the other? Or the trouble from her own hurts inspired her desire to bring joy to others through her stories? Just maybe we were both managing our wounds in the same way. "Do you write all the stories you hear?"

She turned toward me, her wet hair curling into waves around her face, bringing out the depths of those eyes. Or perhaps it was the knowledge of what she held behind those eyes that gave them depth and feeling and attractiveness.

"Only the best ones. Or the ones with that golden lining of beauty." She shrugged a shoulder. "And sometimes the funniest." Her gaze grew distant for a moment, and her countenance fell. "Some stories are too raw to re-create."

Her own? Some unspoken grief held behind those eyes.

Rain still pelted the window, and I wasn't anywhere near ready to have her leave just yet.

"Would you like some tea?" The request came out all raspy and gruff, so I shrugged a shoulder. "The rain's not let up yet, and the tea will take the chill off."

Her smile returned with a nod. "Thank you."

She followed me into the kitchen, where my breakfast table stood to one corner, some bric-a-brac littering one side of it. I turned to apologize for the mess, but Katie had walked to a cupboard against the wall, gaze intent on a few of my carvings there.

"Really, Graeme." She touched a sculpture of Wedge on point. "As corny as it may sound, why would you ever choose to hide this gift?"

I rolled my shoulders to keep them from stiffening at the assumption, or was she hitting too close to the mark? "I'm not hiding it." I filled the kettle with water. "It's all there online."

"Okay then . . ." She turned those large eyes on me, one ginger brow raised. "You hide yourself?"

Myself? Paired with my thoughts from earlier, I felt God was hammering the point home a little too repeatedly. I almost groaned. But my stubborn head likely needed repetition.

"Though being invisible is a perfect butler move, from what I hear. And it adds a sense of mystery."

Her humor eased the sudden tension in my neck but didn't ease my mind. One of Allison's arguments resurfaced. *"You and your parents never leave Mull, Graeme. You tie yourself to this island like the outside world will swallow you up if you leave. I need room for more. And I think you do too."*

I'd gone to university in Inverness and traveled to doctor's appointments on the mainland with Greer. My thoughts came to a halt, confirming my earlier revelation. I'd never been the traveling sort, but since Greer . . . I'd changed.

No wonder I wasn't a hero. They were bold, daring. They faced their fears.

Had I let Greer's death kill something inside me too, and in the grieving process I'd turned things around? Into a lie I now believed?

Katie moved to another sculpture. One of my favorites I'd made for Greer three years ago when she'd first gotten her cancer diagnosis. A shepherd cradling a lamb. I'd carved it with care to communicate to my best friend that no matter the storm, she was held safe. It became as much a comfort to me as to her. A reminder of the truth when I lost faith so many times along the way.

As Greer had said, *"Graeme, it's not about your hold on God. It's about His hold on you."*

And I'd never both challenged and understood that truth more than the last few months of her life and the year after her death. I'd let go so often, raised my fists to the sky, refused to pray. And yet, God held on to my broken heart until the raw, cracked-wide grief began to heal. Even now, as it continued to heal. Every day.

And as strange and braw as it seemed, God had brought Katie into my life to remind me of things my heart once knew. Once believed it wanted.

I poured the hot water from the kettle over the tea leaves into a teapot my granny used to use. Greer too. My history was all around me. Everywhere. My job and family too. Could it be that I'd closed myself in with my trusted few as a way to shield myself from the hurt of Greer's loss and Allison's leaving? Tucked myself away from the world to "protect" my heart? But those things—my family and home—were never meant to be shields. Not from living life.

Why had I not considered it until now? Had it truly taken some American travel writer from across the world literally falling into my life to get my attention?

Katie smoothed her thumb over the lamb's head and glanced over at me. "I think I could handle a sheep like that . . . small and sweet." Her voice shook a little.

"Not a fan of sheep?" I swallowed through the hoarseness in my voice.

"They're not fans of me. Although I can completely understand the biblical analogy as I'm so prone to wander and clearly"—she shrugged a shoulder—"lose my way."

Biblical analogy? That reference, along with some of her other comments, piqued my curiosity. "If you're also prone to search for a place of worship, you may want to steer clear of the church in Glenkirk."

She wrinkled her nose with her frown. "Already been."

I grunted my thoughts. She'd only been in Mull a week, so she must have visited this past Sunday. Very purposeful.

"It was a pretty small crowd, and nobody talked to me." She raised her palms in defense. "I get that I'm a stranger, but I was hoping for a little camaraderie among kindred spirits. It's what I loved most about my grandparents' church—that sense of family." She slid down in a chair at my little table, and the sight warmed my heart. "Good teaching, good people." She wiggled her brows. "And lots of eating."

I coughed out a laugh and poured her tea, pushing the plate of biscuits toward her. "With those preferences in mind, I have a place for you to try then."

"Really?"

"'Tis called Livingston Chapel and it's just beyond Glenkirk. We use an older building, but the congregation is fairly new within the last ten years."

"We?" Her brows rose as she watched me and then took a drink of her tea. "That's your church?"

"Aye." My lips twitched. "God's not finished knocking the eejit from my head just yet, as you, no doubt, have noticed from my agitation at times. I need the help."

"Don't we all?" Her smile spread across those lovely pink lips and brightened her eyes in a fascinating way. "Sounds like the kind of place I should certainly visit, because I'm pretty sure there's still some eejit to knock out of me too."

Katie

Classes didn't start until after lunch on Wednesday, so I took the opportunity for a morning walk since the sun shone fresh upon the wet ground, beckoning for some photos. After yesterday's storm, the already lush colors of Mull shimmered in richer hues.

Or maybe part of it was my dazzled brain.

I'd barely slept last night after Graeme drove me back to Craighill. Mrs. Lennox even enquired after my health at dinner because I remained so quiet. Not to worry, though, because she became distracted by Caesar skittering across the floor during the third course and nearly derailing the entire fish dish as a faithful footman danced around the furry creature to keep from spilling everything on his tray.

I could at least write that the Edwardian Experience oozed with the humorously unexpected. When Mr. Lennox mentioned how he was glad it was Caesar who had gotten loose instead of his pet python, Monty (very clever, Mr. Lennox), Mark turned twenty shades of pale.

But as I walked through the lovely morning, I just couldn't get the previous afternoon and Graeme MacKerrow out of my head. Sure, he had great shoulders. And I often got distracted by his eyes. And the way he rolled those *r* sounds reverberated in my chest like a warm bass drum. But there was so much more to him—grief and gentleness and creativity and humor. Depth and humility. Ach! Tenderness.

My palm flew to my chest as I took the path into Glenkirk.

And he'd invited me to his *church*?

How is a girl supposed to go back to a normal way of thinking after such a combo? But that was completely ridiculous because I was leaving and he was clearly linked to Mull. He even owned an ancestral manor house! If that didn't shout *tied to Scotland*, what did?

But . . . I just couldn't shake this connection with him. I liked him. Not just the shoulders and the accent, but . . . *him.*

It's like God put every possible combination of my daydreams together, including cute kid and dog (which I hadn't even considered before) and formed a perfect specimen of all my star-bright wishes from the last ten years.

Similar to one of those rare and childhood-defining moments when you actually won the coveted stuffed animal from one of those claw machines in the store after spending much more money than the toy even cost. Except this was a million times better.

I looked up to the sky as I stepped onto the main street. *Not fair, God. You can't just dangle him in front of me, knowing I'm going to leave soon.*

Oh, but what a view!

My face heated at the very idea. And my eyes got a little watery too, so I shook away the thought—mostly—as I entered Mirren's bookshop. And immediately realized it was Wednesday . . . at ten.

A rush of welcome exploded from the group of ladies in the corner, all waving me forward with their free hand as the other hand held some knitting object or other.

"We knew you'd come back to join us, Katie Campbell." This from Maggie, who tucked her chin with her nod. "I saw it in your eyes."

Mirren rolled her gaze heavenward and approached me as I came forward. "It's a braw day for a wee dauner." My brain interpreted the sentence in slow motion. *A good day for a small walk?* "I'm happy you dried out well after the dreich day yesterday." And then Mirren turned to the group of ladies and thoroughly tossed me into the lions' den of matchmaking. "Katie rescued dear Lachlan after a fall and walked with him in the rain all the way to Graeme's cottage."

"In the rain. Poor lass." This from Lori, who offered the sweetest smile.

"Then they had a spot of tea." Mirren's knowing look brought out a collective "ah" from the other ladies, as if Graeme had asked me on a date or something.

Which he hadn't.

He'd invited me to church. But that's not a date. Is it? It felt wrong to think of an invitation to church as a date.

Mirren gestured for me to sit and promptly placed a cup of tea in my hand. "And Graeme said Katie was attending Livingston Chapel on Sunday next."

The audible appreciation rose in volume. I could practically feel these knitters envisioning me in a wedding dress.

"How is Lachlan?" Maybe I could deter the flock of yentas from their current course.

"He's healing nicely, thanks to your quick response," Mirren answered.

"But let's hear the other bits." Bea scooted to the end of her chair like she was watching a suspense movie. "Mirren said that you and Graeme were cooried up at the table when she arrived."

My brows shot high. We were having tea and the table was small, so we sat a little close, but no coorieing like the twinkle in her eyes suggested. "I don't think *coorie* is the right—"

"I fell in love with my husband the first time we had tea together." Lori sighed as if recalling the moment in her mind.

"He's a fine catch, Katie. Good heart." Bea tapped her lips. "Strong jaw."

He did have a nice jaw.

"And his heart needs tending with your sunshine, you ken," Lori offered, her sweet smile full of daydreams. "The last lass broke it thoroughly."

"But she didnae belong, and we all knew it," Maggie added, pointing toward her eyes. "Something in the eyes."

"Now, ladies, she was a fine lass." Mirren's voice smoothed out the conversational ruffle. "But she didnae belong with Graeme in all the ways they both needed." Mirren sent me a look. "Their worlds didnae fit."

Neither does mine, I wanted to say, but swallowed a sip of tea instead.

"The high and mighty sort, she was," Maggie continued, sniffing the air as if the very memory of this lady carried a bad smell. "She wouldnae have ever thought to wear plain and practical clothes like our Katie does."

I looked down at my smudged jeans and yellow wellies. Plain and practical. Exactly what a girl wants to hear about her clothing choices. Not sure if that helped my confidence or not. But the "our Katie" part softened the comparison a little.

"You'll be a fine match for him, Katie," Maggie added with a stiff nod. "Even if you are a Campbell."

I pinched my grin into submission. "Thanks, Maggie."

"And he's in need of a charming lass like you. Adventurous, kind, tall . . ." This from Bea.

Tall mattered in romance? I shrugged. Well, it certainly could make kissing a little easier. Heat leaped into my face, so I took another sip of tea.

"Wear blue on Sunday to ensure you catch his eye," Lori said. "He's right fond of blue."

Did all these ladies know him *that* well? Small town took on a new definition, though I'd never truly experienced it since the first ten years of my life. Dad had us moving all over the world with his chaplain duties.

"Oh, and we'll collect you some heather to wear to lure him in."

Lure him in? With heather?

"It's a potent flower and pure Scot." Maggie winked, and I basked in the camaraderie, even if my cheeks were on fire.

Was this just a normal part of life for these ladies? The happy busybodying? The advice? The . . . care? My chest pinched a little.

"Dinnae fash, Katie-girl," Bea added. Oh great, the nickname was catching on. "We've all been married long enough to know how to catch a lad."

"Catch a lad?" The phrase tumbled out of me in a laugh.

I wasn't even planning to stay in Scotland. I didn't need to have needless ideas of catching a lad rolling around in my head or heart. But arguing with the matchmakers seemed futile.

The pleasure in my grin spread all the way through my chest. I hadn't had people this invested in my life in . . . a really long time. And nothing quite like this. The feeling pressed in on me like a great and long-overdue hug.

So I gave in to the flurry. Just for now. Just to feel connected for the short two weeks I had left.

And as dangerous as the notion was to my heart, the idea of not embracing it for a little while hurt worse, because my lonely heart wanted to hold on.

Even temporarily.

And I'd deal with the consequences later.

CHAPTER 14

Graeme

"We will be eating an early supper tonight so you can get to bed early." Lennox's voice traveled through the ballroom, echoing off the oak-paneled ceiling and matching floors I'd spent part of the year repairing. "We leave by nine o'clock sharp for our surprise outing, and you are encouraged to wear modern clothing."

Surprise outing? Ah, right. As part of the experience, each set of guests would have the opportunity of engaging in a special activity offered on Mull based on the time of year of their visit—Christmas festival, annual spring music festival, Mendelssohn on Mull, flower show, or whatever Mull had to offer.

But in July? My stomach dropped a little. The only real option had to be the Highland games. And with a little help from Dad, I'd gotten quick approval for a demonstration tent to show how my sculptures were made.

I didn't have to leave Mull in this case.

But I was determined not to bury my life along with my sister. Mum and Katie's words stuck like a splinter, and I had to work it out.

This opportunity would prove a test.

And that was all.

My attention traveled back to Katie, who stood beside me as my dance partner, since Mark the Eejit had rewounded his ankle by trying to slide down the stair railing.

He injured more than his leg. Men weren't meant to straddle railings and slide down them.

However, it assured me of my solid building skills, because the new railing didn't so much as shake.

Would Katie's eyes hold the same fascination at watching me create the sculptures as they had when she viewed the completed projects in my cottage? Holding her in my arms again was no hardship. This time we danced a quadrille, which I'd only seen on YouTube last night after some subtle questions to Lennox about the dances for today. The waltz, I knew. Greer had taught me.

Which made the idea of dancing it a little sweeter.

And she'd have gotten a laugh at the idea of me, dressed as an Edwardian butler, dancing it with an accident-prone American. Actually, I could almost hear her laughing as Lennox droned on about the history of the dances.

Greer would have found the language of fans class humorous as well. The only two moves I cared to remember were the ones that communicated "kiss me" and "I fancy you." At one point, Katie's eyes met mine as I waited by the door at my butler station and her fan flashed wide. She began raising it to her lips in the signal for "kiss me," when Miss Dupont slapped Mark the Eejit because evidently he'd given off some rather unflattering message.

But had she fancied a kiss? Because the more I spent time with her—and with each dance—the kissing idea had grown into a full-on need.

So as the next dancing lesson began, Miss Dupont was paired with Logan, and if my fan-reading skills proved acute (a thought I actually hated to have floating around in my mind), she kept repeating the phrase "I fancy you." Either that or she had an itch on her cheek.

Logan appeared either unfazed or unaware of her message, but the too-serious man acted like he was long overdue for a date. Miss Dupont might not prove to be the right choice, but someone needed to help the poor lad.

"For this dancing lesson, we will be learning the quadrille and the waltz." Mrs. Lennox scanned the room, as proud as the peacock who gave up his feathers for her hat. "I see you've already found your partners."

Katie raised a brow as if in challenge, so I sent the same look back to her, bringing on her smile. And fool that I was, I wanted to keep seeing it again and again. The fact that I brought it out of her only made it better.

"Face your partners, everyone." Lennox went around placing people in position. "Yes. That's right. Now gentlemen bow and ladies curtsy."

I folded my arm across my waist and offered an exaggerated bow, while Katie dipped into a slight curtsy, her smile quivering as if she wanted to laugh. "What a heroic bow, Mr. MacKerrow!"

"Only the best for my dance partner, Miss Campbell."

Wake grinned at the other corner of the little box we'd made with the two couples. Maybe he saw something betwixt me and Katie. Maybe not. At the moment, I didn't care.

"Now, bow or curtsy to the person at your other corner," Lennox continued. "No, Miss Dupont, not Lady Lennox. You will bow to Lord Wake. Yes."

And that was only the beginning of our muddled attempt at the quadrille.

We began with a few moments of stumbling since the partners crossed other partners over and over again. At one point, Logan tripped over Wake's shoe, hitting Miss Dupont and sending her off-balance. Katie lurched forward to grab the smaller woman to keep her from crashing to the floor, which sent them both teetering. I was able to rescue them from actually hitting the floor, but I heard someone's clothing rip. I couldn't figure out where, and I really didn't want to know, but Katie's wide-eyed gaze shot to mine. She'd heard it too.

And I almost laughed. This entire production needed a solid laugh. Lennox took it much too seriously for anyone with half a brain. We were a mess.

As if for proof—and never one to allow the ridiculousness to pass her by—Ana "tripped" over the air and landed quite decorously in Wake's arms, adding a hand to her forehead in a swoon. Wake looked at Lennox for help.

The woman quickly clapped her hands together. "I believe we shall move on to the waltz, everyone. Perhaps it will prove less . . . injurious."

Now this one I'd been hoping for because, unlike the quadrille, where Katie left my arms in the dance, the waltz was meant for two. The same two. In fairly close proximity.

"I havenae danced the waltz in a long time, so I'm giving you fair warning." My palm slid to the waist of her yellow gown well before Lennox encouraged pairs to take their positions.

The slightest hitch in her breath at my touch sent a little uptick to my heartbeat. This woman was driving me mad, and I was willingly along for the ride.

She kept her eyes on mine as she slid her palm over my shoulder, causing my own breath to falter. There was no denying the draw between us. It glared as brightly as Ana Lennox's pink dress.

With a raised brow, Katie leaned close, filling my lungs with honeysuckle and sea. "It's a good thing I've danced the waltz regularly for the past few years then."

Ah, a bit of competition? She wanted to play this game, did she?

I tightened my hold, drawing her deeper into my embrace, and her smile slowly faded as she stared up at me, her increased breaths pulsing her chest. Her height brought her lips temptingly close, and the rest of her filled my arms in a perfect fit.

"I imagine I'll remember the steps quickly enough."

Watching her response to me nearly undid every logical thought in my head and sent me breaching the distance to claim those parted lips of hers. I'd never known anyone who needed rescuing more than her or offered so much with her personality, and I kept wanting to show up for it. For her.

I was mad.

And fascinated all at the same time.

"So should I let you lead, or do you need me to show you the ropes first?" Her rasped question added a little extra heat to our nearness. Heaven and earth! "Until . . . until you remember the steps?"

My arm slipped from the side of her waist fully around her back, nearly bringing her flush against me. "I'll remember."

Her breath stopped altogether. Perhaps mine did too, especially when her attention dropped to my lips. And then I nearly *did* lose all sense and give her a thorough smuirich in the middle of the ballroom.

"Mr. MacKerrow, that hold is much too close for a proper waltz." Lennox tapped on my arm, and I drew out of my trance, pulling my attention from Katie's lips to Lennox's pinched expression. "Only arms are touching. We are not in a taproom." She gestured toward Wake and Ana. "See there. Ana has always excelled at waltzing."

Because Wake knew how to lead.

I drew back from Katie into a "proper" hold, garnering Lennox's nod of approval as she walked back to the center of the group.

When I looked back down at my partner, my gaze fell on her crooked smile. "I have a feeling you were a wee bit of a troublemaker when you were young."

"Aye." She made it too easy to flirt. Too easy to enjoy the banter. "Perhaps more than a wee bit, especially when I had a goal in mind."

Her cheeks flushed, but she lifted her chin in defiance, taking my challenge like the lass I knew she was. "And what about you? Do you have a goal in mind?"

"Oh, aye!" I wiggled my brows and leaned closer. Her breath hitched all over again. "Leading you in the waltz."

She released a chuckle, regaining her composure much too quickly for my pride. "That remains to be seen, Mr. MacKerrow."

With her challenge spurring me forward, I took the first step. Now, I'm not too stubborn to admit that she graciously followed and even pressed a hand here and there to keep me in the right direction until I found my rhythm. We worked well as a team. I imagined we'd match in many other ways too.

And then, well, I started wondering just how long I could convince Katie Campbell to stay in Mull.

Katie

Some things in life you're prepared to witness and remain somewhat composed. Weddings. Scuba diving (lesson learned). Middle school musicals when your oldest niece dies as Juliet.

But watching Graeme MacKerrow compete in the cannonball throw competition discombobulated me entirely. I mean, I resorted to some teen version of myself, cheering and occasionally swooning from the sight. I think I may have drooled a little, but I wasn't ready to admit that yet.

The Mull Highland Games brought an ambience of festivity and cultural pride. From the processional led by chieftains in their traditional dress to the parade of dancers, bagpipers, and a few dozen brawny-looking men in T-shirts and kilts, the entire experience showcased the pride and love of the Scottish heritage I was beginning to understand a little more every day.

It reminded me so much of my own Appalachian heritage and the way my grandparents celebrated the rich history, lore, and people among the Blue Ridge.

The same confidence and grounding of the soul was interwoven through the people participating in the games, as well as through the spectators hovering on a nearby grassy field.

And I was *definitely* taking in the view.

Of one Scot in particular.

Unapologetically and, perhaps, a little slack-jawed.

After the waltz and a conversation in the hallway later about his sister, Graeme MacKerrow took up more and more space in my mind.

Dave and Brett kept sending me texts teasing me about the growing hashtag use of #katieshotscot. And then there were the hundreds of comments on my posts matching me with the Scot over anyone else in the comedy Clue movie of my life. And the Clue theme had worked in my latest post, introducing the "characters" in Craighill without using their names or real photos. Only fun descriptions to give readers and followers the chance to get involved in choosing their favorite "actors" in the Edwardian Experience and to draw positive attention to Craighill.

My consistent readers usually left tips and comments, but this response well exceeded anything I'd seen so far. In fact, I had a few rather bossy readers giving me their directives about "The Scot." In short: "*Marry him!*"

I couldn't even think long-term like that. I shouldn't even have been contemplating short-term. But I loved spending time with him.

I'd run my post ideas by Mrs. Lennox first, and she'd approved, with the caveat of no photos of people or real names, except my own, of course.

So now I had a massive online conversation happening about the "fictional" folks of Craighill, an adorable little ginger-headed boy, and a hot Scot. I mean, he *is* hot, so it makes sense to refer to him that way. In my head.

And as I watched him throw some galleon cannonballs from a historical shipwreck while wearing a blue T-shirt, kilt, and a broad smile, well . . . I may have started envisioning a lot of things about my future I hadn't thought about before. Especially when paired with his teasing, gentleness, and the feeling of his arm around me during the waltz.

Have mercy, what would a hug from him feel like? I sighed like the hopeless romantic I rarely acknowledged in myself.

I pushed down a swallow of my egg roll sandwich with a big swig of the "fizzy juice" I'd bought at the nearby food tent. Graeme MacKerrow was pure kryptonite for a girl who was running away from home. I should steer clear of him.

My attention landed on his shoulders and skimmed down to his kilt.

With a sudden rush of volcanic heat in my cheeks, I looked up to the sky and offered God a silent apology for ogling like the Scot-struck gal I was. *But really, Lord. You made him that way.*

And I'm really sure you said, "It was good."

"Katie!"

I turned to the sound of my name and caught sight of Lachlan and another boy running toward me, Wedge leashed at his side. Lachlan limped only a little, as proof of the quick healing of youth. A sweet warmth replaced the spiked heat from only a moment ago. How could this little boy wiggle his way so deeply into my heart already?

Kind of like his uncle.

And his grandma.

I was surrounded by people who were becoming important to me, when I usually left everyone behind. *Stop being ridiculous, Katie.* Attraction and friendship did not warrant changing one's entire life! I kept in contact with several friends I'd met along the way as I traveled. Family members too. None of them had given me reasons to consider altering everything I loved.

Yet the dimpled grin on Lachlan's face, the way I cared about what happened to him, sent me into pondering the what-ifs like never before.

I met him at the bottom of the hill, near several of the other tents. Some held food, some sold handcrafts, one offered to find your Scottish heritage, a few were empty, but all proclaimed the pride of this heritage.

"This is Jamie." Lachlan thumbed toward the boy as they neared. "I told him how good you are at getting lost."

The smile on my face stilled and then . . . nearly turned into a laugh. I coughed instead. "That's true."

"But you're good with bandages."

Jamie crossed his arms, examining me with a pair of brilliant green eyes. Next to that disheveled dark hair, he gave off his own kind of faerie vibes. Maybe one of J. M. Barrie's lost boys?

"And you don't like Irn-Bru."

Both boys stared at me, shaking their heads as if beyond disappointed.

"Maybe the taste will grow on me." I shrugged. I mean, what do you say? Probably not "It tastes like bubble gum." I got a good tongue-lashing from Maggie of the Stories and Stitches book club when I mentioned my thoughts to her on Irn-Bru.

"But I *do* like fishing."

That won a small grin from the boys, and without hesitation Lachlan grabbed my hand and pulled me forward. "Granny told me to bring you to see the sword dance."

I didn't fully comprehend his words because the sweetness of him taking my hand and guiding me somewhere lodged in a special place in my mind. A new significant memory to press back some of the less favorable ones.

"Sword dance?"

"Aye, you'll have to see it to know," Lachlan answered. "Uncle Calum's books are in the book tent too, but you cannae tell anyone he wrote them."

My brows rose. How did that work? And wasn't Calum Graeme's brother? And there was a younger one too, if I recalled. Peter? Who was away at college or something?

"It's a secret. He likes to be mysterious." Lachlan nodded as if repeating something he'd heard before. "But you must see the sword dance first."

"My sisters are 'bout to compete." This from Jamie, who trailed behind. "They've been taking Highland dance in a club after school for years." He lengthened the last word as if his sisters were about a thousand years old.

"Ah, Katie-girl." Mirren greeted me and ushered me forward near a set of tents where an upraised platform stood. "With your love of stories, I thought for certain you needed to see a bit of traditional Scottish dance."

She linked her arm through mine, as if I belonged right there with her, and drew me closer to the platform near another small group, one of which looked familiar. Lori, another of the knitters—the sweetest of them, besides Mirren—said, "Oh, Katie, good to see you, dear. Isn't this lovely?"

And again, I was embraced into this community as if I fit. As if . . . they wanted me here.

Me! With all my troublesome . . . ness.

"I'm telling her about the history of the sword dance, Lori." Mirren gestured with her chin toward the platform.

"Oh, aye." Lori nodded. "It has stories back to Macbeth even."

"Macbeth?" I laughed.

"And is a long held dance done before battles," Mirren continued. "Battle swords would be laid on the ground, and the warriors would dance around the sword, trying not to step on it as they danced. If the warrior's feet touched the sword, it was considered an ill omen for the upcoming battle."

I lifted my gaze to the platform where two young girls in colorful dresses and ballerina-like slippers took their positions. Sure enough, large swords were laid at their feet. I whipped out my phone to video a little.

"Uncle Graeme says it all started when Scot warriors took the swords of the opponents they'd defeated, placed their own sword at their opponent's sword in the sign of the cross, and danced around them in victory," Lachlan added. "See there."

Lachlan pointed, and Jamie added, "Mum can't watch them perform. She gets too nervous they're going to fall, and I've tried to remind her that they've danced it dozens of times without dying, but she doesnae listen."

Mirren and I exchanged smiles, stifling our laughter. Gah! I loved kids.

I spent over an hour of the four-hour-long festivities with Mirren, Lori, the boys, and Wedge, watching everything from Highland fling dancing to hammer throws and bagpipe competitions. I'd always expected the bagpipes to grate on my nerves, but instead, they grew on me, creating a background of sound ingrained in the life and culture of this world. Fresh air, laughter, accents, and bagpipes.

"And how are you liking your first Highland games, Miss Campbell?"

I turned from my first bite of a jammy cream doughnut to find Graeme approaching in full and glorious . . . Scottishness. Kilt, tight T-shirt, wind-tossed hair. I don't think I'd ever thought knees could be sexy, until now. Heaven help me.

Needless to say, as I bit down on my doughnut, the massive amount of cream inside squirted around the edge of my mouth in perfect middle school embarrassment fashion—basically giving me twin trails of cream down the sides of my chin.

I was an accident-prone, redheaded, cream-toothed walrus.

Excellent way to impress a guy.

It's a real wonder I'm still single.

I attempted to catch the dripping cream with my hand as Graeme rushed forward, pulling a handkerchief from the top of his kilt and . . . laughing? More like a rumbly sort of sound, like the percolation of a coffee machine, but it still almost made me smile.

Which would have been a very bad idea because . . . cream.

"First jammy cream?"

There was no way I was taking the bait and answering him with my mouth as full as it was. I narrowed my eyes, only to have his percolating chuckle take on more volume. "Did no one warn you about the size of these things?"

"I can nearly cram a whole one in my mouth if I try," Lachlan said, wrinkling his nose and looking from Graeme to me.

Graeme caught some of the cream dripping off my chin that my palm missed.

Stellar romantic moment, Katie. The stuff to relive for decades to come with sweltering embarrassment and the desperate desire for the ground to swallow me whole. The humored expression on his face had me snatching the handkerchief from his hand and taking care of the mess myself.

"She's just enjoying it as she ought!" came Mirren's encouraging response as she placed a hand on my back. "Jammy creams, cream buns, and the like aren't meant to be eaten without a mess. It makes them taste better."

I smeared some cream across my face with the handkerchief to prove her point. It was tasty, but the mess I made didn't improve its flavor. It only increased my humiliation.

"A little warning would have been nice," I murmured after a swallow or two. "But it's delicious."

"Aye." His gaze dropped to my lips before dragging back to my eyes. "It is."

My face flamed for a whole new reason, and I forgot about my walrus appearance, the smeared handkerchief, and maybe even my name. I needed distance from this man just to protect my IQ.

With powers Superman should envy, I pulled my gaze away from his and turned back to Mirren, who stood sporting her own massive smile. Maybe she was trying to hide her laugh too. "But"—I waved toward the field with his handkerchief—"in answer to your question, this has been amazing. The dancing, the heavies, the piping." I raised my half-eaten jammy. "The scran."

He rewarded me with a wide grin I felt all the way down to my wellies. "You're speakin' like a Scot now, lass."

Lass. That word from his lips and paired with such a look. Heaven above!

I glanced down with a loose hold on my composure and finished wiping my face. "Mirren has helped. Lachlan and Jamie too. Maybe they didn't warn me about the jammy, but they've given me lots of other information, from the types of dances to the songs the pipers played." I nodded over to Mirren, and the tender look in her eyes gave me pause for only a second.

She cared about me. And she'd sent Lachlan to seek me out so I could spend time with them. *Me.*

As weird and disastrous as I am. As tall and troublesome.

Without expecting me to be anyone else.

And Graeme had looked at my mouth as if—my face reheated enough to sizzle any residual cream—he were hungry. And it certainly wasn't because I gave off seductive vibes. Could he really be attracted to *me*?

"Aren't you meant to be off somewhere about now, Graeme MacKerrow?" Mirren's question sliced into the stare linking my boiling body temperature to Graeme's eyes.

He hesitated before pulling his attention from mine.

"What?" He blinked as if the contact impacted him as much as me. And then he gave his head a shake and looked down at his watch. "Aye." The word shot from him, and he took a few steps backward, his gaze finding mine again. He even added a knee-weakening grin, as if to hold me over. "Come see how well I am at taking advice?"

"You'd better see it now because it may never happen again," Mirren shot back, receiving a frown from over her son's shoulder as he disappeared into the crowd at almost a run.

"What in the world is going on?"

"It's a surprise." Mirren linked her arm through mine and pulled me between the tents. "And you'll want to have your camera ready because it'll be worth givin' folks a glimpse of your talented Scot, now won't it?"

"*My* talented Scot?" But my protest disappeared into the noise of the passing crowd as Lachlan took my other hand and pulled me forward.

We stopped in front of a tent with a hand-painted sign that read: "Wildlife Sculpture Demonstration." And beneath those words: "Watergaw Sculptures Demonstration."

Watergaw? Was that some sort of family name?

"What sort of wood do you use?" The question came from an older man who stood among the group of observers facing the single occupant of the tent.

Graeme?

My bottom lip dropped. He sat behind a table beneath the tent with a finished sculpture of a barn owl on one side of him and directly in front of him an unfinished . . . puffin? Wait. Had he planned to show his work here? It didn't sound like it from our conversation at his house. Had he taken my words to heart?

Mirren pulled me among the throng, closer to the front.

"In answer to your question, Mr. Cane"—Graeme patted the puffin—"I typically use tupelo wood since it's a soft timber that still holds its strength." He wiped his palms down the sides of his kilt. Was he nervous? I stepped closer, hoping to catch his eye. Reassure him. "But if I'm not painting the work, I tend toward oak or chestnut. The wood is good for carving and has some beautiful colors and grains."

"You been doin' this for years, have ye?" An older man waved toward the tent. "And we didnae know?"

"I began taking it seriously about five years ago, but . . . well, I . . . I've only been selling for about three years." He cleared his throat, his smile tight.

"What a wonder!" came an older woman's response. "Your grandpa would be fair proud of you, lad."

Graeme's gaze shot up to the woman. "Thank you, Mrs. MacRay. I hope so."

"His *grandpa*?" Another man called out. "The lad's done us *all* proud with such work. The owl looks so lifelike I'm tempted to go hide my chicks."

The crowd laughed and Graeme's expression grew a little more relaxed.

"There's no greater compliment to Graeme than that," Mirren whispered. "But Mr. Cane is right. My father couldnae have come close to the skill Graeme's shown."

Silence settled over the group crowded around the tent, and Graeme shifted a little, obvious discomfort growing with each extra second. I knew this feeling. It happened the first few times I interviewed people. The awkward shift from what I knew in my head to actually engaging with the person. All I needed at the time was a little boost to get started. A question here. A comment there. A smile from someone in the crowd.

I stepped forward, gaining his attention, holding his gaze.

"So, how do you get started? Do you have a picture in your mind already, or do you create as you go?"

His shoulders dropped a little with his growing grin. Relaxing, I hoped. "I . . . I usually have a type of creature I want to know more about and start by researching photos of my subject and take a few of my own, if I can." Graeme reached for a paper on the table. "And then I'll sketch out my design."

The paper showed a beautiful pencil sketch of a puffin standing on a rock, reflecting what the unfinished wood already revealed in rough form. Amazing.

And he drew as well?

"I rough out the design first, usually using my chisel, and then refine the piece with more detailed tools." He took a seat in front of the puffin, a small tool set scattered atop the table.

"You sell them, do ye?" a lady asked.

"Aye," he answered, taking up a small knife-like tool.

"Do you just sculpt birds?" another man queried.

His gaze found mine again, eyes lit, before turning to answer the man. "A few other things, like sheep, foxes, rabbits, but birds mostly."

"Have you done a gull?" someone asked.

"Aye. Several."

"What about doves and starlings? Those are near my house," a young lady asked.

"I've carved a few," he answered. "And some mistle thrush, sparrows, even a golden eagle." He raised the knife to the wing of the puffin. "And for my demonstration, I'm going to show you how I create the finer parts of a wing using my burn pen. It's very effective."

A murmur went through the crowd as he lifted the strange knife for everyone to see, then began detailing the wing.

"Look at him. He's getting comfortable now," Mirren said. "And see how proud he is. All he needed was a little nudge in the right direction, Katie-girl."

I still couldn't believe I'd been that nudge. That he'd valued my words enough for them to . . . matter. My throat closed up, my heart shook. Something inside me gave way to a feeling I tried to ignore, teasing a hope I didn't fully trust, so I decided to go for what I knew.

Distraction.

"What does watergaw mean?" I whispered down to Mirren, and the way her eyes softened at the edges hinted at her answer.

"'Twas one of my daughter, Greer's, favorite old Scottish words. She was always finding old words to revive in our vocabulary because she loved the language so much. No wonder she loved unique words. She and Graeme had their own twin language for so many years, and none could understand except the two of them." Mirren sighed with a smile and then gestured toward the sign. "Watergaw means a part of a rainbow. Only part. A broken piece one might see through clouds.

Greer garnered hope from it as a way to search for beauty, even within brokenness."

A piece of rainbow. Shattered light but still beautiful.

"Life is filled with broken pieces, and we're bound to have more hurt and brokenness along the way, but she always searched for the small pieces of beauty and held on to them."

I was choked up and couldn't respond with anything but a nod, so I looked back at Graeme. His hands carefully and gently moved over the wood. My eyes burned. *Watergaw.* He was making something exquisite out of a broken piece of wood.

I was broken. Down deep. In places I couldn't touch. But was it possible someone like Graeme or his family found me . . . beautiful? Enough to care about me in all my fractured past and chaotic present?

How many times had I missed finding out the answer to that question because I ran away? Because I never stayed long enough for relationships to take hold?

And what would I do now with this knowledge? What if this attraction and interest proved truer than I could imagine and knocked all my fears to the curb? What if I'd convinced myself that I didn't need what my heart truly wanted or needed most?

Would I run away like I always did?

Before I messed things up worse. Before I didn't meet expectations.

Before all the charm and delight of the newness of a place and relationship dulled with familiarity and reality.

Because the very real fear lay between wanting to believe in the beauty but seeing only the brokenness. Maybe *that* beauty was worth being brave for.

And if Graeme MacKerrow and this little world on Mull proved to be all the wonderful things I feared it might be, would I be brave enough to trust them with my brokenness . . . and choose to stay?

CHAPTER 15

Katie

My phone was exploding.

And I was stuck inside an Edwardian-era swimsuit with no hope of escape.

It had been interesting enough to put on the worsted wool serge suit (say that three times fast) when dry, but now that the outfit pressed damp against my body, un-sausaging myself while my phone kept buzzing about a certain emergency left me tangled with my arms stuck over my head, my belly in view, and my lower cello still covered with "ruffled bloomers."

No way was I calling for help.

There were some images *no one* needed to get stuck in their minds.

Me as a headless Edwardian belly dancer was one of them.

At least the beach outing had been relatively trouble-free, except for the instance when Miss Lennox fell out of the bathing machine (read changing room on wheels) into the cool loch water, garnering plenty of attention and a rescue by Logan.

She seemed a little disgruntled that Mr. Logan hadn't attempted CPR on her.

From the way she was clutching his shirt while "unconscious," he may have thought she hoped to give *him* CPR. I feel certain all sorts of Edwardian etiquette was broken when Miss Lennox's strength proved greater than Mr. Logan's resistance and mouth-to-mouth took on a little less life-saving quality and a little more scandal.

My phone buzzed again, and I suddenly envisioned poor Emily finding my tangled dead body already mummified inside the vintage swimsuit.

Lord, help me.

With another tug and a pulled muscle, the cloth freed me and I sighed down on my bed. *Worsted* wool serge, indeed!

While sliding into some blessed dry, though still Edwardian, clothes, I reached for my phone. Ten messages popped up on the screen. Most from my mom.

My stomach tensed.

Oh no! Who was hurt? Dad? Brett?

Mom: Katherine, I cannot believe you'd attack another person! I was sure you'd grown out of your volatile teenage phase.

What?

Mom: I just can't believe it. For all the world to see! I knew all along traveling all the time couldn't be good for you and your mental health.

Where was this coming from? I never hurt anyone—at least on purpose.

Mom: All the ladies at the club are appalled. I'm horrified. How am I going to explain this one?
Brett: Hey, sis. Looks like you've got an online enemy among your ranks.
Dave: Are you okay? This isn't your usual way to get viewers!
Brett: Here's the link.

I clicked on the link just as another text came through from Mom.

Mom: Is there a way you can get those photos and the article removed? It doesn't look good, Katherine. Everyone loses their temper sometimes, but as I've told you on several occasions, living in the spotlight places you in a vulnerable situation. You have to be aware of how you present yourself even more. I'm sure you'll clear this up.

Article?

I closed out the texts and opened the link. A photo filled up my screen of the waltzing lesson from the day before when I was reaching down to help keep Miss Dupont from falling, but someone had taken the shot and put a very different spin on it. The headline of the post read: "Miss Adventure Turns Nasty."

I skimmed over the article. *Someone* had spun the lie that I'd gotten jealous of the other guests and started a fight. Another photo from the tennis lesson, with Graeme holding his eyes right after I'd hit him with the tennis ball, read: "The true colors of Miss Adventure shine during competition. She may smile on the screen, but she's seething beneath the surface, waiting for the opportunity to strike."

Other photos from different moments over the last few days had been twisted to suggest sabotage of other people's clothing, tripping Mr. Logan (with a photo of him at the dining table after the big spill), and stealing food.

Stealing food? I mean, that's the only believable one, but still!

Only one person would do such a thing. Someone inside Craighill. Someone with online connections, plus a bone to pick with me.

I growled and nearly threw my phone. Mark!

I immediately sent off two quick messages to Dave and Brett to provide some clarity, but I paused before responding to Mom.

Appearances were everything to her. Presenting as fine and perfect was everything. She didn't ask if the information was true. She didn't ask for clarification. She just wanted me to fix it, because it all boiled down to how it made her look in front of her country club friends and the ladies at church.

I pinched my eyes closed against the pain of another conversation about "appearances." My life-in-accidents stood in stark contrast to her pristine world—another reason I never lived up to my sister's perfect reputation. I was too painfully authentic, whether I meant to be or not. The longer I stayed away from home, the more I saw how toxic her mindset was. How debilitating to relationships, especially for those closest to her.

I should have been used to it after years of never measuring up to Sarah's ghost, but it still stung. It was so easy to make a memory into a saint. As the only other girl in the family, the comparisons fell on me.

Fury wound its way through my chest, but the hurt ached even deeper. Hurt that she'd jumped to the wrong conclusions. That she automatically believed the lie.

I placed the phone down and took a deep breath. I couldn't change her.

The phrase pinged in my mind. *I* couldn't *change her.*

God knew I'd tried. Brett too. Even Dad, when I was younger.

But her mind was too mixed up in how she and her family were perceived. And then, after Sarah died, we all walked around on eggshells, waiting for Mom's outbursts, trying to dodge them, hoping her sudden reactions didn't land on us. And then we all started avoiding her. Dad stayed at the office. Chase and Brett joined sports and then went off to college. I ran away. First to my grandparents and then . . . around the world.

It would have been simple to blame her reactions on the death of her child, but the unpredictability was there before Sarah died. Death just made things much worse. A few of us suggested she seek professional help, but she said the problem wasn't her. It was everyone else.

The weight of it pressed on me.

My gaze flew to the cloudy sky out my window, searching, pleading. What was I supposed to do?

And then, the mantra I'd repeated to myself for years hinged into place with a different click.

I *couldn't* change her.

And then, *I* couldn't change her.

My breath burst from me like a hit to the stomach.

It wasn't *my* responsibility. A knot in my chest began to unravel.

It wasn't my *fault.*

And it wasn't something I had the *power* to control.

I pulled up her text and steadied my mind. *Keep the response simple, and say more when you've had time to think.*

Me: The information is false. I'm working on fixing it, but keep in mind that people can say whatever they want online and I have no control over it. Traveling is not the problem—a jealous writer is. I'll send more later.

I reread the post and made some mental notes before grabbing my Edwardian boots and hat and dashing from the room, braiding my damp hair as I went.

I refused to count how many times I almost fell on the way downstairs toward the back garden. Thankfully, I found Mark on his way to the back lawn for our archery lessons and pulled him into the library.

"Why are you such a jerk?" I pressed the corner of my phone into Mark's chest so effectively, he stumbled a step back.

"Jerk?" The guilty look on his face negated his defensive raised-palm posture. "That's not a very nice way to say good afternoon."

"Good afternoon, my eye!" I turned my phone around so he could see the screen where the article glared its full and horrible headline. "You know as well as I that I was trying to keep Miss Dupont from falling, not knock her down because I was"—I looked down at the text and quoted—"'jealous of the attention being bestowed upon the other media guests in the house.'"

He skimmed over the screen as if he'd never seen the words before. "That's not a good look for you, Katie. It could really hurt your ratings."

After controlling the urge to slap him, I almost corrected him to say that any news increases visibility, but since he didn't take the time to learn the ins and outs of social media, why try educating him now? "Ohhh!" The word emerged like a fighting roar. Would Mr. Lennox loan Monty the Python to me for just a few minutes? Just a few. "I cannot believe you'd stoop this low. This is like something a third grader would do to cheat in a schoolyard game. Not a grown man."

His jaw tensed, but he shrugged his shoulders. "I don't know why you're blaming me. Anyone from the house could have posted that."

I rolled my eyes so hard it hurt my head. "Mark, everyone else is *in* the photo. And you were standing at the perfect angle to take it." I scrolled down and showed him the photo from the lawn tennis match—a photo of Graeme holding his eye after I'd accidentally hit him with the ball. "And you *know* this was an accident. Everyone knows this was an accident. You are aware these links can be traced, right?"

His face paled. Got him!

"You accused me of some pretty rotten things, Mark." I shoved my phone in my pocket. "And the only reason you could have done so was for the Vision Award. You slandered me because of an award!"

He folded his arms across his chest and looked away like the stubborn child he was.

He had no defense. I shook my head and stepped back. "News flash—you didn't just slander me, but there are several instances where you imply that Mrs. Lennox is not managing her business as she should and that the Edwardian Experience isn't fair or safe."

The arrogance on his face melted.

"How stupid was that, right?" I backed away from him. "Here you are, up for a prestigious award for your content, and you let a bout of jealousy strip you of one of the things that put you in the finalist category to begin with—your professional integrity."

With another glare, I marched around him—as best I could in my "sports skirt" and heels—and entered the back lawn. I'd had bad things written about me before, so this wasn't a first, but those negatives always seemed to weigh heavier than the hundreds of positives out there.

And it just stung a little more from someone I actually knew.

Even if that *someone* was Mark.

Dave's text oozed with his usual balanced approach, offering some suggestions to help curb the spread through a clarification post and video. Which I would do after archery. Brett's text only wanted to make me aware of it . . . and praise the fact it was creating such visibility. The man really was the most optimistic optimist in the whole world.

Mom hadn't responded.

No surprise. She said her piece, dropped her bomb, and waited for her offspring to respond with dutiful obedience to *her* demands.

Lord Wake and Lady Lennox were already in position with bows when I arrived in the garden, with Mr. Logan and Miss Dupont having some sort of side discussion over one of the arrows, it seemed. Graeme hadn't joined everyone for the beach trip, but evidently he'd been asked to assist with archery.

Um . . . and then I immediately wondered what he'd look like in swimming attire, Edwardian or not. Heat shimmied up my neck like the teenager my hormones wanted to be, and my attention focused on his well-suited self. It was enough to almost distract me from my frustration.

Almost.

But not enough to stop my forward momentum toward a physical release of my ire. I slipped on my glove and bracer I'd packed for the trip, then snatched a bow from the nearby collection, took up a few arrows, and stepped to the designated shooting spot. A round straw target was positioned about, what, forty yards out?

I breathed in the familiar feel of the bow in my hand, clasping my palm around the grip. My body instantly relaxed. A long bow. My favorite.

Perhaps I couldn't dribble a basketball and walk at the same time, but I knew how to do this. And right now the frustration buzzing through my veins needed an outlet.

Mrs. Lennox had even chosen wooden arrows? Some of my ire dissipated. Grandpa would be impressed. I tilted the bow slightly and slid the arrow on the shelf, smiling as I raised the bow. Thankfully, this certain dress had more give in the sleeves, so I could take a proper position and have full range of motion as I pulled back the string. My fingers slid over my cheek, anchoring my placement, and as I followed the arrow point to the target, I drew in a breath.

I released my frustration in one breath as I relaxed my hold on the string. The arrow swished off with barely a sound and pierced near the center of the target. Without a pause, I took up another arrow and repeated the movements, releasing more anger and securing another bull's-eye.

"Well, Miss Campbell, this isn't your first archery lesson." Lord Wake smiled, moving to stand between me and Ana and gesturing toward the target. "Or is it beginner's luck?"

With a grin, I swept down to take another arrow and replicated my movements, landing the next arrow between the first two. "It's my *one* sport." I lowered the bow and turned to Lord Wake. "I'm pretty lame at the rest."

"But how do you get it to go so straight?" Ana whined her question, waving the bow as she spoke. "Mine keep flying off in all directions!"

She fired off an arrow that soared high and far to the right of the target, and no wonder. Her body faced forward instead of sideways, she overdrew the string, and she used a low anchor.

With a few pointers, and after about three tries, her arrow finally struck the far side of the target. "Did you see that?" She spun around, eyes bright, and nearly decapitated me with her bow. "I *did it*."

And then a realization clinked into place in my mind. Was Ana Lennox trying painfully hard just to do something right? Sure, she was immature and silly. Sometimes a bit desperate and dramatic. But were all those things how she grasped for self-worth and approval?

And Lord Wake looked down at her with a little pride on his face—not like an adoring lover, but more like a happy uncle. Had he taken on the responsibility of Ana's companion so she wouldn't make even more desperate decisions, since her mother was hyper-focused on the Edwardian Experience and her father so relaxed he was almost horizontal?

"You did!" I nodded. "And I bet you could do it again too."

"Would you take a video of me, Katie?" Ana's eyes brightened with her smile. "So I can show my dad?"

My heart softened completely. "Of course I will."

And she hit the mark again and again, her success continuing to deflate my annoyance.

It wasn't that I hadn't dealt with bad publicity before. Having a presence on social media or anywhere online pretty much guaranteed that unless you were Julie Andrews or Jennifer Garner, you weren't going to make everyone happy.

But the betrayal of a colleague just ruffled my fury feathers in all the wrong ways. And it took another ten to twelve shots with the bow—and a few prayers that only God needed to hear—before I finally felt calm enough to stop.

I shot a few more arrows, lowering my blood pressure to a less volatile level, and then moved to sit in a nearby chair. Miss Dupont took my place at the shooting spot with Mr. Logan joining, her much more attentive than usual as he helped guide her in the archery lesson. My gaze shot to Mrs. Lennox, who failed to correct the inappropriateness of their nearness and whispered conversations.

Mark didn't show up to the lesson.

Coward.

It would have done my heart good to best him at archery.

A shadow fell over me, and I looked up to find my favorite Scot staring down at me. He studied my face and then took the seat next to mine.

"Are you sure it's okay for the butler to sit during working hours?"

His lips crooked and he relaxed in the chair as if in answer . . . or as proof he didn't care what the answer was. My whole body warmed at his closeness and that grin. "You looked fairly scunnered when you came out of the house."

Scunnered? Must mean annoyed. Or furious. "A wee bit." I imitated his accent poorly, but it inspired a playfully jutted eyebrow, so I took it as a win. "Mark is jealous and trying to hurt my online reputation by sharing false information."

I knew it would blow over. It still stung though.

Without hesitation, the butler pulled his phone from his jacket pocket. Within ten seconds, a low growl rose from his throat.

A sound I felt in my chest . . . and shoulders. All the way to my less attractive kneecaps. Heavens.

"Where is he?" Graeme sat up, ready for the attack.

I stopped him with a hand to his nearest tree-trunk size arm. Number one, how was it possible to feel his muscles beneath a butler's jacket? Number two, Graeme could squish poor Mark to jelly with one foot. Maybe one look. "Don't waste your time on the Great Disappointment. Once Lennox finds out, he'll likely be kicked off the island anyway, unless he can do some major groveling."

Though the idea of someone coming to the defense of my reputation left a soft and wonderful mark right in the center of my chest. In fact, I almost got a little teary-eyed.

Why?

Because my emotions were all over the place. That had to be it.

"It's not the first or last time I'll have to do damage control for online slander." I shrugged. "The way of the cyberworld, I'm afraid."

He relaxed. "Does it bother you?"

"Sometimes." I leaned back in the chair. "I think it might bother my mom more though. Image is a big deal to her." I blinked. Had I just said that out loud? I rarely talked about my mom to people, especially anything that could be perceived as dirty laundry. "But it will pass. I know my boss would love for me to make some posts or write an article to counteract or distract from it, if possible, so I'll think of something. I've had a lot of questions about how these gowns hold up on long walks, so I may try that."

He nodded, squinting as he looked ahead at the archers. "I read a few of your posts online. You're a braw writer."

Ah, *braw* I knew, and my happiness meter kicked up to thrilled. "Not too sappy for you?"

"Well, you're not a Sassenach."

And then all happiness dropped. I had completely forgotten about *those* posts!

The "Hot Scot" posts.

The comments debating my future love life with said Scot. I turned my face away from him to grimace my displeasure before returning with a smile. "My editor chose the titles."

He kept his face forward but said nothing.

"I . . . I never mentioned your name, and I haven't even put any of the photos up from the Highland games yet."

He ran a hand over his mouth and nodded. "But you did mention I was hot."

My jaw slacked. And my face took a fevered trip to sunburn hot. I sure had. More than once. I held in a little whimper. The semi-confident flirt had been vanquished by Miss Humiliation. "I was recovering from a near-death experience."

He coughed. "Of course."

I shrugged to try and play cool. "I described things for the readers so they could use their own imaginations. You know—poetic license and all. And the weather's been rather warm the last few days."

He seemed to have a wrestling match with his grin for a minute and then nodded again, keeping his gaze forward. "I also read some of the comments."

The desire to cringe began a whole new war with my shoulders. The comments! My followers had always been active before, but add a life-saving, dancing, woodworking, single Scot into the mix, and they'd become ravenous. However, Graeme really had an amazing fan club right now, plus his own hashtag: #Katieshotscot.

Did God read hashtags? Because I could count that one as a prayer.

"And read about your fear of sheep."

Not the response I was expecting. I stared over at his profile. Great nose, BTW. "Sheep and I have a long and somewhat troubling history. I would share it with you, but I'm not sure you'd recover."

His lips twitched. "Since your followers know about your sheepish past, it might be just the right time to distract them from the bad press by overcoming your fear."

Sheepish? (I ignored his clear desire to distract folks from my love life.) Had this wonderfully burly man just tried a pun? Seriously? Mr. Tree-Trunks-for-Arms tried a pun? "And you have just the right place for me to overcome my fears?"

"It's not a *baaad* idea."

I tried to catch my laugh from escaping, but it just sounded like a tuba failure. "What's your idea? I've *heard* facing your fears is a good thing."

He turned in the chair, gaze locking with mine. "You have an early supper this eve, and then I'll show ye. Interested?"

In more ways than one. "Okay."

His smile spread wide. "The servants' entrance by the kitchen. Meet me there after supper." His gaze trailed down to my impractical shoes, leaving a little fire trail in its wake. "And wear sensible clothes too."

Graeme

Dancing with Katie Campbell fed my dreams.

Bantering with her from across the table in my kitchen fed my heart.

Having her "rescue" my awkwardness in demonstrating at the Highland games deepened my interest in her all the more.

But watching her shoot a bow like a warrior maiden—and then teach ridiculous Ana the basics—had my thoughts lodged somewhere between kiss-the-woman-senseless and hold-her-in-my-arms. She came with the wildest combination of ridiculous humor, kindness, intelligence, and beauty. A wonderful combination.

And she didn't even know it.

After having read a few dozen of her articles and watched a few of her reels, something became clear—Katie didn't take herself seriously enough to believe she was attractive or desired.

And she was both. *More* than both. The longer I observed her and the more conversations we had, the more my brain started entertaining her future with mine in every scenario. Her heart kept proving more and more worth the winning. She fit in a way Allison never had.

Into conversations.

With Lachlan.

In Glenkirk.

And it didn't make sense at all because her life contrasted in every way with mine.

But as she rode alongside me in my car toward our surprise destination, the conversation only made me like her more—though she tended to turn the topics away from her family. She mentioned her editor, Dave. And a brother named Brett. Even showed me a photo of the farmhouse she'd inherited from her grandparents, called Lark Hollow Farms. But any probing questions about other family members or her past she met with a deflection back toward me or by sharing a story from her travels.

What was she hiding?

"So where are you taking me to help me overcome my fear of sheep?"

I nodded ahead to a sign along the road. McClean Farms.

She followed my direction and then turned back to me. "A farm?"

"A sheep farm."

Her eyes rounded. "A sheep farm."

"Aye." And my grin tugged wide.

"You're taking me to an entire farm of sheep?" The pitch in her voice rose.

"Aye." I nodded. "To show you they're not to be feared."

Her bottom lip dropped, and she slapped my arm. "I trusted you, and here you go taking me into the very heart of sheepland."

"It's not like we're going to Mount Doom or anything, Katie. They're just sheep."

"That's what I'm worried about." She pinched her fingers together in her lap so tightly her knuckles turned white. So I reached over and placed my hand over hers.

Her gaze shot to mine.

"I'll be with ye."

She blinked a few times, those captivating eyes of hers glistening for the briefest moment. "Okay." Her voice was barely a whisper.

I slid a thumb over the back of her hand, her skin soft, cool.

She froze a moment and then cleared her throat but didn't pull away. "However, I hold you eternally responsible for any *baaad* thing that happens."

And whatever hesitation that had been keeping hold of my heart pinged its release. Puns weren't my humor of choice, but when her eyes lit up from me using them, they suddenly took on new appeal. "*Ewe*"—I lengthened the word and raised a brow, watching comprehension dawn on her face with her smile—"can count on me."

Then she looked down at our hands and, ever so slowly, turned her palm over so that our fingers entwined. Nothing prepared me for the sense of rightness in her hold, the strange sort of certainty. And I wished we weren't so close to the McClean house. That we had another half hour to ride and talk with her hand in mine. That there weren't questions between us about futures and homes and where the two would meet.

But Maggie McClean already had the front door open before the car even came to a stop.

"Wait." Katie looked over at me. "This is Maggie, the Knitting Nazi's farm?"

My laugh burst out, and I gave her hand a squeeze. "Knitting Nazi?"

"Have you seen her knit?" Katie's eyes widened again. "Oh, I understand now. She must be taking out her sheep frustration through knitting. It makes perfect sense. If I worked with sheep all day, I'd find a way to release my frustration too."

I chuckled, reluctantly let go of her hand, and exited the car, meeting Katie on the other side.

"Well, let's see what you're made of, lass" came Maggie's first words as she approached, pulling her sweater around her shoulders and giving Katie a look from head to toe. "And if they don't kill you the first time, it's a good sign."

At first I feared Maggie had destroyed any chance of Katie stepping forward. The older woman wasn't known for her bedside manner. But Katie must have caught the glint in Maggie McClean's eyes, because she plucked up and placed her hands on her hips.

"Maggie, I'm sure that if I have you as a guide, I'm going to be just fine."

The woman's smile crinkled her entire face and she looked over at me. "You've got a smart one here, Graeme. Flattery will get you everywhere." Her expression sobered. "Except with sheep. They take a calm approach, and the fewer words the better."

Katie

"I think Maggie's taken a bit of a fancy to you."

I chuckled and looked over at Graeme as we drove back toward Craighill, his teasing more recognizable now that I knew him a bit better. Plus, his lips crooked ever so slightly on one side, confirming his humor.

Not that I focused on his lips a lot. Sometimes I got distracted by his shoulders or eyes, and now the new sense of holding his hand.

But little clues certainly helped a girl out. Especially a girl who was trying to figure out if this whole "Falling for a Scot" thing was real, or just a fragment of my online persona.

"Do you mean from the way she failed to warn me that one of the sheep had a tendency to ram strangers with his head?" I narrowed my eyes at him. "Or was it the way she placed a little feed on the back of my sweater so one of the sheep kept trying to eat my clothes?"

His grin spread wide. "Maggie McClean is known for her teasing nature, and the fact she did so with you only proved how much she likes you."

"She tortures those she loves, is that it?"

"Aye." He nodded. "In the best way. Very Scottish."

I pressed my body back into the car seat, the happy hum of a satisfying day calming my racing heart. Despite the antics of Maggie and her sheep, I had to admit, I'd tiptoed toward overcoming my sheep terror.

"Well, I don't plan to flock toward buying a sheep farm in the future, but I have to admit, it wasn't *so* bad." I sighed. "And Maggie makes some of the best . . . what was it called?"

"Tipsy laird," he offered.

"Oh my goodness, yes." I placed a palm over my happy stomach. "I've had trifle before, but that one? I love raspberries. Thank you, Maggie!" I sighed. "And I loved the tea. Did you say it was heather tea?"

"Moorland tea can be made from heather, aye."

This place oozed with discoveries. Around every corner. From the food to the landscape to the history, culture, and people. It's as if I could never learn enough. The videos Graeme took of me and the sheep were bound to be a great distraction from Mark's post, but they'd also answer a challenge from some of the readers to face my fears.

The readers always loved when I took their requests or considerations into account while traveling. And their votes for the Scot in my life certainly matched my own.

But the scariest part was, I didn't want the match to be a fling or something temporary. Graeme and Lachlan and Mirren—even moody Maggie—were starting to take up space in my heart in a way that hurt when I thought about leaving.

And I knew women gave up their dreams all the time for love. The movies and fiction spoke of it in spades, but I loved traveling too. Finding stories brought me such joy. But in my limited experience, men didn't want a woman who traveled around the world.

Ah! What was I even thinking? Graeme hadn't asked me to stay. He'd held my hand. That was it. Hand-holding didn't equate to a lifelong commitment.

Deep breaths, Katie. You're overthinking like a pro.

"You never got to finish telling me about heather's legend."

Graeme had stayed beside me when meeting the sheep and almost kept guard while Maggie introduced me to the beasts in her own special way. He was a good man. Sure, a little grumpy around the edges, but good.

He caught me staring, and I looked back toward the view. A misty rain fell, the weather that seemed the most predominant to this place. "I refused to look up the story because I figured your version would be much more authentic than a Google search."

I almost felt him smile.

"Legend has it—"

"Do you realize how incredibly tantalizing those words are?" I sighed back into the seat and closed my eyes so nothing would distract me from the sound of his voice.

"—there was once a lass named Malvina who loved a warrior named Oscar, but before they could be wed, Oscar was killed in battle."

I sat up and looked at him. "There are a lot of really sad Scottish stories, Graeme."

"We try to keep things real. Life is filled with both bitter and sweet."

I relaxed back, sending him a frown. "I'm waiting for the sweet part then." I closed my eyes again.

"A messenger from the battle delivered the bitter news to Malvina, along with some heather flowers as a token of Oscar's love. It is said that Malvina wished that whoever received heather flowers would know happiness and luck for their days since she'd known the happiness and love of a good man, despite having lost him."

Bittersweet for certain. "So heather means love and luck?"

"Different types of heather have different meanings, I suppose."

The car wound up the drive to Craighill's back entrance. "White is usually in reference to purity and happiness. It's also thought to protect, which is why Scottish warriors often wore it into battle." He sent me a wink. "It's also believed that white heather grows over the resting place of faeries."

"Ooh, now that sounds like a great post idea."

He brought the car to a stop by the side entrance of the house. "There's some up along Tearlach Path, if you fancy a look."

"The place not too far from your house where you can see the Gribun cliffs?" I turned toward him. Light from the house was playing with evening shadows across his features. "That path?"

"Aye, but be careful when you visit faerie places. You never know what may happen." His eyes twinkled as he exited the car and made it around to my side before I even gathered up my camera bag, an umbrella in hand.

"I suppose the other colors of heather have meanings too?"

He frowned as he looked down at me. "But you dinnae expect me to know them, do you?"

"Of course I do." I rolled my eyes and stood. "You seem to know everything else."

He released a loud sigh as if I were the most "bathersome" creature and then slid his arm around my waist to pull me nearer beneath the umbrella. I sucked in a deep breath of his leathery-sea scent and his touch, and decided to take the slowest walk in earth's history toward the door of the house.

Tarry, just like Grandpa taught me.

"The heather on the far side of the loch that I can see from my window, it's purple."

"Ah, the most popular color." He didn't seem in a hurry either. "Purple can mean admiration or beauty. Usually offered to let the person know how much you value them in your life."

"Oh." A soft touch of rain hit the top of the umbrella, and Graeme tugged me a teensy bit closer. I "cooried" in like the enthusiastic co-orieer I realized I was. "And pink?"

"Pink?" Had we gotten even slower? "It means love."

Love. My breath hitched on the word and my heart took the hint by racing into a faster rhythm. Was it even possible to love someone you'd just met? To feel a kinship more real than with some of the people you'd known your whole life?

I stopped and looked up at him, the house entrance too close. Too clearly an ending to the evening. "You are all sorts of surprising, aren't you?"

"Surprising?" The question brewed off his tongue in that wonderfully Scottish way that I somehow felt in my chest.

I cleared my throat in an attempt to get my emotions under control. "Well, it's just that you started off all grumbly and 'Have you got two left feet, woman?'"—this said in my best Scottish impersonation.

"That was horrible."

"My point was made, however." I shot him a grin. "You're not all grumbly and irritating. You're actually really kind and funny . . ."

"Incredibly handsome."

I laughed, and he sent a look of mock offense.

"Okay, yes. In a rugged, rescue-the-damsel sort of way."

One brow shot high at that last part.

"Well, you have. Several times." I chuckled. "At least you won't get bored hanging out with me, is all I'm saying."

He chuckled, low and deep and oh-so deliciously. "You rescued me at the Highland games."

I turned toward him, my breath shaking a little at the nearness of his face to mine. "Maybe everyone needs a hero in their life now and then, right? Even fumbling ones."

"Katie."

His voice cradled my name. My breath shivered out as I stared up into his face, searching those eyes for an answer to the next steps in this very unexpected and unfamiliar dance.

Faint lights from Craighill glowed warm against the rising dusk and fog, encouraging me even deeper into his hold. The air tinged with the orangey sweetness of primroses, the gloaming whispered of magic, and all of it wrestled through my nomadic heart as if to offer an unsettling what-if.

Those two words whispered through my mind, almost like I was answering some unvoiced call from the highland mist.

One of his dark brows took an upswing along with the corner of his lips. "Will you hold this for me?"

I swallowed, crawling my way through the mental cloud his stare had on my comprehension. "Um . . . sure." I took hold of the umbrella, keeping it carefully perched over the two of us, and then, with his hands free, he placed them on either side of my face.

He was going to kiss me.

Me.

And him.

Kissing.

With the slightest hitch in his growing smile, he lowered his head, and my entire body paused in sweet anticipation.

And then—

"What are the two of ye doing out in the—"

The cook's voice broke off as she likely interpreted the intention of our position, and we pulled apart.

I think the cook was probably part pixie.

"Thank you for this evening, Graeme." I handed him back the umbrella, holding his gaze.

"See you Sunday?"

"Aye," I answered, inciting the smallest smile from him.

And then I turned, with one last look to him, and entered the house.

CHAPTER 16

Katie

It was a good thing the kiss didn't happen.

Excellent, actually.

Because I didn't need to go around kissing a man when a future with him seemed improbable. The Edwardian Ball was Wednesday, which meant I left on Thursday. Less than a week from today. And people didn't go around changing their entire lives over a man they'd only known for nearly three weeks.

The feel of his most recent note in my jacket pocket pricked my palm, and my fight against improbabilities dwindled.

Drochaid nan sithean

Bridge to the Faerie Hill

But be careful. Faeries can't be trusted with directions or gold.

Then he'd drawn a little map to show me the way.

It was the closest things to a love note I'd ever gotten.

The stone bridge had been beautiful and isolated from the world as if someone just decided to create this work of art out in the middle of nowhere for their own benefit. A few waterfalls tumbled over rocks nearby, an island of trees nestled between the bridge and the loch, and the mist fell over everything as if it had been waiting just for me.

I'd even discovered Bea's cottage—one of the knitters—on my way back to Craighill. She'd welcomed me inside for tea and to meet her husband and cocker spaniel, then gave me a tour of her art studio filled with acrylic and watercolor paintings of so many of the places I'd seen on Mull.

The instant welcome to draw me into her house for conversation and tea settled over me like so many other things about this place.

And I'd written about it, trying to put into words this intangible something only Scotland possessed. The mystery-infused air, the history-laced earth, the legends in the fog. All of it fueled my writing.

Words for *Katie on the Fly* came with maddening speed too.

Dave liked my most recent article, "The Sheepish Adventure to Fearlessness," and felt it should help curb some of the backlash from Mark's post. But he still encouraged me to continue to put out more content. "Bring back the Scot if you can. He seems to be a crowd favorite."

No duh! What I needed was a really spectacular story to share about "The Scot" if I wanted to overshadow Mark's meanness. Maybe he'd let me write about his sculpting? Or maybe I could write the legend of heather, as he told it? "Pink Heather and a Hot Scot"?

Ugh. Love? I wasn't in love with Graeme MacKerrow.

Definite *like* though. So maybe a light pink heather?

Dave praised my edits to the articles I'd sent back to him, encouraging the three newer writers to reach out to me for further discussion. The idea of mentoring them wasn't so bad either. Maybe I could offer some encouragement like Dave had given me.

Badly needed encouragement that had changed the trajectory of my career.

Hmm . . . Hadn't Gran once talked about giving out of our own gifts and lessons? Being little rescuers of others in a world where people looked out for number one?

I grinned at the thought. Yes. I might not be able to rescue in grand gestures, but maybe I could keep being a little heroine for others. Like Graeme had said. What seemed so small in helping him had mattered. And maybe encouraging these new writers was a way to do that too.

As I got ready for church, my phone buzzed on the bathroom counter beside me.

Mom: Did you get my last message?

Code for: *Why haven't you called?*

How was she even awake right now? Wasn't it five in the morning for her?

I drew in a deep breath and pressed her name, then the speaker button.

"You're up early." Starting the conversation usually ended better for me. It stalled her questions.

"I'm always up early. It's the province of the elderly." Which she wasn't, but she liked to play that card when it worked in her favor or sounded funny. "Did you know that Brett and Jessica are contemplating moving away from Atlanta?"

Ah, she wasn't just calling about the online slander situation. She had news. "Brett mentioned something about it on his last call."

"I hope you advised him to reconsider. His banking job is the first step to climbing the corporate ladder like his brother. We both know his art will never amount to anything, Katie. So I need you to back me on this before he makes a huge mistake."

I stiffened at her utter dismissal of Brett's abilities. Surely she knew her own son well enough that he'd never drop everything to pursue his art. He had a family to provide for. But if his plan to move away from a higher cost of living to try to save money and heart in the long run . . . "Mom, I think Brett's old enough to figure out what he and his family need most."

"No, he's not. He's always been led by his desire to paint and it just won't amount to anything."

"You told me travel writing wouldn't either, and look where I am now."

"Yes. Look where you are now." Her voice edged with familiar disapproval. "Having your name maligned for all the world to see. If you'd just pursued nursing like I'd recommended early on, then you wouldn't have to worry about those things."

Sarah's goal. To be a nurse.

Another thing I failed to accomplish, among the dozens of expectations Mom placed on me in Sarah's shadow.

"Nursing was Sarah's dream, Mom. Not mine."

Silence greeted me. I'd mentioned her name. The one we didn't mention. The one our family hid beneath the grief and unspoken memories as if she never existed. But we all knew. She had lived. She'd breathed and laughed.

But two weeks after her death, Mom stripped the house clear of any trace of Sarah, except for her bedroom. Every picture with Sarah in it, every award or medal, all took up a new space in Sarah's room, like a little shrine that no one visited or talked about but everyone knew was just behind a closed door.

"Nursing was your dream. Don't you remember? You used to try and treat your siblings' wounds?"

Sarah.

I was usually the one she was treating. "That wasn't me, Mom."

"Of course it was. You were top in all the science classes."

How many times would I have this conversation with her? Me and science had a really bad teenage relationship. "Mom, I barely passed my science classes in school."

"Why are you contradicting me? Are you trying to upset me?"

I pinched my eyes closed.

I couldn't change her.

It wasn't my fault.

"I've gotta go, Mom."

She huffed. "Of course you do, but will you at least talk to Brett about what I said?"

"I'll talk to him." And boy, would I. He understood.

"Good. And I do hope you're able to clear up the mess about your online presence. You know that everyone at the club follows your journey and wants to see you succeed in the best way."

I stared at my reflection in the mirror, one eye with mascara, one without. Both watery. The mantra had helped a little, and usually I shrugged off her ridiculousness. Ignored the hurt. But the brokenness in our relationship felt bigger today.

What I really wanted at this moment more than anything was a mother who'd just take me in her arms and love me as me. Not as the memory of someone else. Not as the "reputation keeper." Not as the "good girl."

But me, in all my messy, ridiculous self.

And if I accepted that I couldn't fix my mom, then I had to accept the fact that my wish would never come true.

"Bye, Mom."

It took me too long to pull my mind from the residual foggy effects of my conversation with Mom. And I almost canceled attending the MacKerrows' church.

Because I could just run away and hide. Stay safe. Disappear.

But my heart ached for light. For Mirren's companionship and Lachlan's teasing and Graeme's smile and God's hope more than the desire to turtle up under the covers and cry for a few hours.

But I shouldn't rely on them. It wasn't their job to be my pick-me-up. And it was too early to call Brett. But with all he had going on, it wasn't his job either.

The sunshine out my window brought the warmth and birdsong of the day, almost as if God was trying to get my attention. I chuckled. And maybe that's exactly what He was doing. Reminding me not just of the beauty of the day, but that He was here.

And maybe the love I needed to linger in most was His?

The idea of the watergaw hit me all over again.

Fear kept me in check for so long, moving me away from relationships, keeping me on the run, feeding my insecurities. Fear of letting people down. Fear that my perfect little dream of home and love and happily-ever-after would never measure up in reality.

But love was messy. Life was hard.

Forgiving and being forgiven.

Falling and learning from the fall.

Breaking and healing through the love of others.

Even if I only had a little while with the MacKerrows, their brand of care shored up my fearful heart like nothing I'd known in a long time.

And I didn't mean the swooning.

Or the shoulders.

But the real sense of belonging.

So I embraced the forthcoming sadness just to enjoy the present. Watergaw.

I quickly finished getting ready, choosing a blue blouse to wear with my skirt. With a smile to myself in the mirror, I slung my bag over my shoulder and slipped from the quiet manor house.

The sun shone clear and beautiful upon the waking world. For now. Who knew what the weather would be like in an hour?

So I borrowed one of Craighill's bicycles and started down the hill.

The fresh air provided the morning perspective I needed. And the beauty of the surroundings pulled my mind toward better things. Higher things. Truths I needed to fill my head and aching heart with after a phone conversation with my mom.

My value wasn't measured by her behavior. Or my mistakes. It was measured by God's love. A love I couldn't out-fail. Ever. I needed the reminder so badly, and it was almost as if every flower and sea-scented breath joined in a massive chorus to remind me.

Graeme's directions (including another self-drawn map) led me to an iconic view to add to the many I'd seen so far. A stone chapel hovered between a rocky hill on one side and an open glen full of flowers on the other. It welcomed me forward with the same sweetness as Mirren and Graeme, who met me at the door. After the phone call with my mom, sitting between Mirren and Graeme in the little chapel as songs rang out and sunlight filtered through stained glass windows, a battle between longing and belonging wrestled in my heart. I hadn't shared a moment this intimate with other people since my grandparents died, and the memory sank deep into my home-parched soul.

At one point during the service, Graeme's arm came up to rest on the pew behind me, bringing an extra waft of his yummy scent, and then Lachlan offered me a piece of gum, and Mirren gave a comment or two about the "Scottishness" of the pastor. I wanted to nestle into the experience like a warm blanket on a cold night and never emerge.

So I held on. Daydreamed. Hoped.

What could my world look like if everything turned out like the storybooks? If Graeme offered me his heart and his family embraced me and my traveling? If my fear, clumsiness, and unintentional troublemaking didn't derail any possible happily-ever-afters? If home came with more of a Scottish accent and salt-sea air than anything I'd ever envisioned for my life?

The temptation to give in to the what-if tugged me deeper into a hope that terrified me and enchanted me all at once. And promised me that if I fell this time . . . I'd never recover.

"I cannae believe you've never had steak pie." This from Lachlan, who'd sat across from me at the long dining room table in the MacKerrows' cottage. "You've lived a poor life in America, and that's a fact."

"Come now, lad." Kenneth MacKerrow, the patriarch of the family, and the leader of the gene pool where his sons were concerned, chuckled as he served some of the steak pie on a plate for me. "Katie's scran in America mayn't be as tasty as what we have here in Scotland, but I doubt it's poor."

He winked over at me, the ease at which this family moved among one another giving off all sorts of snuggly vibes. They loved one another.

I don't know if they realized what they had, but any onlooker with a history like mine saw it glaring in neon from every side hug or easy exchange. The gentle way Mirren placed her palm on Kenneth's shoulder as she stood near him, and the instance when he tugged her against him as she asked if anyone needed more to drink.

The way the brothers shoved one another around in playful annoyance and everyone kept an eye and ear out for Lachlan. *This* was finding the needle in the glen.

"I'm pretty sure Lachlan is questioning all of my food choices at this point." I grinned as much at Kenneth's wink as at the overall joy of being in the thick of such a place. "Especially since not finding Irn-Bru to my liking."

The men all groaned in response.

"Not to worry, Katie." Calum leaned closer from his place beside Lachlan. "If we keep you here long enough, Irn-Bru will grow on ye."

Clearly, Calum inherited the charm gene from both his parents, but his darker eyes were from his father. He teased often, laughed readily, and flirted shamelessly with me, which wasn't necessarily bad when it meant Graeme kept finding a way to stay close.

The whole day kept warring between my hopes and fears. Church and now a family lunch. I almost sent a gaze heavenward to question God's faith in my personal strength and self-control.

"Where do you travel next, Katie?" This from Mirren.

"I actually am attending my first Renfaire in Kentucky for two days, followed by a special alpaca festival for another two before I return home for a couple of weeks."

"An alpaca festival?" Graeme cleared his throat, his grin hiding none of his amusement. "I can't imagine any trouble happening to you there."

"Right?" My gaze caught in his, attraction pinging between us like a pinball machine. "Now that I'm a sheep master, my Jedi powers should transfer to other creatures automatically."

The family laughed, and I took a bite of steak pie with a sigh. Boy, this reminded me of my grandparents' house so much. Even the food. I'd thought meals and families like this had disappeared with them, but here I was, living in a scene so familiar yet so different. The closeness. The ease. I hadn't realized just how much I ached for it—the depth of what I'd lost when my grandparents died—until this reintroduction.

And I wasn't quite sure what to do with the discovery. It was almost too much. Too wonderful. Overwhelmingly sweet.

"Do you ever rest?" Kenneth asked, offering me a basket of bread.

"I feel pretty rested right now." I took his offering.

"Now, lass, you ken what I mean. Everyone needs a time and place to settle."

"Says the man who works about ten hours a day," Mirren said, raising a brow toward him.

He pinched his lips tight with a fake frown. "Now, my heart, I take days and hours when I'm needed or wanted, don't I?" His cooing endearment melted Mirren's ire like ice cream in an Arizona summer. He turned his attention back to me. "University hours can be long, especially when I must take the ferry to the mainland each day."

"He's such a good professor, he keeps getting promoted, and there's naught I can do about it, Katie-girl." Mirren kissed the man on the head, resulting in him pulling her into a side hug.

"But I am home *every* night to settle my heart, Katie." His gaze caught mine and held, much like Mirren's. Mind-reading skills must run in the family. "It doesnae sound as if you're home very much at all."

I failed to mention the idea of "home" was just that to me. An idea. Though the scene before me looked and felt a whole lot like what home should be.

I was saved from responding by Calum. "You must really like traveling then?"

He was clean-cut and his hair hung a little longer than Graeme's—not quite to the shoulders but close. And he wasn't quite as tall or broad as his elder brother, but not far off. Both got their stature from their dad. Mirren barely came to five foot four.

"I love it. It's been an amazing part of my life, and I've finally gotten to a point where I'm not having to race around like a starving rat to find the next story." I took a drink of my sparkling pressé. "My editor even has me doing a trial run at editing."

"So there's good money in it?" he continued. "Writing?"

His eyes took on a strange glimmer as if he meant something different than he said.

"There *can* be if you cobble together different sources of income, as I have over the years." I studied him. "And if you can find your niche and write well."

"He's making sport of you, Katie." Graeme nudged my shoulder with his own. "Because he's fairly exploding with the need for you to ask him about writing."

"Och, Graeme. Dinnae give away my secret." But Calum's exclamation came with more drama than real frustration.

"Your secret?" I laughed out the question. "Oh right. Lachlan mentioned something about your books being for sale at the Highland games."

"Aye." Mirren topped off my water. "Calum's a fiction writer, and his first series has been very popular. Fantasy, they are."

"Really?' I swung my attention to him. "That's fabulous."

"You can't go off telling it though, Katie, because my agent has made it a point for no one to know the true author behind my pseudonym." Calum wiggled his brows. "He thinks it adds more mystery to my brand."

"I'm glad it keeps any fans away," Kenneth offered, filling his fork with some more steak pie and sending another grin to me. "But I reckon the anonymity keeps Calum humble, which is a feat all on its own."

"Dad." Calum pressed a palm to his chest as if wounded and then turned back to me. "Dinnae believe a word from them about me, Katie. I'm the very model of a modest man."

"You know God hears ye talkin', don't cha?" Graeme shot back across the table. "And right after a sermon on meekness too."

The family's laughter erupted again, and my heart filled almost to overflowing with it all. In fact, I had to take a few extra drinks of my flavored water to get my emotions under control.

"Truth be told, my agent has some braw scheme to reveal my true identity"—he straightened with a bit of exaggerated pride—"through some brilliant marketing idea. I'm not sure what it is yet, but he's always full of grand ideas."

"Sounds familiar." Graeme rolled his eyes heavenward as he shook his head in exasperation. "True identity? You sound like a bloomin' superhero, Calum."

"Who's to say I'm not?" He wiggled his brows at Graeme. "Saving one uninspired reader at a time."

"Och, away with ye!" Graeme shot back, sending a wink over to me as he scooted a teensy bit closer.

Maybe I was dreaming. A wonderful dream. "Fiction is a fantastic genre to choose, especially fantasy," I finally added to the ongoing conversation as the men kept ribbing one another. "But I didn't realize how difficult and exciting it would be all at once to make the stories and characters come to life."

"Oh!" Calum gave the room a look before settling his eyes back on me. "Are ye writing somethin' then?" He leaned close, his flirt vibes on display from the twinkle in his eyes. "Care to share with a fellow writer?"

"If you lean any closer over the table, Calum, you're going to get your shirt in the sauce." Graeme ground out the words and rested his arm on the chair behind me.

Staking his claim a little, maybe? Because I was, well, pretty good with that.

"It's nothing as impressive as writing adult fiction." I shook my head, butterflies taking off in my stomach. I'd only shared my little stories with Brett and his kids. They're the ones who inspired the idea to begin with.

"Don't sell yourself short." Calum's expression sobered. "Writing good fiction for children can be as difficult if not more so than for adults."

"What's it about?" Graeme's voice pulled my attention to him. His arm propped up behind me, his face so close, I hesitated a little in his gaze.

Struggling with my thoughts.

And then actual words.

"Um . . . it's a middle reader series." I turned back to the other people at the table, hoping my face didn't match the color of my hair. "A little secret project I've been working on for a few years."

"We writers and our secrets, eh, Katie?" Calum wiggled his brows and Graeme proceeded to, apparently, insult his brother in Gaelic, if Mirren's slap on Graeme's shoulder gave any indication.

"And?" Graeme gave my arm an encouraging squeeze, the motion gently placing his arm against my back.

I considered myself "claimed," if he was interested in a traveling daydreamer with a tricky past and a clumsy future.

"And . . ." I drew in a deep breath, attempting to manage expectations. "It's about a girl who goes on marvelous adventures with her dad who is a travel writer. It's my way of helping kids explore the world."

"I like that idea," Lachlan offered, before cramming a large piece of bread in his mouth. "I like adventure books."

Or at least that's what I thought he said.

"Are you keen to share any of it?"

I'd just taken another bite of steak pie, and my attention swooped to Calum. All the newfound heat drained from my face. "What?"

"I'd be happy to read some of it, if you're willing."

He looked serious. And interested.

I pushed through a swallow. "Oh, I . . . I . . ."

"He's a very good writer," Mirren added. "And I woudnae just say so because he's my bairn."

"Despite being a numpty most of the time, he's good at encouragement and writing." Graeme's words emerged by my ear and sent delightful happiness spilling through me like a drug.

His voice could get me to agree to just about anything. Jubilantly.

"I've only ever shared it with my brother and his family, so . . . so it's probably not what—"

"None of that." Calum waved away my words. "I know—hand me your mobile, and I'll add my email address." He held out his palm, gaze switching from me to Graeme, almost in challenge.

"None of *that*," Graeme growled.

"Are you serious, Calum?" I laughed my surprise. "You *want* to read it?"

"Cross my heart." He made the motion. "And you'd better take the offer because I'm only serious on special occasions."

"Truer words . . . ," Mirren added, topping off Calum's coffee.

"Okay. If you're sure." Was I ready to have someone besides Brett read—and possibly critique—my stories? "I . . . I could share my document with you, and then you can transfer it to whatever device you need."

"Aye, that'll work." And he rattled off his email—which I hastily entered into my phone—then winked, clearly pleased with himself.

"And I just turned in a book, so I'm keen to have something new to read."

"Stop latherin' on the charm." Graeme shook his head. "She's too smart to fall for your ways. You're pure gallus, you are."

"Och, away with you both." Mirren stood, waving her napkin at the two men. "Katie and I'll wash up to get away from you lot, while you set up the room for some music."

Music? I took the last drink of my water, picked up my plate, and followed Mirren into the kitchen, taking my place drying dishes as she washed.

It was simple. Should have been drudgery.

But I'm pretty sure I grinned like the idiot I was through the whole thing as Mirren talked about growing up on an island east of Scotland called Skymar, then meeting Kenneth.

"Where did Lachlan get such red hair?" I asked, taking a bowl as the strains of a fiddle began playing from the next room. I turned toward the sound, the music drawing out my grin. "Ah, that'd be Calum. He also plays the bagpipes, of course." Her smile crinkled. "Graeme plays the guitar, so you're bound to hear it—" A guitar joined in with the fiddle, playing a lively tune that sounded a lot like the bluegrass music back in the Blue Ridge Mountains. "Lachlan'll join in with his banjo and Kenneth on the bass."

"How wonderful." I laughed, listening as each instrument picked up pace into some Scottish melody I thought I'd heard at the Highland games.

"Lachlan got his ginger hair from my side of the family." She handed me a glass. "Peter, our youngest, has the same."

I didn't know much about Peter, except that he was attending seminary somewhere on Skymar, the island Mirren had just mentioned.

"And Greer," Mirren continued, holding out another glass for me. "She had a wee bit of red in her hair, but it was mixed in with the darker brown. Beautiful though. Long and healthy like yours until the chemotherapy started."

Greer. The name carried the same indefinable presence as Sarah's.

I didn't know what to say, so I just took the next glass.

"She played the fiddle too." Mirren's smile never waned. "And had the voice of an angel." She chuckled. "I s'pose she truly does now." She held out a bowl. "What about you, Katie? Do you play any instruments?"

And the conversation moved right along. Without a fight or breakdown or tongue-lashing. Greer slid in and out of the sentences as if they talked about her regularly. As if she might walk into the room any minute.

"I . . . can play the guitar a little, but I mostly learned so that I could best my brother."

Mirren chuckled. "'Tis the way of it with girls with brothers, isn't it?" She dried her hands. "They tend to foster a strong constitution and either a good sense of humor or a constant state of mistrust."

I laughed. Accurate. "Very true."

"Greer had a good sense of humor, like you." She pointed her towel toward me before tossing it onto the counter. "Evidence of brothers and a wee bit of a cheerful heart, I'd say." With that, she slipped her arm around my waist. "Now let's see what the lads are up to."

We walked into the living room where the chairs had been pushed back to make an open space on the floor.

"Katie can dance the Gay Gordons, Mum." Graeme's gaze caught mine as we entered the room and he set down his guitar. "Bragged about it even."

I opened my mouth in protest, sending a mock glare that bounced off Graeme's crooked grin, but Mirren clapped. "We can make two partners work, can't we? Kenneth?"

Without hesitation, Kenneth set aside his bass and came to Mirren's side, taking her hands.

"Come on, Katie." Calum paused his playing and grinned. "Dinnae tell me you're afeart of dancing with my eejit brother, are ye?"

At the moment, I wasn't even sure what emotions I felt. Fear, wonder, longing . . . all tangled among one another.

Graeme came to my side and took my cold hands in his big warm ones. Then Calum began the melody with Lachlan joining on the banjo. The steps came back so easily, especially with Graeme as my guide, and I almost laughed . . . and cried at the same time.

As the music continued and Kenneth and Mirren started the round, emotions kept clashing inside my chest. The warmth of family and the sweetness of their love. Greer's easy presence in conversations. My inclusion and belonging. Graeme's secure hold on my hands and tender look. The impossibility of how any of it could last.

It all pressed in on me. I wanted to hold on forever and run all at the same time.

Belonging? Was that the elusive something I'd been missing for so long?

But I couldn't belong here. I didn't live in Scotland. And this wasn't my family. And . . . I was leaving.

We kept dancing, with the family's teasing and encouraging comments to one another like some sort of verbal tennis match. And I was actually not too bad at this sort of tennis. Encouragement. I could handle that version.

"You're a good dancer, Katie," Lachlan called from his seat, his eyes wide with surprise.

"How about you, Lachlan?" I held out my hand to him. "How is your Gay Gordon?"

The boy's chin raised as he stood, and he marched over to my side as if trying to stretch up a few more inches.

"Your granny said you're even better at checkers than you are at fishing," I said to him as he attempted to spin me around, but his arms just didn't reach that high.

"Och, Graeme. I'll have to try again when I've got some more inches to me."

Graeme stepped back in, and Lachlan nodded as he completed my spin. "Aye, that's the way it's done." He folded his arms in front of him as if examining the situation. "I'm a sight better at checkers than dancing, for sure."

Graeme's arm came up around me to turn my steps backward so I couldn't see Lachlan again until he'd spun me back around.

"But not as good as Mum," Lachlan continued. "She beat everyone at checkers, except Peter."

"Your mom did?" My gaze moved across the room to a photo I'd seen when I first entered. The seven of them, all together at some sort of Christmas function, Lachlan clearly a few years younger.

"We always said that Peter intentionally talked so much while playing any game that he distracted his opponents into delirium," Graeme added, evoking a chuckle and an "aye" from Kenneth ahead of them in the dance.

"But Greer was determined to beat him at the game before she passed." Mirren tossed a smile over her shoulder. "And she did. With two weeks to spare."

"And Uncle Peter didnae go soft on her either," Lachlan added with a nod. "She won fair and square. We celebrated with ice cream and a bonfire."

His little voice speaking about his mother so effortlessly broke the last of my grasp on any emotional control. Graeme turned me into a spin and I took my chance. I had to get away.

"I . . . I'm sorry." The words shuddered out. I released his hand and ran for the door—away from the warmth, the emotions, the incomprehensible sweetness of it all, and right out into the rain.

CHAPTER 17

Graeme

The barmy woman had run out into the rain like a loon.

And it would take her a half hour to make it back to Craighill on foot.

The music came to an abrupt stop with the slam of the front door.

"What on earth?" Dad's question likely voiced everyone else's thoughts.

She'd seemed so happy.

What had gone wrong? The dancing?

My gaze shot to my brother. Calum?

"I think Katie might be a better lass for you than me, Uncle Graeme." I blinked and looked from Lachlan to Mum and back.

"And why do you say that, lad?"

"Because you're a faster runner than me." He set his banjo down and shrugged. "And taller. And don't mind a wee bit of crazy."

Calum's brows rose as if he wanted to laugh, and the nudge somehow set my feet in motion. I grabbed my jacket and car keys and ran out the door into the rain, searching for a sign of her. We'd left her bicycle at church because of the rain, so she had to be on foot.

I caught sight of her red mackintosh up the drive, farther than I imagined her capable of walking in such a short period of time. But she *wasn't* walking. She was nearly running.

Away.

What had happened? Everything seemed to be going fine. Well, in fact. Mum had cooked one of her best meals. Dad brought in added humor and warmth. Calum was . . . Calum, but he wasn't usually too off-putting, except when he lathered on the charm.

Eejit.

And I'd mostly behaved myself. My manners could always do with some improvement, but I'd not made a mess of things. Or so I thought.

Her pace had slowed by the time I pulled beside her in the car. I rolled down the window. "Katie."

Which caused her to speed back up.

So did I. "Whatever it is, we can talk it through."

She shook her head and walked faster, her shoulders shaking.

This was getting me nowhere, so I put the car in park and stepped out in the rain after her. "Did I do something to hurt you?"

Which was the most likely option.

She shook her head more fiercely, and her feet faltered because she turned around to face me, her eyes red-rimmed, tears mingling with rain on her face. My chest crashed from the sight.

"Your . . . your family is . . . wonderful."

Not what I'd expected. "What?"

She sniffled, pinching her eyes closed. "Like . . . like a dream. Absolutely wonderful."

"You're greetin' over how wonderful my family is?" Her brow creased and I rephrased. "My family made you weep?"

"No." She gave a helpless shrug. "And yes." She covered her eyes with one of her hands, and another sob shook her shoulders. "You . . . you can't understand. I've . . . I've only imagined a place so warm and sweet as your family. Where parents love and respect each other. Where there's . . . joy."

I took another step nearer, trying to understand.

She looked up at me, the pain on her face nearly slicing my middle. "I don't—"

"I know what it's like to lose a sister." Her words stilled my forward motion. "She . . . Sarah . . . she was nineteen and I was thirteen. First year of college for her, and a crazy drunk driver hit her head-on. In a moment she was gone." The words poured out of her, as if she needed to say them. "And . . . and it's hard enough to deal with the grief of a missing life. I know you understand that." Her voice wavered, her gaze searching mine. "But what's worse is never being able to talk about her because it will upset your fragile mother too much. And your dad can't handle your mom's emotions, so he just works more, leaving the kids to try and sort out an upside-down world."

"Katie—"

"And your family . . . they . . . they're healthy, even as they grieve. You talk about Greer and laugh as you share memories of her." She raised her wet sleeve to her face. "Mom removed all of Sarah's photos. All of them. And refused to talk about her, ever, because grieving in real time didn't fit with her country club lifestyle. And if we did, Mom would break down on us and blame us for her response."

She pressed her palm into her chest. "And . . . and I was . . . the only other girl. Sarah and I were nothing alike in size or interest, but Mom started manipulating situations to try and force me to . . . to almost become another Sarah. And it's impossible. Sarah was beautiful and graceful and intelligent and . . . perfect." She shrugged. "And I was me." She waved to herself. "There's no hiding who I am." Her breath shook. "I'd always had trouble fitting into my mom's world of pretense, so trying to measure up to Sarah's memory only made things worse. I *always* failed. And I knew I'd keep failing because no one can ever measure up to a perfect memory."

The confession, the pain spilled out of her. I shifted another step, trying to infuse some sort of comfort into my expression.

"And I'm sorry." She wiped at her face with her hand. "I'm sorry I don't know how to be normal about it. And I act weird because I'm so afraid of caring too much and failing." She sniffled again and waved back toward the house. "So when I witnessed how things could be . . .

how they *should* be, it . . . it was too much." Her voice broke with another sob. "And now, your absolutely lovely parents are going to hate me because I was so rude to leave their wonderful house, and Lachlan's going to be worried because I'm so messed up"—she looked up at the sky—"and you're getting soaked by the rain." Her voice disappeared into a squeak and my heart squeezed.

In two steps, I pulled her into my arms. Her body tensed against me and then she released a sob and burrowed into me. My thoughts reeled through what she'd said. Emotionally fragile mother and absent father. Impossible expectations.

Was that why she traveled? And rarely talked about her family? Or home?

Running away from more than just her past but . . . the expectation of failure?

I tightened my hold on her, raking my mind for the right words to say, hoping my arms offered some sort of reassurance that she wasn't a failure at all. She bloomed with life and care. Humor and goodness.

Beautiful . . . and stronger than she even knew.

I lowered my chin to her hair, attempting to shield her from more of the rain, and she released a shaky sigh I felt in my chest.

Perhaps I didn't need to say anything.

"I'm sorry, Graeme." She looked up from her place in my arms. "I ruined one of the most lovely days I've ever had by—"

"Katie." I waited for her to meet my gaze. "You've ruined nothing. At all. You're doing what most creatures in the world do when they're afeart. They try to escape."

"But why? Why would I run away from something I want so much?" Her palms came up in a helpless motion. "I didn't even know how much until today. It's crazy."

"It's human." I swallowed through a tightening in my throat. "I think you've needed someone to hear your heart for a long time and it hasnae happened because you've never stayed long enough in one place for people to care." I pushed back her damp hair from her cheeks, searching her face. "But ye dinnae have to run from me."

Her eyes filled with tears all over again and she looked down, her palms resting on my chest. She sniffled. "I . . . I don't want to run from you."

I breathed out a sigh and pulled her back into my arms, allowing a few more tears to join the others on my shoulder. How long had it been since someone held her like this? Listened to her fears?

Too long, from the sound of it.

"We . . . we need to get you out of the rain." She sniffled into my shoulder.

Of course she'd focus on me when *both* of us stood under the same downpour. "Do you want me to drive you to Craighill?"

She nodded. "If we can take the long way?"

I wiped my palms over her cheeks as she looked up at me, attempting to dry away the mixture of rain and tears. "Aye, we can do that."

I led her to the passenger's side and then took my place, allowing the silence a little room as we traveled across the narrow roads. I wasn't sure what to ask or say, but the longer the silence continued, the more wrong it felt.

God, help me.

I drew in a breath and ventured a question. "What was your sister like?"

I wasn't sure if she'd heard me at first, but after fidgeting with the zipper of her mackintosh for a moment, she cleared her throat. "Um, well, petite. So, not like me." She chuckled. "When Mom tried to get me to sign up for cheerleading after Sarah died, it was a nightmare. I mean, look at me. No one's going to want to try and hold me at the top of one of the stunts. Oh no! And as clumsy as I am, the idea of being a base or spotter was kind of iffy too."

She rubbed at her eyes again, her hair falling in fiery ringlets around her face, those eyes so large and vulnerable, they pulled me in with her to this pain. I could almost imagine her stumbling through life, trying to appease her mother while pushing her grief deeper and deeper until it waited like a bomb to explode.

"I imagine you would have been the first to help a fallen cheerleader though."

My comment brought her gaze back up, her brow creased. "I . . . don't know. Maybe?"

I felt her stare. Did she not see her own self? I'd had the opportunity to observe her for over two weeks, even more so when becoming the butler, and she never failed to be the first to offer assistance or encouragement to the others in the house. She'd rescued Miss Dupont from a dress malfunction, offered her plate to Logan when one of the footmen spilled some of the contents from his, redirected Wake when he'd gotten lost in the garden, and even saved the Eejit from Kirsty. And those had only been a few of the many instances, offering kindness with her own brand of humor on top.

It was a part of who she was.

"But . . . but Sarah was someone who made a room better just because she entered it. She had a way of putting people at ease and bringing joy. Sometimes very bossy joy, but it ended up being a good thing." She sighed. "And she could sing! When Mom asked me to join the choir like my sister, I tried to talk her out of it because I really can't sing. I didn't last very long."

A lightness entered her voice as she spoke, so I kept with the conversation. "Did she look like you?"

"Ha! No." She shook her head. "Sarah would have been like one of your Scottish faeries. She had this magnificent blond hair and blue eyes. Effortlessly beautiful, elegantly slender."

"I'm fond of gingers, myself." I shot her wink. "Tall ones."

She looked over at me, those quivering lips of hers tipped upward a little. "Nice move for the weepy woman whose face probably looks like the inside of a watermelon right now."

Her description unleashed my grin, but I mastered it back into a serious expression. "I mean it, Katie."

Her gaze held mine, searching, as if for the truth of my words. "I don't know why."

"Would you believe me if I told ye?" I looked over at her from my periphery as I drove.

Her brow crinkled anew. "I . . . I don't know."

I drew the car to a stop at the front of Craighill and turned to face Katie. "I have some orders to make tomorrow, but will you join me for supper on Tuesday?"

"Mrs. Lennox has us booked up with lessons in preparation for the ball, but maybe lunch on Wednesday?"

"Aye." I grinned. "That will give me even more time to make my list."

"Your list?" She wiped at her eyes with her fingers.

"Of all the reasons I like you, so you'll have a different voice in your head than your mum's."

She shook her head as she looked down, but her smile spread. "You don't have to do that, Graeme."

"I want to. And I want to spend as much time with you as I can, Katie. If you fancy spending time with me."

And maybe that was the trouble. Me.

She looked back up, her fingers twisting together again. "I'd fancy that."

"Good." I released the breath I hadn't realized I was holding. "Lunch? At the cottage?"

"Aye." The word shook out in a small laugh, and she reached for the door handle. "And thank you. For everything, Graeme, but especially for welcoming me into your home and family and . . . chasing after me. That . . . that means a lot. Please apologize to your family for me."

"My family was glad to have you, Katie." I took her arm as she made to move, pausing her escape to add emphasis. "And so was I."

Her smile flashed wide for a second. "See you Wednesday?"

"Aye." I released her arm. She exited the car, and something in me wondered if I'd see her again or if she'd resume the escape plan she'd started when she left my parents' house.

I prayed she'd be brave enough to stay. To finish out her plans.

Even if her plans didn't include me.

Katie

Monday started delightfully relaxed.

Mrs. Lennox gave all the guests the morning free in preparation for a visit from the new fashion expert, who was due to arrive and fit us for our ball gowns. Evidently Mrs. Lennox had made an agreement with her from the beginning to design original ball gowns for each of the ladies at the house as part of the experience. And as a historian and designer, her dresses would not only promote one of the benefits of visiting Craighill but would work as cross-promotion for the designer's skills.

Evidently she was an up-and-coming fashion genius.

And what girl didn't get a little giddy now and again about wearing something she could never normally afford? But since *World on a Page* was paying, I'd bask in the opportunity.

I'm sure Graeme was glad to have the morning away from his butler duties, but with this being the last week, at least the end was in sight for him.

I frowned. It wasn't an ending I liked to think about.

An uncomfortable ache settled in my middle, and I dropped down into my desk chair.

I couldn't shake the feeling of Graeme MacKerrow's embrace.

And I didn't want to.

Even now as I closed my eyes, the strength of his arms around me, the tenderness in his touch, burned into my memory. I wanted to stay in those arms forever, draw from that strength. My heart panged against the idea. But I couldn't.

I had a job to do.

Trips to make.

Stories to tell.

And after yesterday, no matter how sweet Graeme's response, nobody wanted me and all my brokenness in their family. The scene came back to my mind in horrific detail. They'd been so sweet to me, and I'd run out into the rain to escape. I was a disaster.

But what if Graeme and his family wanted me?

The question weaseled up through my doubts. What if . . . ?

I'd bared my soul to Graeme in a way I had never to anyone except my grandparents. I'd entrusted him with parts of my heart no one else knew, and—I winced—there was more where that came from.

And instead of leaving me standing in the rain alone, he'd asked me on a date.

Who was this guy? A glutton for punishment?

It was a good thing I wasn't seeing Graeme today, because my emotions weren't fit for a view of those shoulders and arms. Especially when I knew what they felt like around me now. Nope. Any resolve I had wouldn't stand a chance against his brogue and his grin.

And that look in his eyes.

My throat squeezed at the memory. But wrapped in his arms was where I wanted to tarry for a very long time. Maybe even forever.

Was Graeme MacKerrow what home felt like?

I shook away the thought and sat down at my computer to make a few notes. I'd just sent off an email to Dave and was getting ready to close my laptop when I caught sight of my open Katie book document where I'd left it the day before.

After yesterday, would Calum still want to read this? I checked my phone for Calum's email address and stared at it for a little while before setting in on the desk and closing my computer.

That was a lot to ask a man you just met . . . and possibly even emotionally scarred.

A knock pulled me to the door, but instead of finding Emily with a breakfast tray in hand, Mrs. Lennox greeted me with a trained smile. And beside her stood a strikingly beautiful dark-haired woman, a good five inches shorter than me, with the most amazing green eyes.

"Ah, Miss Campbell." Mrs. Lennox gestured toward the woman. "This is Allison Duncan, the designer from Edinburgh who has been working on all the gowns for the ball on Wednesday evening. She's here for your fitting."

"It's nice to meet you, Ms. Duncan."

The woman took my outstretched hand. "I'd expected you to be tall from your measurements, but now I'm even more excited about your fitting."

Definitely a different response than expected, and delivered in a Scottish accent too. "Really?"

"Aye." Her eyes glistened like a kid's at Christmas. "The color and style of my design for you is going to prove a stunner. Without a doubt."

Stunner? Not the usual description for me, but I was intrigued.

"Miss Lennox will expect you in an hour, Miss Duncan, and we are all looking forward to seeing your designs on display." Mrs. Lennox nodded and then left us.

"So, Miss Duncan—"

"Please, call me Allison." She hung a long garment bag on my closet door. "The only part I play in the charade is as a designer."

"You're one of the few Scots Mrs. Lennox has brought on, so she must really like your work."

"I think she liked my price even better." Allison unzipped the bag to reveal a shimmery confection of warm teal. "But I need the visibility, and I have a soft spot for Mull."

I stepped closer to the gown, mesmerized. "You . . . you think that's the best one for me?"

"Oh, aye." She ran a hand over the slim bodice, beaded with darker teal to make delicate vertical rows that gave off an almost elegant, corseted look. "You have curves we can certainly complement with the right gown."

I refrained from sharing that I'd tucked a curve or two into my jeans.

"It's beautiful. Like something from a movie."

"Which is what I hope to do in the future, if I can continue getting my designs out for the world to see."

"Design for movies?" I stepped forward and fingered one of the elbow-length lace sleeves. This? For me?

"As you well know, visibility takes time and lots of hard work, but my work is poised to be noticed right now, and this extra opportunity is just what I need." She tugged the full length of the gown out from the bag.

"It's not as puffy at the bottom as some of the other evening dresses I've worn."

"There was a slimming to the bottom of the gowns as the Edwardian era neared its close, and I thought that with your proportions you would showcase this certain style quite well." She raised a dark brow, examining my face. "It hints toward the flapper gowns of the twenties and will certainly accentuate your silhouette."

Accentuating my silhouette didn't sound as flattering as her expression conveyed, so maybe I needed to reevaluate.

"The difficulty so often associated with women of your body type is that you try to minimize what you have." She waved to herself, a much slimmer but still hourglass shape. "Would you tell me not to wear things that showcase my shape?"

"Of course not, but you're—"

"The same shape as you, except to fit my height. And your body type fits your height beautifully, so let's celebrate it." She scanned the room. "Come now, I'm excited to see how it looks, so put it on for size."

I took the gown into the large walk-in closet and slipped out of my jeans and T-shirt and into the shimmery combination of soft cloth and delicate beading. Thankfully, both the bottom and top of the cello fit with only a slight catch on the upper quadrant.

"Ah yes." Allison brought her hands together in clear delight as I walked into the room. "The color is perfect and the sweetheart neckline complements the straighter lines on the rest of the dress. Oh, it's even better than I imagined."

"You really have a gift."

"It's a special compliment when the wearer brings out the best in my designs." She took her fingers and pinched in various places on the gown. "Only needs a tuck here and there for the bodice to maintain the slip look around your waist."

"Did you say you have a soft spot for Mull?"

Allison kept her head bent as she pinned the cloth at my waist. "I've spent a great deal of time here in the past. It's a brilliant island to visit, but not the kind of place most people choose to stay."

"No?"

"There's not much here, and people are stuck in their old ways of thinking and living." She looked up. "The villages are quaint and sweet but small, with limited options. The landscape is gorgeous but desolate at times. And if you really want any variety, you must travel an hour or more to reach the nearest city."

Variety? My walks along the countryside in the misty air, the vastness and somewhat intimidating mountains. The winding paths and roadways that led to untold adventures that kept unfolding around every turn.

And the people?

Sure, this island and its "small" life wasn't meant for everyone, but the appeal to my heart kept growing.

It felt more and more like the home I was beginning to want for my future.

If home could include frequent-flyer miles.

"You've traveled all over the world," she continued, moving to pin the other side. "Do you think you would be satisfied living in a confined place like this?"

"Living somewhere doesn't mean you're trapped there, does it?" I stared down at her bent head. "Coming home to one of those little cottages with a handsome Scot to welcome me sounds pretty appealing on every level."

Her gaze came to mine, and her smile crooked. "Ah, have you found someone to share a cottage with, then?"

My face flushed hot. "Not necessarily." Though the memory of being in Graeme's arms came to mind, causing my insides to conveniently melt. "But the idea is nice."

"I see the way of it. You *do* fancy someone." She stood and stared up at me, her smile firming into a line. "Then let me give you fair warning about the men of Mull."

I raised my chin to brace myself.

"Their hearts are bound to this place, and they're not too keen on the ones they love having a wanderlust."

Graeme's lack of desire to leave Mull to feature his art came to mind. "You seem to know from experience."

"Aye." She nodded. "I was engaged to a good man here on Mull. Great family. But my dreams were elsewhere, and he wouldn't support those dreams, not if it meant leaving Mull."

The thought pinched against my newfound giddiness. "People change," I offered in defense of her fellow, but also to protect my hopes. "If you cared about each other enough to become engaged, then maybe time has helped soften his heart to the idea. I mean, if he's such a good guy."

"He is." She studied me a moment, and then her expression softened. "And perhaps I can take the opportunity to find out how much he's changed while I'm here."

I never made claims to being a matchmaker, but offering encouragement for two formerly connected hearts to find their way back to each other certainly sounded like a good idea. Especially if the guy she left was anything like Graeme.

"Well, I think I've gotten everything on the gown ready for adjustments. You can change if you like."

My gaze fell on my rust-and-cream walking dress lying across my bed, and my plans for today came to mind. "Since historical dress is your specialty, would you mind if I asked you a question?"

"Of course."

I gestured toward the walking dress. "A few of my readers keep asking me questions about these types of dresses holding up for the long walks that we see Jane Austen or Brontë's characters make in the Regency era. Do you think this would make a good comparison?"

She ran a finger over the skirt of the dress. "It's made of sturdy cotton, which would have been similar to some of the day dresses of the time, so a fair comparison. Why?"

"I was thinking of going on a walk in costume this morning before our activities begin and documenting it for my followers."

She chuckled. "Well then, don't forget a hat and sturdy shoes, because it looks like rain."

CHAPTER 18

Katie

It seemed to rain about 80 percent of the time on Mull, or at least while I'd been there.

But I liked the rain. And the morning mist failed to stop me from making the walk to find the puffins and search for the sea caves Lachlan had mentioned.

The fresh air cleared my head.

Praying along the way helped too. Of course everywhere I looked inspired some sort of awe at creation, so turning my thoughts in a heavenly direction came fairly easily. And boy, did I need some heavenly thoughts with all the chaos going on inside my head and heart.

I wanted what I experienced yesterday at the MacKerrow house. I wanted the safety of Graeme's arms. I wanted that sense of belonging.

But what I didn't want was to give up my job or give away my heart, only to have it smattered across the glens. Or royally mess up a relationship with Graeme and smatter *his* heart across the glens . . . and hurt Lachlan and Mirren in the process.

Why was I even considering any sort of romantic-something with Graeme when so many things were at stake?

What am I supposed to do, Lord?

A gentle breeze answered with a whiff of honeysuckle in the air, and I breathed it in. Grandpa would have loved this place. The quiet, the vastness, the earthy feel of connecting to nature and history. Perhaps the faeries played their games with me as I moved up the hillside, stopping at several points to take photos or videos, but when I finally reached the summit, I'd gone much farther than I'd expected.

Down below on one side, I could still make out the tip of Craighill's tower, but on the other side, the loch spread out and widened. In the distance, a cliff branched outward like an arm into the water, revealing caves beneath with water crashing up against them. I moved forward, taking a few more photos and holding my hat during my video as the wind whipped around me.

And then, up ahead, in a little flock, waddled one of the goals of my walk.

Puffins.

I slipped as close as possible to the stocky little birds, their black-capped heads bobbing as they huddled together near the cliff's edge. A strange, almost comical, collection of sounds emerged from the birds. Like they were having some sort of humorous gurgling conversation with one another. It fit them.

As a few puffins flew in to join the rest and proceeded to stumble into their landing, I felt an immediate kinship to these creatures. Another took off nearby with an equally bumbling liftoff. Yep. I'd found my spirit animal.

"Aren't you guys the cutest things ever!" I drew closer, with my camera taking in as much as I could. And, I suppose, most Edwardian ladies—and maybe even Lizzie Bennett—didn't crouch, because the attempt stretched dangerously at the cloth of my walking dress. (A note for a future video.)

The cliff view in the background with the puffins in the foreground really made for some spectacular shots. Brett would love them.

A few of the larger puffins caught sight of me and waddled closer, giving me amazing pictures of their unique coloring of black, white, and that interesting orange. Another landed nearby, tripping along in a way I understood down to my big feet.

And then . . . their comical conversations became frantic.

I stood from my crouched position as they scattered away from me, some taking off and leaving the ledge, others dispersing in opposite directions from one another.

"Hey, I'm not scary," I called, stepping a little closer, and they scattered even faster, a few staggering into flight. "In fact, we have a few things in common. Funny-looking. Clumsy."

They continued their retreat. Hmm . . . I'd heard puffins were social and curious. Not skittish. Maybe it was the hat?

And then I heard it. A deep snort-like growl behind me. I froze and closed my eyes, drawing in a slow, deep breath. Keeping my movements small and deliberate, I turned toward the sound.

Air stopped in my lungs.

Standing less than twenty feet away, growing larger the longer I stared, was a Highland cow. His rust-colored fluffy coat rippled over him as the wind hit it. He stared back at me, with the one black eye not covered by the wooly bangs dangling across his forehead. Handlebar horns protruded from his fuzzy head as he lowered it a little, stomped the ground, and offered another intimidating snort.

Although referred to rather adorably as a hairy coo, the way his cold eye bore into my face, I wasn't getting any "adorable" vibes from him at all.

And was this Highland cow (I refused to refer to such a terrifying beast as the sweet-sounding "hairy coo") the same one Lachlan had referenced? What was his name? Seamas?

I shifted a step back, much too aware of the cliff not too far behind me, as the puffins took off in quick succession, their little wings doing much more than my hat would do for me.

I took a step to my right with the purpose of making a run for it back down the hill, but Seamas stomped a few steps closer in that direction, so I stopped again. Okay, did you do the same things with Highland cows as bears? I raised my arms into the air to make myself bigger.

Nothing.

So I roared.

He flinched and then snorted but didn't move.

I roared again.

He lowered his head, and a chill moved up my body . . . just before he charged directly toward me. In the distance—as I saw my life flash before my eyes for the . . . sixth time—I heard a dog barking, but I didn't have time to contemplate the direction.

I stumbled with the grace of a puffin a few more steps back, trying to gauge when to jump to the side in order to dodge those horns, when the foot I'd placed my weight on slipped.

And then the rest of me followed.

Over the edge of the cliff.

I wasn't dead.

That was my first thought as I blinked my eyes open. Because, from all I'd read about heaven, pain wasn't a part of it, and the ache rising up my backside, not to mention in my ankle, confirmed a very earthly habitation.

But where was I?

I sat up on my sore derriere and gasped. Nothing but sea and sky and distant cliffs met my view. I looked up the way I'd fallen. A six-foot drop—or more—left me on this tiny ledge on the side of a cliff in the rain.

Which had increased from a mist to a solid pelting.

Squinting up at the offending rain, I stretched out my back and tried to sort out what in the world I was going to do. Ah, was that thunder?

Perfect.

I think this moment easily topped the Peruvian sheep one. Especially with my lack of options for escape.

Highland cows were my new nemesis.

I lowered my face into my hands for just a moment, thankful for my hat giving a little buffer from the rain, and . . . laughed. Laughed at the ridiculousness. Laughed that God saved me "by a ledge." Laughed that, after all my worries about falling in love, I never contemplated actually falling off a cliff.

Again.

Maybe God was trying to prove a point, that instead of relying on my own directional abilities, I should pay attention to His course. Wasn't there a verse about that somewhere?

I steadied myself against the cliff wall and stood, holding in a wince when I pressed weight on my ankle. Not bad, but not good either. Especially if I hoped to climb up the side of the ledge toward freedom.

Just in case someone had walked near enough to hear me over the rain, I called out a few times for help and then reexamined my game plan. I'd learned years ago not to panic. Panicking only muddled up my thinking. And worst-case scenario, I'd sit on the ledge of this cliff for a few hours in the rain before someone came looking for me.

I'd left my whereabouts with Emily, so at least someone knew my *general* location.

And if I didn't show up for my date with Graeme tomorrow, surely he'd search for me. Right? I mean, he wouldn't think I ran away again, would he?

My stomach twisted. Because I really wanted that date.

And running away didn't look as appealing as it usually did.

Thoughts of the date spurred me back into my plan of climbing up the ledge, so I studied my options. A few of the rocks may prove to function as little stepping stones to assist me in gaining height, right?

And I'd climbed worse.

My attention dropped to my clothes. Except, I hadn't been wearing a pretty gown on my last climbing excursions, and the idea of skimming down to my drawers and corset for all the world to see felt a little scandalous by anyone's standards.

I glanced around. Okay, so my viewing audience was severely limited to fowl.

Though the dress was smudged with dirt from my chest downward, it didn't show one tear. My followers would be happy to learn that bit of information. Very sturdy, indeed.

I stood up on a rock, keeping my hand against the cliff, and tried to raise up on my elbow by hooking my boot on a slippery stone, only to get my knee caught in the folds of my skirt while trying to raise it. I slipped back down to the ledge to land on my backside . . . again.

Ugh. My bum did not approve. At all. In fact, it strongly protested.

I looked down at my skirt and sighed. Scandalous, here we come!

Tugging off the cute thin jacket covering my blouse, I folded it and gently placed it on a little tuft of grass nearby. Then I unfastened the skirt and placed it on top of the jacket. Thankfully, the mock blouse covered my top down to my hips, so instead of standing on a cliff in my corset, camisole, and knickers, I at least added a thin white blouse to the ensemble.

Plus my hat.

I probably looked ravishing. Especially with the garters holding up my stockings.

Just as I stepped back up on the rock, a head popped over the top of the ledge. A fluffy, familiar head, with tongue on full display and two-toned eyes staring down at me.

"Wedge?" Relief swept through me. "Did you come to my rescue, boy?"

If I couldn't have a knight on a white horse, I'd take a cuddly sheepdog.

Wedge yipped his response and then released a whine, pawing at the edge of the cliff above me and sending dirt tumbling onto my upraised face. I dodged part of the avalanche and wiped my eyes.

"What ya doing down there, Katie Campbell?"

Well, if that voice wasn't one of the best!

My grin spread, and I looked back up to find Lachlan peering over beside Wedge.

I cupped my eyes in a futile attempt to shield my upturned face from the rain. "I met Seamas."

The boy's eyebrows rose. "And he pushed you over the ledge?"

"He charged me, and I fell."

Lachlan looked out over the horizon and released a low whistle. "The good Lord sure wants you alive, Katie Campbell. This is one of the only places with a ledge near the edge of the cliff. Otherwise, it's just a pure drop down to the rocks and sea."

My stomach plummeted. I didn't necessarily *need* that information.

"It's good to know God's not finished with me yet, then."

"Aye" came his quick reply. "Granny would miss you fiercely. Uncle Graeme too."

The simple statement spread the sweetest warmth through my chilling body. I love kids' honesty sometimes.

"Well, let me see if I can get out of here so I won't be missed any longer. Would you take these for me?" I tossed the jacket and skirt up to him, and after a few tries, he caught them and placed them on the grass above. Then I clutched the cliff and took position to try to climb again.

I made enough headway to almost get an elbow over the lip of the cliff. Lachlan grasped around my arm to assist, pulling till his cheeks grew redder than they already were.

"You're heavier than a sack of potatoes, ye are."

I laughed. Okay, maybe their honesty wasn't always my favorite.

And I slid right back down the cliff side.

"Och! This is no good." He released a loud sigh and raised his slender arms in defeat.

"We could try again." I righted myself and reached for the ledge, but Lachlan frowned.

"I know what is to be done," he said like the grown-up he wanted to be. "I'll run for help and leave Wedge here to keep you company." He peered down, a sudden glimmer lighting his sprite-like face. "Dinnae go anywhere."

"Funny," I called as he disappeared from view.

Wedge sent a few more sprays of dirt down to me and finally gave up digging to take a seat. The rain picked up a little more, and the air cooled another dozen degrees. Or at least it felt like it. I rubbed my palms against my bare arms and tried to think of warm fires and hot chocolate . . . which automatically sent my thoughts to Hot Scot, which helped a little with the internal cold feeling.

I sighed out to the horizon. Maybe I should have at least kept the jacket.

Brilliant and graceful. Me to a T.

I waited a little while, occasionally finding Wedge peering down at me before he'd disappear from view again. And then I decided to try to climb again. I mean, being the literal damsel in distress didn't mean I couldn't put forth a little effort.

After a few false starts, I finally hooked one elbow over the summit as the rain pelted my soaking hat. At least the brim kept water from blocking my vision, except when the wind blew rain into my face. I sputtered out another unwelcome taste of the storm and tried to get my other elbow over the rim, and had almost succeeded when two things happened. A movement in the distance distracted me *and* the wind blew so hard it sent my hat soaring over the cliff side and into the sea. Or, at least, I assumed a sea still swirled beneath the thick fog shrouding whatever lay below.

Just lovely. Hatless, skirtless, and completely prideless.

I blinked my vision back to the approaching distraction above the cliff and almost lost my grip on the rim. Galloping through the blinding rain, in my direction, was a horse with a rider. A white horse.

I squeezed my eyes closed and reopened them. Did hypothermia cause delusions? Or were the faeries at work?

Wedge yipped, and the rider veered his horse in our direction.

Definitely the faeries.

Every Scottish legend I'd read over the past week burst through my mind, intermingled with a few BBC costume dramas. My Scottish folklore knowledge didn't go that deep. The scenarios included my being turned into some weird creature—or possibly sea-foam—or being stolen away to the faery kingdom to live out my days without a memory of the human world. Or I would be driven into the sea by kelpies. Or, my favorite of the scenarios, I'd hear the sweet tones of my dream guy's Scottish accent recounting his fear of losing me and my love in the form of a sonnet.

Did kelpies have riders?

The hoofbeats grew closer, and through the clearing of the mist came Graeme MacKerrow.

I blinked. Graeme MacKerrow on a white horse in the rain wearing an open-collared blue shirt.

My jaw dropped. Dream-status achieved.

Maybe I had died and gone to heaven.

And proved a Scot on a white horse swoonier than any other knight.

By lots.

Thank you, Seamas.

"You're the most troublesome woman I've ever met."

So much for the undying love sonnet.

At which point I lost my hold on the cliff's rim and slid right back down to land quite dramatically on my softest spot.

Maybe I'd rather face the kelpies.

I pushed myself back to my feet, groaning as the bottom of my cello protested the movements. The wind from the sea brushed up with a fury, tossing its cold chill all the way up my damp and thin Edwardian undergarments.

Why did every one of my mishaps end in meeting him somewhere along the way? Couldn't I, at least once, show up without a catastrophe in my wake? I'm sure I'd look more appealing. And actually dateable.

I desperately wanted to tell him that I was much smarter than these encounters suggested, but Gran's adage "Actions speak louder than words" stilled my defense.

A rope dropped in front of me, and I looked up to find Graeme staring down with Wedge at his side. One boasted a very bunched brow.

Not the furry creature.

"This wasn't my fault."

His gaze caught mine, and he blinked. "It's no time for a conversation. Take the rope."

With a grumble, I took hold of the rope, and within less than a minute, Graeme held me in his arms again. I nestled into the familiar hold with renewed appreciation, pressing my face into the side of his neck and burrowing as close as I could.

"God help me, woman, you're determined to die." His bass tones reverberated in his chest, his arms tightening around me.

"I'm not really *trying* to die." I sniffled, refusing to move from this cocooned spot. "I just have bad timing."

A growl-like snort, very similar to that of Seamas, rose from him. "Aye, that's a fact." And he pulled me away from him, giving my body a quick once-over. "What on earth are you wearing?"

Before I could answer, he grumbled out something in Gaelic, I presumed, and jerked his collared shirt off to reveal a white T-shirt beneath. "We need to get you to the cottage straightaway."

"You . . . you have a horse." My whole body shivered as he wrapped the shirt around my shoulders.

"'Tis Greer's." He took my arm and stared down at me, rain dripping off those curls. "And my sister must be watchin' out for you from heaven for you to have fallen on that ledge instead of . . . "

He didn't finish but merely shook his head and marched with me to the horse.

The very idea of the alternative sent another shiver through me. And then, as if it were the most normal thing to do, he placed me on his horse, mounted behind me, and raced up the hillside.

With me.

On a horse.

With him.

In the rain.

Wow. I loved Scotland.

And I tried really hard not to think about how this mishap reduced my attraction points into the negatives.

"You found her," Lachlan announced as we entered the back of the house.

"Aye." Graeme tossed the boy a nod. "Put a kettle on, Lachlan." Then he turned to me, his gaze trailing over my scantily clad (for an Edwardian) self. His jaw twitched. "Follow me."

The brusqueness in his actions fizzled away all romantic notions.

So much for a repeat of those hugs. Or hooded looks. Or near-kisses. I had failed with him just like I knew I would. Stupid, stupid to get my hopes up.

I followed behind him down a narrow hall to a small bedroom. "I'm sorry, Graeme. I only went to see the puffins and to make a few videos."

He opened a drawer and drew out a pink sweater, some black leggings, and thick wool socks, giving me another look from top to bottom as he did. His entire body tensed, and I rushed forward with my defense.

"Then this massive Highland cow came along and charged me."

"Put these on. They were Greer's and should fit." He sighed. "We've got to get you warm, Katie. You've been in the wet too long and your skin is ice." He walked to the door. "I'll put the horse away and add some wood to the fire."

With a brand-new sense of humiliation and defeat, I slipped into the wonderfully dry clothes and carried my wet underclothes and shoes with me back into the living room. The heat from the fire drew me forward, exhaustion suddenly overwhelming me from the inside out.

"The tea should be ready in a trice," Lachlan called from the kitchen as Graeme reentered the house, his wet T-shirt doing nothing to hide the rippled form beneath.

"Thanks so much, Lachlan, but I have to get back to the house. Mrs. Lennox is having a photo op for some of the local newspapers, and we're all supposed to be there."

Graeme stared over at me, his disapproval almost palpable.

This was what I feared most. Tasting just a teeny bit of what being cared for by him would feel like, only to fumble it up in grand and glorious Katie style.

The sooner I got out of here the better.

"Thank you for rescuing me, Graeme."

His gaze flipped to mine, and his shoulders slumped a little. "You need someone in your life who will, ye ken?"

"I've survived this long." I shrugged a shoulder. "But . . . you're really nice to have around. I promise I'm not an idiot. I am clumsy, but I'm not usually stupid."

"I dinnae think you're an eejit, Katie." He released a long sigh, and those lips of his twitched. "But I am beginning to wonder if death is haunting your heels." He released another snort-like sound. "Because I've never in all my days known anyone who falls into as many predicaments as you."

"My granny used to call it a gift."

The snort happened again.

"So why not use your gifts to your advantage, right?" I shrugged. "And become a social media phenomenon."

And then he laughed. Shoulder-shaking, belly-holding, sweetly contagious sort of laughter. Deep and rumbly and oh so wonderful.

With the memory of his arms around me and the tingle of his voice still warming my neck, this delightful addition to all the things that made up Graeme MacKerrow pushed my interest over the proverbial ledge into something much more lasting than simple attraction.

I cared for him all the way to my shivering bones.

Soul-deep.

Like, grow-old-together deep.

My palm went to my stomach. "I'd much rather stay here all cozied up inside your cottage." Had I just said that out loud? And rushed ahead, "But I have to get back to Craighill."

He studied me, his expression softening for an instant, and then he nodded. "Lachlan, will you run to the barn and turn off my machines, lad?"

"Aye" came the boy's quick reply, and he dashed between me and Graeme out the door.

Graeme shook out a T-shirt on the back of the couch and looked over at me. "I'll drive ye." And as if it were the most natural thing to do after making such a statement, he pulled his wet T-shirt over his head.

After the tangle of emotions I'd experienced over the last twenty-four hours, adding such a sight to my psyche didn't bode well. Because I may have survived falling off a ledge and nearly drowning in a loch, but glimpsing Graeme MacKerrow's fine torso nearly slayed me on the spot.

Now, some gals may possess the ability to ignore an excellent male physique of refined muscles, tan skin, and well-placed traces of chest hair—I was clearly not one of those ladies. In fact, my eyeballs must have been so glued to his mighty-fine torso that his frown deepened to such a degree that his brows created a little V in the middle.

I cleared my throat and looked away.

For a second.

"Whoa, um . . . I think you need to . . . um . . . put all of that away."

The V tightened the teeniest bit. "You can't expect me to drive you to the house when I'm nearly as soaked to the skin as you were."

"I . . . I, well, of course not. But you can't go showing off all"—I waved a palm toward his well-sculpted (not that I was looking) self—"*that* in public. Have you no pity for people's eyes . . . or brains?"

Or walk with God.

The V completely disappeared from his forehead, replaced by something almost as dangerous as the perfect pectorals. A slow and steady smile curved from one corner of his lips to the other, lighting his eyes in a way that sent my pulse into a mad dash for the finish line. A red warning light went off in the back of my mind.

He looked around the room, which was as empty as my airway at the moment.

"Public?"

And he took a step toward me.

Have mercy. I was a goner.

"I mean . . . you are . . ." I swallowed the help-me-Jesus lump in my throat as my attention dropped back to his chest. "*Those* are dangerous and probably distracting for . . . people."

His hooded look ratcheted up my heartbeat into a sure-fire gallop. "Dangerous, are they?"

My stomach dropped to the octave level of his voice.

I should probably retreat. Dash back into the rain.

Seek the assistance of a passing adult.

But my traitorous feet refused to do anything but take another step back.

He slipped the dry shirt over his head as he drew another step closer.

And my back hit the wall.

I was living proof that a human could survive internal combustion of the emotions. I'd experienced almost all of them within just a few seconds.

And survived.

But with the heat scorching my skin, I wasn't sure for how long.

My gaze dropped to his fully *covered* chest, and I nodded about three times. Maybe eight. "Good. Great. All . . . fixed now." Was that my high-pitched voice? And then my shoulders slumped with a sudden realization. "Oh man, but you realize, every time I look at you, I'm going to have X-ray vision. Which means I'll never get anything useful done in your presence for the rest of my days on Mull."

Maybe for all eternity.

His smile only grew more breathtakingly threatening with each step.

And I was pretty sure I was nearing maximum hyperventilation.

Every bit of spice-leather-ocean yumminess of his scent wrapped around me in his next step, and my knees paid homage in protest of gravity.

Thankfully, maybe, he caught me midswoon and drew me up against his now-shirted chest. But with my X-ray vision in working order, I knew what hid beneath.

I swallowed and, like the complete glutton for punishment I was, I rested my palms against his chest. Those electric blue eyes of his bore into mine, searching, waiting.

I raised my chin, all ability to verbalize as nonexistent as his shirt used to be. But evidently he saw whatever he needed because his palm tightened against my back, bringing me flush against him at the same time his mouth captured mine. Every muscle in my body joined in my knees' revolt, and I gave in to the tug.

His firm lips knew exactly what to do. Caressing my shocked and dazzled ones to life . . . and response. My palms moved up his chest to frame his face, fingers sliding over his ears in such a way that caused a deep sound to reverberate from his very impressive chest into mine.

I should stop.

But he'd become my gravity. Holding me up. Keeping me afloat from the inside out. And the fact his body encapsulated mine in this protective sort of hold while kissing away every thought in my head flipped something over in my chest.

A feeling I didn't fully recognize branched through me, as if it had to travel so far to make it to identification. His warm kiss. His strong hold. His scent and protection and rescue and humor, all twined together into the far-off feeling of . . . coming home.

I pulled back, barely two inches, my fingers refusing to release their grip on his shirt. "Mrs. Lennox would not approve. At all." My whispered breath pulsed between us. "Not Edwardian. Especially the shirtlessness."

The slightest twitch tipped one corner of his lips. "Do you think I'm concerned about Lennox, lass?"

Lass? The word left his lips and rammed right into my cracked heart. A simple, common word, but rumbled low from his throat and paired with the searching sweet look of his, the combination of four letters declared war in my chest.

Fear.

Hope.

I shouldn't have let him kiss me. It really was the most ridiculous thing I'd ever done (apart from the horrible decision I made on a paraglider in Iceland), but in all honesty, I was under the influence of hot Scotness . . . or Scot hotness. That was my only excuse for not running away as soon as his tenderness threatened to undo my carefully honed flight mode. Either way, I shouldn't be held responsible for the actions that happened next. Because, without one bit of consideration for Edwardian appropriateness, I took his wonderfully bearded face in my much-too-eager hands and pulled him right back in for more.

Bad idea.

Very bad.

And I kept encouraging this very bad idea with a great amount of zeal.

Graeme didn't seem to mind at all. He growled his pleasure and wrapped me in those massive arms of his as if I weren't too tall or too clumsy or too broken.

I was just right.

An amazing rush of heady happiness swirled up from my stomach to my brain as his lips claimed mine, taking over the kiss.

I gladly relinquished the power. Letting go had never felt so good, so easy.

Heaven, help me.

Kisses shouldn't be this deadly. This consuming.

But here I was, snogging like one of the most appreciative snoggers in the whole world, without a care about what happened when I stepped out of these strong arms and entered the real world again.

Was I intoxicated by a hot Scot?

Without a doubt.

Would I regret it once I sobered up in the light of day?

Without a doubt.

But just for this moment, this amazingly marvelous moment, I embraced the feeling of being protected and cherished and safe . . .

Of coming home.

"You realize I can never see you again, right?" The words rasped from me as we pulled apart again and I rested my head back against the wall. "Because I don't go around haphazardly kissing Scotsmen or butlers or anyone else."

One of those dark brows of his took an upswing as he brought his palms to rest at my waist. "You think I do?"

I searched those eyes as they searched mine, and emotions began to gather in my throat at the answer I saw there.

A kiss like that wasn't commonplace for him either.

"Probably not the 'butlers' part."

His lips quirked, and he moved to breach the distance between our lips again only to stop at the slamming of a door.

"All done!" Lachlan called.

Graeme stepped back, releasing his hold around my waist, but not my emotions.

Oh no.

To use the local vernacular, my heart was in a fankle. Double-knotted. No return. Heartbreaking fankle.

And the realization didn't stop me from wanting to kiss Graeme MacKerrow one more time.

CHAPTER 19

Graeme

I was caught.

Likely to my demise, with her track record, but caught nonetheless.

Even before the kiss, when I'd held her in my arms in the rain, some part of my heart recognized a missing piece her presence filled. And I wanted that rightness all the time. Her.

Her past, her misadventures, her kiss, and her future.

All of it. Like I'd never wanted anyone else in my life.

I couldn't explain why I'd been drawn to her from the start. Was it the need to help her? The way she lived without pretense and slipped right into my life and family so easily? But now, knowing her tender heart better, her courage and teasing ways—well, I'd gone as mental as the folks in Craighill, I s'pose. Something in the broken pieces of her heart matched mine, and we made a whole.

I don't know how it worked. I had no scientific or psychological explanation.

But it did. Or could.

Perhaps I was a different person than I'd been two years ago with Allison—more mature. More aware of seizing life as it came. More inclined to trust a higher hand to help with the weak spots, instead of allowing my pride to rule my head.

But watching her at my parents' house with my family, seeing how she fit in a way Allison never had, solidified everything.

I couldn't let her go.

Lachlan's call as he'd burst into my workshop the day before and recounted finding Katie on the ledge squeezed in my chest. I knew what it was to lose someone. Too well, I knew it. And perhaps I'd come across as irritated at first, just because the pounding in my chest at how I might find her didn't cease until I held her safely in my arms again. But finding Katie safe and whole, and being able to bring her home healed something in me.

She helped heal something in me.

I paused on the idea. No, not necessarily her.

Love did.

Air burst from me as I took another walk around the main corridors of Craighill in search of her. Love for her wound its way into the bruised and scarred places I'd pushed to the side since Allison—and deepened by Greer's loss—and shored them up. Braced my heart to love again, whatever may come.

Her weaknesses, her genuineness, even her ridiculous mishaps, called for love—practically pleaded for it.

And I wanted to give it. To her.

I nearly laughed again. It didn't make sense. It seemed too impossible in such a brief amount of time, but there it was. I wanted more conversations. More teasing. More laughter. And definitely more of those world-shattering kisses.

Dressed for my butler duties, I watched out for her at breakfast, but she didn't show. With the house buzzing about the end of the inaugural Edwardian Experience, the wrath of Lennox on Mark the Eejit (who was sent packing yesterday), the upcoming ball, and the special gowns created for the women from some designer in Edinburgh, the morning class on ballroom etiquette had been moved to the afternoon. So, perhaps, Katie hadn't left her room.

But with her penchant for running away, I imagined she was trying to avoid me.

And to avoid a determined butler took quite the feat.

I could be as stubborn as her, if not more so.

I was in this chase for the prize—Katie Campbell's heart. And I might not know how it would all turn out—including the possibility of getting my own heart thoroughly smashed—but I knew I'd regret not trying at all.

Her care for others, her humor, her intelligence and passion.

And just the thought of such passion turned my thoughts directly back to kissing her quite thoroughly in my house and wishing for a repeat as soon as possible.

It was then I heard her voice coming down the hallway. A one-way conversation. Possibly mobile?

"And this is the hallway to the ballroom, everyone."

Was she making a video? I slipped into the narrow door of the linen closet and waited.

"Tomorrow the grand ball will happen, bringing this marvelous Edwardian adventure to an end. I can't wait to show you the gown specifically designed for me. If I ever hoped to feel like Cinderella, this dress is the one to do it. I'll also be interviewing the designer tomorrow so you can learn more about her vision for the dresses and what led to her design choices." She drew closer. "I'll pop in later today to give you a tour of the ballroom as we take our next class. See you later, and may you turn your misadventures into the best adventures."

Her sign-off line. I'd heard it several times since following her online. And I smiled. Despite the hurts she'd known and her proclivity toward disaster, she aimed to take the difficulties and find the good within them. Perhaps we wanted exactly the same thing. Making something beautiful out of something broken.

Her cleverness and kindness shone through in the videos and articles as clearly as in person, proving her even more genuine.

Beautifully genuine.

Just as she made it to the open door, I slipped my arm around her waist and pulled her inside the closet. Her eyes widened just before I claimed her lovely, shocked mouth with my own.

A hum of appreciation curled up from her, and for a second she melted against me like she had yesterday, giving me full permission to tug her even closer. But then she pushed back.

"What—" she sputtered, blinking. "Why are you kissing me?"

A laugh burst out of me. "Because I like kissing you?"

Her bottom lip dropped again, and I moved in for another taste, but her palm stopped me. "But . . . but you're not supposed to like kissing me. Not after yesterday. You're not even supposed to really like *me*."

"I assure ye, yesterday only made me like you—and kissing you—even more."

She shook her head, her brow puckering with wrinkles. "But . . . Graeme." She looked at me as if trying to console me. "I'm a mess. A big mess. I even make messes. You said so yourself that death is practically nipping at my heels. You can't"—her voice trembled ever so slightly, and my chest ached—"you can't like me."

"Prepare yourself, Katie." I raised a palm to her cheek and smoothed back a few stray hairs that had fallen from whatever hair twist she wore. "I like you. A lot. And I'm not certain why trouble likes to follow you, but I *am* certain that I want to be there to help you out of it. If you'll have me."

Katie

If I'd have him?

Lord above. A perfectly delicious Scottish man shouldn't go around saying things like that to an emotional American woman who found him dangerously attractive, without fully counting the consequences.

So I did what any self-respecting woman would do.

I grabbed his face and pulled him right into another kiss.

Which he didn't mind, because neither of us pulled away for . . . well, I'm not sure, but I was rather breathless and so was he.

"You're crazy," I murmured, patting the front of his shirt as my eyes started burning. Why in the whole wide world would a man like him want to be with me?

"Aye." The simple word, spoken so confidently and with such a grin, nearly sent me vaulting right back into giving him a vigorous reward.

But my vision blurred instead. "I don't understand, Graeme. What could you possibly see in me to counteract my bent for mayhem?"

"What do I see?" His hand slipped to my neck, his pale gaze roving over my face as if searching for an answer. "Can't I just like you because of who you are? How much I enjoy being with you?"

Could he? My history of fleeting—and sometimes catastrophic—romantic relationships provided no assistance . . . or point of reference. "You did say you have a list at some point, if I recall. And it would be helpful in believing you, because . . . the only thing I've really done to impress you is attempt to die."

He laughed. "You've done a little more than that."

"Okay, accidentally wound others, including you."

His grin spread all the way to his eyes, and from the way he looked at me, I was beginning to think he enjoyed self-harm. "Katie." He laughed again, bringing his other palm to caress my cheek. "You're funny."

"You like me because I'm funny?"

"Aye." He shrugged. "And you're kind."

Not what I'd expected.

"You don't see it, do you?" He shook his head, still staring at me with such intensity and tenderness, I barely held on to enough brain power for comprehension. "You help those around you all the time, like it's the most natural thing to do. I've seen it with Dupont and Lennox. You even saved Mark the Eejit from being overrun by Kirsty, at your own peril. You're smart and clever, which anyone can tell from talking with you, but especially when reading your writing."

He'd read more of my writing?

"And, whether it's from what you're searching for in life or your faith, or maybe a wee bit of both, you bloom with this sort of"—he waved his hand a little as if searching for the word—"hope about you. Even when the eejit betrayed you, you didnae really want him hurt. And unlike him, you're not seeking to steal attention from others or puff yourself up. Even in your online presence, you're promoting other people and their stories or the places they live. Not yourself."

My grandparents had seen those things in me and told me so, but their voices had been gone from my life for almost seven years. And it was easy to forget the good parts about yourself when the record playing in your head only recounted all the clumsy, ridiculous, broken parts on repeat.

He framed my face with his hands, but this time his approach came slowly. Gently.

Maybe there was something to the magic of this place. Even their Scottish closets. Because once his lips touched mine, any doubts about our compatibility disappeared against the warmth of his mouth against mine. As large and gruff a man as he appeared, his lips moved with infinite tenderness, kindling a slow and wavering spark into a full-blown bonfire in my chest. I wound my free hand into the folds of his butler's jacket. Holding on? Oh yes. Afraid I might wake up? For certain.

He wrapped me in an earthy-sea scent, which seemed so at home in these wild highlands. Woodsy. Him and his work, blended together with the stories and tales pouring through these mountains. I'd never thought how a person could belong somewhere so certainly, but he did. Here. And maybe I belonged with him.

His thumb stroked my jawline as he took his time, teasing my lips with his, and I gave in to it all. The touch, the tenderness, the overwhelming sense of being found. Seen.

I could have blamed the faeries.

Or thanked them.

But if yesterday's kiss kindled my blood, this one captured my heart.

And I realized how very dangerous Graeme MacKerrow was. He'd just killed all of my ready-made plans. Everything I thought I believed about myself and my future? Dead.

Mr. MacKerrow. In the linen closet. With a kiss.

Our date was still on!

I hadn't ruined it.

After kissing me senseless in the linen closet (which was not Edwardian appropriate at all), Graeme renewed the invitation for lunch at his house the next day before I needed to be back at Craighill to get ready for the ball. When he'd sheepishly added that Lachlan would be joining us, my quick enthusiasm garnered me another round of kisses until we both parted ways, me for the class and him to . . . watch the class.

Well, he watched me some too.

Then practiced the waltz with me.

I couldn't wrap my mind around the fact that I cared for such a man.

And he cared for *me*.

And of course this realization didn't happen last week when I had time to make decisions. No, I had less than two days left to sort out what we were supposed to do about all that caring. Because, for better or worse, I was due to leave Scotland the day after the ball for an assignment I couldn't change.

So, maybe I had to tone down my happily-ever-after mindset to something more . . . realistic. Something temporary. Fleeting.

I took the following morning's relaxed schedule to walk down to Mirren's so I could have a last chat with her before I headed to Graeme's. Craighill was aflutter with activity in preparation for the ball, and I needed to apologize for my flight from Mirren's on Sunday. Explain.

As soon as she saw me through the window, she opened the door and drew me into a hug. "Ah, hen, I hoped you'd pop in."

"I just wanted to apologize to you before I leave. I doubt, with all the activities going on at Craighill, I'd have a chance to talk to you before the ball, and I leave on Thursday for my next assignment."

"Come in. The knitters will be here in a few minutes, and they'll want to see you too."

She led me back to her office, leaving the door open to listen for any visiting patrons. Her tenderness and welcome smoothed over my worries. No guilt or manipulation. No hesitancy in her affection. Just . . . acceptance and care.

"I wanted to thank you for how wonderful you've been. Your whole family." I accepted the teacup she offered. "I don't have words to express how special it has been to know you."

"Do you not plan to come back?"

I paused my teacup to my lips, the question a lingering unknown as far as "coming back" in a way to fit permanently into their world and Graeme's life. Of course I'd come back to Scotland. It had seeped into my soul. Beguiled me. I had to come back.

"Of course." I took a sip and lowered my cup to the little table. "I'm just . . . well . . ."

"You're afraid. Aye," she finished, nodding, her expression softening with a knowing smile. "And rightly so. Love isn't easy."

"Especially when you add two totally different worlds to the mix."

"True. The best loves are made up of a fair bit of challenge. There's sacrifice and longing and hurt and hard choices."

I had the sudden urge to come to love's defense, even though I felt every one of those things deeply. Her smile tipped a little. "But"—she raised a finger in dramatic emphasis—"there is also joy and affection and laughter and friendship."

And kisses, but I'd keep that one to myself. "And . . . belonging," I added, my eyes stinging a little.

Which I'd felt here. With her family. With Graeme.

Her gaze sharpened on me. "And that scares you most?"

"I want it so badly, I'm terrified." Her face blurred in my vision. "That I'll bumble it like I do so many other things. Like I did on Sunday."

"Katie, darlin'"—Mirren reached forward and took my hands in hers—"when someone loves you, truly, no amount of your good-hearted bumbling will steal their love from you."

"But . . . but how can you be sure? I've felt it happen in my own family. What if . . . what if I'm not enough?"

She tilted her head, searching my eyes. "How badly do you want to belong? To be loved?"

The taste of it teased an almost insatiable desire. "A lot."

She squeezed my fingers and released my hands, sitting back in the chair. "There is a castle in Perth that has two towers with a gap between them of about two and a half meters or more. What would that be for you in American measurements?"

I calculated, trying to follow along. "Eight feet? Nine?"

"'Tis said that years ago, Dorothea, the daughter of the Earl of Gowrie, who lived in the castle, fell in love with a man her parents didnae wish for her to marry. Some say he was a tradesman who worked at the castle. However, being the hospitable Scots they were, they placed the man in the West Tower opposite Dorothea's East

Tower, with no connection between the two towers for them to meet at night."

Where was she going with this? Did she want me to stay away from Graeme? Or vice versa?

"One night Dorothea slipped from her bedroom with the plan to visit her lover in the adjacent tower. But Dorothea's mother expected some shenanigans and came to the adjacent tower's stairway just as Dorothea had begun climbing it. Hearing her mother's call, Dorothea had to act fast. What was the lass to do?"

If I answered, "Run away," would that prove my cowardice?

"There was nowhere to hide on the stairway, and she couldnae be found in her lover's room, so Dorothea ran up the rest of the stairs to the battlements on the top of the West Tower. With her mother approaching, Dorothea only had one chance of escape."

I felt my body tense. "A leap of eight or nine feet?"

"Aye, and at night too. And in a gown." Mirren raised a brow, adding her own bit of tension to the story. "But she made it, and her suspicious mother returned to the East Tower to find her daughter fast asleep in her bed."

"What happened to the lover?"

Her smile tipped. "Dorothea and John ran away the next day and eloped to live happily ever after. Or at least that's how the tale goes. But even to this day, the gap between a battlement and a nearby tower is known as the 'maiden's leap.'"

"Maiden's leap?" I repeated, watching her, the implication pinching.

"Love is always an act of faith because we cannae see the future. But there are some leaps that seem impossible and others that are not. What makes the difference?"

"What?" I whispered.

"The strength of character of the lovers and the choices they are willing to make. If the two people are willing to make the hard commitment to each other and do the work love requires, the leap isn't as far. And doesnae have to be as frightening either."

"How do you know if the people have strength of character?"

Her smile gentled. "Well, part of that is the leap, the other part is using your eyes, ears, mind, and heart to make a good guess. But love gives you the strength to leap, and faith gives you the vision to believe that the one you love will be on the other side to catch you. So the question does come back to what sort of person are you? And what sort of person are you willing to leap for?"

Mirren gave my shoulder a squeeze and left me to contemplate her story as I sipped my tea. The Stories and Stitches book club ladies arrived soon after and pelted me with their special brand of affection and dozens of reminders that I had a place in Glenkirk whenever I wanted. Maggie even offered me a job on her sheep farm, to which I smiled and politely declined.

Mirren laughed.

And as I made my way back to Craighill, I knew Graeme was worth leaping for.

But was I brave enough to leap?

CHAPTER 20

Graeme

I had a little over twenty-four hours to convince Katie Campbell that a future between the two of us wasn't impossible. Whatever it looked like in the long term, I had no idea, but what I did know was that I cared about her enough to sort it out.

I set out a few ham rolls and crisps. Too simple, but I somehow knew Katie wouldn't mind. It was another assurance of how she fit into my plain and quiet world. No wonder things with Allison failed to fit, despite my trying over and over again.

My world and hers, our futures, never really fit together. Our goals mismatched.

And then here came some cheerful, accident-prone American whom I never would have thought twice about if she hadn't captured my attention by falling on me, and she matched me in ways I never imagined.

I sent a grateful look heavenward and walked to the refrigerator to set out some juice when a knock came from the front door. I glanced at the wall clock. Early? I grinned. Perhaps she was as eager to spend time with me as I her.

After all, with her leaving the day after the ball, we didn't have a lot of time to work with.

My welcome smile stilled on my face as I opened the door.

Allison Duncan? Here?

"Hello, Graeme."

I gave my head a shake and looked past her to see a silver Kia Sportage in the drive.

"Allison? What are you doing here?"

She pulled her suit jacket closer around her slim body, her smile hesitant. "I was at Craighill working on dress designs and thought I should take the opportunity to . . . see you."

Designs? Lennox had hired Allison to design the gowns?

"Before you ask, I used your name to get the job. When I heard someone was looking for designers for the Edwardian Experience, I jumped at the chance. Mrs. Lennox had gotten down to three choices, so I"—she looked away—"I mentioned knowing you to see if it would help me get the upper hand." She raised her gaze again, chin high. "I'm not proud of it, but I needed this job in my portfolio, so I thought I'd better clear the air on that before you heard it elsewhere."

She looked good. Great, even. My attention swung back to her face. She'd cut her hair shorter, shoulder length, but the style looked good on her. Every bit the elegant woman I'd known and loved in the past, with a little extra class in her wardrobe. She'd even worn heels. To my house. And a picture of Katie stumbling into the same door drenched, muddy, while supporting a limping Lachlan almost inspired my grin.

Her confession only dug the truth deeper.

The heartbreak of nearly two years ago actually turned for my good in the long run. Her goals hadn't changed. Neither had mine.

But I had. I knew better what I wanted and how to compromise.

"I hoped to have some time to speak with you." Her gaze implored. "To . . . apologize and, perhaps, I don't know . . . sort out things in a better way than we did two years ago."

I hesitated. Katie was due to arrive in a half hour, and I still had to sort out my arguments for how we could stay together. Whatever they were. Whatever she'd be willing to sacrifice for me and Lachlan.

But it shouldn't take long. And maybe I needed this too.

I stepped back and welcomed her in, gesturing toward the living room.

"It's not changed at all, has it?" She chuckled, glancing around the room before dusting off one of the chairs with her palm to take a seat. "I suppose that answers one of my questions."

"You had a question about my furnishings?" I kept my stance at a distance.

"Not your furnishings, but they do reflect one of the things that pushed us apart, I think."

Lachlan came down the stairs, his expression slow to register recognition.

Allison stood. "Oh, well, but you've changed."

"Lachlan, you remember Allison?" I offered, watching the lad slowly comprehend. His frown deepened, especially when Allison stood and offered her hand to him.

"You've grown three inches or more."

"Aye." The boy looked to me and, with my encouraging nod, took her hand in a brief and awkward hold.

"Why don't you and Wedge take a wee dauner until Katie comes."

Lachlan sent Allison another look and then headed for the door, his sharp whistle calling Wedge to follow.

"I thought perhaps you may have given him over to your parents to raise." She sat back down, smoothing her palms over her skirt. "To have two parents for him."

Interesting assessment. "They're well in his life still, but I gave my word to Greer. Besides, I love the lad like he was my own."

She nodded, the previous smile not as warm. What had she been thinking?

"I shouldn't have left the way I did." Her declaration came slowly, soft. "I'm ashamed of leaving when I did."

"Thank ye for that." I rounded the couch and sat down across from her. "I can be a very thrawn person, especially when I have a hard time dealing with changes. So much of my world had been turned on its head."

"I was stubborn too. I know it." She raised those green eyes to mine. "But you weren't willing to compromise. On anything. And I felt suffocated."

I took the accusation. It was partly true, as far as having difficulty with compromising. The deepest pain of change had just happened—had been happening for a year as I watched my sister die. My heart couldn't manage another change. Another shift in what felt like a sinking world at the time. "I was barely holding on within the familiar, loving world I had here. I cannae imagine how I or Lachlan would have healed as well anywhere else."

"But you didn't even try." Her gaze pierced into mine. Hurt? Anger?

"Try?"

"To give me space. Freedom." She shook her head. "If you'd just let me know my work and dreams were important to you. That you were as willing to sacrifice yours as I was mine."

"You knew it already. We'd discussed it before Greer became sick. I'd always supported you."

"Everything changed when she got sick. You barely left the island. Never had time for me." She folded her arms across her chest. "It's like I lost you long before we split up."

I wasn't sure how to respond. I'd put so much of myself into the relationship with Allison to promote her design goals and travel with her to her events in an effort to further her career. And then Greer received her diagnosis. And all I could do to keep my sanity was make my world as small as possible. Keep my family nearby. Serve my sister and nephew.

I'd continued coming and going with Allison when possible, but those opportunities became fewer as Greer's disease progressed. And Allison drew further away. Complained about my absence at her events.

"My whole world had turned upside down, Allison."

"What about mine?" She stiffened. "You'd been my biggest fan, the strength I needed when I was afraid to try. And then you were gone. Or worse, you were hateful."

"Hateful?"

Her eyes grew glossy, her pain still on the surface. "Do you even realize how you were then?"

Air burst from me. "Allison, I barely remembered how to breathe each day for a few weeks, so no, I don't remember."

Her eyes widened and then her jaw tensed. "You gave ultimatums. It was either give up my career or leave forever." She stood. "That wasn't fair."

I slowly came to my feet. "As I recall, you weren't willing to compromise either. It was follow you to Edinburgh straightaway or don't ever come at all."

"You pushed me away."

"Did I?" I raked a hand through my hair. "Or was I trying to keep you close because I needed you?"

Stating the truth hit me. I had needed her. And she'd left. The pain had turned me inward, and I withdrew from everyone but my family. Then I focused upward when I realized no earthly being had the strength or ability to heal my heart. And that's when I changed. When I found peace. When I began to heal.

I drew in a breath to steady myself. Perhaps Allison hadn't found her own peace. "I'd just lost my twin sister, Allison. My head wasn't working and I may have pushed too hard for an answer because I . . . I wanted you near."

Some of the fight drained from her posture. "And I couldn't handle being in the middle of all the . . . sadness. I had work I needed to do."

And the picture came clearer with each sentence. Mum had been right. We both were at fault. Her selfishness. My grief and need to control. It created a cataclysmic encounter where no one won. "I'm not the same I was then." I sighed. "I shouldn't have pressed for an answer, to expect you to stay. But I had a grieving little boy to think about and—"

"I . . . I didn't have the energy to manage you and your grief. The timing of everything was just . . . well, hard for everyone."

Katie would have stayed.

The thought pushed through my mind. She would have given up everything to stay. I just knew it.

"We both were wrong, Allison. And I'm sorry for my part." I pushed my hands into the pockets of my jeans. "You were asking more from me than I could give. You wanted me to leave my family in the middle of our grief. I couldn't."

Something shifted in her expression, a pleading sort of look. She took a step forward. "Are you saying that if you hadn't been grieving, you'd have left Mull and come with me?"

"Hadn't I shown you enough? How much I loved you?"

She drew another step closer, her eyes watery. "Then come with me. Let's start over. You can craft and I can design. We can have the life we dreamed together." She took my hand. "I . . . I've never stopped loving you, Graeme. I've tried to have other relationships, but no one has loved me the way you did. Can we have a second chance?"

Katie

I pulled my bicycle to a stop at the side of Graeme's cottage and studied the silver SUV in the drive. Had I seen that car before? At Craighill?

Mrs. Lennox? Seemed unlikely with only a few hours before the ball.

Which reminded me of why I'd shown up a little early to the lunch date—I needed to cut it short because all guests were encouraged to be ready for promotional photographs an hour before the ball began. I looked down at the clock on my phone.

Which meant a half hour for lunch, at most, and then I'd need to ride my bike back to Craighill to get a shower. I grinned as I thought about Graeme seeing me in that ball gown. I'd never had a Cinderella moment, but to be honest, I related the most to that particular princess because of her losing her shoe.

Belle was way too clever to be relatable.

Aurora too elegant.

But a poor girl who kept soot on her face, occasionally talked to animals, and had a tendency to lose footwear? I could see myself in her.

A half hour was enough time for some much-needed conversation with Graeme though.

And maybe a snuggle with Lachlan and Wedge? Okay, Wedge snuggled. Lachlan wrestled.

My phone buzzed in my hand and an unfamiliar and local number popped up.

Katie, it's Calum. Your book is brilliant. You are one of the most natural storytellers I've ever read.

I stared at the phone for a good fifteen seconds, rereading the text. Seriously? He thought my book was "brilliant."

Me: Are you serious?
Calum: I know it's hard to believe with my ever-ready wit, but I am very serious. And I want your permission to share the book with my editor.

It took about twenty seconds to comprehend that one. I'd looked up Calum—or his pseudonym, C.J. Cunningham—and he was published by one of the top publishing houses in the world. And he thought my book worth a look by them?

Calum: It's a great opportunity. Even if he doesn't take it, which I highly doubt, he'll give great feedback.

And opportunities like this never came for new authors. Ever. Not that I was completely new, but definitely new to fiction.

Calum: Katie, it's a braw story.

The compliment alone had me a little lightheaded.

Me: I don't want to miss the opportunity, Calum. And if you think it's really worth a look???
Calum: I do! I'll send it right now to prove my point.
Me: Are you serious?
Calum: I don't joke about excellent writing, Katie. That's just rude.

I chuckled, half because of his humor and the other half out of sheer disbelief.

Me: Thank you so much. I'm a little astonished.
Calum: Thank you for allowing me to read it. I see excellent possibilities here and will let you know what I hear. Is there another phone number or email address I could use to contact you after you leave Scotland? (Assuming you're going to leave?)

I had to leave. I had a job to do.

Me: Was that a threat, premonition, or wish?
Calum: I can see why Graeme likes you. Quick wit is a winning feature.

Calum: But not a threat. I only make those in fiction. But as for the latter two? Perhaps. You do fit in rather well with our family, and it would be nice to have another writer around. No one else understands the plight of imaginary friends.

I grinned, touched and amused by his words. The idea of leaving kept getting harder. But I . . . I didn't want to give up traveling. Graeme had a hard enough time just talking about showing his work abroad, so how on earth would he handle a girlfriend who spent a large portion of her time as a nomad?

Of course, if this turned out to be true love, I'd be willing to make certain sacrifices. But would he ask me to stop traveling entirely?

I shook the thoughts away.

You're getting ahead of yourself there, Katie-girl. You've only had some life-altering kisses so far, not a proposal.

With quick work, I sent along my email address and dismounted the bike I'd been using as a stool during my text conversation. I'd barely turned the corner of the house when Lachlan and Wedge came into view, the former scowling. The latter ran up to me for a greeting.

"What's the matter with you, Lachlan?"

The boy rolled his eyes. "Lunch is going to be late."

I laughed. "That's okay." Then I frowned. "Hmm . . . but I may have to miss it because I have to get be at Craighill earlier than I thought."

"I'd rather be with you at Craighill than here. Uncle Graeme's got a visitor, and I don't like her."

Her? "Oh, I didn't realize someone else was joining us for lunch."

"She just showed up, and Uncle Graeme sent me for a walk to get me out of the way."

I looked back at the cottage. "I don't want to interfere if it's something serious. Maybe I should just head on back to Craighill and talk with your uncle tonight."

"But you're leaving tomorrow." The little lilt in his voice twisted my heart into knots.

I knelt down in front of him, and Wedge took the move as an invitation to lick my face. I nudged the dog aside and placed my palms on Lachlan's shoulders. "I promise you that I'll be back, if for nothing else than to visit you and your granny."

"And Uncle Graeme."

I nodded. "And Uncle Graeme." If Graeme wanted that too, because I sure did. "I still have more Scotland country to see."

"And you haven't even eaten at Lochside Café or Shona's Bakehouse. That's a crime."

I nodded, happy to have distracted him from those watery eyes. "Or Fishnish."

"Och, aye. You haveta try Fishnish."

"See?" I squeezed his shoulders. "How can I stay away?"

For being such a little boy, those eyes of his caught on to my meaning, because in a very unexpected turn of events, he reached over and hugged me.

My whole body froze for a second. My heart nearly exploded.

And that's when I knew, whether Graeme and I sorted out a future or not, I had to come back to Mull.

For Lachlan.

And Mirren. And the crazy book club.

But I really hoped for Graeme too.

I stood up and walked back toward my bike. "Once your uncle finishes his conversation with his friend, would you let him know I'll see him tonight?"

"Aye." Lachlan slipped his hand into mine as I walked, and I saved the feel to memory. Another sense of belonging washed over me, and I sent a thankful glance heavenward. "But she's no friend. Not anymore."

"Oh." I looked back over at the house. *Who could it be?*

"And I'm glad they didnae marry."

My feet came to a stop. Marry? That was unexpected. "Marry?"

"Aye, Allison and Graeme were set to marry a long time ago, before Mum died. I dinnae ken why she showed up now after being gone for so long."

Allison.

My bottom jaw loosed.

Allison Duncan. Practically perfect in every way Allison Duncan? Classy and gorgeous designer Allison Duncan?

Graeme was engaged to *her*?

The thought took a few seconds to congeal. I mean, opposites attract and all, but . . .

"She wants to sort out things, whatever that means," Lachlan continued as we came to a stop beside my bike. "But I think Uncle Graeme is too smart to go with her when he can keep someone like you."

I almost pulled the little boy into another hug. The idea of Graeme keeping me did have a nice ring to it.

"If *he* kept me, you'd have to keep me too, you know."

"That's all right with me." He nodded his disheveled head of ginger hair. "I wager it would take the two of us to help keep you alive anyway."

My smile flared so wide I almost lost control of my laugh again. "That's probably a good idea."

I leaned down one more time and gave Wedge a scratch behind the ear, then pulled Lachlan into another hug. "I'll come back, Lachlan," I whispered into his ear. "I promise."

He looked up at me, his smile so trusting.

As soon as I got my next break. Right back across the ocean.

I hopped on my bicycle and started back down the drive. Even if Graeme reunited with Allison, I could still come to see Lachlan. And Mirren. And even Calum.

Because the truth was, Graeme and Allison could be reconciling right at this very minute. I swallowed through my tightening throat and gave my head a shake.

Don't be illogical, Katie.

You are a sensible adult.

Graeme is a good guy.

This is not a Hallmark miscommunication scene.

I looked back at the house.

But this was real life. And it was always a risk.

And sometimes the girl didn't get the guy.

Dave: You won again, Katie! You won the Vision Award for your category.

I should bask in the excitement of it all. Of the recognition of my work. Of my princess moment. Of finally realizing that my heart could belong somewhere again!

But the potential ship of Graeme and Allison—Graemison?—tempted to sink my wavering confidence. I pushed the thought away.

You are more than a relationship with Graeme MacKerrow.

Me: Oh wow, what an honor! I hadn't seen the announcement yet because I've been so busy getting ready for the ball.

Dave: Ball? Oh, right. The Regency thing.

Me: Edwardian, Dave. It's Edwardian. You've read all of my articles about it. You should know by now.

Dave: They're not the same? Well, anyway, I hope you've been really considering the editing position, Katie. You're a natural. The other writers love how you've taken a special interest in helping them grow. I knew you were made for this.

And I *had* enjoyed it. More than I thought I would. But enough to fully replace traveling to be with Graeme? He probably wasn't even that serious about me, even if he wasn't kissing Allison right now.

I cringed at the visual, along with the feeling of a fist tightening around my heart.

Dave: Well, enjoy your evening and plan to rest up on the plane tomorrow, because you won't be taking a breath for a few days.

Oh no. What did that mean?

Me: Why did I just get a really bad feeling, Dave?
Dave: I've rearranged your schedule a little and booked an 11:00 a.m. flight for you out of Edinburgh tomorrow morning.

Eleven in the morning? It was easily over four hours to Edinburgh from Mull, and that's if I caught the ferries at the right time.

Me: Dave, that means I'd have to leave Mull by four o'clock in the morning to even attempt to catch my flight.
Dave: It's the only way you'll make the awards ceremony in New York.

I groaned. The Vision Award ceremony. This was crazy.

Me: When will I sleep?

Though I already knew the answer.

Dave: Attend the ceremony tomorrow evening, fly to Kentucky for your next assignment, and then you have the next two weeks off.

This shouldn't sting so much, but it did. I was hoping for a few more hours in the morning with Graeme and maybe Lachlan. Leaving at noon from Mull provided much more of a farewell cushion than before dawn.

Dave: You weren't able to attend the ceremony last year.
Me: I was in the rainforest without phone reception, Dave.
Dave: Right, but you promised that if you won again, you'd accept in person. World on a Page gets great publicity from this. And it would be good for you too. You should be proud.

He was right. I'd promised. And I *was* so proud of my writing and the stories and the people I got to celebrate.

Me: I am proud.
Dave: And if you take up editing (which you should), it will naturally reduce your travel time so you're less likely to be up for another Vision Award. Sleep afterward.
Me: I got it. Butt-crack of dawn it is!
Dave: That's my girl. I'll email you all the travel details. Can't wait for the final Scottish installment. It's been some of your best work to date.

I'd loved writing it. I wasn't usually featured so prominently in my stories. My mishaps were more anecdotal to the stories I collected and retold along the way. But I'd loved *living* out the adventures during my time on Mull, even if there were a few moments I wasn't sure I'd survive. A smile pulled at my lips. They were *my* near-death moments, part of my story here in Scotland. For a long time I'd skirted around being the focus of my own story. After all, I'd never really fit into my mom's world or Sarah's shadow, and social media gave me the unique vantage of redirecting the interest toward others.

That had worked. Because who would want to hear about me?

But maybe, when you start figuring out where you belong, you start falling in love with your own story too. Because . . . love does that. It changes everything.

My phone blinked with a message.

Dave: Your loyal fans want to know what happened with the #hotscot.

I released a sigh and stared over at the ball gown waiting for me to tuck, fasten, and squeeze into.

I wanted to know the same thing.

CHAPTER 21

Graeme

I was in no state to attend a ball.

In fact, I'd never thought of myself as the type to attend one in the first place.

But after Allison's visit, then the message relayed by Lachlan about Katie—and the added worry that whatever I said to Katie could possibly scare her away—I was left flummoxed. I couldn't seem to get anything right.

I almost forgot my kilt pin. Couldn't find my sporran. And nearly walked out of the house without attaching my fly plaid. Thankfully, Mum had stopped in to take Lachlan for the night, so she caught my oversight and proceeded to attach the cloth to my shoulder. Someone would have thought I was getting married, I was so off my head.

The conversation with Allison proved all the more how badly I needed to ensure Katie of her freedom—that I'd support her future. That I wasn't trying to tie her down or squelch her dreams. The last thing I wanted to do was scare her away. I wanted to create tomorrows with her.

I drew in a deep breath as I walked through the doors of Craighill. And I'd embrace whatever those tomorrows might look like.

And then I entered the ballroom into a surprising host of people. Two dozen, at least. They had to be acquaintances of the Lennoxes, from the accents I heard as I walked through the room. I even noted a few reporters.

I steered clear of them.

As I studied the space, I had to admit I was chuffed at the look of the room. Seeing one's ancestral home adorned and celebrated in such finery did any Scot's heart good. Even if the adornment came in Edwardian fashion.

It meant the place wasn't sitting abandoned and forgotten. Someday, if God allowed, the MacKerrows would run their own business from these walls, celebrating the culture and history, hosting weddings, welcoming visitors.

It was a brilliant plan with the family all in.

Katie could bring her own creativity to it all too. As part of the family.

But for now, even if it involved an extended partnering with Lennox and her dramatics, the house was well cared for and brimming with people who appreciated it.

So where was my particular person of interest?

And then, as if my thoughts materialized into reality, my attention caught on a shimmery sea of teal and ginger locks.

All thoughts of Craighill, kilt pins, and ex-fiancées disappeared. In fact, most everything cleared from my head at the sight of Katie Campbell coming down the stairs in a gown of sea and starlight.

My life had been filled with many bonnie things, but the longer I looked at her, the dimmer those other things became in comparison. Her hair was piled in fiery curls atop her head, leaving ample view of her bare neckline.

My feet responded of their own accord, approaching her.

She caught sight of me as she neared the last step and froze for a second before stumbling.

But I caught her. And immediately my lungs filled with honeysuckle and sea and Katie. Losh, I wanted to catch her over and over again. Right into my arms. And never let go.

Allison's blame immediately came to mind. But I couldn't hold on too tight, could I? I had to grasp her and this future loosely, and

I was poor at that. Because when I held on to someone, it was for keeps.

"That stumble was your fault this time," she whispered, her gaze trailing over me as her smile crooked like a temptation. "I got distracted by how braw you look."

"It's no comparison to you, Katie Campbell. I've never seen such a bonnie lass."

Her brow raised as if she didn't believe me. "I would argue with you, but the word *lass* from your lips is kryptonite to my sarcasm." She sighed. "It's pretty much kryptonite to my logic too."

"Ah!" I held out my hand to her with a bow. "Then I'll make wise use of it, as long as I'm able. Might I have this dance?" I wiggled my brows. "Lass?"

Katie

No man should show up dressed like that and not bring a marriage proposal with him.

And then he goes and looks at me the way he does while adding "lass" in his excellent, deep-voiced accent!

How was I supposed to let go of this . . . of him, tomorrow? How could my life take a full 360 from travel writer with no roots to Scotland-has-my-heart-and-future-forever? Well, not Scotland. Graeme.

And Lachlan.

And Mirren.

But my love for them all blended in with moody lochs and heather-cloaked hillsides and faery stories and rainy days. They seemed to complete the jigsaw puzzle of my heart, and I just wasn't sure if all the pieces would end up coming together in the end.

Not when I had to leave so soon.

Graeme drew me into a waltz as a stringed quartet played from a balcony above the room. Mrs. Lennox had outdone herself. And even with all her fumbles and mistakes, her Edwardian Experience deserved a raving review from this travel writer. In fact, after taming her prejudice about working with the locals and hiring a few for the house, she'd even begun to endear herself a little to the community.

"I'm sorry about Allison." Graeme's voice pulled my attention away from the room and to his familiar eyes. "I didnae ken she was here."

"Well, she's an excellent designer." I dipped my chin toward my dress, not sure how to turn the conversation. "I've never worn anything as elegant as this before, and I refuse to drink anything for fear of spillage."

"Katie." The way he said my name held some sort of homing ability to eliminate words from my head. "You're beautiful already, all the way through."

All the way through? No one had ever said that to me. Or looked at me the way he did. My breath hitched in my throat, and I lowered my gaze, his tenderness too much. Too tempting to fall into without any certainty. And that's what I wanted from him. An assurance that he was as committed to figuring out how to make this relationship between us work as I was.

I was already reordering my future. And the realization shocked through me with a few amazing tingles in its wake.

I loved him.

I loved Graeme MacKerrow.

And it wasn't just because of the kilt.

Though that helped a whole lot.

Or the shoulders.

Which were incredibly easy on the eyes, with or without the shirt.

But my heart knew. With him was where my heart belonged.

"Are . . . are you okay?" My brain had been reeling with plans since last night. "With her . . . and you?"

Excellent command of the English language there, Katie.

"She came to seek closure, I believe." He searched my eyes. "And I needed it too, because it's sometimes difficult to move forward when you have loose strings from the past."

"Move forward?" That sounded good.

"Aye." His grin crooked, and my heart stumbled even more thoroughly than my feet.

"Miss Campbell." Mrs. Lennox stepped up beside us, pausing our dance. "May I steal you away for a little while for an interview? Your boss informed me this afternoon that you were the winner of the Vision Award, and a few reporters are here for the ball and would like to interview you."

I looked over at Graeme, who only nodded.

"I'll be back as soon as I can."

But "as soon as I can" turned out to be much longer than I'd hoped. Graeme and I got in another dance, then a conversation at one of the nearby tables, before we were pulled away to help teach some of the English guests how to perform the Gay Gordons.

And then an American reporter wanted to interview him about his regalia.

When we finally found time alone again together, the night had waned into early morning, and I knew my time was running short. We started another waltz in the hope that dancing would deter anyone else from interrupting us.

"It has to be one of the last dances of the night," Graeme said, lowering his mouth close to my ear. "And I'm happy to spend it with you for as long as I can."

The idea of forever teased my happy heart.

"That sounds lovely to me." Because tomorrow was already here. And words needed to be spoken.

"Graeme—"

"Katie."

We both chuckled at our twinned responses, and he nodded for me to continue.

I held his gaze and squeezed his hand holding mine in an attempt to break the news. "I . . . I have to leave earlier than planned."

The V in his brow made an appearance, so I explained the change only to have the V deepen. "How early?"

I cringed. "In a few hours."

"*That* early." His shoulders dropped with his sigh. "I'd hoped for more time to talk."

"Me too."

He nodded. "But we could phone each other?"

I smiled at the suggestion. A definite start in the right direction. "That sounds great. I'll be in constant work mode for the next three days, but after that, I'm back at the farm for a while. And I'd love to . . . talk."

"Aye." His gaze roamed over my face, saying things I wanted to interpret in the most forever of ways.

"My schedule isn't ideal, I know, but I'll make it work out."

His expression suddenly shifted. He firmed his jaw as if preparing for battle. "I want you to know that we can take this between us . . . slow, easy-like." He released a long breath. "With no strings attached."

The sweet warmth of all those happily-ever-afters sudden came to a screeching halt. No strings attached? I'd been living with no strings for so long, it was the last thing I wanted. I wanted declarations. Promises. Strings so tight that they tied me to him for as long as we both shall live.

But I swallowed down my disappointment. My job wasn't an easy pill to swallow for someone whose heart and life was grounded in one place. No wonder he wanted to take things slowly. "Well, I definitely plan to make another trip to Mull really soon."

"That's good to hear." His palm tightened on my waist, and he looked away. "We'll take the time we can find with each other and see how it works out. Nothin' serious. Free to follow . . . our . . . dreams."

He grimaced as if he didn't like the taste of those words.

Well, I didn't like the sound of them. Nothing serious? I'd never wanted anything to be more serious in my life. For the first time in a long time, I was ready to stop running away and run *toward* exactly what I wanted.

Him.

But I needed to readjust my expectations because, clearly, he wasn't as sure.

He faltered.

Was it doubts inspired by his meeting with Allison? Or him second-guessing my ability to survive another year? Or maybe he really wasn't sure about the fact that my life consisted of social media videos, strange conversations with a phone screen, and multiple flights away from home.

It all made sense. Every hesitation.

His heart was tethered to this land. Lachlan needed something stable.

And . . . maybe what I had to offer *wasn't* enough for him.

Maybe I wasn't worth the risk.

Because me, my life, and my brokenness were a lot to take on.

So I sighed out the dream and willed, unsuccessfully, my heart to stay in one piece.

"Okay," I whispered. "We can see how it will work out."

Graeme

"You said what?" Mum's voice took on the sort of edge that usually sent me running to my room as a lad.

Calum buried his face in his hands.

Dad grimaced and looked away.

I'd fallen into trouble and I didn't even know how or why. "What pushed Allison away two years ago was me holding on too tight. Not giving the freedom to grow and not supporting her dreams, so I told Katie those things. The things she needed to hear. Nothing serious. Free to pursue her dreams. No strings."

"You have a good heart, lad." This from Dad, who recovered the fastest. "But you're fair dafty sometimes when it comes to women."

"You're not alone, brother." Calum sighed as if he understood from experience. "All men are when it comes to women, especially the right one."

I raised my arms in defeat and slid down in the nearest kitchen table chair. "What else was I supposed to say? I didnae want to suffocate her or scare her away. And I didnae want her to think she had to change everything for me to care about her."

Mum stared at me as she poured a cup of tea, her expression doubting any intelligence behind my eyes.

"What do you want, lad?" This from Dad, who relaxed back in the chair and crossed his arms. "Do you want a serious relationship with Katie or no?"

I scanned the faces at the table in front of me as if they were the ones who'd lost their minds. "Of course I do. If I had my way, I'd have asked her to stay forever. I dinnae love by halves, ye ken. It's all or nothing. I nearly choked on the words as I said them to her anyway."

"Och, Graeme." Mum took a large drink of her tea.

"She's not Allison." Calum leaned forward, hands folded on the table, his attention intent on me. "Not even close."

"I know that." I wasn't that much of a numpty. "She's better. Worlds better." Why did romance have to be so tricky? "For me anyway. For Lachlan too."

"Exactly." Mum placed her cup on the table with a clink. "But think about her past, Graeme. It's been filled with people who treated her as if love wasn't serious. The strings she needed to tie her to a place were cut. She's spent years looking for somewhere or someone to keep her. A place to belong. And I believe she saw that in you."

Mum's words barbed through my chest.

"Strings dinnae have to mean tangles or knots." She shook her head. "They can be the threads to help her find her way home."

The implication, the realization, knocked the air from me. In my attempt to make things right, I'd gotten it all wrong. Blundered like the clumsiest man on the face of the earth.

I groaned and planted my face in my hands. How did I not see it clearly? What had happened to my head? Katie may stumble on her feet, but I'd caused her heart to stumble. And that was a thousand times worse.

"Does being in love make every man an eejit?" I mumbled, looking back at my family.

"Aye," Dad answered, putting his hand on my shoulder in solidarity. "But we improve with age." He shrugged. "Most of the time."

"In love, is it?" Mum's grin lit her eyes as she raised her tea in salute. "Now I see your brains starting to move in the right direction. What do you plan to do with all the sudden brilliance?" Mum folded her arms, a challenging tilt to her chin. "Because I know you're smarter than what I've seen today."

"I think I need you to keep an eye on Lachlan for a few days." I stood from the table.

"Is that so?" Her grin grew. "And why is that?"

I met her stare for stare and raised my chin. "Because I need to go catch me a very particular lass."

Katie

I'd barely been back for one day, but my progress showed in each room of the farmhouse. Of course working from before daybreak probably helped.

My addled brain refused the respite of sleep.

And counting sheep never helped.

So I put my plans into motion, a little giddy at the design and the headway I'd already made.

A chair gone here. A set of dishes there. Granny's china removed. My favorite pieces of furniture carefully curated and removed.

My favorite things. Only my very favorite. All carefully packed and stored in the two-bedroom apartment over the garage I'd stayed in when I came to visit for summers in college.

That place was all I needed anyway. For just me.

The farmhouse deserved a family.

I dusted my hands off on my jeans and gave the living room another look, my smile spreading into a chuckle. I should have done this years ago.

A car door slammed from outside, and I walked to the porch as Levi and Chrissy pummeled into my stomach for double hugs.

"Hey, guys." I laughed and looked up as Brett and Jessica approached, little Ryan on Jessica's hip. "I'm so glad you were able to come up for a few days. Thanks for making the trip."

"It's good to be here." Brett's gaze roamed over the house, nothing hiding his admiration for this place. The memories here held the same sweetness for him as for me.

I barely kept my grin from tipping into the ridiculous category. This gift was long overdue.

"Hey, kids." Brett turned to Levi and Chrissy. "Run on inside and choose your bedrooms."

It was a game they always played because the farmhouse had six bedrooms, and each held its own special charm and uniqueness. The kids screamed out their excitement and dashed inside as I turned my attention back to their parents' sober faces.

All giddiness shifted into cool warning. "What is it? Is something wrong?"

Jess and Brett paused on the porch and exchanged a look. "We have more than a *few* days to stay, if you don't mind, that is." Jess shook her head, leaning in for a side hug, at which time Ryan took a handful of my hair. "Brett's job laid him off last week."

"What?" My gaze swung to my brother. "Why didn't you tell me?"

He ran a hand over his face. "I didn't want to cast a shadow over your trip."

"But we could have brainstormed some ideas together. Made some plans for your family." I stepped forward.

"I've looked into a part-time remote job that I can work around my schedule with the kids," Jess added, shifting Ryan to her other hip before sending Brett a gentle smile. "We'll find a way to make it work."

Somehow, her confidence transferred over to Brett so much that his posture even straightened a little. The tenderness of their willingness to fight for and encourage each other was definitely relationship-goal worthy.

And adding my own special surprise to their lives at this particular juncture only made it ten times better! A little twist in *their* story—a good twist.

"I've already had a few businesses near here show interest," Brett added, his smile much more hopeful than it had been a moment before. "So I think I can at least find something to keep us from increasing our debt."

They followed me inside as my grin fought for release, the anticipation nearly exploding inside of me. We walked down the hallway and turned into the living room.

Three . . . two . . . one . . .

"Wait." Brett's response came first. "What's going on in here?"

"Are you moving?" Jess asked, her gaze taking in the much less cluttered space. "Did you have a garage sale? I thought you just arrived last night."

I turned toward them, bringing my palms together like the delighted genius I was. Okay, overdue genius, but didn't that still count as genius? "I just moved my personal things into the garage apartment, since that's the only space I really need when I come back to the farm."

"Oh!" Brett nodded, resting his palms on his hips and surveying the room. "You gonna use this place as an Airbnb, then? Smart way to get extra money."

"Well"—I pulled the house keys from my pocket—"that's something the two of you will have to decide." I tossed the keys to him, and he stumbled back as he caught them.

"What?"

I laughed. "I'm giving it to you."

"You're giving what to us?" Brett looked down at the keys in his hand, completely confused.

"What do you mean?" Jess shot a look from me to Brett and back, eyes widening. "The house? Katie, you can't. This is your inheritance."

"This is *our* inheritance. Grandpa and Gran only wanted it to stay with a family member who would love and appreciate it. You both do that." I waved toward the room. "And I don't need it. I'm keeping the garage apartment and some acres connected to it, but I'm deeding the rest of the farm over to you." I shrugged. "If you want it."

Brett's jaw dropped. Jess caught her laugh with her hands, her eyes shimmering with fresh tears.

Yes. This was right. Perfectly right.

"Katie?" Brett ran a hand through his rust-colored hair. "Are you crazy?"

"We know I am." I raised my palms in helpless acceptance. "But are *you* interested?"

"Why would you do this?" Jess shook her head, tears brimming until one spilled over. "This is your home."

"No, it isn't." I stepped close to her, taking her hand. "Maybe it was once upon a time when Grandpa and Gran lived here, but it's only been a big holding spot for me for years now. It deserves better. It needs a family to fill it with love, and I can't think of a better one to do that."

Jess looked over at Brett, whose own eyes were a little red-rimmed.

He stepped closer, searching my face. "Are you sure?"

"Without a doubt." I laughed. "A hundred percent."

"We won't have a mortgage, Brett." Jess placed a palm on his arm. "And you can practice all those handyman skills you love so much."

"And the cottage on the back acres would make a great Airbnb for extra money," I added, unable to stop my grin as the joyful reality of it began to dawn more and more on their faces.

With a sob from Jess and a laugh from Brett, they both took me into their arms, leaving baby Ryan to double-fist my hair with great zeal and me to join in a little crying myself.

Without a doubt, *this* story was going to be one of my favorites. "I'm going to take that as a yes and will drive into town to get the paperwork started tomorrow."

"Thank you, Katie." Brett took hold of my shoulders, his gray eyes watery and sparkling all at once. "This . . . this has always been a dream of mine."

"I know." My vision blurred. "And I'm so glad to make this dream come true for you. I'm just sorry it took me so long."

Jess spoke through a sob, still shaking her head in disbelief. "What caused you to make this decision?"

Or who.

"Well, Scotland." I wiped a hand over my eyes and squinted as I confessed. "And a certain guy who I hope will become more than just a memory, if I have any influence at all."

"Ah, I thought I heard something special in your voice when you talked about him," Brett said, taking Ryan from Jess's arms.

"You mean the guy who rescued you from the loch?" Jess's eyes widened.

"And the cow," Brett added.

"The hot Scot?" Jess finished, eyes wide, with Brett sending her a curious grin.

"The same." I drew in a deep breath. "I'm heading back as soon as I can because I need to let him know how I feel."

"Katie, that's fantastic." Jess pulled me into another hug. "And if he's smart, he'd never let you go."

A crash sounded from upstairs, followed by a scream, and Brett shot Jess a look before both of them dashed off in the direction of the noise. With all the curious nooks and crannies of this turn-of-the-century home—and over fifty acres to explore—this was the perfect place to raise an energetic family who had a whole lot of love in them.

I chuckled again and started toward the kitchen when the sound of another car door detoured my steps to the front door.

I froze.

My breath caught.

Standing in my front yard near a little red Toyota was Graeme MacKerrow, looking a little lost and a whole lot of gorgeous. I gave my head a little shake. Graeme? Here? I pushed open the screen door and stepped out on the porch, still unsure whether I should believe my eyes or not. After all, I'd not slept very well for a few days, so daydreams were possible.

And daydreaming about him was unavoidable.

His gaze held mine, as if measuring my response to him being here, but my pulse seemed to know the rhythm of this meeting.

He wore jeans and a blue button-down, which did his shoulders and chest all sorts of favors. Not that they needed any help. As a matter of fact, fatigue hadn't hurt my X-ray vision one bit. I took a few slow steps forward, making it to the bottom of the porch.

He neared, hands in his pockets, before stopping a few feet from touching distance. "This . . . this place is fair impossible to find."

I loved his voice. "It can be," I rasped, afraid to blink.

We stood in silence. I just kept staring because I wasn't quite sure if what I was seeing was real. Graeme MacKerrow in little old Waynesville, North Carolina?

And then the implications of his traveling across the world to this tiny part of the Blue Ridge Mountains registered in my mind. It could mean only one thing.

He'd come for me.

Me.

The man who didn't leave home. The man whose heart had a triple-lock hold on the Highlands. The man who offered a no-strings-attached relationship?

"It's a lovely place." He gestured toward the house with his chin. "And the mountains remind me of home."

I smiled then. "Yeah, they do." I shifted a little closer, stuffing my own hands in my pockets. "It's been in the family for over a hundred years."

He nodded, looking away and back. "Family land is good to have."

"Yeah, gives a sense of roots, I've heard."

His lips quirked up on one side, and he studied the landscape with renewed interest . . . avoiding my face. Was he nervous? My heart swelled with so much emotion my chest ached.

I loved him.

"But it's not going to be mine for much longer."

His gaze fastened on mine. "It's not?"

"I . . . I'm signing it over to my brother Brett and his wife, Jessica, because"—I drew in a breath, taking the risk—"I realized that this place isn't really home for me anymore."

"No?" He edged a step closer, the wariness in those eyes shifting into something much more confident. Knee-weakeningly confident.

I shook my head. "I've fallen in love with a different place." My voice shook as he closed the distance with another step forward. "Different people."

"Have you now?" The dip in his octave stole my breath a little.

"Aye." My word shivered a little. "With . . . with Scotland."

He paused only a second before taking another step. "Scotland?"

I shrugged. "And Lachlan."

"Aye." His grin tipped. "He's one to love, and that's a fact."

"And I adore your parents." I pressed my fist into my chest as tears blurred Graeme's face in my vision. "Especially your mom."

His next step brought him within touching distance, those mesmerizing eyes of his searching mine. "I'm pretty sure they like you better than me right now."

A quiet laugh shook from me, along with a few stray tears. I braced myself and took the maiden's leap across the impossible space between reality and hope. "I've been wandering a long time, trying to find out where I belonged, but I've never felt so much at home as when I'm with you."

Without another hesitation, Graeme pulled me into his arms, wrapping me in the warmth of his body and scent. "I'm sorry I fumbled through what I wanted to say to you during the ball, Katie." He whispered the words near my ear. "I was an eejit."

I drew back, looking up at him. "Do you want to try again?"

"Aye." He ran a thumb over my cheek, catching a tear, his gaze never leaving mine. "I want you to belong with me. To rely on me to catch you."

He caught my sob with his lips, cradling my face in his large, tenderly rough hands. And I kissed him back between laughs and sobs. Held him close. Breathed in his familiar nearness. The taste of his lips on mine, the strength and security in those arms only pinned my heart more tightly to him.

When he pulled back, he brushed my hair from my face, his look intent. Filled with love. "I want you to travel the world, Katie. Gather your stories. But let me be the home you always find your way back to."

Have mercy, what a beautiful collection of words spoken directly to my heart. My palms slid from his neck down to rest on his chest, emotions strangling my voice into a whisper. "Strings attached then?"

"Double knotted." He raised a brow, one corner of his delicious lips teasing northward. "And tied with a bow."

I tugged him into another kiss, my heart filled to overflowing. Even in my wildest dreams, I'd never imagined the story of my own life could look this good—my X-ray vision kicked in—okay, this great.

Or that a man like Graeme MacKerrow waited on the other side of the globe to lead me to the place I belonged.

Home? Oh yes.

"Why don't you bring the man inside before the neighbors start talking."

I looked back toward the house to see my brother and his entire family standing on the front porch watching our little rom-com scene. Graeme looked from me to the porch and then took in the surrounding forest where nary another house could be seen.

"I think we'll take our time, Brett." I waved away my brother, and he chuckled as he walked back into the house.

Arm in arm, we eased our steps toward the porch, stopping to indulge in a few more kisses along the way. "When do you have to go back home?"

One teasing brow tipped upward. "I expected having to spend a week finding you in the middle of this massive country, so I have a little time."

"You planned a whole week to find me." I sighed. "Your chivalry knows no bounds."

He sent me a mock frown, and I kissed him.

The frown softened considerably, so I kissed him again while we stood on the front porch of a farmhouse I loved with a man I loved even more.

Despite all my fumblings and mistakes, my adventures . . . and misadventures had led me home. And as Graeme kissed all my worries away, I welcomed the sweet beginnings of a new story for me. Aye, there was no place like home.

EPILOGUE

Katie

Ten months later

I turned toward the camera I'd poised on my tripod. "We are at the Fraser River today with expert fly fisherman Joe Lawrence, who will be teaching us the art of fly-fishing." I held up the rod. "Already—much to his possible peril—Joe has given me a fly rod, which is different from spin fishing, mostly because of the line we use, right, Joe?"

"That's right." The man adjusted his ball cap and then reached out to tug at the line of my rod. "In fly-fishing, lines are weighted so that you don't need to use a bobber or heavy bait. Lines can be any weight from one to twelve, one being the lightest. We're using a six weight on your rod for small bass or trout you might catch in this river."

"And this is the fly." I raised the fake bait up so that I could edit it later into a closer shot. "As you can see, these flies look a lot like lures we see in spin fishing, but flies are practically weightless."

"Which is why the line needs to be weighted—so your cast will reach its goal," Joe added. "Now casting is a fluid motion where you try to bend the rod to create energy. That's called 'loaded.' You want the rod to come to a stop twice."

He demonstrated the action with his own rod, and it looked a whole lot prettier than what I'd tried to do off-screen. I should have brought Graeme and Lachlan on this assignment. They loved fishing.

I, however, loved the idea of fishing more than the actual action. Especially when it involved finesse.

"Keep the line as straight as possible as you move it from behind to the front with your aim on the fish you have in your sights."

I attempted to replicate his movements, only to have the line fall kerplunk at my feet.

"You need to strengthen your wrist a little, Katie," Joe said. "You don't want a noodle wrist."

I looked in the camera. "Save the noodles for your spaghetti, folks."

"And make sure the rod doesn't go too far behind you or too far in front." He adjusted my hands. "That's a better grip. Now tuck any of your slack under your finger." He nodded, glancing over my head for a second before continuing. "Ready to try again?"

"Sure am!" I looked back at the camera. "Because I'm sure everyone is waiting with *baited* breath."

Joe rolled his eyes with impressive dexterity.

"Okay, let's practice again." And with my usual excitement, I swung the rod back and forward as practice, heeding his ten o'clock–two o'clock rule . . . or at least I tried. The line made it a little farther this time.

Joe looked just over my head again, his grin broadening ever so slightly.

"You know, I think you need to lean back a little this time."

"Lean back?"

Third time's a charm? And so I did, but the line must have gone too far back because it snagged on something. (This was not the first time I'd caught a tree today.) "Um, Joe, I think I leaned so far back I caught another tree."

He shook his head, grin perched beneath his mustache. "You didn't catch a tree."

Oh dear! What did he mean? (Please say it doesn't require stitches!)

I turned and a laugh burst out of me. Along the tree line with Lachlan by his side stood Graeme MacKerrow, my line in one hand and a large box cradled in the other.

"Oh my goodness!" I called, dropping my rod and laughing again. "Best catch of the day."

Lachlan's giggle hit me in the heart. For the past ten months, Mull had become my home base as I continued my travels, and I'd only fallen more in love with Graeme, the MacKerrows, and Scotland every day. Dropping my assignments to one a month helped a lot, because it had given me time to work on my book series, since Calum's publishing house offered me a contract only a month after he'd sent in the story. Dave celebrated my new love for home by giving me the editorial position he'd always planned. And it worked. All of it. Mull, my job, and my loves.

Graeme and Lachlan met me halfway across the rocky river beach line, Graeme looking delicious in his jeans and sweater. I glanced down at my waders, jeans, and rain jacket, and wondered how in the world he could still be attracted to me. Praise God, he had some sort of hero complex, because I certainly kept him fulfilled.

"I thought you guys weren't joining me for a few days yet. I still have some filming to do before we go to your art show in Vancouver."

"It couldnae hurt to show up a few days early to see you." Graeme slid his free arm around me and touched his lips to mine for a quick embrace. "Besides, I'd like to try my hand at fly-fishing. What about you, lad?"

"I'm always ready for fishing."

I grinned at my men and waved back toward Joe. "You know folks will love to see you on my videos. They always do." I started to walk back when the box in Graeme's arms caught my attention. "Did you bring some of your sculptures out here to show Joe? Because I know he'd love to see them. Especially your small birds. He's a fan."

Graeme shook his head and shifted the box nearer. "This is actually for you, lass."

The word from his lips never got old. Or stopped sending sweet tingles down my neck in welcome. "For me?" I searched his face, but his expression gave away nothing. So I looked down at Lachlan. His expression was positively impish.

"What are you guys up to?" I narrowed my eyes and gave them another once-over.

"A surprise." Graeme wiggled his brows and offered the box. "One of the best."

After taking another look at each of their suspicious faces, I lifted the top off the box as Graeme held it. And then I gasped so big, I started coughing.

My book cover for *Katie on the Fly: An Egypt Adventure* stared back at me.

"Oh my goodness. The author copies are here!" I pulled out one of the books. "Can you believe it? Isn't it beautiful?"

"Like the author," Graeme added in low tones, which immediately sent me rewarding him with a kiss to his cheek. If he found wellies, rain jackets, and occasional mud smears attractive, who was I to argue?

"Lachlan, look!" I opened the front of the book to the dedication and read the simple sentence written there. "To Lachlan, who made the story better."

"Me? That's me!" Lachlan's grin spread all the way across his face. "But why me, Katie?"

I knelt down to wrap my arm around his shoulders. "Because once I added a redheaded sidekick for Katie in her adventures, the stories got even better."

"I bet she didn't get lost as much either." He nodded, taking the book in hand and looking down at the page with a little wonder taking up space among those freckles.

I sighed and stared down at the cover again before turning back to Graeme. "This was the best. Thank you two so much for bringing them to me."

"Of course, Katie," Graeme said and then tipped his chin back toward the box. "But you missed something."

I studied him a moment and then looked back inside. In the far left corner, on top of another copy of *Katie on the Fly*, sat a small square box. A little black, jewelry-shaped box.

My gaze flashed to Graeme. We'd talked about marriage dozens of times. I knew we were going to spend the rest of our lives together. But he'd never given me any clear indication of when he'd ask. "Graeme?"

He took the little box out and gave the big box to Lachlan to hold, and then . . . my hot Scot lowered himself down onto the pebbled beach, with the river roaring behind us and an excited ginger-headed boy nearby, and opened the box to reveal a simple but beautiful diamond.

"Katie Campbell, I love you. I want to build a home with you." His beautiful gaze held mine, his smile creasing the corners of his eyes. "Would you share a lifetime of adventures and even misadventures with me?"

I covered my mouth with my hand and lowered to my own knees to touch his wonderfully handsome face. "All of them. Every day."

And he kissed me. Short and sweet, his hooded look giving me a promise for a more thorough celebration later. And I pulled him and Lachlan back into my arms and thanked God.

This, by far, was my best blunder of all.

Falling . . . in love with my Scot.

Author's Note

This book! Oh, I had such a fun time bringing Graeme and Katie to life! And, even more so, bringing you guys with me to Scotland! I hope y'all find many reasons to laugh in this book, many reasons to cheer, and many reasons to find hope. I wouldn't mind if you swooned once or twice either because . . . um . . . #hotscot :)

This story is filled with little hints about finding home or sibling grief or self-confidence—things I've experienced personally and that found their way into Graeme and Katie's story. The weirdest part about this book for me is that I started writing it in April 2021, and my brother unexpectedly died in May. I stopped writing this book then, but getting to come back to it later, with a deeper, more personal, and healthier knowledge of grief, really grounded this story in a way it hadn't before. At that time, I didn't have a solid setting for the story yet, except Scotland, but a wonderful trip in 2022 with author friend Laura Frantz helped me find my location in Mull. So many places in Scotland are captivating, but something about Mull just really cinched the decision for me.

Life is hard. Grief is hard. Feeling unworthy or unwanted is hard. Which is why I love how this story takes all those "hard" things and bathes them in hope and community. We were not meant to live this life alone because of how hard things are. Katie's discovery of belonging is, in part, due to finding her community. I will also add that, personally, faith provides a comfort and strength within those hard times. It's like a sturdy rock beneath all the emotions and conversations and disappointments that doesn't move so that during the "storm" we have a security. St. Augustine of Hippo famously said, "Our souls are restless until they rest in you." May your heart and soul find where it belongs.

Thank you for joining me on this writing journey!

Acknowledgments

As always, a book may start in an author's crazy brain, but it really does take an entire team to make it come to life. I am beyond grateful for my amazing team at Thomas Nelson. Their encouragement, support, and enthusiasm are not only contagious but really make the nuts and bolts of this process easier. Becky, I cannot thank God enough for allow me to work with you!

I also have a little group of early readers/encouragers, who keep (or try to keep) me on the straight and narrow of finishing a book. Thank you so much to Beth Erin, Joy, Alissa, Tiffany, Becky Y, Katie (no relation to Miss Adventure), and Anndrette. Seriously, when I feel like my story stinks, you all swoop in and encourage me to keep going. THANK YOU SO MUCH!

Despite our differences, I am incredibly grateful for Jaime Jo Wright in my life (did you notice the shoutout in this book?). Even though writing romance makes her want to stab herself in the eye with a fork and writing creepy makes me want to bury myself beneath a mountain of pillows, we've developed this fun and supportive friendship. I just always make sure she walks in front of me.

I am so thankful for my agent, Rachel McMillan, who is one of the loudest and proudest cheerleaders in the entire world. Oh, how she champions her clients! If I could have dedicated this book to two people, she would have been the second.

As ever, I could not (and wouldn't want to) walk along this writing path without my amazing family. Some like fiction, some don't, but they all love me and celebrate the good, bad, and frustrating along with me in this journey. I LOVE YOU ALL!!!

P.S. My dad would have liked Graeme MacKerrow, not only because of the woodworking aspect and the faux-grumpiness, but he would have appreciated the beard.

And I am just in awe that God allows me to create stories that entertain but also touch the heart. His strength has definitely gotten me through so much, but it also undergirds each story that I write. I'm so grateful that my ultimate belonging place is with him. "See what great love the Father has lavished on us, that we should be called children of God." (1 John 3:1 NIV)

Discussion Questions

1. Have you ever visited somewhere (abroad or local) that gave you a sense of wonder?
2. If you could be any character from *Clue*, who would you choose and why?
3. Katie struggles with a sense of belonging. Some of her struggle is because of fear and insecurity. Have you read another book that deals with a character finding a place to belong? How was it similar and/or different from Katie's journey?
4. Katie and Graeme have both had a sibling loss. What are ways in which each of them has dealt with their grief in healthy and unhealthy ways?
5. Quirky characters can bring such joy and community to a story. Did you have a favorite book club member? Why?
6. What are some things about Lachlan that add to this story? How does he help both Graeme and Katie in their journey toward each other?
7. Faith takes a quiet motif in this story, but it is still something that plays a part in the characters' lives. In what ways did Katie and Graeme's faith help them in their grief?
8. Why do you think Katie and Graeme's personalities complement each other?
9. If you were a travel writer, what would be the first place on your list you would travel to?

About the Author

Michael Kaal @ Michael Kaal Photography

Pepper Basham is an award-winning author who writes romance "peppered" with grace and humor. Writing both historical and contemporary novels, she loves to incorporate her native Appalachian culture and/or her unabashed adoration of the UK into her stories. She currently resides in the lovely mountains of Asheville, North Carolina, where she is the wife of a fantastic pastor, mom of five great kids, a speech-language pathologist, and a lover of chocolate, jazz, hats, and Jesus.

You can learn more about Pepper and her books on
her website at www.pepperdbasham.com.
Facebook: @pepperbasham
Instagram: @pepperbasham
Twitter: @pepperbasham
BookBub: @pepperbasham